MIDNIGHT DESIRE

Deidre's eyes flew open. Wolfram was at her side. It had not just been a dream of her senses. She sat up in bed and smiled at him.

"I have missed you, Deidre," Wolfram said huskily.

"And I you, my Viking," she answered softly.

"Deidre!" he moaned, burying his face in the softness of her uncovered breasts. She reached out and clasped him to her as he ran his tongue over the softness of her skin.

"You are so beautiful, so very beautiful," Wolfram murmured.

He kissed her then, molding his lips to hers, and Deidre sighed as waves of sensation swelled within her. His hands moved upon her body, touching her mouth, her throat, her belly, her thighs until Deidre felt her limbs grow weak with yearning for him.

"Love me, Wolfram. Love me," she moaned.

FLAME FROM THE SEA

KATHRYN KRAMER

CHARTER BOOKS, NEW YORK

FLAME FROM THE SEA

A Charter Book / published by arrangement with
the author

PRINTING HISTORY
Charter edition / August 1987

ISBN: 0-441-24067-4

Charter Books are published by The Berkley Publishing Group,
200 Madison Avenue, New York, New York 10016.
The name "Charter" and the "C" logo
are trademarks belonging to Charter Communications, Inc.

PRINTED IN THE UNITED STATES OF AMERICA

10 9 8 7 6 5 4 3 2 1

To Marcia Hockett, my mother, whose love and wisdom have guided me all the years of my life. I never could have finished this story without your efforts and advice. This story is for you with special love.

The poem in Chapter Two, quoted in part from "Deidre's Farewell to Alba," is an old Gaelic song.

Author's Note

They came from the cold north on ships dancing on the waves. For two hundred and fifty years the people of Europe trembled at the name "Viking." "From the fury of the Northmen, deliver us, O Lord" was one of the prayers of the Christian churches. Yet we owe them a great deal, these fearless and skilled sailors. Our very language is filled with their words and historical and geographical names. The English-speaking nations are bound to these colorful peoples.

They were brave as lions and as fierce. They came to raid and colonize Scotland, Ireland, Iceland, Greenland and half of England, to fight with bravery and spirit and establish their homelands. It is rumored that America itself was first discovered by Vikings.

Although these Norsemen began as raiders, they became skilled conquerors, lawgivers, and administrators. They took on the Christian religion and became traders, traveling from Iceland to China and as far south as Africa.

The Irish, too, have touched us with the beauty of their culture and left us a rich legacy. The skillful blending of these two has enriched our lives.

Flame From the Sea is the story of a young Irish woman and a bold Viking who find the magic of love despite the differences of their worlds. Together they mold the destiny and future of the New World.

-Kathryn Kramer

Prologue

The changing colors of the Irish sky lit up the rocky shoreline and cast a glow upon the dark-haired, thirteen-year-old child who sat upon a cold damp rock gazing into the swirling waters of the ocean. She hugged her thin arms around her bony knees and breathed deeply of the sea air. Already the cold of winter approached, and yet she was somehow unable to tear herself away from this spot even though her hands were numb from the chill.

"I must do something to save him!" she thought frantically, remembering again the eyes of the man her people held captive—eyes as blue as the sky and just as stormy.

She seemed to live only for those moments when she would see this young man, and the sudden thought of his powerful arms and shoulders, his golden hair, and the strong set of his chin made her stomach dance with butterflies. Her kinsman Maddock and her father told her that she should hate him, for he was a Viking, one of the hated Northmen who raided their shores, but she could not do so. This Viking was not cruel. He was brave and strong and pleasing to the eyes.

The first time she had seen him her kinsmen had dragged him to the hall with his hands tied by thick ropes behind his back.

"We have a slave!" she heard the men cry. "Now we can make this one suffer as our sons do who are sent over the seas to slavery by these Viking bastards."

Curious, she pushed through the crowd to take a look at this fierce Northman and was surprised by his youth. He was no more than four or five years older than herself. His face bore the mark of strength, a young face not yet old enough to grow a beard. He was handsome. Looking straight at her with his

1

head held at a proud angle, he appeared to be the conqueror, not the conquered. But she had read pain and disillusionment in those eyes, and as she did sorrow and compassion washed over her.

"One of his own people sold him into slavery," she heard one of the Irishmen say. "Well, we will see that he earns his bread." The man kicked viciously with his foot, sending the captive Viking sprawling.

With an aggressiveness that was foreign to her nature, Deidre rushed forward. "He is a human being, not an animal," she cried out. "To strike a man who is bound makes you as barbaric as the Vikings are said to be." Reaching out and clasping the Viking's strong hand, she helped him to his feet and his touch stirred her deeply. The Viking looked at her again, and this time his gaze was bright with gratitude, his eyes speaking words that his mouth dared not utter.

That was nearly two months ago, and since that time, Deidre had watched him. She brought him food whenever she could because she feared that the gruel and water he was fed were not enough. She would either steal it from the table or, more often than not, give him her own portion. His thankful smile made a great tenderness well up inside her.

Now the wind swirled about her, whipping thick strands of long black hair into her face. Reaching up, she brushed the silken threads away and was not surprised to find her cheeks wet with a mixture of light rain and tears. Tears for the captive.

"I must free him," she thought again. And yet to do so would incur not only Maddock's wrath, but her father's as well.

The Irish girl rose from the rock and looked at the emerald green fields of her kinsmen's lands, planted all the way to the cliff's edge. Arable soil was scarce on this shore, which was several miles to the north of these lands owned by her father. Though she missed her own lush land, she had come to dread leaving here. All too soon the meeting of the clans that had brought her family here to this region would be over. Who would protect her Viking when she was gone?

In the distance she could see mean-spirited Maddock and his men pushing and shoving the Viking youth, and she felt a surge of anger well up inside her, a protectiveness which sent her scurrying toward them. Maddock's figure loomed before the prisoner, a whip held high in his hands.

"Obstinate Viking bastard!" he shouted. "I said pick it up." He meant to humble the Viking by making him grovel before him. A large pile of cow dung lay in the road, and it was this that Maddock bid him lift.

"He doesn't understand our language!" Deidre shrieked. "How can he obey you?"

She found her kinsman's angry eyes upon her. "This does not concern you, Deidre," Maddock said, lifting the whip up with the intent to strike.

Springing up with the grace of a deer, she placed herself between the two men. "Don't hurt him. Please."

Maddock tried to push her away, but she stood her ground. Nothing mattered at this moment but that she keep him from beating this man who had suffered torment enough already.

"Move!" Maddock commanded.

Her eyes were pools of anger. "No! I won't let you do this," she replied. "You will have to strike me first, and I have no doubt that my father will take retribution if you do so, kinsman or not."

He stood and glared at her before he eventually turned and walked away. Deidre had won this time, but again she wondered what would happen when she and her family returned to their own lands. She knew she had to set the Viking free.

Later that night when the moon was hidden by clouds and the path misted by fog, she came to him. Hearing a sound behind her, she ducked quickly behind a bush, but it was only a night bird taking flight. Clutching the knife she held in her hand against the folds of her cloak, she breathed a sigh of relief and opened the door of the hovel which housed the Viking slave.

He smiled when she entered and took from her hand the piece of bread and slice of cheese she brought him. He ate with the greedy haste of one who has been deprived of ample fare. His eyes appraised her. She was a slender, lovely child with a heavy mass of black hair, a straight nose and eyes of a violet hue. Such a brave little thing, this dark-haired Irish child. How could he forget the way she had shielded him from a beating this day?

He spoke to her in a language that blended his own tongue with a few of the words he had learned from his captors. His voice was soft but deep.

Deidre tried to ascertain his words, but couldn't quite understand and she was too shy to say anything herself. This young man was an enigma to her. Hard and strong one moment, yet gentle whenever she was near. His strength seemed so great but it was not great enough to break the bonds that held him. That she must do.

She took a step toward him, intent on freeing him, when a voice calling her name from the distance urged her to caution. In an effort to avoid giving herself away, she ran back outside.

"Deidre. Deidre." It was Maddock's voice and she hastened to meet him. It was too late to hide, she had been seen.

"I thought I saw you come this way," he scolded. "Why do you spend time with that brute? I know you steal our food to bring to him." He gripped her by the shoulders. "He is an enemy, a heathen. He doesn't worship our God, the blood-thirsty brute. You would not coddle him so if you had ever seen the horror of a Viking raid."

"I cannot stand to see him go hungry." She sought to wriggle free of his hands, but he held her fast.

"He's fed enough to keep him alive so he can work. More than that he does not deserve." He eyed her suspiciously, then deciding it was only childish fancy that she would soon outgrow, released her from his grasp. "Well, feed him if you must, but I warn you . . ." Muttering beneath his breath he took his leave of her and Deidre returned to the hut, crouching as she entered.

A small slit in the wood allowed the moonlight, which had now escaped from its cloak of clouds, to shine in the dwelling. Deidre looked over at the Viking's form. No doubt the toil of the day had exhausted him for he was asleep. His face looked so young, so vulnerable. He smelled of sweat and of the sea air; no other scent had ever stirred her more. Although she could not completely understand her feelings, she knew it pleased her to be near him. Thus thinking, she sat down beside the young man to watch over him in his slumber.

The young, blond Norseman cried out in his sleep, tossing and turning against the surging tide of a nightmare. Was he dreaming about that time when he was betrayed by his own kind, captured and sold to the Irish? She sought to offer her comfort. Staring at his bare chest, her eyes were drawn to the muscular narrowness of his hips and suddenly she wondered what it would be like to hold him close. In a selfish way she wanted to keep him here with her, and yet she knew that this could not be. Reaching into the folds of her cloak she took out the knife and moved closer to the sleeping form.

Bringing the sharp object up to his wrists, she sawed at the bonds which held him, her mind made up now. She would face her punishment bravely, knowing that her beloved was free. He stared at her as he understood what she was about, and a strange warmth sparked inside her as he returned her smile.

It took several minutes to work through the ropes, and all the while Deidre listened for any sound outside the hut. Had Maddock suspected her real intentions? His eyes had seemed to watch her every move tonight and even when he had scolded her and gone his way, she had sensed something about his stride.

At last, the Viking was free, standing up and drawing the Irish child to him. He gathered Deidre into his arms, not in a gesture of desire but of sincere love and affection. He would never forget what she had done for him. He wanted some token to give, some way to thank her, and at last was satisfied. Breaking free from the embrace he bent down and picked up a rock, exposing the hiding place, where he had managed to keep the things he did not want his captors to take from him. Oh, how clever he had been, hiding the small items he treasured in the stockinged feet of his braccae until he could find a safer way to keep them from the grasp of his master. Now he withdrew from the hole in the ground a brooch that he had fashioned with his own hands. Among the Norsemen these golden objects were treasured. He sought to give it to the Irish girl as a gesture of his gratitude for her kindness to him.

Deidre reached out her hand and took it. It felt cold in her palm and its edge was sharp. Looking at it in the moonlight she wondered at the workmanship, the swirls of design upon it. Never had she seen anything so beautiful. She would cherish it always.

"Thank you," she whispered, averting her eyes lest he know how deeply she cared about him. She felt him gather her into his arms again and she buried her face against the wide expanse of his chest to cry her tears of love and sorrow. If only he could stay . . . but that was not possible.

The Viking suffered in her embrace for a long moment, telling himself that it was a child he held in his arms, a beautiful one to be sure, but a child.

"What a woman she will become," he thought, regretting that he could not be there to see her mature.

He lifted her face to his gaze and she felt his lips on her forehead, heard words of endearment in his strange Viking tongue before he broke free from her. Then he was gone.

Deidre would never forget that night. She watched in grief as he left her and felt her heart torn from her body as he walked away. Almost reverently she touched the brooch and whispered, "Good-bye. May God be with you until we meet again."

The Viking looked back at the lovely waif and felt a great sadness. He would never see her again, her hair hanging about her shoulders like a raven black cloak. He wondered what punishment she would suffer at her kinsman's hands for freeing him. He paused, tempted to go back to save her from any pain, but a rustle in the bushes alerted him that someone was coming. The lust for freedom pounded in his heart, surged through his veins. Turning to run, he put the Irish child from his mind.

PART I

The Sword and the Flower

PROVINCE OF MUNSTER
SPRING, 845

"Thou canst not stir a flower without troubling of a star."

THE MISTRESS OF VISION
Francis Thompson

1

The first flowers of spring filled the cool morning air with their fragrance, as the wind blew across the green land of Ireland. The winter fog which had covered the land like an unearthly mist had now faded, leaving the sky clear and blue.

Rising from her resting place upon the soft grass, the young woman lifted her face to the warmth of the sun and gloried in the caress of its shining rays. The early morning chirping of the birds filled the meadows with music as beautiful as the sound of the finest lute, and she smiled at the song that met her ears.

"What a glorious day," she cried out, as her long, raven-black hair whipped around her shoulders and tickled her bare arms. Turning her eyes toward the sea she watched as the foaming waves hit the stone cliffs with noisy fury. The expanse of water had always impressed the people of her land of Eire with its darkness. Perhaps that was why, in the days long gone by, her people had feared it, and the gods and goddesses it gave birth to. Now, however, they worshiped the Christian God who had come to the island with the blessed Saint Patrick.

Reaching down, the young woman picked a flower from the ground and tucked it behind her ear. Today was to be her wedding day. She would be given in marriage to her betrothed, Phelan, as had been promised so many years ago.

Her father and Phelan's father were two of the greatest landowners in this part of Eire. Long ago they had discussed the joining of the two clans by marriage, and since her oldest sister, Bridget, was already spoken for, Deidre, the second daughter, was promised to Phelan, the oldest son. Deidre had not seen Phelan very often until recently, and so she neither

9

liked nor disliked him. He and his family would profit mone-
tarily from the marriage, and Deidre's father would benefit by
acquiring more power and prestige as leader of a larger clan.

After tonight, Deidre reflected, she would no longer be an
innocent maiden. The thought brought a small stab of fear.
Would she feel the same surging desire for him that Bridget
did for her husband? Would Phelan be gentle with her? Closing her violet eyes to the bright light of the sun, she gave
herself up to dreams and visions of her coming marriage. She
wanted so to believe in love.

A shadow of doubt was cast on her lightheartedness suddenly as she remembered the large dowry of sheep and cattle
her husband would be receiving—not to mention a large portion of land.

"Perhaps Phelan is marrying me for my father's wealth, not
because he loves me!" she said aloud. Perhaps love was only a
foolish dream. If she herself did not love the man she was to
marry, she could say truthfully that she was fond of him. Yet
she could not help but wonder what really being in love would
be like, to feel the wondrous joy the bards sang about. She had
felt that magic briefly once for a young Viking slave. Sighing,
she looked wistfully out to sea again, so deep in thought that
she did not hear the footsteps behind her.

"Deidre, there you are! I've been looking all over for you,"
a voice scolded behind her. Turning, she saw the familiar face
of her sister Bridget.

"I'm sorry, Bridget. I just needed to be alone for a while
this morning."

"There's so much to do yet to prepare you for the ceremony," her sister scolded gently, understanding her sister's
feelings.

But Deidre barely heard Bridget. She was lost in reverie
about her ancestors the Celts, those ancient peoples who had
lived upon this land long before the coming of the Christian
monks. Even now pagan customs were practiced by some during the four seasons of the year, much to the anger of the
priests. And the old gods and goddesses still lived on in the
folklore and stories. She had tried to explain to the kind old
priest, Father Finian, that the old ways were as much a part of
her people as their very breath and blood, even though they
now worshiped the one God, but he had not understood at all.

"I can almost imagine those days of the past, here on this

hillside," Deidre said softly. "What would my life have been like then? Would I have given myself to a lover during the Beltaine fires?"

Bridget crossed herself hastily as if to banish any thought of such pagan frailties from her mind. "We must not think of such things!" she said. Deidre often marveled at her sister's piousness and wondered if she might have entered the convent had she not been betrothed to Ian. Ian had courted her sister with a fury that had banished all thoughts of a celibate life from Bridget's mind. Deidre could not help but feel a small twinge of regret that Phelan's courtship of her had not been as passionate.

"Deidre, come back to the hall with me," Bridget persisted, putting gentle hands upon her sister's shoulders. Then they both turned away from the sea, walking arm-in-arm back to the stone building which had been Deidre's home since she could remember. They did not see the red and white striped sails upon the horizon, which were coming closer to the shore.

The Viking ships dipped and pitched like monsters from the sea, flashing their overlapping shields in the cold glint of the sun like scales. The ferocious, carved dragons and wolf heads were covered so as not to frighten the land spirits. Aboard the ships the seamen watched as the gulls circled and screamed their warning to the shore beyond. In an effort to quiet their screeching, several of the Vikings threw bits of fish overboard to them, yet the birds would not be silenced.

A tall blond-haired man stood on the steerboard of the lead ship looking toward the shore, squinting his blue eyes against the flaming light of the sun. He was a man of pride and of courage. Wolfram the Bold was his name.

"It's as the traitorous Irishman said," he murmured to himself. "We will take them unawares." He watched as the land's green vastness came into view. Would he ever cease to love this emerald-green isle? He who had sailed to many lands beyond the sea in search of treasures, including the great empire of China, still felt excitement whenever he came to the mist-filled land he now called home. For five years he had raided these shores, returning to his settlement Dubh-Linn, on the opposite side of this huge island. Forgotten now was all the humiliation and pain of his younger days, days spent as a slave. Someday when he was rich and powerful he would re-

turn to the Northland and revenge himself upon the man who
had sold him into slavery.

Wolfram gave the order to drop the sails and the men bent
their backs to the many oars and rowed toward the shore. As
the ship approached land he could hear the waves beat against
the rocks and the wind hum its ancient chant. In spite of his
courage, a shiver went up his spine. Here on this shore, he
somehow knew he was to face his destiny.

Wolfram lifted his eyes toward the sky in an effort to dispel
his uneasiness. "Odin," he called out. "Odin, be with us this
day."

The men hearing his words took up the chant. "Odin, Odin,
Odin, Odin." As their voices blended with the wind.

In the small room that was her sleeping chamber, Deidre stood
beside Bridget. She could hear the voices of the guests arriving
at the great hall. The sound of laughter and profanity told her
that the men had already taken up the cups of mead offered to
them and were feeling the effects of the brew.

"I hope that they are not all drunk before the ceremony
even begins," she grumbled to her sister.

Bridget laughed knowingly. "You'll soon learn the ways of
men, dear sister," she said. "Drink relaxes them, loosens their
tongues, and gives them added courage. I imagine even Phelan
has had a drink or two."

Bridget gently combed her sister's shining blue-black hair.
She entwined the soft, waist-length midnight strands with
flowers and ribbons and plaited the crown of the hair in
braids.

"I'm a little frightened, Bridget," Deidre said softly, turning so quickly to look at her sister that she felt the tug of the
comb as it caught in a snarl of hair.

"Don't be," her sister reassured her, giving her a hug
before she held her at arm's length to appraise her. "Don't
think of all the old wives' tales you have heard. What a man
and woman do together is beautiful, a wonder beyond belief."

Bridget studied Deidre's beauty knowing that Phelan would
be well pleased. Deidre possessed a beauty no man could
resist, with a fine chiseled nose, high cheekbones and large
dark-fringed violet eyes. If her eyebrows were a bit too thick,
well, that was her only imperfection; and there were those who
would say that her brows framed the splendor of her enor-

mous eyes. A slender waist and long legs were the envy of many of the women, and Deidre's well-formed breasts and slim hips were a poet's dream.

Deidre felt the cool linen of her gown as Bridget slipped it over her head. It touched the ground and covered her thin chemise, its long split sleeves showing the fair skin of her naked arms. The white material was a striking contrast to the darkness of her hair.

"I want everything to be perfect—your hair, the garments you wear, the wedding feast. Everything. It is only right that the youngest daughter of Llewellyn the clan leader be given the best," Bridget exclaimed.

Deidre belted her fur-lined robe around her small frame. Bending down, she pulled on her fur-lined leather shoes.

"Are you ready?" Bridget asked, giving her sister one last inspection. Never had she seen a more beautiful bride.

"I think so," she answered, fighting against her foolish fears. She reverently touched the finely wrought gold brooch with which she had fastened the neck of her gown, and remembered a time long past and a young man who had once touched her childish heart. That time was so long ago, or so it seemed.

"You still treasure that brooch, don't you?" Bridget's words sounded like a reprimand, but as her eyes met Deidre's she smiled. "Soon your Phelan will chase all thoughts of anyone else from your mind."

Deidre silently pondered her sister's words, wondering what it would be like to go to the marriage bed with the man who had been her betrothed since she could remember.

"I'm ready," she whispered at last.

Together the two sisters walked to the main hall, little realizing just how greatly their lives would change after tonight.

2

The large hall was bathed in an orange light cast by the flames in the vast hearth. Fires from the many candles danced along the tables and illuminated the fine tapestries that hung from the walls. The tables were covered with meats, fruits and vegetables; venison, pheasant, roast pig, succulent lamb and chicken. Garlands of flowers and ropes of laurel hung from wall and ceiling alike and combined their fragrance with the tantalizing aroma of the bridal feast. All the clans of Munster were represented by the banners of the invited guests who looked forward to the ceremony that would unite two of the most powerful families in the province.

Deidre's eyes darted back and forth as she searched for the familiar forms of her father and mother among the shadows of the great hall. She spied her father talking with Phelan, no doubt still discussing the dowry she would bring. Llewellyn smiled at his daughter and raised his hand in greeting but then turned back to his conversation. Fighting her wounded pride, Deidre left the room before she succumbed to nervous tears. Because she was a girl, she was not deemed as valuable to her father as his sons, though that he loved her she knew for sure.

"Mother!" she called, longing to feel her mother's arms around her before the ceremony began. How she would miss that comfort when she was no longer under her father's roof. She searched for the matriarch of the family and found her in chapel. Beside her mother stood Father Finian in his somber robes of the church—a white tunic and a Romanesque embroidered cloak. Both had their eyes closed, and Deidre knew they were saying a silent prayer for her happiness.

"Well, little flower," the priest intoned as he opened his eyes, "shall we begin?" Since their first arrival on the isle ten

14

years ago, he had called her 'little flower' because, he had told her, she was fragile and beautiful like a rose.

The chapel was not large enough to accommodate all the guests and so the ceremony would take place in the hall. Like a sleepwalker, Deidre walked toward the great hall again, her arms entwined with the old, white-haired priest's on one side and her mother's on the other. It was from her mother Tara that she came by her midnight hair, no doubt from some Iberian ancestor. Her mother's long hair was now streaked with gray, which added to her regal bearing.

Faces turned toward Deidre as she entered the room again. All activity and chatter ceased at the sight of the priest. Looking the proud father, Llewellyn was seated in his hard-back, thronelike chair, and Phelan was seated beside him on his right hand. The two stood up as the priest, mother, and daughter came before them.

Phelan, dressed plainly in a tunic of white with a fur-lined cloak, took the hand of his bride as he stood smiling beside her in front of the priest. This short, stocky man would soon be her husband. Deidre looked upon his face. It was round with a flat nose and eyes a little too far apart to make him really handsome, although his smile was pleasant enough.

"You are lovely," his deep voice rasped, as his eyes swept over her, taking pleasure in her womanly curves. He knew he had made a fine match in this one. A comely woman and one who would bring him land and livestock as well.

Deidre cast her groom an apprehensive glance. *Forever*, she thought, *we will be bound forever*. She seemed not to hear as Father Finian spoke the words which would join her to the man at her side. When the brimming chalice was lifted to her lips, she was unable to sip at first, until Phelan's touch broke the trance she was in, his hands assisting hers to lift the cup. She stared at him as if he were a stranger, apprehension written on her face. Her fingers were icy as he took her hand. Phelan swore beneath his breath, forgetting for the moment where he was.

Such a timid creature, he thought, anxious to be rid of this pomp and ceremony so that he could lay claim to his lands.

The priest concluded the marriage rites and the bride and bridegroom found themselves surrounded by well-wishers who congratulated them, pounding Phelan on the back and kissing Deidre on the cheek. Now the feast would begin at which the guests would hear the reading of the signed marriage contract.

Deidre sat between her father and her bridegroom at the
long table. She nibbled on a pheasant wing as she listened to
the terms of the marriage agreement. Her father had been very
generous, but then he was a clan leader, a man of great wealth.
Would Phelan have married her if she had been from a lesser
family? She would never be quite sure.

After the contract was read, there were great festivities—
eating, drinking, music, and dance. It was late in the evening
when Phelan's father, mother, and brothers left Llewellyn's
hall. By this time many of the other guests had already retired.
One by one the smoldering candles died, the logs sputtered
and burned low. The hour was late, shadows crept about the
room.

The dogs snapped at the table scraps tossed to them, fighting now and again over a tasty morsel. Deidre looked around
her at the glazed eyes and bowed heads of the intoxicated
guests and was eager to be away from them. Even her father,
he who was usually so clearheaded, was unsteady upon his
feet. As he rose to give another toast to the young couple, he
nearly fell upon the table and was saved only by Phelan's
steadying hand.

Reaching for a horn to blow to bring the drunken revelry to
an end, Llewellyn said in his slurred speech, "I have ordered
the shanahy to recite the story of Deidre, for whom my daughter was named. Then we must all retire."

The shanahy stood and began strumming the strings of his
harp, his hands gnarled with age. Despite his years, however,
he brought beauty to the strings with his touch.

The shanahy told the sad tale of the ill-fated Deidre who
was foretold to bring death to many heroes, and peril and sorrow to Ulster with her beauty. Upon hearing the prophecy, the
Red Branch warriors demanded her death, but their king,
Conchobar of Ulster, gave the female infant instead to a
trusted serving woman to hide away until she was of an age to
be his own wife. When she became a woman, Deidre wished
for a man to love who had hair as black as a raven, skin as
white as snow, and cheeks as red as blood and found such a
man named Naoise who took her away with him to Alba. The
vengeful Conchobar, through cunning, arranged for the
brothers of Deidre's beloved, and Naoise himself, to leave
Alba. Deidre, with her second sight, implored them to remain

there but they would not listen, so homesick were they. As they all put out to sea, Deidre sang farewell to the land she would never behold again.

The shanahy's old voice was remarkably strong and clear:

> "A lovable land is yon eastern land,
>   Alba, with its marvels.
>   I would not have come hither out of it,
>   Had I not come with Naoise.

> "Lovable are Dun-fidga and Dun-finn,
>   Lovable the fortress over them;
>   Dear to the heart Inis Draigende,
>   And very dear is Dun Suibni.

> "Caill Cuan!
>   Unto which Ainle would wend, alas!
>   Short the time seemed to me,
>   With Naoise in the region of Alba."

Deidre had heard the story so many times that she fought against drowsiness. The wine she had sipped had relaxed her but as she looked in Phelan's direction she felt a mild anxiety. What did she really know about this man who was now her husband? As if sensing her searching eyes, he looked in her direction and she could tell that he was edgy, too. His eyes kept darting toward the door, and Deidre blushed as she imagined that he, like her, was anxious to be rid of the remaining guests. She saw him nod, then, in dismissal to his soldiers and retainers. Soon they would be alone.

What will it be like to share my life with this man? she wondered, looking into his brown eyes. *Will I like his lovemaking and moan with pleasure at his touch?* As if reading her thoughts, Phelan grinned at her, causing Deidre to blush to the roots of her hair. She couldn't help but wonder if his fiery red hair bespoke a temper. Would she experience it in the years that lay ahead? With a sigh she turned her attention back to the shanahy, closing her eyes, her mind gently drifting with thoughts of what was to come tonight.

The sound of broken wood shattered Deidre's dream. Her instincts warned her of danger as the fearful words sounded in her ears from across the room.

"God help us. The Vikings are here!" an old man shouted.

"It's not possible!" she heard her father cry out, struggling to stand and retrieve his sword. He had not time to arm himself before the nightmare descended upon them like a demon from hell.

A scream tore from Deidre's mouth as she saw the gleam of upraised swords shining in the light of the fire. Her heart instantly filled with terror, not only for herself but for all her loved ones.

"It can't be happening! It can't!" she cried, yet as she spoke she could see the fearsome warriors break into the hall, their long hair flying wildly about as they ran shouting their harsh battle cry.

"O-O-Odin!"

Deidre longed to flee into the night, but her feet froze and her voice was paralyzed with fear. Her eyes met those of one of the Vikings, a tall, blond-haired, bearded man whose craggy brows arched above piercing blue eyes, as blue as the ocean around her beloved home. What was it about those eyes that stirred her, that drew her to him with a swift rush of emotion that shamed her? She tried to turn away, but she could not. There was something so striking about his arrogant face, despite the scar across his forehead, that she fell captive. His bearded face bore the stamp of power and strength as if he were born to be a leader of men. His full lips smiled at her as if to say that he would conquer her as easily as he was conquering her people.

"No!" she exclaimed, finally finding her voice. She felt herself being separated from her father and husband by huge grasping hands, brutal hands, and fought like a wildcat protecting its young as she saw their swords drawn against her father. They were going to kill him, cut him down as he stood defenseless in his drunken stupor before them. She could see her mother being pursued by a grinning, monstrous-looking Viking with a blood-spattered helmet.

"Deidre, get back!" It was her father's voice. He did not want her to come to any harm. Didn't he know that without her family she would not want to live. She could not run away and let him meet his death alone. She would not flee as many others had done.

Her father's eyes pleaded with her to do as he asked, yet she could see that he admired her spirit and loyalty. Several pairs of hands grabbed hold of Llewellyn, keeping him helpless to defend his family. Not one to give up without a battle, he fought furiously with his captors, but he was greatly outnumbered.

Deidre hurled herself forward, screaming and lashing out wildly. Grabbing up a candlestick, she swung it like a club.

"Phelan!" she cried, her eyes pleading with him to help her father. Why was he just standing there? She was grabbed from behind and held securely by hands which bruised her tender flesh. The screams of her mother and sister tore at her soul.

A dozen more men with their axes and swords raised, their crazed blue eyes lusting for blood, burst through the shattered door into the hall. With loud cries they moved forward, bringing with them death and terror.

Deidre saw her father fall and she fought like one possessed. Her shrieks captured the attention of the broad-shouldered, blond Viking leader who moved slowly toward her, his manner regal yet fearsome. Her eyes pleaded with him to end the bloodshed, and for a moment it seemed that his eyes were troubled too.

"Please!" she begged, wondering if he would even understand her words. Was it her imagination, or did he start to answer her before his attention was turned once again to battle?

Deidre's eyes searched for Phelan, but he was nowhere in sight. Had he fled or was he a victim of this death and destruction? Was she so soon to be widowed, she who was not yet fully a bride?

"Mother! Bridget!" she screamed. Calling upon God to aid her, Deidre made one last lunge against her captors, kicking out with her foot and catching one of the Vikings in the groin. He issued a curse and raised his sword against her. Knowing she could not escape, she closed her eyes and awaited her executioner's blow.

3

The noise of battle surrounded Wolfram as he stood looking down at the small form clothed in white. The beautiful young woman's long black hair spread out like a mantle around her shoulders, her dress spattered with blood.

"By Thor she's lovely!" he thought, looking down at her. Drawing off his helmet and throwing it to the stone floor, he realized that this girl who had fought like a vixen would have met her death had he not intervened as Sigurd raised his sword.

He looked about at the bodies littering the room. The fighting was nearly over, the Irish subdued and the treasures of the great hall taken. It was a rich household; the traitorous Irishman had been right.

The young woman stirred and Wolfram looked at her. Why had he saved her life? There were many slain this day. What was it about her that touched his heart? Why did she seem familiar?

"Father. Father," the young woman murmured. Seeing her eyelids flutter, Wolfram bent down upon his knees beside her.

The clink of metal on metal, the cries and groans of the wounded, and the laughter of the men taking their pleasure upon their victims sounded in Deidre's ears as she opened her eyes. It was as if she were in the midst of a terrible nightmare. She could hear voices and smell the smoke from the flickering fire. Tears flooded her eyes, a sob tore from her throat, as she struggled to sit up. It was then that she saw him, the blood-stained sword still in his hand.

"Are you going to kill me too?" she gasped. She could not scream, she could only look at him with stricken eyes. All that she held dear had been taken from her this night.

"No, I have something else in mind for you." She was surprised to hear him talk to her in her own language. His eyes wandered over her like a caress, as if he could look upon her naked flesh with those sea-blue eyes. Deidre knew nothing of lust and yet somehow his bold look shamed her.

She tried to speak, but she could not. Fear strangled her heart. This Viking wanted her. He looked upon her with a smoldering look that spoke clearly of his desires, yet only moments ago she had been at her husband's side. That time now seemed like an eternity away.

Wolfram, reaching out, touched Deidre's arm as she shrank back. Her eyes traveled the length of the room looking for her father in the hall. Not seeing him, she supposed him dead by these heathen hands. Bridget's husband lay upon the ground, a large wound in his chest. Her sister too was on the earthen floor, her fiery tresses spread beneath her. Atop Bridget lay a huge Viking, his braccae down around his ankles as he moved up and down, thrusting in a brutal manner.

"Bridget!" she screamed, struggling to rise to her feet. The hand of the Viking leader stayed her. "Let me go to her," she pleaded, but the cold look in his eyes told her that he would prevent her from doing so. Fighting her tears, she resolved to be strong. Taking a deep breath, she waited in terror for this Viking to do to her what she had witnessed the others of his kind do.

Forming a circle around Wolfram, each man leered at Deidre as they waited for their Viking leader first to have his sport. To their disappointment, he made no move, though his eyes blazed with desire to touch this dark-haired woman. She had sparked a fire in his loins. "This woman is mine alone," he said in a loud voice, asserting his claim upon Deidre. As he brandished his sword, one by one the Vikings walked away, none willing to fight Wolfram for any woman, no matter how tempting.

Deidre had no doubt now that this man was the leader. His air of power, the way the other Vikings had obeyed him, told her as much. She knew nothing about men such as this, yet she felt his strength, his authority. Before she could protest, Wolfram had picked her up in his arms, as if she were a mere child. He held her against his muscular body as cheers rose from those Vikings watching.

"Let me go!" she cried out, fighting, pushing at him with

her small delicate hands in an effort to escape his powerful
arms. The Viking only laughed.

"You cannot escape me. I will have you."

Deidre was torn between terror and a strange excitement.
He was handsome, and there was an attraction between them
that at any other time she might have responded to. But she
could not give herself to him now. The memory of her marriage to Phelan, the sacred vows they had spoken, made her
fight Wolfram all the more fiercely.

"No. Put me down," she wailed.

His laughter was her only answer. His moist lips sought her
neck, his arms tightened about her, one strong calloused hand
cupped her breast and she gasped in shock.

Wolfram strode from the room with Deidre in his arms.
Walking up and down the hallway he soon found what he was
seeking, the bridal chamber. It pleased him to think that he
would be this lovely woman's first lover. Her husband had not
had time to sever her maidenhead.

The room was ablaze with candles. New linen sheets scented
with sweet herbs were in readiness for the bridal couple.
Throwing Deidre down upon the bed, slamming the wooden
door shut with his foot, he turned toward her.

"I am a married woman!" Deidre said foolishly, thinking
to cause him to leave her. She had no way of knowing that
Vikings honored no Christian vows.

"Your beauty is wasted on that Irishman!" Wolfram
growled. He stared at her from across the room with eyes
which nearly mesmerized her, then quickly he came to her
side.

"I will never let you touch me!" she cried out, making a
mad dash for the door.

Wolfram had anticipated her thoughts and caught up to her
before she was able to open the thick wooden portal. He stood
blocking her way. Deidre fought like a trapped wildcat, kicking and clawing him and beating at his chest with her fists.

"I like a woman with spirit!" Wolfram shouted. His voice
nearly deafened her and added to her fear, but she did not
cower. Struggling in vain against his power and strength, she
at last collapsed upon the bed in dry wracking sobs.

"Why don't you kill me? I would rather die than suffer
your touch. You who have murdered my kinsmen and raped

my sister. I only pray that my mother escaped your foul villainy," she gasped. The rise and fall of her chest gave truth to her exhaustion.

"Kill you? I think not. It would be too great a waste of beauty." Wolfram caught her arms in his strong hands as he spoke. Such a tiny creature, she barely came to his shoulders, yet she raised her chin in defiance.

"Then I will kill myself." She looked longingly at the sword at his waist, and slowly he handed her the cold metal.

"Go ahead," he challenged. "For by Odin I will have you this night. I have claimed you before all and it is my right."

Deidre took the sword. Her hand trembled as she lifted the weapon to her breast. Then suddenly Father Finian's words rang in her ears: *Thou shalt not kill.* Could the blessed Christ forgive her for such an act of cowardice?

Deidre remembered her father's face as he fought for his life, and the screams of her sister as she lay abused. She saw again her brother-in-law's face with its mask of death and her mother's figure running toward the chapel with a Viking in pursuit. It was written *an eye for an eye and a tooth for a tooth.* If anyone was to meet death this day, it should be the Viking.

Slowly she moved the sword in her hand in a circle, pointing it not at her own heart but at his. It would be so easy to avenge her family here and now.

Wolfram's mouth spread in a grin. This one was feisty. She was not the sniveling kind of woman who succumbed to tears and begging. He wondered if she might follow through with this act.

"Vikings are not afraid to die by the sword," he said calmly. "If you kill me, I will join Odin in Valhalla." He made no move to take the weapon from her hands as he played a deadly game.

"I can't!" Deidre cried at last. She flung the weapon to the floor and turned her back upon him. No matter what he had done she could not take his life nor her own.

"Ah, you Christians. It is against your laws to take a life. Even your own," Wolfram whispered, turning her around to face him.

"Especially our own," Deidre answered angrily. His tone of voice seemed to be mocking her.

"Then glad I am that you follow the ways of these foolish monks," he said huskily, taking her into his arms. "For I would not see you dead."

Wolfram pulled her up against the hardness of his male body and bent to kiss her. His lips were soft, yet firm, taking her breath away. It was Deidre's first kiss. Not even Phelan had dared to take such liberties.

His mouth was gentle against hers and moved softly as his tongue parted her lips to explore the softness of her mouth. Her blood coursed through her veins. His nearness made her dizzy, yet in spite of the fire that was burning in her soul she pulled away, wiping at her mouth with her hand. "I have told you that I will never let you touch me in that way. I will not come to you willingly."

Wolfram was on fire with his desire for this girl, yet he would never resort to rape. He would woo her and win her. "I'll be gentle with you. I won't be brutal and cruel like those of my men you saw today. I swear it," he whispered breathlessly, wondering at the tenderness she inspired.

"Gentle? You. A Viking?" She sought to calm the trembling of her hands. His kiss *had* been gentle.

He pulled her to him for another kiss. He knew about women and how to spark their desires. He had more than his share of women clamoring for his bed.

Deidre felt his lips caress hers with a tenderness that shook her. So warm, so sweet. His hands roamed over the soft curves of her body. He was her enemy and yet she enjoyed this closeness. Yea, she welcomed it.

"You taste sweet. I want more of you," he breathed. His lips brushed her hair, traveled to her ear, to her neck, tracing a path of fire wherever they touched. "I will bring you pleasure, you will see."

His voice came to Deidre as if through a fog. He stepped closer, cupping her hips with his hands and drawing her close against him. His swelling manhood pressed against her belly as he caressed her with mouth and hands and she fought to regain her senses. This very day she had spoken vows before God to remain true to her husband!

"No!" Her innocence had been shattered forever by the sights and sounds she had witnessed and now her soul would be lost if she gave in to the Viking. She tried to pull free of his grasp and was surprised when he let her go.

Wolfram couldn't hide his smile. The woman was not totally immune to his charms and this pleased him. Somehow she had become an obsession to him, not only to take her, but to bring her pleasure as well. It would be his victory.

Slowly he began to disrobe. He removed his leather corselet from his chest, and his stout ornamented belt from around his waist. The bindings of his braccae he slid off and threw into a pile at the foot of the bed. He removed his leather shoes and the tunic of coarse wool, all the while watching her with his eyes.

As he pulled off his trousers with their strange stockinged feet, Deidre noticed that his legs were well formed and muscular. Her eyes were drawn to his chest and the tuft of hair which trailed in a thin straight line down his navel, to his manhood. She found herself mesmerized by his male beauty. She had never seen a naked man before, naked to the waist, perhaps, during the summer months, but she had never witnessed a man's private parts. He was so huge, so frightening yet at the same time fascinating. Suddenly ashamed to be so boldly gazing at him, she looked away.

Standing before her like some heathen god of fertility, Wolfram ordered, "It is your turn to disrobe now." He took it as a matter of consequence that she would obey.

"No!" She stepped back from him, pulling her cloak tightly against her bosom as if to hide herself from his smoldering eyes.

"No?" Wolfram lost all patience with the girl. Virgin or not there was not much more he would take. Did she not realize how he had controlled himself? Were she to have been taken by any other of his men, she would not have been dealt with so kindly. He had wanted to be gentle with her, but he was tired of begging her. He would have her any way he could. She belonged to him by right of conquest.

"I am tired of your virginal games!" he roared, losing all control of his temper. "Stubborn woman." He took a step toward her, reaching out to take hold of her cloak, the material ripping as he tore it roughly from her shoulders. "I did not want to have to force you but by Odin I will!"

Deidre put her hand in front of her breasts, seeking to keep her gown intact. "Please, don't do this," she implored.

Heedless of her plea, his eyes seeming to bore into her very soul, telling her that any words she might utter would be useless, Wolfram reached out for her again. She would feel his sword this night, the sword of his manhood.

Deidre made one last effort to free herself of the Viking's hands, but it was useless to fight him. His fingers wrapped around the cloth at her neckline. A sob tore at her throat. As she strove to maintain her dignity, the gleam of her metal brooch caught in the glow of the candlelight.

Pulling back his hand abruptly, Wolfram stared at Deidre as if hit by Thor's hammer. "Loki take me!" he swore beneath his breath. His face was grim, he ran his fingers through his long blond hair. His heart beat fiercely in his chest as memories assailed him. No more did he seek to touch her. He was fighting his own private demon.

Turning his back on her, the Viking strode to the door. "Your purity is safe from my touch," he said over his shoulder, not even looking at her. "There is none here who will dare harm you. I will see to that."

Deidre was confused by his actions. Her voice shook with emotion, her hands trembled. "I . . . I . . . am grateful," she breathed.

At the door the Viking paused, then retraced his steps toward her. The fear touched Deidre's heart that he had changed his mind, but it was his garments and not her charms that he was after.

"Stay in this room. I cannot guarantee your safety if you are wandering around. Sleep. I have no doubt that you have need of that sweet slumber." He would not look at her, yet she could sense a sadness in his countenance and wondered at the reason. She had no idea why he had spared her, nor what he had seen when he had looked at her. Had it been her God who had intervened?

Picking up his sword, trousers, and tunic, Wolfram took his leave of the Irish girl.

She heard the door behind the Viking slam with a loud thud as she was left alone in the room to seek her solitary slumber. Throwing herself upon the bed she finally gave vent to the tears she had fought for so long.

"Sleep!" she sobbed. Until she found out the fate of her loved ones, sleep would be long in coming to her.

4

Deidre tossed and turned upon her bed, fighting the turmoil within her breast. Outside she could hear the laughter of the brutal Vikings and the sound of tramping feet. How she hated their strange jibberish.

"No doubt they strip us of all we hold precious," she thought in anger. And yet, hadn't they already taken that which was the most valuable, the lives of those she loved?

Rising to her feet Deidre made her way to the door, fully intending to leave this safe haven to go in search of her family members. No longer would she be such a coward and hide inside these walls.

It was all she could do not to cry out as the images in her mind tormented her. Her father, her husband, her mother, her sister and brothers—what had been their fate? Taking a deep breath, she vowed to remain strong no matter what she found beyond the door of this room.

Slowly she pushed open the portal and peered out. Seeing two stocky Vikings with their swords in their hands walking toward her, she quickly closed it again.

"Oh my God, how could you have forsaken us?" she questioned aloud. Would these cursed heathens never leave? She suddenly remembered Father Finian. Had the Vikings murdered him, as they had so many of the monks and men of the cloth in Munster during the last fifteen years?

A shriek tore from Deidre's lips as the images again floated before her eyes. She longed to awaken from this nightmare and find herself among her sister and brothers, sitting at her father's feet, listening to his lusty tales of the Fenians and other stories of her beloved island of Eire. But those days were gone. Would she ever truly be happy again?

27

Again she opened the door, determined that this time she would let nothing prevent her from searching for her family. An eerie silence met her as she stepped through the doorway. No longer were these conquerors laughing and jabbering with their piercing, guttural language, no more did she hear the sound of sword upon sword. This time there were no Vikings in sight.

Deidre ran down the hall toward the chapel, the only sanctuary. The rest of the house was filled with Satan's devils. Opening the door, she was engulfed in the darkness of the room like a warm mantle. Reaching out she felt the warmth of a hand brush her flesh and felt her sanity flee her.

"Who is there?" asked a voice she knew so well. It was her mother.

"Mother! Is that you? Are you unharmed?" She was afraid to hope.

"Deidre!" Her mother's soft comforting arms embraced her. She stroked Deidre's hair as if she were still a small child afraid of the dark. Their tears mingled as they each told the other what had befallen them. Deidre's mother had been fortunate. Escaping the cruel arms of one of the marauders, she had hidden in the chapel beneath the altar and thus been saved.

"Father?" At last Deidre asked the question, fearful of the truth.

"I know not. Many have been wounded or killed. I only hope that he was not among them," her mother answered. Her fingers tightened on Deidre's shoulder as she told her daughter of her fears.

"How I hate these Viking heathens!" Deidre swore.

"We must not hate, Deidre," her mother said softly. "We must love our enemies as it is written in our Holy Book."

Deidre's hands wiped away her tears. It was so easy to recite the words the monks and priests intoned, but difficult to really feel them in one's heart after all that had happened. She longed to utter curses at these sea rovers who had taken all from her, but she held her tongue and said only, "We must find Bridget."

"Aye," her mother agreed. Together they walked the long distance to the hall. There was no sign of any of her people. It was as if they had vanished like the gods of old. They had naught to celebrate now.

"Oh no." The gasp of her mother caused Deidre to start. Looking at the hearth she saw the cause of her mother's alarm. The great hearth fire had gone out—a bad omen. Since the days of the Druids it had been thought that the spirit was in the fire. It was important to keep the flame kindled.

Deidre gathered her cloak about her as a sudden chill crept through the room. Hastily they sought to light the fire anew, then walked from room to room in search of Bridget.

A noise behind her caused Deidre to start. Turning she saw a tall, red-haired man. His conical helmet identified him as Norse. His face was young and boyish, with dark-blue eyes. He did not appear to be one who could plunder and kill, yet she knew that he must have done so. He spoke to her in his foreign, guttural tongue.

"I do not know your language!" Deidre murmured in mild irritation. If only he could tell her where her family was. As if reading her thoughts, the young Viking pointed toward one of the overturned tables. Deidre ran toward it and there beneath found her sister.

"Bridget! Oh Bridget!" She crooned to her sister, rocking her to-and-fro. "Mother, I've found our Bridget."

Tara ran to join her daughters and looked down upon the face of her eldest who looked into space as if they were not standing near her.

"What's wrong with her, Mother?" Deidre cried. She wanted to scream and never stop.

"Go back to your room." Her mother's voice was stern. "Bridget will be all right. I'll tend to her."

Deidre wondered at the command in her mother's voice. Why was she treating her like an errant child? A look toward the doorway answered her questions. Standing there like ancient war gods were three fierce Vikings. One of them smiled, showing missing front teeth. Deidre fought against her panic, remembering the blond Viking's words to her to stay in her room. It was too late now.

"Go back to your room!" Tara again commanded. She seemed to be telling Deidre to ignore the leering heathens and walk quickly by them.

Years of obedience won out over fear as Deidre did as her mother demanded. She held her head high as if she were the conqueror and not the conquered.

The man with missing teeth grinned and his bold eyes made

her flesh crawl, yet she did not flinch. He said something to his companion and laughed. Deidre wished she could understand what the foul man was saying.

At the doorway she turned around. "Mother, I cannot leave you. What if they hurt you?" Again the man grinned at her. This time Deidre could not hide her fear.

As if sensing her feelings, the young Viking stepped in front of her, a human shield.

"We won't harm them, Rorik," one of the men said with a smile to the young man, his words unknown to Deidre. "We have had our fill of lust and looting for a while and besides, she belongs to Wolfram."

The young Viking motioned to Deidre to go, then lifted Bridget up in his arms to carry her toward the sleeping rooms. Tara following in his wake. Although she did not know him, Deidre felt in her heart that she could trust him. Strange, to feel so about a Viking.

Walking to her own room, Deidre fell upon her bed. No longer able to fight the needs of her body, she fell into a deep sleep as soon as her eyes closed.

5

Like a restless and prowling wolf, Wolfram strode up and down in front of the doors to the great hall. Somehow he could not bear to be inside the walls where his men had wreaked their pillaging and violence. Not since he had lain eyes on the brooch and looked into those violet eyes filled with fear. This young woman had once shown him kindness and he had unwittingly repaid her by harming those she loved most and robbing her family of its treasures.

Little had he known that he would find her here in this hall. That *she* would be the bride of whom the traitorous Irishman spoke. In all these years he had wondered what had happened to the Irish child, if she had blossomed into the beauty he had foreseen. She had exceeded his expectations now that he found her.

"But she was far to the north of here when last I saw her," he cried aloud. Even with his anger at her kinsman he had not raided those northern shores from fear of causing the Irish child some harm, and now without meaning to he had come upon her here and done that which he had feared.

"Oh, gentle god, Balder, how could this have happened?" he murmured. He rubbed his sleepless eyes. How fitting that his lips had called upon Balder. That god too had been betrayed just as the dark-haired Irish beauty now was. How he loathed the traitor Irishman. What kind of man brought death and violence to his own? One such as he who had betrayed me, Wolfram answered.

He closed his eyes and could again see the face of the lovely child looking at him with her wide violet eyes. How could he ever have failed to recognize her?

Because all these years I have remembered the child and

31

now that child is a woman. A very beautiful woman, he
thought. He was not surprised that she had not recognized
him. He too had changed greatly. At seventeen he had not yet
been fully a man. He was taller now, battle scarred and more
muscular, and whereas before he had not had facial hair, he
now wore a beard.

*She offered me water when I thirsted, gave me her own por-
tion of food to ease my hunger. I, who was then only a slave, a
thrall,* he thought. How could he ever forget her
bravery—stepping in front of the whip when his owner had
been ready to give him the fell of the lash.

Closing his eyes he remembered the night she had freed him.
For just a moment he had been tempted to turn back, fearful
of the punishment she would receive for helping him, but the
longing for freedom had won out and he had fled, running
into more danger in the hostile Irish land. For a time he had
wandered, lost, alone and hungry, but he had the will to survive and indeed he had. Living on wild animals and any edible
vegetation that he could find, he had slowly made his way
across the land to the new Viking settlement of Dubh-Linn
and there made his home. For a time he had been wary, even
of Vikings, knowing that one of his own had betrayed him,
but at last he had taken to the sea and until this moment had
been content.

"By Odin's breath, what are you doing out here?" The
voice of his friend Sigurd broke into Wolfram's reverie.
Sigurd was his childhood friend, a man who had proved his
loyalty by coming in search of Wolfram when he had not
returned to the Northland. They had met at last in Dubh-Linn
and since that time had sailed the seas together. Sigurd had
gladly relinquished his authority over the Dubh-Linn Vikings
to Wolfram, for he was the son of a Jarl.

"I couldn't sleep." Wolfram answered with a scowl in his
friend's direction.

Sigurd raised his brows in surprise at Wolfram's bad mood.
Laughing and pounding him on the back, he tried to lighten
his spirits. "If I had bedded such a lovely wench as that dark-
haired Irish lass, I too would not be sleeping, though I would
not be found out here. Tell me, was she an ice maiden? Is that
the reason for your foul temper?"

"No!" Wolfram shouted, turning his back. He didn't want

to talk about it. How could he explain his feelings even to Sigurd?

"Aha, she was so hot-blooded that you were no match for her fire!" Sigurd teased, continuing his attempts to learn why Wolfram was angry.

Wolfram hit the outer door of the wooden and stone building with his fist, nearly breaking his fingers in the process. Somehow the pain it caused him seemed to atone for a little of the wrong he had done this night. "It is none of your concern, Sigurd," he said sternly. His blue eyes met the eyes of the other man and was a mirror of his torment and guilt.

"What is it?" Sigurd asked, ignoring his friend's words. "Are you angry with me because I nearly struck the Irish girl down? I would not have killed her. I sought only to wound her. Never yet have I spilled a woman's blood."

"That is not what is troubling me."

"Did you harm the girl? Is that what is wrong?"

"I did not touch her!"

"Did not touch her? You must have the sun fever or be addled in your wits! She's a beauty."

The words tumbled forth from Wolfram's mouth then, telling all about his days as a slave, a story Sigurd had heard before. Wolfram had sailed from the Northland on his first voyage, hoping to prove his manhood. Instead he had been taken into bondage when the ship had touched near the shores of Britain. At first he had been in bondage to other Vikings, made to row their ships, but when they landed on the shores of Ireland he had been sold to the Irish as part of a peace settlement. But he had found no peace. He had found himself bound to a cruel master who had taken out his hatred of the Vikings who raided his lands upon the back of a young slave. He had spent two months in that living Hel, suffering the blows of this lord. Two months of wanting to die with a sword in his hand, to leave the realm of the living, but he had been saved from despair by a gentle smile and eyes which had looked upon him with kindness.

"She brought me water and food everyday, this Irish child, and became my only link with the outside world," he whispered. "If not for her I would most likely be dead and with the goddess Hel herself."

"And this Irish woman is that same girl?"

"Yes. Although I know she does not recognize me. I have changed." Wolfram touched his beard. "This hair hides my face." He was silent for a long while, then continued his story. "One day she could not bear to see me in chains any longer and unbound me so I could escape."

Sigurd whistled. "No wonder you are in such a mood, my friend. What do you plan to do about this woman?"

"No further harm will come to her or her family. Nor shall we take any of their goods, except that which we need to survive. I can do no more, though I wish all this could be undone." Wolfram gestured with his hand. "How I wish we had not come here. But how was I to know? How was I to know?" He was silent for a time then said, "On the morrow we will be gone from this shore." He wondered at the pain his words brought forth in him, to be gone and never see those violet eyes again.

Long after Sigurd had left him, he gazed up at the sky, at the twinkling stars which always guided him. Wolfram knew in his heart that he would never forget this day nor the sight of the woman who had this night stolen his heart once again.

6

The mists of Ireland fell from the skies like tears a mother shed for her children. The downpour lasted but a short time and when it had ended, the glittering beams of sunlight streaked through the gray of the early morning.

Opening her eyes, Deidre looked about her. For just an instant the fury of the night before was forgotten and she imagined herself to be in familiar surroundings with Phelan. Last night had been her wedding night.

"Phelan!" she called out as sudden remembrance of the Vikings' terror returned to her. She looked around, her eyes wide with apprehension. Seeking the Viking's leather corselet and metal studded belt, she knew that it had been his lips which had tasted hers, his arms which had branded her with their touch—not those of her wedded husband's.

She wished that last night had been only a nightmare, a strange, twisted dream. And yet she knew that it had not. The absence of her husband beside her attested to that as did the scarlet upon her gown.

Rising from her bed, she remembered seeing her mother and Bridget last night. At least they were alive, but what of her father and her brothers. Where was Phelan?

Stepping through the doorway, she was surprised to see several Vikings roaming about. Last night before finally closing her eyes to sleep it had been quiet. Now the giants were awake. Several of the Norse warriors rose to their feet from their beds upon the rush strewn floor, grabbing for their swords and scurrying about with loud voices.

"I see that you are not so frightened of us this morning," a voice said. Turning, Deidre saw the blond Viking leader standing behind her, hands on his hips.

35

Remembering what had nearly passed between them the night before, Deidre's face flushed at the sight of him. Trying to maintain her dignity she hid behind a mask of anger.

"No, I am not afraid. Now I only long for you and your wolves to leave these shores and let us try to piece together the shards of our lives."

"We are leaving this very day," he answered softly. He flashed her a gentle smile in an effort to still her stern words, hating for there to be this bitterness between them although he could hardly blame her. Deidre coldly turned her back upon him. Somehow his smile tugged at her heart, and she was furious at herself for her weakness. How could she forget so easily all that he and his men had done?

Deidre left to seek out the familiar figure of her mother and sister among those women tending the wounded and the dead. She found Tara bending over the still form of Ian, bathing his limbs and preparing him for burial.

"Oh, Ian," Deidre sobbed, touching her brother-in-law's cold face. He had been like a brother to her, always laughing and showing her great kindness. The pain of her sister's loss made her eyes brim with tears. Bridget had loved him so.

As if sensing her question before she could ask it, her mother said, "Bridget has not accepted all that went on here last night. Perhaps in the long run God has been kind to her. It is as if she is in another world right now, one where we cannot go."

"God has closed his eyes to us, Mother," Deidre answered bitterly.

"It is not for us to judge the Lord's ways, child," her mother answered softly. "It is only for us to have faith and patience."

Looking about the hall Deidre searched for Phelan. Would she too be a widow?

"No one has seen Phelan, Deidre," her mother said, hiding her own fears.

"And Father?"

"They are not among the dead. Let us be thankful for that and pray that they did not suffer any grave injuries."

Deidre could not be as calm as her mother. She wanted to cry out, to fight against these invaders who had brought such sorrow. She counted nine dead and knew there would have been more if the others had not left the celebration early. How many wounded were there? Was Phelan among them? Her father? Her brothers? How many more tears would she have to shed?

"Come help us, Deidre," Tara's voice was soft yet held a note of authority that Deidre heeded. With a sigh she joined the others who cared for their dead.

Together in silence they adorned Ian with black ribbons according to tradition, and covered his body with white linen. Father Finian came to stand beside the body and Deidre was overjoyed to see that he had escaped the carnage unharmed. He touched Ian's forehead and whispered his sacred words while Deidre gathered and lighted candles around the corpse. From this moment forward Ian's body would not be left alone until he was put to bed in the ground. Later in the evening after the preliminary rituals were observed, the Caointhe or leading keener of Llewellyn's household would sing a lamentation for all those who had perished, as the surviving women of the house gathered to join in the wailing cries.

Roaming about the grounds of the great hall, Deidre renewed her search for her father and her husband. She had heard that the Vikings often gathered slaves from the Irish shores and transported them over the broad green sea to lands to the south. She prayed fervently that this was not to be the fate of her father and Phelan, nor of her two hearty brothers.

Finding no sign of her menfolk, she sat down upon a large rock and gave vent to her grief. Deidre did not see the tall, dark-haired young man who came up behind her.

"Deidre, lass. What are you doing out here? You should be inside with Mother where it is safe from these marauding barbarians." It was Brian who spoke, Deidre's eldest brother.

"Brian!" she shouted in her joy, throwing her arms around the tall young man whose eyes and hair were so like her own. He clutched her to him as she asked him nearly a hundred questions. When at last they drew apart, she noted the blue circles under his eyes and his arm wound, oozing blood from beneath the white linen of his bandages. "You're hurt!"

Her brother told her that he and Colin, her older brother, were both wounded in the fighting. He in the arm, Colin in the leg. Colin was in the storehouse unable to move on his own from the soft bed of flour sacks. Llewellyn and Phelan were alive also, though her father was unconscious from his head wounds.

"I must go to him!" Deidre cried ignoring her brother's pro-
tests that she should seek the safety of the hall. Seeing several
Vikings walking down the rocky hillside toward their dragon
ships, she quickly dodged out of their sight, hiding behind the
open door of the storehouse which held the large barrels of ale
and mead. She heard the din of voices, though her eyes were
not yet accustomed enough to the darkness of the windowless
dwelling to allow her to see those who spoke.

"You have done well by us, Irishman. You will be well
rewarded." It was an unfamiliar voice talking in her language
of Gaelic. The accent was that of a Viking.

So, we have been betrayed by one of our own. Deidre
thought in fury. She strained her eyes against the darkness for
a glimpse of the traitor. It was no use. She had to move closer.
Stumbling in the blackness she tipped over a small keg.

"What in the name of Thor was that?" boomed the voice
she had heard speaking. Fearing discovery she found refuge in
the only hiding place available, a large empty barrel. Carefully
she replaced the lid, hoping that she would not be discovered,
and knowing well that to be found would mean her immediate
death. She could hear the sound of footsteps beyond her small
refuge and the sound of scuffling as the men beyond overturned boxes and barrels in an effort to find the source of the
noise they had heard.

"Must have been a rat!" she heard the voice say.

She waited then as silence once more pervaded her senses.
Was it safe to leave her haven yet? She waited a few more
moments, wanting to calm her trembling hands. Reaching up
she touched the lid of the barrel just as her entire world was
tipped upside down.

"Dear Lord!" she whispered under her breath. Her empty
stomach threatened her with nausea as she was swung up in
the air by strong hands, the barrel she was riding in swaying
to-and-fro. She could hear the guttural language of the Vikings through the slits in the wood but she bit her tongue in
order not to cry out. Her world was spinning as she was carried down to the shore.

With a heave the Viking threw the barrel to the deck
unaware of the cargo within. Deidre struck her head upon the
side of her wooden prison and sank into the cold darkness of
unconsciousness.

7

Hidden in a tree-shrouded cove, the dragonship and longship waited, now boarded with their Viking crew. Standing with his legs straddled, Wolfram looked like a pillar of strength as he shouted his orders. His men were no strangers to his barked commands, having sailed with him many times before. The men on board the dragonship bent to the oars.

Wolfram was proud of this ship which measured a full one hundred sixty feet long and twenty-five feet wide. He had lost several men in the battle and so there were less than the usual seventy-two oarsmen. Several oars were in place without a man to pull them. It had been the Irish, however, who had suffered the most in the battle.

Behind him, Wolfram could see the smaller ship, the longship, being pushed clear of the land by several of the men who rode her. The longship was finely built also, ninety feet long and fourteen feet wide with fifty oars to move it through the ocean's waters.

As they pulled away from the shore under oar power, Wolfram looked back to the mist-shrouded province of Munster and thought of the violet-eyed beauty he was leaving behind. How he had longed to take her with him, but he had brought her enough pain without also taking her from her homeland.

The wind gusted from the northwest, blowing Wolfram's blond hair into his eyes. He could taste the salt in that wind and smiled. It was good to be on the sea again. Perhaps now he could forget what had happened here on this shore.

"We have made the sacrifice to Thor," Rorick shouted, waving his sword in salute to his leader from the next ship. "We will be assured a safe journey."

The helmsman swung the prow around to face the open

ocean. The ship dipped and pitched in the blue-green waters, then Wolfram himself took the steerboard.

"Hoist sail!" Wolfram commanded. The oars were run in and stowed as the sail was unfurled. Each man sat on a sea chest or large barrel as they worked with the oars. It was best that it be so, in order to save space so precious on board the ship.

The *Sea Wolf* glided over the waves as Wolfram left his post and walked to the prow of the ship. Looking at the carved head of a wolf, he felt fierce pride in this ship of his. Watching the wolfhead as it nosed its way through the sea spray, he thought it looked like a cunning animal as it moved through the white waves. A wolf who would continue to seek vengeance on his enemies. Now they were returning to Dubh-Linn, but one day soon he would be returning to the North-land that was his home, bringing many riches with him as well as bitterness.

And when I return I will find out who sold me into slavery, he thought to himself. He had his suspicions. Would they prove justified?

Wolfram felt a hand on his shoulder and looked into the smiling eyes of Sigurd. The man's beard was streaked with gray that looked like silver in the sunlight. As if reading his thoughts Sigurd clucked his tongue sympathetically. "When we are back in Dubh-Linn, you will soon forget the Irish woman."

"Ah yes, Dubh-Linn." The settlement had become a second home for Wolfram. It had been established over four years ago at the fort of the River Liffey, named for the dark waters there. It meant "Black Pool."

The ship sailed on through the rolling ocean, headed toward the Irish Sea. Wolfram had insisted, as he always did, that his men have a clear head as they sailed, lest some severe storm take them unawares. When they pulled ashore during the night to eat, they would be free to indulge in merrymaking and mead. They had taken plenty of strong brew from the Irish storehouse along with dried meats and pickled fish.

Seeing a look of fear on the men who stood there with fingers pointed toward one of the barrels, Wolfram strode toward the middle of the ship where the precious brew was stored.

"It's the daughter of Loki herself, moaning inside that

keg," shouted one of the Vikings. "We must throw it overboard, lest the goddess Hel take us to her realm of the dead."

Another Viking laughed, "It is not Hel but Aegir, God of the Sea that you hear."

"If it be Aegir, we must watch carefully for his wife Ran, lest she drag us down to drown in her net," a third man argued.

Wolfram was amazed to find his brave men shaking in their leather shoes over such nonsense. "Be silent!" he commanded.

The men stopped their squabbling for a moment but resumed their babbling as the sound of a moan came again to their ears. Losing his patience, Wolfram shouted at his men to get back to their places aboard the ship. He was not sure whether to be amused or angered by the men's superstitious mutterings.

"It would be a shame to throw this lusty brew into the waves just to calm your coward's hearts," he thundered.

He turned to go, but then he too heard the soft groaning from within the wooden container. Fearing that he had lost his wits, he bent his ear to the side of the barrel. Again he heard the sound, but unlike his men he knew it to be a human murmuring.

"Odin's bones!" he swore. Again he heard the moaning. Reaching out, he tore at the top of the large barrel, splintering the wood in his haste to see what or whom was inside. Throwing the lid aside, he peered down and gasped at the sight which met his eyes. It was a raven-haired woman. Gently he lifted her out of her small prison and laid her upon one of the warm furs on the deck. She was light as a feather in his arms, like a child asleep.

"It is the Irish woman," he murmured, looking down at her face. He could hear her deep breathing and knowing that she was alive, sighed in relief. He was torn between joy and anger as he looked back toward his men. "Which one of you is responsible for this deed?" he asked with flashing eyes.

"Not I, Wolfram."

"Nor I," came the voices.

"I told you that the woman and her family were to be left ashore, that no more harm was to come to them. Is this how my orders are obeyed?" He strode the deck looking into their faces to ascertain their guilt or innocence. He turned toward

Sigurd. Could his friend have done the deed thinking to please him? The look on Sigurd's face put to rest Wolfram's suspicions.

"Perhaps the young woman was more taken with your charms than you supposed and stowed away," Sigurd finally ventured to say. "Or perhaps Freyja, our lovely goddess of love, has taken a hand in this matter." He fought the smile which threatened to come to his lips. It was the first time since he had known Wolfram that the handsome leader of men was so flustered. Truly the young woman was close to his heart.

"Freyja? Yes, perhaps." Wolfram hastened to the side of the dark-haired woman. Laughter filled his heart. She was here, with him. He had not left her behind. It did not matter why she was here, only that she was on board the *Sea Wolf* with him. The gods must have willed that she be his.

Deidre's eyes flickered for just a moment and she moaned again, fighting hard to escape the darkness and return to consciousness, but her eyes remained closed.

Hearing her murmurs, Wolfram pulled her to his breast. Deidre in turn snuggled close within the warmth of his arms.

"I don't even know her name," Wolfram whispered. How he longed to call to her. Instead he merely mumbled, "Wake up, little one." He looked down at her eyelids and could see them flutter open. He saw the shadow of her lashes as she blinked and tried to focus on him and found himself looking into their violet depths. Instinctively he drew her closer, his hands brushing the softness of her face.

As her vision began to clear, Deidre found herself looking into the piercing blue eyes of this man and froze in shock. What was she doing here with him? Every muscle of her body stiffened as her eyes wandered over the deck of the ship, encountering the Vikings surrounding her. An ear-shattering scream tore from her lips as she realized what had happened.

8

"You!" Deidre gasped. As she looked at the face before her, she felt sure that all the blood had drained from her body. Reason fled her mind as hands reached out to grasp at her shoulders. Jumping to her feet, ignoring the pounding in her head and the whirling of her senses, she made her way to the ship's stern. Looking down at the foaming waters she closed her eyes, preparing to jump. She would not stay among these warlike, ruthless heathens one moment longer.

"No!" Wolfram's strong arms reached out just in time to keep her from a watery grave. The force of his pursuit sent them both sprawling to the wooden deck of the ship.

Deidre wept and fought the arms which held her. "Let me go! Let me go!" she cried. All that happened the day before came back to haunt her, the killing, the destruction, the rape of her sister. It was as if she were in the clutches of some ferocious monster, so deep did her hatred run for these foul Vikings.

"Be silent!" Wolfram ordered as he clung to the thrashing girl. He had no words to tell her of the remorse he felt for all that had happened to her people.

It was as if something snapped deep in Deidre's brain. A scream again came to her lips, a sound which cut through the silence of the sea air like a sword.

"Silence her!" shouted one of the Vikings. "She will bring evil upon us with her wailing."

"Throw her overboard," shouted another.

Deidre could hear the voices but was powerless to silence her cries. She fought again and again to rise to her feet, but the weight of the hated Viking kept her from being able to move.

Was it his hand which silenced her outcry? Yes, she knew it to be his.

"Listen to me. Listen to me well," he nearly shouted at her. "We will not harm you. We are not wolves to devour a lamb. We fight against lions, it is true, but upon my oath you will come to no harm!"

At his words Deidre's cries stopped, as reason slowly flooded through her again. Her eyes met his once more and she could read the truth of his promise within those eyes. Her chest rose and fell as she breathed in the nectar of life, but her shrieks had ceased.

"We did not seek to take you with us," Wolfram said softly. "It seems that the gods have willed it to be so."

"No God of mine . . ." Deidre choked. She wanted to be angry but knew instead that it had been as the Viking had spoken, they had not forced her to come with them. Of that at least this Viking was innocent.

All was silent as Deidre looked about her. The eyes of the Vikings surveyed her with curiosity, yet there was no bloodlust in their eyes. She was grateful that the Viking leader had kept her from jumping overboard, for life was always a precious gift and at this moment she knew that she wanted to live. Perhaps it would take far more courage to live than to die.

As if sensing her thoughts, the Viking loosened his grip on her. "If I let you go do you promise not to try to end your life?" he asked.

Deidre nodded. "I promise. Christians live bravely."

"I would hate to see you die, little one," Wolfram said, releasing her. She was so small, yet her strength had been great when she fought him before.

Deidre rose to her feet, looking out at the wide expanse of ocean. "Take me back." The words held no pleading, were in fact a command.

"No!" Wolfram could not take the chance on doing such a thing. No doubt the word had spread throughout Ireland of the raid he had led. They would be met with swords and axes were they to return to the shores of Munster. He could not so endanger his men. First and foremost his duty was to them.

"You cannot think to take me with you!" The thought of this fate made Deidre's blood run icy cold in her veins.

"I have no other choice. I don't want to cause you further unhappiness, but we cannot go back." The words were spoken as gently as Wolfram could manage. He did not want to cause this one grief but he had to do what he must. Besides, his greatest treasure from the shores of the emerald island was this beauty. He would have given all he owned to possess her but now she was his without one measure of gold changing hands. The child he remembered had grown into a beautiful, desirable woman and she belonged to him.

"My father would give you great reward for my return!" Deidre again felt panic rise within her heart.

"Your father would no doubt see us all killed." Wolfram shook his head. "You have no choice but to be a Viking now—at least for a while."

"Never Viking!" she spat her defiance at him.

With that he turned away from her. The hatred in those large eyes was more than he could bear. He could remember another time when there had been softness in those violet depths and yes, love. He had not been blind to her childhood fondness for him. How he longed for her to love him again.

Leaving the Irish woman behind, Wolfram strode the deck of his ship to seek escape from the memories which flooded his brain.

9

The sun looked like a golden coin balancing on the dark blue of the silken waters as the sun set. Deidre sat curled up on the thick pile of furs near the sternpost and watched as the ship swayed up and down. Trembling, she pulled one of the furs up closer around her face and enjoyed the feel of its warmth and softness against her skin. She could hear the rhythmic thrashing of the long oars as they swept through the water and the voices of the Vikings intoning some old melodic chant as they pushed and pulled the ship through the waves. Each stroke of the oars took Deidre farther and farther away from her parents, her husband, and the familiar shores of her youth.

"Just like the Deidre in the song," she whispered, glancing back as if she could still see the coasts of her homeland of Eire.

Deidre reached up and brushed a strand of hair from her eyes. It was sticky from the sea spray, a strong reminder that this was not a dream at all but reality. When she awakened on the morrow she would find herself still on this ship among the very men who had raided her people.

"Oh God, please be with me," she said softly, making the sign of the cross.

Deidre's eyes were drawn to the tall form of the Viking leader, so powerful as he stood near the mast. What kind of man was this Wolfram the Bold, as she had heard him called? What would be her fate when they reached this Viking settlement of Dubh-Linn? Was she to be the blond leader's slave? His woman? Either fate sent shivers of fear down her back and yet she could not hate him. No. It was not he who had brought her aboard this pagan ship, it was instead another

46

who earned her hatred—the man known as the "Irishman" who had betrayed them all. Someday she would return to her home and learn his identity. Only when he had been punished for his betrayal would she be able to feel peace in her soul again. She closed her eyes tightly as if to conjure him up.

"Are you hungry?" The voice startled her and caused her to jump. She opened her eyes to Wolfram's sea-blue gaze.

She shook her head "no," though her stomach rumbled with its want of nourishment.

"You do not have the sickness of the sea, do you?" he asked touching her stomach gently with his large, strong fingers.

Deidre pulled away from his touch, remembering another time he had put those hands upon her. "No," she said, averting her eyes. His presence beside her unnerved her, yet it was not fear that she felt. She shivered as a cold gust of air whipped the fur from her shoulders. Wolfram bent to pick it up, his hand brushing hers as he did so. For a moment their eyes met and held, then Wolfram looked away.

"This fur is from a land far to the north of your Ireland," he mumbled, placing it back upon her shoulders. Her skin was so soft that he longed to reach out and caress her trembling body, but he held himself in check. He would not frighten her, but would woo her slowly, gently until she felt for him what he did now for her. There was all the time in the world for him to claim her. Hadn't Freyja herself decided it would be so?

Deidre pulled the fur cloak tight against her body. She was suddenly tongue-tied, like a silly school girl first learning to read from the kindly nuns of the abbey. The silence between them made her all the more conscious of his maleness and set her heart to beating rapidly in her breast. At last she asked, "How long will our journey be?"

"Several days," he answered softly. He looked down at the Irish beauty. Her midnight dark hair nearly blended with the night. She held her chin up with pride like a true Viking woman. At first she had cried at the thought of leaving her homeland, but now she seemed to have accepted her fate with dignity and grace. He made a silent vow to protect her.

"Several days?" she repeated in awe. She remembered the few ships of rawhide stretched over wicker frames which belonged to her people. They were nothing like these great ships.

A sudden thought came to her. "What if we sail over the edge of the world?" Her eyes grew enormous as they looked into his.

Wolfram threw back his head and laughed. "We will not fall off, little one," he said. "The world is nearly round, like an egg, not flat. Haven't your Christian monks taught you that?"

Deidre blushed at his guffaw, then turned her back upon him in anger. How dare he act as if she were ignorant. She could read and write and had been taught history by Father Finian himself. Her people had the most culturally advanced civilization north of the Pyrenees. Could this big lout read the Holy Book? No. Most likely swinging his sword was all he could boast about. Hadn't Father Finian told her that the heathen Vikings were illiterate?

Sensing her irritation at his laughter, Wolfram laid a hand upon her shoulder. "You have much to learn about the world beyond Ireland," he said gently. "Soon you will understand our Viking ways."

"I'll never understand robbing and killing others," she said bitterly, pulling away from his touch.

He grabbed her shoulders and forced her to face him. "That is the way of the world, to be strong. Your people too have preyed upon others. You Scots curse us now and yet you raided the British coasts. How then are we different from you?"

Deidre cringed at his words. She could not deny what he said. From the third century onward it had been so, although now her people had ceased their roving ways and settled down upon the land. To those outside her land "Scots" meant the people from Eire. She could think of nothing to say to him. How could she deny the truth?

"I too have been hurt by you Irish," he said softly. Looking into his eyes Deidre could see pain written there and wondered at the cause. Before she had time to ask him about his words, Wolfram had turned and gone.

Deidre returned to her place by the ship's stern and closed her eyes. Her stomach grumbled and she chided herself for her foolishness in refusing to tell him of her hunger. Again she wondered what was to be her fate when they arrived in the Viking's land. Like a lost child she gazed at the churning waters deep in thought. She fought against the tears which threatened to fall from her lids. She would be brave and not give into womanly weakness.

"Mother," she whispered, "farewell." Perhaps of all those she was leaving, she would miss Tara the most, with her wisdom and her love. So thinking she curled up on her pile of furs and slept.

10

Deidre was awakened by the fierce rocking of the ship. Opening her eyes she saw the thick gray clouds which billowed about the sky like the smoke from a hearth fire. She tried to stand up, but the movement of the boat and her lack of nourishment made her dizzy. Instinctively she looked for the now familiar form of Wolfram, her only rock in this tossing sea.

As usual Wolfram was shouting his commands as his crew hustled about with poles and rope. How she wished that she could understand the strange language he was speaking, the Viking tongue. Her instincts told her that there was danger afoot, but all she could do was watch and wait. When at last the Viking leader came in her direction she again tried to stand, was again overpowered by her whirling head. How could he stand when the deck plunged and dipped so beneath his feet?

"A storm is brewing," he said sternly, lifting his head to the sky. He could tell a great deal from the changes in the winds and wave patterns as well as from a look at the cloud formations. Over his shoulder he barked another command at his men.

"What did you tell them?" Deidre asked, her voice rising against the wind.

"To get busy rigging the tacking spar," he answered gruffly, then bent down beside her. "I have not asked how you fare this morning."

"I'm fine," she lied, not wishing him to concern himself with her.

He bent down to help her stand but a giant wave lashed out like a hand, throwing their bodies together with such force that Deidre was winded. She gasped and choked, trying to catch her breath as another wave drenched them with its fingers. Deidre grasped desperately at Wolfram's arm, clinging to him like one about to drown. Her breasts pressed into his chest and in spite of himself and the danger, he was aroused. Through the water-soaked linen of her gown he could feel every curve and swell of her body as if naught separated them and was engulfed in his desire, though he fought this rising tide as surely as he fought the waves. Now was not the time.

Reaching for a length of rope and picking Deidre up in his arms, Wolfram made his way to the nearest ship's crutch, that rising beam of wood.

"I'm going to tie this rope around you and join you to this pole," he said in an effort to assure that she would not panic. "This way you will not be swept overboard."

"No!" Deidre shouted.

"It is the only way, woman. It could mean your life if you do not trust me. Please, trust me." In spite of her fears his voice seemed to calm her. She would let him do what must be done.

"All right," she exclaimed. The rope bit into her soft flesh. She feared that at any moment her strength would fail her but she did not cry out again. Wolfram bound her by the waist, leaving her hands free to clutch at the wood of the T-shaped crutch, then he returned to his men.

It was as if the ocean were a live being, tossing the ship to-and-fro as one would a plaything. Deidre watched as the ship's crew of fierce Vikings struggled desperately to survive. Loose rigging snapped and slashed in the savage winds and indeed Deidre thought that at any moment the ship would turn face down into the churning water. She clung to the pole of the ship until her hands were numb, thankful that Wolfram had been wise enough to secure her with the ropes. They now became her umbilical cord to keep her on board the haven of the *Sea Wolf*.

All the while Deidre fought her terror, she could still not seem to take her eyes off of Wolfram. He showed no fear as he moved about the ship. After a time he took his place at the stern, heaving on the tiller to keep the ship from broaching to in the fearsome waves. Beside them the other ship also fought the waves and looked to Deidre like a leaf in the winds.

The rains came, pouring down upon the ship like water from a barrel. Never had Deidre faced anything so terrifying. Even the Vikings' raid had not filled her with such fear. She heard a mournful cry and looked up in time to see one of the Vikings fall into the ocean surrounding them.

"Sigurd!" Wolfram shouted. He had seen the beam swerve, landing with full impact upon his friend's skull with a force that sent him over the edge. Sigurd, his loyal follower, his comrade, who had saved his life a hundred times was now in danger of being lost to this world. Having fallen without his sword in his hand, he would not go to Valhalla. Quickly without another thought Wolfram stripped off his oil-skin garments, his protection from the gale, and dove like a god into the swirling waters.

"Mother of God, no!" Deidre gasped, seeing his act of self-sacrifice. She wondered why the death of this Viking she scarcely knew, this Wolfram, caused her so much pain. Only now did she give vent to her fears.

Too late the storm abated. Too late for the two men who had been claimed by the cruel Aegir, god of the sea. Or so it seemed to those on board the *Sea Wolf*.

"God, be merciful to him," Deidre prayed, hoping that her God would take this heathen to his bosom. "And God be with me," she added, looking about her at the Vikings. She did not even speak their language. What was to become of her now?

Wolfram used all the strength in his arms and legs to stay above water. He ignored the icy cold waves, moving closer and closer to the figure of Sigurd, which was bobbing up and down in the water like a piece of driftwood. Reaching him, he grabbed him around the neck, swimming back in the direction of the ship. Only when he reached the side of the boat did he dare to stop. He gave a shout and grabbed hold of the steering oar.

Several of his men looked down upon him as if seeing Aegir himself. But Wolfram's bold grin told them of his successful rescue. Amid cheers and shouts, Wolfram was dragged back on board the *Sea Wolf*, a hero once again.

Deidre looked in the direction of the laughing men. How could they be so cheerful when they had just lost their leader? What kind of men were these Vikings? What kind of a man was this Wolfram the Bold who would give up his life in an effort to save another? It was then that she saw him, her heart quickening in her breast.

"Wolfram!" He was clad only in his braccae, the trousers clinging to his powerful body.

Hearing her call to him, Wolfram ran to her side, leaving behind a coughing Sigurd who was being carefully tended by his shipmates. Wolfram untied the ropes that bound her and gathered her into his arms, pushing back the hair from her face.

Deidre clung to him. "Hold me close!" she sobbed, overwhelmed by the feelings which stirred within her at his touch. For the moment she forgot all about her parents, her homeland, and her husband as she gave herself up to the precious ecstasy of his embrace.

"It is over," he said then. "The storm has abated."

His words cut through the fog of Deidre's dreams and she struggled in his arms. How could she have forgotten so easily that this man was a Viking, a heathen and an enemy of her people? The storm which raged within her was far more dangerous, she knew, than the storm which had blown in fury about them.

11

The ship skimmed through the water as if there had never been a storm. Forgotten now was all else but the longing to reach land. Deidre could not help but admire the skill of these heathens for upon the great ocean there was no equal for their mastery. They seemed to be at home upon these fearsome waters. The ship itself showed a craftsman's skill and care.

The ship's captain, Wolfram the Bold, also drew Deidre's admiration, though she was careful not to show it. She had seen his ruthlessness in battle, it was true, but there was also another side to this man. He had risked his own life to save the life of his friend.

"And he has a gentle side to him," she mused, her eyes raking over his well-muscled body. She remembered the look on his face the day of the raid on her people. Was it regret she had seen in his eyes that night he had left her untouched?

As if sensing her appraisal of him, Wolfram the Bold looked at her and their eyes met. Deidre hastily averted her eyes lest he know of her interest in him.

"He is a Viking, an enemy of my people," she reminded herself. "His Viking band killed Ian and others and raped my sister." She could never forget what he and his people had done, no matter what kindness he had shown her these past days. Not even the ocean itself could wipe the blood from his hands, the blood of her family.

Deidre made her way toward the crude tent in the stern of the boat where she could have some privacy. The sight of this Viking, this Wolfram, unnerved her. It had been this same Wolfram who had erected the tent for her to shield her from the elements and to give her the privacy she so desired. He had found her a dry gown among the sacks and barrels upon the deck taken from her father's storehouse.

"He is only giving me that which is by rights mine," she had thought wryly to herself. Still, she had welcomed his thoughtfulness, surprised that a Viking could think about her comfort. Indeed the last few days he had been a hospitable host, bringing her food—cold ham, fish, bread and mead; and tending her as gently as a father would a child. At times Deidre nearly forgot all the carnage that had been wielded by this Viking's sword.

"Why is he acting thus?" she wondered. Now he was busy with the sailing of his ship but no doubt he thought to find her a more willing concubine once they landed and were away from the others' prying eyes. But Deidre would never give in to him. Never! She fought hard within her heart to forget how she had felt in his arms, yet the memory still haunted her. Over and over again she reminded herself that she was a married woman. Her father had chosen Phelan and she had spoken Christian vows. She was a good Christian. It was a sin even to imagine what it would be like to make love with this heathen. One day she would escape these Vikings and return to the arms of her husband.

Wolfram had watched the Irish woman return to the tent and he smiled. He was no fool. Her hatred was softening. He looked upon her as his; he did not consider her another man's wife. She had ceased to belong to that other man the day she had been brought aboard his ship. Soon, when they reached Dubh-Linn, she would be his wife. And what a Viking wife she would make! To imagine her arms waiting for him after a long journey would bring him home much the sooner. Huddled in his skin sleeping bag during the long cold nights, the Irish woman haunted his dreams.

Wolfram set about to win the woman's heart and as they traveled, Deidre began to let her guard down. He was, after all, the only one who spoke her language. One could go mad with no one to talk with. She was surprised to find that this Wolfram was not at all the ignorant barbarian that Father Finian had told her all Vikings must be. She found out that he, like many in his family, could read and write his native language and that he had been given some training in the law of his people.

"How is it that you know my language of Gaelic so well?" she had finally asked him on the third day of the voyage.

"I spent the last five years in your country," he answered. She wondered at the cloud which seemed to come before his eyes.

"In my province of Munster?" she continued, undaunted by his frown.

"Nearby," he answered. A hundred memories assailed him, bringing old hatreds to the surface again. He had been beaten, humiliated, spat upon by those who were Irish like this dark-haired, violet-eyed woman. He had sought his vengeance by raiding and pillaging Irish shores. Indeed, it was more than a thirst for wealth which brought him to the hall of Deidre's father and made him succumb to Sigurd's plea to listen to the traitor Irishman. It had been a hunger for revenge. How was he to know then that the taste would be as ashes in his mouth when he found that in so doing he had brought this woman pain?

Deidre asked the question she had to know the answer to. "Did you raid my land before? Is that how you speak my tongue?" How many times had he brought death and destruction to her people of Eire? Bridget came to her mind and the memory of Ian's pale face. All the resentment for the Viking seemed to return once more, and she turned her back upon him.

"It is a long story. I will tell you about it one day." He reached out to turn her toward him again. He looked at her face and was reminded once again of the wide-eyed child who had shown him kindness. Noting that she still wore the brooch he had given her long ago, he smiled. Soon, when she had softened her heart toward him, he would tell her who he really was.

There was silence between them as each was deep in thought, a quiet broken only by the sound of the waves splashing against the side of the ship. It was as if they were not in the real world but instead in a world of their own. The ship was a haven from reality, but once they came to dry land Deidre knew that she must face her fate.

"When will we reach this Dubh-Linn?" she asked fearfully, the spell broken.

"Soon," he answered.

"And will I then be sold as a slave?" She asked the question in fear of hearing the answer. The appraising look in many of the Vikings' eyes had led her to ponder her future. For how

many years now had she been told the fearsome tales of the
Viking slave traders?

"You will never be a slave!" Wolfram answered, reaching
out for her hand. He found it cold and sought to warm it.
"You belong to me."

Deidre pulled her hand away. "I belong only to myself!"
she said curtly. Without realizing it she gently stroked the
brooch. She had wanted to belong to someone once, so long
ago. He too had been a Northman but killing had not been in
his blood. He had suffered for his youth and gentleness.

Wolfram reached out to touch the precious object. "You
always wear that piece of jewelry. Why?" he asked softly.

"Of all that I have owned, I treasure this the most," Deidre
answered. "It was given to me by one of your kind."

"Then you do not hate us all?"

"He was kind and handsome and everything my girlish
heart could ask for. I only hope that he is happy now,
wherever he may be."

"I'm sure that he is," he whispered. He longed to take her
in his arms, tell her that he loved her, that he was that same
man she had once idolized. But as she backed away from him
he knew he could not. How could he tell her of the change
wrought in his soul, his heart? Gone now were his boyhood
dreams. He had known betrayal.

Deidre started to ask him about himself, curious about this
fearsome, handsome man, but before she had the chance she
heard the sound of the Viking horn, signaling the men to
assemble.

"We will soon be upon dry land again," Wolfram said with
a smile. His eyes looked boldly into hers and she wondered
what he was thinking. Could he understand her fears at leaving the security of the ship? Was he trying to put her at ease?

Deidre tried to smile, but instead her lips managed only a
grimace. Surrounded by his men, Wolfram had not tried to
claim her body. What would he do when they were upon land?

I cannot let him touch me, she thought, looking away from
his searching eyes. *It would be a sin against my holy vows to
do so.* And yet she could not deny that his nearness fired her
blood as Phelan had never done. *Viking. He is a Viking, not
one of my own people,* she scolded to herself. Somehow the
fact that he spoke her language had formed a bond between
them. He was the only one she could talk to in Gaelic and thus

somehow he nearly seemed to be an Irishman. But he was not! She must remember.

Wolfram stood up to leave the small tent where they had been conversing, but he paused to look over his shoulder, overwhelmed by his emotions. Always before, a woman merely warmed his bed, and that was all. With this woman, Deidre, it would be different. Her name sounded well upon his tongue. Perhaps this one could put to rest forever the ache in his heart for Erika. Erika who had claimed his heart only to leave him for another. For Everard, his brother.

"Deidre," he whispered softly.

She turned around and looked at him. It was the first time that he had spoken her name. Before now he had called her "little one."

It was then that Deidre knew she would never be able to forget this Wolfram the Bold. She might meet others, but never would she forget him.

As he walked through the small opening, Deidre knew that it was not Wolfram she would have to fear in the days to come, it was herself.

12

The ship touched the shore at dusk. The helmsman guided it to the land, bumping into the rocks. The Vikings preferred to run the ship aground so it was not a gentle end to the voyage. When the ships were safely at anchor the men began to unload the cargo.

Wolfram was the last to leave the ship, lifting Deidre up in his arms, he carried her to shore with him. There were times when he was so gentle with her that it was hard to imagine him as the fearsome Viking she had seen that night in her father's hall. Even with his kindness to her the past few days, however, Deidre was apprehensive about the days to come.

Looking about her she was struck with how much this land of Dubh-Linn was like her beloved land of Eire. It was just as green, fragrant with the smell of wildflowers, and the mists hung over the land bringing with it the blue, pink, and purple of the same rainbow which had always delighted Deidre when she was a child.

"Why this land of yours is much like my own," Deidre exclaimed to Wolfram as they walked along the well-trod path.

He laughed, "We are still in Ireland. Only we are on the other side in the kingdom you call Leinster."

"Still on my homeland? But I thought . . ." Deidre stammered. Somehow the thought of being on the blessed soil of Eire comforted her. There would be a chance for her to escape after all.

As they walked, Deidre found it hard to maneuver her legs, so long had she been at sea. Her knees threatened to buckle beneath her, but still she trudged along trying to keep up with the long strides of the Viking leader. At last they reached the small settlement with its dwellings of timber, wattle and daub.

The huts seemed to have no windows, and the doors were so low that even Deidre had to stoop to enter.

Why even my father's peasants live in better hovels than this, Deidre thought with alarm. She could see that several cows were sheltered at the other end of the building, separated from the house by only a thin partition.

"Modest, but home," Wolfram said with his brow raised in question. It was as if he read her mind.

"Where will my sleeping quarters be?" Deidre asked, her fingers twisting together nervously.

"There is no sleeping area," he answered putting his hands on his hips in the gesture she was now well accustomed to. "You and I will share this house." He gestured to a pile of furs which Deidre guessed to be the bed. Not far away from this bed Deidre could see a cooking pot hanging over a simple stone hearth. It was suspended from the roof by ropes.

"I cannot share this dwelling with you," she said softly. "Nor can I share your bed. I belong to another."

He took hold of her wrist. "You belong to me!" He kissed her then, his lips firm and strong upon her own as if to assert his claim. Deidre neither resisted nor did she respond. At last he stepped away. "I will not force you," he said. "When I take you it will be because you want me to."

"That time will never come, Wolfram. I was joined with a man before God and vowed—"

"And do you love this man?" His mouth was curved in a smile, sure of his answer. "No."

"We . . . we were promised since I was a child. Someday I must return to him and when I do I will be his dutiful wife." She wanted to run away from him, to do anything to avoid looking into his eyes.

"We will see. We will see, little one." He left her then to return to the ship and help the others unload. Walking to the doorway Deidre could see the gray linen smocks of several of the women of the settlement looking like gray pigeons. She wanted to go to them and offer her hand in friendship, but she was too shy to do so now. Perhaps tomorrow. Instead she busied herself with tidying up this small house which would now be her home.

He said that he would never force me, she thought to herself, but she wondered if in truth he would keep his word.

Deidre saw that the dirt floor of the dwelling was clean and that the room was neat. Finding some meat and cabbage in one of the sacks of food, and water in the cooking pot, she started it boiling over a small fire and prepared Wolfram's dinner. It was the least she could do for him. The smell made her hungry although she thought with dismay that this odor would not be pleasant to have in the house at bedtime.

Outside the door Deidre found a large tub, most likely for bathing. She ran her hand over her bare arms and felt the need to cleanse herself from the voyage's dirt. On the ship she had not been able to wash her hair. It would feel so good to do so now. She eyed the large tub, tempted to bathe, but was afraid that she would catch a chill. Instead she sponged her body clean and washed her long tresses, taking great delight in drying the raven locks before the fire.

Deidre found a large wooden chest filled with silver and gold plates, chalices, knives and spoons, and fine linens. Spreading one of the large linens upon the small table, she set earthenware plates and bowls she found in a large sack near the fire atop it. Near each of the plates she laid down a silver knife and spoon and stepped back to view her handiwork.

"Perhaps living here will not be as bad as I first imagined," she said softly, feeling strangely contented. She was quickly learning that these Vikings were not as different from her people as she had once imagined, nor the heathens she had feared. So far she had not been harmed.

When at last Wolfram returned, bone weary from unloading the ship, he smiled to see that his meal was already cooking. So the Irish woman had more than just beauty; she would be a boon to his lodge as well.

Filling two of the silver chalices from the keg of ale he had brought with him, then sitting down on one of the small benches near the table, he motioned for Deidre to sit opposite him.

They ate in silence, Deidre looking down at her plate all the while, afraid of meeting his eyes. Even though she did not look at him, however, she felt the tension of his presence.

"I have something for you," Wolfram finally said. Pushing his plate aside, rising from the table and stepping outside the low-slung door, he returned with something in his hand. He beckoned to Deidre and she too left her bench.

"What is it?" she asked, feeling like a small child again. Her father had always brought her presents whenever he returned from a journey to the abbey.

Wolfram held it out to her. It was a garment made of the smoothest and softest fabric she had ever touched, a gown of bright blue which seemed to glisten in the firelight.

"It is silk," Wolfram said, smiling down at her. "It comes from China, the land far to the East. I have been saving it until I met a woman like you. Put it on."

"It's beautiful!" Deidre took it from him and held it out in front of her. "Thank you."

"Put it on." His voice was low and husky.

"No . . . no, I could not." She blushed as she thought of him watching her as she disrobed.

As if reading her very thought Wolfram took a step forward. "It is time that you got used to me looking at you, for I intend to do so many times from now on. You are lovely. Do not be ashamed for me to see your body." He repeated, "Put it on," his voice just a whisper.

Deidre stood still, unable to move away from him, yet unable to do as he asked. She felt as if his eyes had already stripped the linen garment she now wore from her slim form.

The minutes passed slowly as Wolfram stood looking at her. Stepping toward her he reached out and cupped her breast, brushing the peak of its perfection with the tip of his finger. His hand moved lower to the smooth curve of her waist, the tautness of her stomach. Deidre shivered as a flame seemed to course through her veins.

"No," she breathed, terrified of those feelings he unleashed in her. She stepped backward, nearly tripping over the wooden chest. "You promised."

"And I shall keep my promise not to force you, though I have not vowed not to caress you or to kiss you." He caught her in his arms then, kissing her with a passion which overwhelmed her. He moved his lips to her neck. "You see, little one, I am no monster. I will give you such pleasure that you will cry out for me to take you."

"Never!" she said faintly, fighting the desire she felt at this man's touch. Her breath caught as he tightened his hold on her, kissing her with a searching passion.

"I will be gentle, you will see," Wolfram said softly as he kissed her again. To her dismay Deidre found her resolve weakening, longed to run her hands over him.

Deidre had to do something to stop this assault to her very

soul. Her body had become a traitor to her mind. "Don't touch me, Viking!" she cried out in mock anger, feeling him stiffen at her words. She stood trembling before him. "I cannot forget that your hands are stained with Irish blood!"

A frown creased his forehead as she broke from his embrace, but he made no further move to touch her. Instead he stood staring at her, his eyes burning into her very soul, then he turned and walked away leaving Deidre all alone.

She collapsed on the small bed, drowning it seemed in her own tears. Thoughts of escape ran through her mind as she gave vent to her grief. Somehow she must find a way!

Wolfram walked far from the hut which lodged the Irish woman. Stripping off his garments he plunged into the cold waters of the seas in an effort to cool his ardor. Why had he made such a promise? Could he wait much longer to have her? It had been long since he had bedded a woman and this Deidre nearly drove him mad with desire. He remembered her small waist, her slim hips, her long legs, the breasts which had felt so smooth under his exploring fingers.

"And her eyes. Surely I could drown in that sea of violet," he swore, stroking the waters of the ocean as he swam about. Why then had he told her he would not force her? "Because I do not want her hatred," he answered, talking to himself. Somehow more than anything it was this that he feared: to destroy forever that bond he had felt for the gentle child who had sought to help him. Deeper than his desire for her, Wolfram knew, ran his love.

Rising out of the sea and donning his clothing, Wolfram spent the hours wandering by the ocean. At last when he returned to the hut, he found Deidre, still wearing the silk dress, her hair spread out around her like the wings of a bird. She lay curled up on the furs of the small bed, asleep. She was lovely lying there with her eyelashes shadowing her pale cheeks.

"Deidre," he whispered, moved again with a great tenderness for her.

Lying down beside her he kept a great distance between them. Wolfram swore silently. "Freyja, goddess of fertility, help me, for I do not know how long I can keep this foolish vow of mine not to claim her." Closing his eyes he tried to sleep, but slumber long eluded him.

13

Drunken laughter awakened Deidre from her fitful sleep. The Viking men were still celebrating their return to the settlement with the mead and wine which had been denied them by Wolfram on the voyage. She could hear giggles from the women and knew that these men were enjoying more than just their drink. She wondered if any of the women were Gaelic born, but at the sound of their gibberish, her question was answered. The women too were Viking.

Wolfram's words came again to her mind that she was still on the land of Eire, though far to the northeast. Perhaps there was still a chance for her to find her way home, to escape from this settlement.

She tried to sit up but was held bound by a weight upon her long hair. *Wolfram. The Viking!* she thought with exasperation. His strong arm was thrown across her raven mane, holding her captive.

In frustration she sank back down upon the bed. When had he returned to the hut? Her heart beat wildly as she remembered the look in his eyes of desire for her, the bold caress of his searching fingers. "I must escape!"

That the Viking had sought to lay beside her, terrified Deidre. How soon would it be before he not only claimed her bed but her body as well? He had promised not to force her, but by his own words he had said that he would not vow not to touch her or tease her lips with his own to spark her desire. How long could she fight against this assault to her senses? A day? A week? A month? Could she bear the shame of weakening to his lust? In truth she had nearly already done so.

"I have to escape. If I have to walk all the way back to

Munster I will!" she vowed silently, forgetful of the danger such a venture would bring.

Deidre sought again to free herself of the Viking's weight upon her hair. With careful fingers she worked to disentangle his hand from her tresses, pausing only when he gave a moan in his deep slumber. Thinking him to be awake, Deidre held her breath, but he merely rolled over on his side away from her, thus freeing her.

Rising from the bed, Deidre peered out into the darkness of the early morning. No one was about the camp; all laughter had died now as the Vikings had finally sought their beds. She knew that she would have to leave soon, before Wolfram awoke.

Deidre assembled what supplies she could for the journey as quickly as possible. Now she was glad that she had familiarized herself with the room during the daylight hours. Still, she found herself fumbling around in the darkness, holding her breath once or twice when her gropings sent something falling to the floor.

Running her hand over the silk dress, Deidre knew that she must leave it behind and don her own clothes for the journey, though she was loath to part with the garment.

"I cannot keep any reminders of the Viking," she scolded silently to herself.

Tearing open a sack, filling it with as much food as she could comfortably carry, gathering her courage, she stepped out into the brisk early morning air. The moon was shrouded by dark clouds, her only guide the light of the fading stars. She had noticed the Vikings navigating by their map of the star-covered heavens, she could only hope that somehow these same stars would guide her too.

Looking back many times to make certain that she had not been seen leaving, was not being followed, Deidre walked until her legs ached and her feet were bruised and bleeding from the rocks of the pathway. Past all logic, she was driven only by the fear of her desire for the blond Viking leader. If only she could put much distance between herself and the one called Wolfram, she would survive somehow.

Deidre knew that she was heading farther inland, but knew not where she would end this journey. At times she nearly crawled along and at times she found herself running wildly as the sound of the night animals frightened her. Was she imagining it, or was she being watched by many pairs of eyes? She cursed herself for being foolish. Why had she left the safety of the settlement? Doubts flooded her mind as she thought about what she had done. There was more than just the danger of the wild animals and rough terrain, for there would be no bold Viking arm to steady her, no sword to protect her. Were she to be captured by any rival Irish clan, her fate could be as foreboding as the one she faced now, perhaps more so.

She wanted to go back but instead pushed on, driven forward by the fear of her attraction to the Viking. Her breath came in ragged gasps, her heart beat within her breasts like the waves upon the shore. As a muscle spasm cramped her ankle with pain, she sank to the ground. A howling like the tortured souls in the purgatory Father Finian had preached to her about pierced Deidre's ears as shivers of terror ran up her spine.

"Oh Wolfram!" she cried out, feeling the sudden longing to feel his strong arms around her. She wondered what he would do when he awoke and found her missing. Would he order his men to search for her?

Deidre listened to the night sounds as she lay there, lost to the visions of her frightened imagination. A blood curdling scream left her throat as something brushed her leg.

"Deidre?" The voice sounded in the distance. Was it another fantasy? "Deidre." Again she heard the voice, Wolfram's voice. He had heard her screams and was even now coming to help her.

She fought against crying out to him again. She could smell smoke, could see the blaze of a torch as he made his way toward her. What would he do to her for running away?

"Deidre, where are you?" he called out, his face showing his agony in the flickering flames of the torch.

"Wolfram, I'm over here," Deidre cried out. He was beside her in a moment reaching out to her. Setting the torch down he held her in his arms.

"Are you hurt?"

"No."

"Odin's teeth, don't ever do such a foolish thing again!" he cried out, holding her tightly against his chest, stroking her hair. "Don't you realize what might have happened? There are wolves out here, all manner of wild beast."

"I want to go home," she managed to say between her sobs.

A stab of guilt knifed through Wolfram. He saw himself not as a brave Viking but as a captor imprisoning a beautiful woman. How easy it would have been to turn back when he had found her onboard his ship, to return her to her people. Why had he not done so? He knew the answer clearly. It was because of his desire for this dark-haired beauty that he had refused to turn back. He had not wanted another man to possess her. He had wanted her himself with a passion which enflamed him beyond reason. His conscience screamed out for him to let her go back, but he could not bear to lose her.

Deidre clung to Wolfram, forgetful now that she had sought to flee from him. Wolfram quieted her sobbing with soothing words and caresses much as a father might do. Only after she had ceased her crying did he seek to look at her, thrusting her at arm's length and holding her shoulders firmly.

"Promise me by the God you hold so dear that you will never run away from me again. Swear it! Promise me," he said.

"I . . . I . . . promise," Deidre answered.

"Swear by your God."

She did not need to swear by her Lord. This night had taught her well the dangers of her actions, yet she answered, "I so swear."

"I ought to punish you for doing such a foolish thing," Wolfram said loudly. As Deidre looked at him with frightened eyes, his heart constricted and his voice became gentle again. "I won't punish you." His arms tightened about her. "I would have died if you had been lost to me."

Wolfram kissed her then, a gentle kiss. Picking her up in his arms, he carried her all the way back to the settlement and the safety of the small bed.

14

When Deidre awoke she found herself alone in the dwelling, the hearth still aglow with the hot embers of the evening fire. Getting to her feet, she poured water in a large bowl and splashed it upon her face. Her hair was matted from the night's tossing and turning and from her early morning flight from the settlement. Picking up the large bone comb that she had used last night, she combed her long black tresses and fashioned her hair into the braids she had noticed the other women wearing.

Looking down at her dress, she appraised the damage done to it by her escape attempt. Between the ocean voyage and the snags and tears of her misadventure during the night, she could see that the garment was beyond repair. Washing herself, she donned the blue-silk dress, remembering the feel of Wolfram's hands upon her.

"Oh why does his touch stir me so?" she cried softly.

Seeking to put all thoughts of the Viking out of her mind, she left the small dwelling and walked a little way from the hut. The green rolling hills of the meadowlands stretched before her, mingling with the dark green of the forests. This Dubh-Linn was different from Munster province, not as rocky, yet just as beautiful in its own way. This land was to be her home now, she thought.

Deidre could hear the guttural chatter of the women behind her as they worked, making preparation for some sort of feast. The noise of their voices sounded like the cackle of chickens. From time to time they looked at her, then at each other and giggled. One of them was even so brazen as to come

68

up to Deidre and tug at her dark braids. She asked a question
of Deidre, raising her eyebrows and waiting for an answer.

"I don't speak your language," Deidre answered, shaking
her head in an effort to communicate in some way with the
girl. It was then that she made up her mind to have Wolfram
teach her to speak his language. If she was going to live among
these people, she would have to be able to talk with them.

Another woman, tall and blonde like the first, tugged at
Deidre's blue-silk dress as if to tell her to take it off. She
pointed to a large crackling fire where a cauldron awaited its
bounty and Deidre knew that the young woman wanted her to
help them with the preparations for the feast.

Deidre nodded her head, "yes," and gestured toward her
small house. The girl smiled and Deidre was struck by the
sweetness of that smile. Perhaps here would be a friend.

Returning to the house, Deidre searched through the large
chests until she found a chemise of lightweight wool and a
long gown of the same cloth. Finding a brooch which was
similar to hers, she paused for a moment staring at it, then
shrugged her shoulders, fastening it with her own brooch to
the outer garment. The chest contained a pair of leather shoes
and Deidre donned these also, turning the fur toward the inside to cradle her feet. Her own were well worn, nearly torn
apart from the rocky path she had trod during the night.

"Now I look like a Viking," she murmured. Somehow after
seeing the women of the settlement, the word did not sound so
fierce. She remembered her promise to Wolfram not to run
away again and wondered where he had gone. But she did not
ponder the question for long; there was work to be done.

When she returned to the women, she was shown how to put
the unleavened bread into flat cakes upon a rock to bake. As
soon as that was done, she was given another chore: to cut up
the large chunks of mutton and put them in a large cooking
pot. As soon as she had finished each task she was given
another and then another. Never had Deidre worked so hard.
She had to admit that her mother and father had spoiled her,
she the younger daughter.

While the women worked they sang and Deidre was soon
tapping her feet and humming the tune of their song. After so
many days on board the ship among only men, it was good
to be among women again. The only thing that marred her

happiness this day was the gaze of one bold Viking, a man short and stocky with powerful arms and a straggly beard. His beady, ice-blue eyes followed Deidre everywhere she went, his grin showing teeth set wide apart as he looked her up and down as if judging her womanly charms. This was the kind of Viking Father Finian had told her about. Thinking about Wolfram she realized how very lucky she was that it had been he who claimed her that night and not such a one as this. The manner of this Viking and his looks revolted her. She wondered who he was. He had not been on Wolfram's ship. She must remember to watch this one closely and never to be alone when he was near.

Later in the day when Wolfram returned, he was covered with dirt and wet with sweat. He appeared in a foul mood. Deidre wondered at the cause. Was he angry with her for running away during the night? Would he now cease his gentle attentions to her?

"I chased a wild pig through the bushes and mud bogs," he finally said, answering her questioning eyes. "I thought I would never catch the creature." Vividly he described his pursuit of the beast, the tale an amusing one. The small boar had slipped through his hands each time he had come upon it and only when the animal had fallen into a hole, had Wolfram been able to capture it.

At the thought of so bold a Viking running after such a creature, Deidre laughed. He seemed like a small boy somehow with the mud upon his hands and face. For just a moment she forgot the wide gulf that separated them one from the other, a gulf filled with violence and hatred.

Wolfram joined in her laughter, not ashamed to chuckle at himself, but when the laughter died down he looked at her with a wistful gaze. "Deidre," he whispered. Her name sounded like a benediction on his tongue.

Deidre sought to relieve the tension in the room by babbling. Walking around the room, she questioned him about the various pieces of furniture and tools. The large chest, he told her, was a collection of treasures he had gathered during his raids.

"But you are my greatest treasure," he said with a smile. "I wanted you the moment I laid eyes upon you."

"Wolfram, please . . ." she began. Oh why couldn't she

hate him? It had been so easy when she had thought of him as her enemy.

"You will never know how my heart nearly stopped beating when I saw that sword descending upon you."

The memory of that moment made Deidre shudder. She had nearly met her death, yet until now she did not realize that it had been Wolfram who had saved her life. Why had he done so? There were so many others who had felt the Vikings' violence.

"Why did you save me?" she asked softly. "Was it just so that you could add me to your collection?" she gestured toward the chest. "I am afraid I will not fit in there, nor will I let you own me." Her tone was gentle, but filled with sadness.

"I saved your life because I admired your bravery in trying to rescue your father. You looked like an avenging goddess with your midnight hair flying about your shoulders. I could not let you die." He spoke the words with such passion that for a moment Deidre was tempted to go to him, to put her arms around him and to forget all else but his touch. How could she hate him? Hadn't he also saved her from the fate which had claimed her sister?

"I am grateful that you saved my life," she whispered, "and my virtue as well." It was as if he were an old friend and not an enemy. She felt drawn to him as she had several times before and wondered at the cause. It was as if she knew him from another time, another place. But that was ridiculous. The first time she had ever lain eyes on him was in her father's hall, though a voice deep within her whispered to her and she refused to listen.

"Come here, Deidre," Wolfram said then.

Deidre was tempted, but the memory of vows taken before God stopped her in her tracks. If she let this Viking touch her she knew she would weaken. Hadn't she nearly done so once before? Instead she busied herself with household chores, hoping that he would leave her, but she was not to be so fortunate.

Understanding well her intent, Wolfram pulled a large tub from the far corner of the room. "I am as filthy as that pig I chased this day. I need a bath. Would you join me?" A wicked gleam came into his eyes as he grinned at her.

Deidre shook her head "no" violently. Must there always

be such strong feeling, such tension between them, as if she were going to lose complete control of herself and fling her arms around him. She could not understand her longing for this Viking Wolfram. He was handsome, yes, but it was something more. Something she could not fully understand.

Though it was woman's work, Wolfram fetched his own water, watching her as she heated it on the fire. When the tub was filled he took off his garments, tossing them to the floor with abandon as if in the midst of some primitive ritual. Remembering another time he had been naked to her gaze, Deidre tried to keep her eyes from him.

He had a magnificent body. Even in her innocence she knew that. Not even the scars on his shoulders and back could mar the beauty of his wide shoulders. She wondered at the cause of those scars. Wolfram's strong arms were corded with muscles, blond tufts of hair covered his chest. Deidre could not help but wonder what it would be like to nestle against that curly hair.

He lowered himself in the tub with a sigh. It would be good to soothe his aching muscles with the warmth of the water. Noticing how Deidre's gaze appraised him, he was pleased.

"Are you sure you do not want to join me?" he teased, laughing at her virginal blush. Silence was her answer as she busied herself by picking up and straightening the garments he had flung about.

From time to time Deidre glanced at him out of the corner of her eye, fearful lest he seek to force her to join him. At last he stepped from the tub and dressed himself.

"If you wish to bathe, I will help you fetch the water for your bath," he said loudly, nearly causing her to drop the earthenware jar that she held in her hands.

"No . . . no . . . I . . ." she stammered, fearful that he would watch her if she bathed.

Handing her a small bar of sweet smelling soap, Wolfram could sense her apprehension. "You must get used to having me look upon you, Deidre. You are beautiful," he said gently, his eyes caressing her.

"Please. Can't I have some privacy?"

He shook his head. "I may not have possessed you yet, but that does not mean that I cannot enjoy looking at you."

For just a moment Deidre's temper flared. "I will not be gawked at, like some slave in the market!" She turned her back upon him.

"Then I will leave you to your solitary bath!" he answered, his temper flaring also. She was a stubborn one to be sure—the only woman he had ever met who seemed immune to his charms. "Loki, take her," he swore softly beneath his breath. Slamming the door behind him, he left the small dwelling.

15

At sunset the Vikings gathered around the large, outside cooking area to observe the feast meant to insure fertility in the soil of the fields. All day Deidre had avoided Wolfram, easing her tormented mind by keeping busy preparing for the evening's feast. Now, the festivities were about to begin, and Wolfram sadly took his place next to her.

In a brown tunic bordered with blue and white embroidery at the sleeves and hem, a brown leather corselet with shoulder straps fastened at the chest with buckles, dun-colored leggings, and silver and gold bracelets arraying his arms, Wolfram looked handsome. He looked every inch the jarl or earl that Deidre thought he surely must be in his homeland far to the north.

"He does not look like the fearsome Viking I gazed upon in my father's hall," she mused, looking at him out of the corner of her eye. Deidre thought him the finest looking man there.

Dinner, or as Wolfram called it, *náttveror,* was filled with much laughter and frivolity as the men told jokes and tall tales about their explorations. Deidre tried to laugh, but the laughter seemed to die in her throat. She felt lonely and out of place among all these people. To feel Wolfram's thigh pressing tightly against her own only seemed to magnify her sense of unhappiness and confusion.

"God help me," she thought. "I am an island unto myself."

Sensing her unhappiness, Wolfram did the best he could to lighten her mood, telling her amusing stories and tales of his gods, of frost giants and dwarfs. Perhaps, he thought to himself, Deidre needed to make friends among his people. He had been selfish these past few days, keeping her all to himself.

"This is Roland, Deidre," Wolfram said, nodding in the direction of a tall, big-boned, blond man. Deidre remembered him from the *Sea Wolf.* "And this is his wife, Signy." Deidre recognized his wife as one of the women who had befriended her earlier in the day.

Roland said something to Wolfram, laughed and slapped him on the shoulder. Deidre looked at Wolfram with questioning eyes.

"He says that Freyja herself could not be more beautiful than you. You have hair as dark as a raven's wing, eyes as wide as the seas and skin as white as a dove's breast, and he says that he envies me my place in your bed," Wolfram explained to her. Deidre's face turned as red as a rose.

The man named Roland chattered on and on in his native tongue as Deidre looked on in confusion. It appeared that he was speaking about the ship, but Diedre could not tell for certain. She looked across the table at Signy who smiled as if to say, "these men and their talk of war." Deidre longed to be able to speak to the woman, there was so much she wanted to know and learn. Instead, she could only remain silent and smile back.

When Deidre could stand it no longer, she touched Wolfram's arm to get his attention. "What are they saying?" she asked.

He was pleased at her interest in his people. Perhaps if he taught her his language, she would soon feel at home in the settlement and realize that she was now a Viking woman, whose only laws and vows were those made between Vikings. "I will have to teach you my tongue, Deidre," he said. "Would you like to learn?" She nodded. "It shall be done."

Wolfram introduced Deidre to more of the Vikings gathered around the table. She met Thurston, Roland, Ulaf, Leif, Rorik, the Viking who had been kind to her sister Bridget that fateful day, and many others who remembered her from the voyage. In addition to Signy there were two other women at the table, Helga, the blond woman who had pulled at Deidre's braids and tried to speak with her and Hildegard, a much older woman with a round face and skin weathered by the sun. Deidre noticed that the men outnumbered the women four to one. Was it like this in all the Viking lands?

As the platters heaped with fish, small game birds, boiled meat and vegetables were passed around, Wolfram taught

Deidre the name for each one. She learned quickly and he praised her efforts.

The food was similar to that which Deidre's family prepared for their feasts except that the Vikings seemed to prefer boiling meat, the Irish roasting it. Deidre thought the cheeses, butter, fruits and long loaves of dark bread upon the plates in the center of the table looked delicious. Beside each plate was a goblet filled with wine, a rare treat and one saved for feasts such as this one, Wolfram told her. Like the Irish, the Vikings were fond of their drink. They raised the mugs and goblets to toast each other and drained the dregs dry.

Deidre had partaken of several swallows of the strong drink and now felt lighthearted and at ease. The flames from the central fire fanned bright, casting a warm glow about Deidre as she turned her eyes toward Wolfram. For one hypnotic moment their eyes met and held. She could feel his closeness, his desire.

Wolfram's senses soared as he looked at Deidre. He could see the deep emotion in her eyes. Dare he hope that her look spoke of love?

A shout broke out among the Vikings, breaking the spell. "To Wolfram. Long may he sail the seas!"

Deidre ate in silence. Sensing that she was being watched, she looked up and was alarmed to find the short, stocky Viking with the cold, ice-blue eyes staring at her. Something in his manner told her that he did not consider her to be Wolfram's property. The lust in his eyes made her shiver in revulsion. She started to tell Wolfram about her fears, to warn him about the man, but at that very moment young Rorik stood up and began telling a tale about the creation of the world. Wolfram whispered in Deidre's ear, translating the words into Gaelic.

"Flaming Fire, burning ice, that is how it all began," Wolfram said softly. "In the south the realm called Muspell flickers with dancing flames. No one can endure this fire except those born to that land. In the north is the realm of Niflheim. It is packed with ice and covered with a vast drift of snow. In the center of this world was a fountain from which twelve rivers poured forth into a large abyss. These rivers became frost, but the fiery clouds of Muspell turned the ice to mists and caused clouds to form. Life quickened in the drops of water from this ice and formed the first frost giant called Ymir."

"Ymir," Deidre repeated, fascinated by the tale. How different it was from the story of creation in the Holy Book, but then coming from a land of ice and snow as these Vikings did, it was no surprise to her that they should believe that the world had been created out of its frozen depths.

"Also out of the clouds came Audhumla the cow, who discovered a man's head while nourishing itself from licking the frost and salt in the ice. This new being married the daughter of the race of Ymir and brought forth the gods Odin, Vili and Ve," Wolfram continued.

Deidre looked up to find Rorik's eyes upon her as he talked. She smiled at him and he smiled back. Feeling a sharp pinch to her arm, she looked behind her to see the frowning face of Helga. Her jealous glance warned Deidre not to show too much interest in the youthful speaker. No doubt the Viking woman was in love with Rorik, Deidre thought, wishing she could assure the woman that she had no desire for her man.

As Rorik continued his tale, Deidre sat with downcast eyes. The strange tale was one of giants and violence, of how Ymir the frost giant was killed and his body made into the earth, his blood made into the seas, his bones the mountains, his hair the trees, his skull the heavens and his brain the clouds. All the while, Wolfram whispered the translation of Rorik's words into Deidre's ears. The soft stir of his breath in her ear sent shivers down Deidre's back and she longed to snuggle closer against him.

"They took sparks from Muspell and placed them in the sky as the sun, moon, and stars, to encircle the round earth and the sea," Wolfram continued. She remembered the day he had told her that the earth was round. Could it be so? Were these Vikings right?

Another man rose to tell another tale and another and another. Deidre found the stories interesting, particularly the exploits of Odin and Thor.

At last the Viking men rose from the ground and walked to the fire, forming a ring around it. Deidre followed, but was pulled back by Signy to stand with the women. Gone now was the relaxed atmosphere, to be replaced by a sense of excitement. Each Viking was now wearing a helmet with horns sprouting out each side. Deidre had not seen this kind of helmet before. During the raid and upon the journey over the sea, the Vikings had worn conical helmets. She reasoned that

these horned helmets must be for ceremonies and thought to
herself wryly that they looked like devils.

The men sang and chanted as if in a drunken frenzy. Upon
the ledge of one of the rocks in the middle of the fire was
placed the statue of a male figure with helmet on his head.
Deidre blushed as she saw that the statue was endowed with a
very large manhood, which was huge in proportion to the
small ugly figure. The men took turns pouring wine over this
ugly statue, chanting all the while, and Deidre knew that this
ceremony had something to do with fertility and the planting
season. Was the wine supposed to signify blood? She felt a
stab of revulsion as she realized that perhaps once long ago it
had been blood which had been sacrificed and not red wine.

"I must get away from this pagan ritual," she thought in
alarm, "lest I be damned by my God." Thinking again of
escape, she turned and fled into the darkness of the night,
heedless of where she was going. After the smoke from the
fire, the air was cool upon her cheeks as she breathed in its
freshness. It soothed her lungs, but nothing could soothe the
pain in her heart. Watching Wolfram participate in this chanting and dancing only magnified the differences between them,
differences that could not be changed. He was a pagan. A Viking.

The wine she had partaken of earlier made her unsteady on
her feet and light-headed, as if the world were haloed in a hazy
glow.

The sound of a snapping twig alerted Deidre to danger. Was
it animal or man behind her?

"I was foolish to come out so far alone at night," she
scolded to herself. Her intentions this time had not been to run
away, but only to get away from the furies of the festival. She
must go back before Wolfram thought her to be running away
again.

Once more she heard a sound behind her. Slowly turning
around, preparing to run, she felt a hand reach out and grab
her.

"Let me go!" she cried out. The hand only held her tighter,
imprisoning her against a rocklike chest. Feeling the brush of
exhaled breath near her cheek, Deidre looked around, struggling to see in the darkness of the night. It was the cold-eyed
Viking staring down at her in the moonlight, the one she had
seen earlier in the day. His cruel eyes glinted at her in the

moonlight. Thrusting his hands to invade her gown, his fingers began kneading her breasts.

Deidre let out a shriek as the Viking grunted and pulled her down to the ground. He ignored the pleading sound of her voice, coming closer and closer to her as he lifted the hem of her gown.

"No! No!" Deidre screamed. The horror of this hulking giant forcing himself upon her was terrifying. Fighting with all her might against the sacrilege of his taking her, Deidre broke away from his grasp with a surge of strength. Stumbling about in the darkness, crawling behind a large tree, she awaited her fate.

16

Through his mead-fogged brain, Wolfram heard the high-pitched sound. He looked about wildly for Deidre. She was gone.

Again he heard a scream echoing in his ears. "Deidre!" he called.

He left the chanting Viking throng, running as fast as his legs could carry him toward the direction of the sound; thoughts of Deidre being mauled by a wolf or a wild cat tortured his brain.

"Deidre," he called out, but there was no answer. Again he called her name and this time he could hear a faint whimper among the bushes. Coming closer he saw the form of Eric Haraldsson hovering over Deidre, clinging to her arm as she tried to hide behind a tree.

A wild cry of outrage tore through the silence of the night. "You son of Hel!" Wolfram shouted, lunging for the hefty Viking.

Seeing the man bearing down upon him, sword upraised, Eric Haraldsson let loose of his captive and reached for his own sword.

Wolfram's ears were attuned to sounds of danger in the darkness of the night, his senses ready to guard him. Hearing the sound of Eric's sword whistling through the air, Wolfram ducked just in time. The sound of splintering wood told him that the blade had found a tree trunk instead of his neck and for that he whispered his thanks to the gods.

Undaunted by his foe's attempt to behead him, Wolfram, swinging his own sword, heard the clatter of metal upon metal as his weapon connected with the hulking Viking's sword. Eric let out a growl of anger, throwing himself forward, swinging furiously, striking in every direction. Wolfram thrust with his sword and felt it connect with the man's flesh. A howl of pain rent the air.

Again and again the two Vikings collided, weapon against seapon in the dance of battle. Wolfram stumbled over a tree branch and fell to earth with such a thud that he was immobilized by the shock of pain for just a moment. The warning of his senses came to his rescue as his sword arm swung forward, blocking his enemy's death blow.

In the darkness, from her place upon the hard ground, Deidre could hardly distinguish one man from the other as she watched the confrontation in horror.

As she rose to her feet, watching the shadowy forms, she prayed, "Oh God, dear merciful Lord, be with Wolfram." The thought of his death caused her pain.

Straining his eyes, Wolfram looked up for just a moment and saw her standing there. The pause gave Eric the chance he needed. Knocking the sword from Wolfram's hand, he bore down upon him to wield the death which would still Wolfram's breath of life.

"Wolfram!" Deidre screamed. She made her way to the spot where the sword lay upon the ground as if in a daze, picked it up and held it with both hands.

"So, I have bested you at last, you son of a dog!" Eric bellowed, relishing his victory.

A thin trickle of blood seeped from Wolfram's throat as Eric pressed his sword against his enemy's flesh. His eyes locked with the other Viking's eyes and he was surprised to see the hatred there. Had Eric always hated him?

"You would send me to death without a sword, without the chance to enter Valhalla?" he breathed, closing his eyes to wait for the death blow.

Deidre moved forward, holding onto Wolfram's sword with both of her small hands. Moving as if in a dream, she raised the sword and struck out with all her might. For one so small her strength was fierce, her aim true as she wounded Eric in his sword arm.

"Ah . . . Ah . . ." Eric shrieked, dropping his own sword to the ground. His chance at life renewed, Wolfram sprang upward, picking up his enemy's sword. It was he who now held sway over life and death.

"Get out of here. Now. Don't let me ever see your face

again," Wolfram threatened. "If I do, I will kill you!"

"Where am I to go?" Eric growled.

"I do not know. Loki take you for all I care." He had a feeling deep inside him that it was a mistake to let the man go free, that surely this dog would come back to haunt them. Yet, for Deidre's sake, he did not listen to his inner voice. Wolfram gathered Deidre in his arms and they watched as Eric Haraldsson slithered away like the snakes Saint Patrick had driven out of Ireland.

"I thought at first I had killed him," Deidre whispered, clinging to his strong body.

"Perhaps it would have been better if you had," Wolfram said softly, suddenly regretting his decision to spare the man.

The stood molded together for several moments, their bodies touching, their hearts fluttering. His lips found the hollow of her throat and he gently traced a path upward.

"Let me love you, Deidre," he said softly. "Let me take you to that world of fire and passion that the bards sing about." He ran his hands over her body, fanning the flames of her desire. How he loved the smooth soft feel of her, the peaks of her breasts, the taste of her skin, the fragrance of her hair.

Wolfram kissed her gently, his mouth tasting of her honey. Deidre gave herself up to the kiss, reaching out to touch him as he touched her, his powerful chest, his flat belly. She could feel the swell of his manhood pressing against her stomach and wondered what it would be like to have this staff within her. Would Wolfram make her cry out in passion as Ian had made Bridget do? So wondering, she snuggled amid the warmth of his arms.

"Deidre," Wolfram's hand slid down to lift the hem of her gown. She gasped in pleasure as his fingers nestled in the silken curls of her womanhood, stroking gently, bringing rippling fire of pleasure to the core of her being. She wanted him at that moment as surely as he wanted her.

He gently pulled her down with him to the soft grass. The stars twinkled down at them like sparkling jewels, making it a perfect setting for their joining.

Wolfram tugged at his garments in a flurry of excitement to possess her, moving away from her for just a moment to again join her, his braccae gone from him now, clothed only in his tunic. His hands worked at her gown, pulling it down around her waist. It was then that reality came flooding back to Deidre.

"No, please," she moaned, rolling away from him.

He reached out for her, but she eluded his arms, pulling her gown again upon her shoulders.

"I love you, Deidre. Don't deny me now. Not now when we are so close to becoming one." He rose to his feet and put his arms around her waist, bringing her close to him once more.

She fought against her own desires as well as his. "What is your penalty for adultery?" she asked him then. It was as if she had doused him with cold water. "Answer me."

"Adulterers are hanged or trodden to death by horses," he answered, loosening his grip upon her. "But you are not committing such a deed by joining with me. You are mine. Freyja has willed it."

She shook her head. "The laws of my people say that I belong to another."

"And your heart?" he asked bitterly.

"My heart belongs . . ." She wanted to tell him that her heart belonged to him, but she could not speak the words. She had taken the vows and did not have the right to love another. For the first time she resented that her father's choice had not been hers. She had not had any say in the matter and yet it was the Irish way. Women before her had always done as their fathers wished. Her mother had wed her father in an arranged marriage. Dare she even question? She forced the thought from her mind.

"Your heart belongs to me. Say it." He reached for her but Deidre escaped his hands, fleeing from him back to the house she shared with Wolfram. Throwing herself down upon the pile of furs she wept her heart out. She *did* want him and the longing made her desperately unhappy.

When Wolfram did not come home that night, Deidre at first felt relieved but then she feared that perhaps she had angered him. How would she feel if he sought out the likes of Helga or Signy? Wolfram was a man that few women could resist. What if even now he was in another woman's arms? The pain of such a thought was like a sword wound to her soul and she wondered what she would do if he became lost to her forever?

17

With the first light of dawn, Deidre was awakened to find that she was not alone. Beside her on the small bed lay Wolfram. He had come back! He looked younger in his sleep and Deidre had the feeling that there was something familiar about him. For the first time she wondered what he would look like without his beard.

Wolfram stirred and, remembering last night, Deidre rolled off the bed. Picking up her garments, she dressed herself hastily before the Viking awoke. Her hands touched the gilt of the brooch with reverence as she fastened it in place. How could she feel desire for this Viking when her heart belonged to another, and her soul was tied in bonds of marriage to a husband across the land?

"What kind of a woman am I?" she whispered, yet she touched the finely wrought object again as if to remember the face of the man who had given it to her. "No doubt he has a wife and many children," Deidre murmured. The ache at the thought pierced her heart.

"Tell me about him?"

Deidre turned with a start to find the eyes of Wolfram upon her. "You loved him, didn't you? Tell me about this man. I know it is not your husband whom you really love, vows or no vows."

"He came from the lands to the North, like yourself," Deidre began. "I was but a child of thirteen, all legs and arms, as awkward as a colt." She wondered just why she was telling this man about her childhood love.

"Was he a slave?"

84

"Yes, how did you know?" She felt her heart skip a beat as their eyes met. What was it about Wolfram's eyes which tore at her soul?

"I guessed as much. How did you meet him?"

"He was sold into slavery to one of my kinsmen by his own brother, or so my father told me. I am ashamed to admit that any of my clan kept another in bondage. It was out of hatred that he did so."

Wolfram fought to control his rage. So it was true after all that his own brother had so betrayed him. He would not doubt her word, she had no reason to lie to him. He clenched his fists and tightened his jaw. Someday his brother would pay dearly for such treachery.

Deidre went on, unaware of the tumult in Wolfram's mind. "He would let no one humble him, though it meant many beatings and ill treatment by my kinsman. When I found out what he was suffering, it was more than I could bear. I brought him food and did what I could to see that he fared well. Then one night I could stand seeing him in bondage no longer and I loosened his bonds."

"You meant for him to go free?"

"Yes. I prayed that he would find his way to freedom, every night I so prayed. It is not right that one man enslave another. Christians do not take slaves."

"No, it is not right. Though we Vikings have our thralls or slaves, I cannot think that it is a thing which should be done. It is taught that each man's class is a decree of the gods and that only the faithless would dare to change such a thing, still I am tempted to do so. All those vanquished in battle are sold into slavery, though I myself have never stooped to do such a foul thing."

"Never?" she asked, amazed that even though he was a Viking and guilty of much, he would speak with such feeling.

"I know how it feels to have the lash upon one's back. So you see, little one, I would never have enslaved you."

For just a moment Deidre wondered if he had in truth been a slave. She looked into the blue of his eyes and at that moment she knew for certain that she had known this man before. Was it possible? No, her mind was playing with her, she told herself.

"Who are you, Wolfram the Bold?" she whispered, afraid

to find out the answer. It would make her denial of him all the
more difficult.

"Perhaps it is time that I shave and let you see what I really
look like," he said grimly. He asked her to bring him his small
dagger so that he could shave his whiskers, and from time to
time Deidre heard him issue a loud oath to his pagan gods
when he nicked himself with its blade.

Deidre looked upon his clean-shaven face and gasped.

"Do you recognize me now?" he asked softly.

Deidre lifted her violet eyes to his face, tracing every line
and curve as if it were a map. She thought surely her eyes must
be deceiving her. It couldn't be, but it was. Why hadn't she
guessed before? Had the beard played tricks on her eyes and
blinded her to the truth?

"It *is* you!" she said softly. Her eyes *had* been blinded to
what her heart had known all along. This then was why she
had been so drawn to the Viking from the moment she had
lain eyes upon him.

"Yes, it is I, your bold slave of days so long ago. When I
saw the brooch that day in your sleeping chamber, there upon
your breast, I knew that you were the child who had once been
so kind to me. That is why I could not force myself upon you,
nor will I ever. I love you, Deidre, and I always will. The tender child has grown to be a beautiful woman I want as my
wife."

Tears ran down Deidre's cheeks. It was too late. She had
found him too late. If only she had known the day of the wedding that he was near, perhaps then they would have had a
chance at happiness then, but now? Her honor and sacred
vows separated them and always would.

Deidre covered her mouth with her small hand and turned
before he could hear her sobs.

"I love you, Deidre," Wolfram repeated. He turned her
around to face him with gentle hands.

"It's too late," she sobbed. "I can never belong to you.
Never. I must go back to my husband, can't you see that?"

"I only see that we have wasted too much time already." He
reached out to take her face in his hands, but Deidre shrugged
free of his touch. "If you have any affection for me, you will
leave me alone."

Wolfram's last hope was dashed like the waves upon the
rocks. He had been so certain that at last she had grown to

love him, that when he revealed to her that he was the same Viking she had once given her heart to, she would do so again. But Deidre was lost to him and the knowledge tore at his soul.

"I will leave, if that is what you want," he exclaimed, hiding his pain in anger. "You may sleep in your lonely bed for all I care. I am tired of your denial of the love you feel for me. What kind of a god can wish you to honor vows which bring such pain and loneliness? As for me, I would rather be a pagan. At least my gods are not so heartless." With that he was gone leaving Deidre as he had said. Alone.

18

Days turned into weeks and still Wolfram did not return. It was as if the sun had disappeared from Deidre's world. From time to time she spotted his tall muscular frame working in the fields or walking by the shoreline, but he never came near the wattle and daub house where she slept nor sought her company. The pain his absence caused was like a wound, a sorrow that engulfed her heart.

During the days Deidre busied herself at the loom, weaving material for a new tunic for Wolfram or helping the other women dry or salt food and hang the various herbs to dry. She made bread, kneading it in the wooden trough, and helped to brew beer and mead, watching the other women to learn how it was done. These tasks helped her endure the loneliness of Wolfram's neglect of her, and during the day she was indeed so busy that her mind was eased somewhat.

It was the nights, however, which were unbearable. She would lie on her fur bed and think of Wolfram—his smile, his courage, his boldness. He was everything she could desire in a man. He was strong yet gentle, handsome though not puffed up with conceit, and he had been so patient with her. And how had she rewarded him for his patience? By refusing to grant to him that which they both so desired, and for what reason? A vow of marriage given, yet not consummated.

"How could my God wish this loneliness upon me?" she asked herself, then answered, "He could not. Wolfram and I are married in our hearts. Phelan never loved me nor I him. How then can it be wrong that I give myself to the man I do love?"

Wolfram too was in agony, watching Deidre from afar yet not daring to come too near to her. His desire was much too

strong to control and he feared lest he break his vow to her not
to use force. His pride too had been wounded by her refusal.
He bent his back at the plow during the day and slept aboard
the *Sea Wolf* at night. But always he kept Deidre in his view or
knew that others were nearby to protect her.

"So, it is here that you hide yourself," Sigurd roared on
finding Wolfram on the Viking ship late one night. "Is it that
the Irish woman snores too loudly?" He chuckled at his own
wit.

Wolfram was in no mood for jokes. Jumping up from the
hard deck he returned Sigurd's jibes with a frown. "You know
very well why I am here. To keep from acting like a rutting
stag. The Irish woman wants no part of me. She will not break
her vows to that Irish dog of a husband of hers."

Sigurd cocked one eyebrow. "Wolfram, my dear friend, I
always knew that you were a stubborn Northman, but I did
not think that you were stupid. That beauty loves you, I have
seen it in her eyes. You of all men should know that women do
not always say what they mean. She wants you to beg her, woo
her and sweep her off her feet. Do that and she will soon
forget that any other man ever existed. Vows be damned, she
will be your woman and plead with you to take her every
night."

"I do not think . . ."

"You are not supposed to think, only to feel and do what
you must to win this woman of yours. Life is too short to let it
slip by without living it to the fullest. As a Viking you know
how soon it is that we may die." Sigurd patted his friend upon
the shoulder. "Now go to that woman. You have wasted
enough time already."

Deidre stood before the hearth fire in the small hut warming
water for her bath. Today she had worked herself into exhaustion. Her back ached and every muscle in her body was sore.
Signy had given her a present this day, a small flagon of perfumed oil which Roland had brought back from raids in the
lands far to the south. Although they could not share each
other's words, they could share each other's feelings by the
look in the eyes. Hildegard too had proven to be a friend. The
older woman was one of the few around the settlement who
knew some words of Gaelic and had helped Deidre understand
a little of what was being said. With Wolfram gone, Deidre

had begun to look upon Hildegard as her only link with the
Viking world.

When the tub was filled, Deidre tossed aside her garments
and stepped inside the perfumed warmth. She leaned back and
enjoyed this peculiar Viking custom of submerging one's entire body in water. Wolfram had told her that he had heard
that his people had learned the custom from those of the land
to the east, the island off the coast of China. She had tried it
several times now and had not caught the dread chill that her
people of Eire always talked about.

Deidre stayed in the tub until the water turned cold, then
stepped out and draped herself in a thick linen cloth. Standing
before the fire she rubbed her skin until it glowed, then sank
down upon the furs of her bed. The soft furs tickled her bare
skin as she pulled them up her body to shield her from
the night air. Enjoying the feel of their warmth, she closed her
eyes to sleep.

Wolfram entered the small dwelling feeling comforted to be
once again home. The embers of the fire glowed like bright red
stars and by the light of their glow he could see Deidre's face
reposed in slumber.

"How I love her," he said softly. Guilt tugged at his heart
as he thought of what he was resolved to do and for a moment
he was about to ignore Sigurd's words and turn around and
leave, but Deidre's soft moaning stopped him in his tracks.

"Wolfram," she mumbled.

Thinking that she was awake, he went to her side, but her
eyes were closed and she was breathing the heavy sighs of
slumber.

Wolfram reached out and touched her bare arm, so soft to
his fingers. It was such torture, wanting her so. He gently
caressed her shoulder, moving up to the slim whiteness of her
neck, entwining his fingers in the glory of her midnight hair. A
desire filled him, a desire so powerful that it banished all other
thoughts from his mind.

Deidre's eyes flew open. Wolfram was at her side. It had not
been just a dream of her senses. She sat up in bed looking into
his sea-blue eyes and smiled at him.

"I have missed you, Deidre," Wolfram said huskily.

"And I you, my Viking," she answered softly.

"Deidre!" he moaned, burying his face in the softness of
her breasts which had come uncovered with her movement.

She reached out and clasped him to her, knowing that nothing else mattered at this moment except his nearness.

Wolfram ran his tongue over the softness of her skin, and she sighed as waves of sensation swelled and surged within her. There was only the feel of his lips and tongue and hands. All remembrance of her vows fled from her mind.

"You are so beautiful. So very beautiful," Wolfram murmured.

Wolfram kissed her then, molding his lips to hers. His tongue explored the recesses of her mouth with great tenderness. Deidre's lips parted to his probing tongue, enjoying the taste of him, the feel of him and the very smell of him. It was as if they had been fashioned, each for the other. Could any wine taste as sweet as his kisses? She knew it could not.

Wolfram's hands moved upon Deidre's body, stroking lightly as if she were a cherished treasure, and indeed she was. He touched her mouth, her throat, her belly, her thighs with both fingers and tongue until Deidre felt her limbs grow weak with her yearning for him. Arching her back she sought to mold her body to his, pressing against him with a groan.

"Love me, Wolfram. Love me." she whispered.

He left her side only for a moment to shed his garments, and for that brief time Deidre mourned his loss, his warmth beside her.

Wolfram fumbled with his clothing, swearing beneath his breath as he yanked upon his lacings and leggings. It was as if he were encumbered with ten clumsy fingers on each hand. When finally he joined her on the bed of furs, he feared lest she now reject him as she had so many times before, but Deidre merely reached out her hand to touch him.

Wolfram kissed her mouth and put his arms around her to draw her close against him. Every part of their bodies touched, blended as if to become one.

Deidre felt the warmth, the maleness of him. His body was so strong and muscular, his mouth so firm yet gentle. She wanted to give him pleasure as he was doing to her. She reached up and ran her fingers through his thick blond hair, amazed at her own boldness. She knew in her heart that this was right. This moment had been destined to be since she had first set eyes upon him so many years ago.

"I want to please you," she whispered.

Wolfram brushed her hair back from her face. "Just let me

love you. What we do will come as naturally to you as breathing, my love." He wanted to be gentle with her, not to hurt her and yet he knew that this first time would bring her some pain.

Wolfram's mouth strayed down her body, his lips searing her skin until she was moaning with pleasure. A warmth, a fire coursed through her body. Her body responded with a will of its own, all shyness forgotten. She returned his touches, exploring his body and felt joy when she heard him moan with desire at her inexperienced touch.

"Yes, yes," he urged as she reached down and ran her hand over his stiffened manhood. Deidre thought of the times she had been so afraid of this sword of his flesh, his powerful maleness. Now she was no longer afraid. Wolfram would do naught to cause her injury. Instead she longed to feel him deep within her. His flesh was warm to her touch, pulsating with the strength of his being.

Wolfram slid his hands across her stomach and tenderly stroked the silken softness of her womanhood. Deidre felt the waves of pleasure flow through her like the ocean's tide and moved her body toward his questing fingers.

Wolfram felt her shiver and knew that she felt the same ecstasy that he felt, a rapture that seemed to entwine their souls as well as their bodies. They had drunk from the enchanting cup of love and there was no turning back now.

"'I love you, Deidre," Wolfram whispered. "Please know that I love you and do not wish to bring you hurt." He had to tell her of the pain this first joining would bring. "There will be pain at first . . ."

"I know. My sister told me," she answered, tightening her arms about him. "I do not care. I only want you to love me."

"And so I shall, little one." He covered her body with his own, gently parting her legs. He teased the petals of her flowery womanhood, entering her easily, covering her mouth with his own as he thrust.

Deidre welcomed him with a cry of joy, seized by a surge of pleasure which was only stilled by the sudden pain as he broke through her maidenhead. Deidre cried out, but her body relaxed as Wolfram soothed her with kisses. In truth once that brief pain was over, only pleasure remained. They were no longer two beings, but one. She welcomed his thrusts, moving with him until they were both engulfed by the flames which consumed them. Wolfram, ever the gentle lover, brought

Deidre such joy as she had never even imagined would be possible. It was as if the stars themselves had come down from the sky to burst within them both. For one blinding moment Deidre thought that she would faint, would die with the wonder of their joining. She called out his name over and over again as the world seemed to quake beneath them and explode into light.

"Deidre!" Wolfram's cry was like a prayer to one of his gods. With a shudder he was still, yet buried deep within her.

In the hazy afterglow of their lovemaking, they held each other close knowing that each had found his mate for life. Deidre knew that she had been loved wholly, as Phelan never could have loved her.

"You belong to me, Deidre," Wolfram said softly. "Only to me. Never to anyone else." And in the saying it was so, a spoken vow between them that could never be broken.

19

Deidre awoke as the first rays of the sun seeped through the small slits of the house, the tiny windows. It felt so good to have the warm rays touch her naked skin as she lay entwined with Wolfram's strong body. She felt a fierce surge of desire to again feel his hands upon her body and his mouth joining hers.

She looked over at him, sleeping so peacefully as he held her in his arms. In the bright sunlight she studied his face. In the quiet of his slumber he looked like a small boy, so vulnerable.

"So this is what love is all about," she thought. Deidre knew that if Wolfram were taken from her now, she would not want to live.

Deidre's eyes traveled down Wolfram's body to the well-formed legs, the powerful chest, the flat belly and trim waist and lastly to the mystery of his manhood, that which had given her so much pleasure. It was also asleep this morning, but upon arousal she knew how powerful it could prove to be.

Deidre snuggled once again amid the warmth of his arms, her head against his chest, wishing that life could always be as peaceful as it was at this moment. If only she could remain in the safety of his arms forever.

"What are you thinking?" Wolfram whispered in her ear, opening his blue eyes to meet her violet ones.

"How happy I am here with you, that I wish it could always be thus," she answered, stroking his sun-goldened chest. With longing she reached down and ran her hand lightly over his manhood, laughing as it roused to her touch. Wolfram in his turn outlined the swell of her breasts and Deidre felt again that rapture she had felt the night before. His mouth covered hers, his hard body molded against her softness.

"I love you, Deidre. Never leave me," he finally said, as they drew apart for just a moment.

"I'll never leave you as long as you want me and love me," she promised, knowing in her heart that she spoke the truth. His people would be her people, his land her own from this moment onward.

Wolfram made love to her then. He did not rush his pleasure but held himself back so that Deidre could experience the full joy of her newfound womanhood. He was amply rewarded for his patience as she met his raging fire with a fire of her own. An aching sweetness became a shattering explosion of pleasure. Deidre gave herself to him fully as a spasm shook her whole being and she seemed to be thrown into the very heavens above.

It was with the greatest reluctance that they parted later that morning, for both knew that their lives would never be the same after this love they had shared. Deidre thought about Adam and Eve, the first lovers.

"The Holy Book says that Eve, the first woman, was brought forth from Adam's rib," she said aloud, wondering if this were true.

Wolfram laughed as he fastened his stout leather belt, watching her fasten her brooch, that token of their first love.

"According to Viking legend, Odin made the man from an ash tree and the woman from an elm tree," he said. "A still mightier tree supports the world, or so it is said."

Deidre pondered his words. There was so much that she needed to learn about his people. She had only begun.

Wolfram walked to the door. He so hated to leave her. Deidre ran to him and wound her arms around him, not wanting him to go.

"Tonight, little one. We will have tonight," he whispered. Tonight seemed like eternity as he stepped out the door.

Tonight soon came and more nights after that as Wolfram and Deidre basked in the glow of their newfound love. It was as if no other people existed except the two of them. Wolfram went about his business of plowing, Deidre her woman's work, but only when they were together were they truly alive. Deidre felt in her heart that nothing could ever happen to shake the foundation of their world; she did not know how wrong she was.

20

On a morning near the end of spring, Deidre was rudely awakened from her peaceful slumber as the sound of broken wood shattered through the silence of the dawn. She sensed danger, yet she barely had time to awaken Wolfram, and indeed cover herself before the nightmare descended upon them like demons from the depths of Hades.

A scream tore from Deidre's mouth as she saw the gleam of upraised swords shining in the light of the sun. Her heart was filled with terror, not for herself but for Wolfram.

In the dull silence the sounds of screams rent the air, the unmistakable clash of sword upon sword. Memories of the attack upon her father's hall flashed through her mind.

Wolfram barely had time to arm himself before the three Vikings were upon him. They were going to kill him if he did not surpass their combined skills and win this deadly combat.

"Deidre, run. Get away!" he shouted, lashing out with his sword at the nearest foe.

Stubbornly she refused. Didn't he know that she would gladly die by his side? She would not leave him to meet his fate alone.

Wolfram stood legs astride, sword in hand, dodging an axe which missed him by a hound's tooth. His sword blow hit its mark and one of his enemies was felled to earth like a massive tree.

Now it was two against one as the Vikings pushed forward. Looking into their faces, Deidre saw the leering grin of Eric Haraldsson. So it was he who had brought this treachery upon them. How she wished now that Wolfram had killed the man when he had the chance.

Eric Haraldsson swung and struck a powerful blow just as

Wolfram ducked out of the way. His sword embedded itself in a small wooden bench, nearly cleaving the wood in two. The other Viking stepped forward to take his place, swinging his battle-axe. Wolfram pushed forward Deidre's loom, nearly knocking the man off balance.

Deidre sought for any weapon that she could use to aid Wolfram. He could after all only face one at a time. He needed her help. Oh that for just a few moments in time she could be a man!

She found the perfect weapon in a long-handled baking plate, made of iron and wood, and swung it like a club. She struck Eric Haraldsson a blow which sent him sprawling and then brought the rounded surface down upon his head to knock him unconscious.

"Well done, Deidre," Wolfram said in praise as he continued his own fight. "At least now the odds are more fair."

The two men crossed the room, back and forth, first one striking out then the other. It was a contest evenly matched. All Deidre could do was stand aside and watch. It would not be well for her to interfere this time. Then suddenly Wolfram's foe tired, losing his reserve of power. In truth he was a man much older than Wolfram. Wolfram's sword struck out and sliced through his enemy's shoulder rendering his sword arm useless. Deidre had no doubt but that the man would bleed to death within a moment and there was nothing she could do to change his fate and wondered if she even wanted to try. Would he not have murdered Wolfram even as he slept?

"I am becoming more Viking than I ever imagined," she said aloud.

Wolfram put his arms around her. "Aye, you have acted this day as a Viking woman should. I could not have asked for greater bravery."

The man who had just been wounded gave a rasping sound, the sound of death and Wolfram knelt down beside him while Deidre tied Eric Haraldsson securely with ropes. He would be killed but not by her hand.

Eric opened his ice-blue eyes and squinted them as he looked into Deidre's eyes. She read hatred there, an urge to cause her injury and she was glad he was bound.

"Irish bitch!" he swore. "You have not seen the end of this."

Quickly she left his side to escape his malice and joined
Wolfram. He was staring transfixed at the face of the dead
man upon the floor.

"I know this man. He was the one who took me captive and
sold me to the Irish as a slave. I could never forget his face,"
he exclaimed as all color drained from his face.

"Are you certain?" Deidre asked.

"As sure as I know that I love you," he answered, rising to
his feet to stand beside her. "If it is the last thing I do, I will
find out from Eric Haraldsson the reason for this foul deed. If
my brother *was* responsible for ordering such a thing done, I
will soon know it."

They walked outside into the light of day. Several bodies lay
on the ground, enemies as well as those from the settlement,
but it was clear that Wolfram's people had been the victorious
ones. Several houses had been burned to the ground and from
afar they could see the blaze of the fields which had been set
on fire. Wolfram lost no time in gathering a party of men to
fight the flames, and Deidre in her stead sought out the
women to aid the wounded.

There was no time for the usual morning meal as women
and men alike fought hard in their own ways to save the settlement. The men returned with faces blackened with smoke but
with the knowledge that most of the crops had been saved.
With his return, Wolfram again turned his attentions to the
man named Eric Haraldsson.

"Tell me who sent you," he shouted, grabbing the man by
the throat. Never had Deidre seen him in such a white hot
rage.

Eric merely smiled at Wolfram and spat in his face. "I will
never tell you," he said.

"And if I threaten to burn you alive if you do not?"
Wolfram countered. "What say you then?"

"I am not afraid of death at your hands. Do it quickly,"
Eric snarled his defiance.

Wolfram loosened his grasp and eyed the other man coldly.
"It will not be a quick death. You will beg me a thousand
times over to let you die. If there is one thing I cannot tolerate
it is treachery."

Something about his voice, his expression, took away Eric's
bravado. He did not mind dying and going to Valhalla, but to
have a slow painful death was another thing. He thought a

moment and then asked. "And if I tell you all that you want me to, what will be my fate then? I will not live one day as a slave."

"I will see that you are sent to Norway, to serve your fellow Vikings there. Not as a thrall but as a peasant bondi. Your sword arm will be severed so that you may never again take up arms against your brothers. It is better than you deserve." He stood with hands on hips, looking down at the traitor.

For a long moment Eric Haraldsson was silent, pondering the matter over in his mind. He chose death over life and Wolfram again stated his terms. "Tell me and I will have you killed quickly."

"It was your brother. Your brother!" Eric finally blurted.

Wolfram was not surprised, though his heart ached to find that there was treachery in his own family.

"When he found out that you had escaped your slavery he bid me to find you, to seek you out and make certain that you never returned to the Northlands. I was supposed to kill you if you ever planned to go back to your home," Eric continued.

"Then why did you fall upon us today?" Wolfram asked.

"My own anger. I hoped to take your head back with me to the Northland and claim a reward from your brother. How was he to know what had passed between us? Someday he will be the jarl in your father's place and I sought to secure a position at his side." Eric was silent then, his eyes cast downward. Was there a chance that he could escape and warn Wolfram's brother?

"So, it is my brother who seeks my undoing," Wolfram whispered. He thought about their childhood days. Perhaps even then Everard was jealous of Wolfram's closeness with his father. Even though Everard was the eldest son, Wolfram had been the son of Olaf's favorite wife and therefore the son he had adored. That Wolfram's mother had died in childbirth had acted to make her son more precious to the Viking Jarl. "No doubt Everard feared that I and not he would be chosen as the next Jarl."

Deidre sought to bring him comfort, reaching for his hand and squeezing it with affection. "Your sorrow is my sorrow," she said.

Wolfram looked down upon her. "I must go back. I have a fear for my father. I have been away too long." He thought about his desire to return a wealthy man. He had spent the years raiding and traveling about after his escape from slavery. Time had gotten away from him in his pursuit of treasures. He had been possessed by the demon of greed. But now he knew he must return.

"If you go, I will go too," Deidre promised. "A brave woman from my Holy Book once said, 'Whither thou goest, I will go.' "

He buried his face in the softness of her fragrant hair. "Then we shall go, little one. Together we shall cross the waters to Norway."

Having made his decision, Wolfram gathered together the people of the settlement. There was much rebuilding that needed to be done and he realized that there would be many who would choose to stay, but there would also be those who would follow him.

Sigurd was the first to step forward. "I will go with you, my friend," he said.

He was joined by Rorik and Roland who stepped forward together. Next came Leif and Sigfrid, Thurston and many others. A chant rose up, saying Wolfram's name.

"Wolfram. Wolfram. Wolfram."

Many women too elected to go. Signy, Hildegard and Helga were among them, much to Deidre's happiness.

Early the very next morning preparations for the long journey were made. This would be no short voyage and thus they would have to bring along many provisions. Food that was dried, pickled herring and other fish, some fresh fruits, grains, and water in skins were put aboard as well as weapons.

And so I leave this land of Eire after all, Deidre thought, watching the flurry of activity from the doorway of her small house. Looking about the room she bid farewell to the memories she had gathered there and looked forward to her voyage which would take her to the snows of Wolfram's homeland.

PART II

The Land of Fire and Ice

NORWAY
SUMMER - WINTER, 845-46

"Ice is the silent language of the peak;
and fire the silent language of the star."

AND IN THE HUMAN HEART, Sonnet X
Conrad Aiken

1

The two Viking ships, *The Sea Wolf* and *The Dragon's Head*, sailed north along the coast of Ireland through the turbulent waters of the Irish Sea, past the tip of Scotland. Although there had been storms on this journey, so far there had been none which could compare with the first storm Deidre had encountered that day Wolfram had dived overboard to save his friend, Sigurd. The ships had stopped briefly at the Orkney Isles to replenish the food supply, then sailed onward through the North Sea toward Wolfram's boyhood home.

It was a comfort to Deidre to have other women aboard the ship. Hildegard had proven to be a help to her. Deidre laughed and told Wolfram that between his teachings and Hildegard's, she would be speaking the Viking language so well that none would dare to say that she had not been born among his people. Although she exaggerated, it was true that she could speak the tongue very well. Now she could understand the Viking stories and jokes and found herself joining in on the laughter.

Deidre found Wolfram's people to be a hardy lot, self-reliant and rocklike. The mountains and sea seemed to be in their blood. Their settlements were often separated by mountains and because of this, they knew the importance of working together for the good of all. They were generous and honest to each other, yet ruthless to those they considered their enemies, Wolfram had told her. Those enemies included other Vikings, particularly the Danes who had now set their sights on the Irish Isle.

The sea was important to the Viking. From the sea he drew food, by sea departed the invaders, and by way of the sea came traders who would bring new riches back with them.

103

They had put ashore near the settlement of Nidaros just long enough to prepare for the final thrust of the journey to Skiringssal, their destination.

"It is good to be upon land again," Deidre thought, trying to adjust to being on solid ground. It was as if with each step she took the earth rose up to meet her like the tides of the ocean.

"Sea legs," Wolfram had said with a smile. "It will take you some time to adjust, my love."

"I am not as sea loving as you, Wolfram," she answered, as they walked along the shore of Nidaros. "But I will try to be a good Viking."

Wolfram brushed back her raven locks as they blew in a swirl around her face, a gesture he had repeated many times while on this journey. Reaching out, he held on to the woman beside him, to warm her and shield her from the wind blowing from the sea. What would she think of his world of sea, rock and forest, he wondered? He glanced down at Deidre, so deep in thought.

"What are you thinking?" he asked softly, brushing her forehead with his lips.

"I know nothing about you or your family," she replied. Turning to him, he could read the apprehension in her eyes. "I fear this brother of yours. My intuition warns me that somehow he will cause us both pain."

Wolfram clenched his jaw. "He has much to answer for, though it will take me some time to prove my case against him." His voice softened as he reached out to touch her face. "But I will not let him harm us. This I promise. He has fooled me once but he will not do so again."

"I too will watch him warily," she said. "How sad it is that there are men who cannot be trusted." For a moment she thought about the man known only to her as "the Irishman." Perhaps one day she would be able to revenge herself upon him as Wolfram sought to avenge himself upon his brother.

Feeling contentment beside Wolfram, Deidre lay her head against his chest with a sigh. If only they could stand like this forever gazing out at the sea, heedless of all worry, feeling only the joy of being together. If they could forget about the two men who had wronged them, about being Viking and Irish, she would have asked for nothing more.

Standing beside him in silence for several moments, Deidre

ended the quiet by her soft question. "What is your family like, Wolfram? Will you tell me about them? What will they think of your Irish woman?"

He reached down to cup her face in his hands. "So many questions." He laughed softly. "I will answer your last question first. My father will tell me that I have chosen a beauty. A perfect mate. My sister Zerlina will mother you as she did me in the past. My younger brother will adore you, my elder brother will look upon you with lustful eyes." His brows furrowed for a moment. Everard had stolen a previous mistress, Erika from him once, but he would not take Deidre. Deidre was his love.

At the mention of Everard, Deidre shivered. She would surely not welcome his attentions.

Wolfram's eyes held a shadow as he looked again at her. Since she had asked about his family, the time had come to tell her something he feared would shock her Christian heart. He had fought so hard to win her love, he did not want to lose her now.

"Deidre, there . . . there is a custom among my people, which . . . which you must understand," he stammered.

She looked at him in puzzlement. Never had he been afraid to speak before. Now he seemed like a boy who must tell his mother he had broken her best flagon.

"I have learned a great deal about your people in the last few months, Wolfram. What more could there be that I must learn?"

He blurted it out, "Both my father and brother have more than one wife. It is the way among my people. The wealthy, the jarls, pride themselves on the number of sons they can beget. With a life as hard as ours, there are women who would be at the mercy of the elements if they did not have a man to care for them. We . . ."

Deidre's heart felt as cold as the mountaintops. She could do many things, but she could not share Wolfram with any other woman. "And you?" she asked quickly, her hands trembling as she waited for his answer.

"I have no wife," he answered. "I have not found a woman I would want until now." He gathered her close against him.

Deidre's apprehension left her. She had feared her happiness would be shattered by the knowledge that Wolfram belonged to another. It was enough heartache that her vows to

Phelan stood between them. Polygamy. Such a strange custom to have more than one wife, and yet hadn't Solomon done so in days of old?

"I care naught what your father and brother do," she said finally. "As long as you do not follow their example. I am, I fear, a very jealous woman."

Wolfram smiled. "And I a very jealous man." How could he tell her that as the son to the Jarl he too would be expected to follow the custom? Would he lose her love?

The blaze of the sun cast a glow upon the water, looking like the flames of a fire. "The midnight sun," Wolfram whispered. "Endless day. Summer sun shedding eternal light. That is how my love is, Deidre. And Loki take any who would seek to part you from me."

2

Deidre found that the land of the midnight sun was no myth but a world of magnificent blue sea, dark green forests, and majestic mountains rising up to the sky proudly displaying their crowns of snow-capped peaks. The fjords, those narrow inlets of the sea between cliffs, cut into the mountains allowing the huge ships to sail between their wondrous towering rock walls. Deidre looked up at these towers with awe.

"I have never seen anything like this before!" she exclaimed as the *Sea Wolf* steered so close to the elongated rock formations that she felt as if she could reach out and touch them with her hands.

The *Sea Wolf* and the *Dragon's Head* moved up the fjord as smoothly as if they had wings. Eager to be home, the men had sailed during the day and into the night toward Skiringssal. Now in the early morning hours with the blue sky overhead and the walls of the cliffs rising about them, the journey was over, they were home.

One of the men on deck drew a curled horn to his lips and blew the signal which meant that they were friendly and intended no harm. The three notes were anwered by another horn high atop the hill. The men began to cheer and shout as the ships pulled into shore, and a crowd of people soon appeared in answer to the shouts. Here and there a dog scampered about, wagging its tail and barking, as women and children came running to the landing to greet the ships.

As the *Sea Wolf* stopped not more than a few feet from shore, the oarsmen stuck the oars out to form a bridge between the ship and the land. Deidre watched with awe as several Vikings danced daringly about atop the oars. Each tried to outdo the other: balancing, stepping high, even jumping up in the air. Wolfram himself joined the festivities, nearly falling into the deep blue waters as he grinned at Deidre.

"Serves me right for my vain folly," he laughed, coming back to her side. As the ship came to a large rock, he took her hand and together they jumped off the *Sea Wolf* onto dry land, running up a curling pathway to the top of a hill.

Some of the Vikings stayed behind to unload the vast ships, but not Wolfram. This was his day. He was coming home, bringing with him his beautiful Deidre.

"Five years since last I saw this place," he exclaimed, pulling Deidre along beside him. "Five long years."

Deidre looked about her at the cluster of houses huddled together. Here and there was a house balancing on the bank of the waterside, another nearly touching the mountain slope, a dwelling perched on ledges high above the water. The green and brown fields about them were dotted with flocks of goats, sheep and cattle.

They walked a long distance toward a group of wooden buildings which Wolfram explained to Deidre were "outbuildings": a byre for housing animals in the cold days of the winter, barns to store their fodder, a stable, a small smithy, and a bathhouse. It was quite different from the settlement at Dubh-Linn.

"Come, my love," Wolfram intoned. "It is time you met my father, Olaf the Red." He led her to the largest building which was the central dwelling house—the *skaalen*, or hall— where cooking, eating, feasting and gaming were done.

The house was made mainly of wood with a turf roof and a stone foundation. Around the building was a planked wooden walkway which led up to one of the two entranceways. Stepping inside the wooden door, Deidre could see that, like the small hut in Dubh-Linn, this large building had slats to let in the light and a hole in the roof to allow smoke to escape and the sun's rays to enter. Because of the cold climate, there were no windows.

A squeal of delight rent the air as a woman slightly older than Deidre came toward them, her red-gold braids bouncing off her shoulders as she hurried forward. Deidre noticed that the young woman had a pronounced limp, her foot twisted out to the side, and she felt a stab of pity for her.

"Wolfram!" the young woman exclaimed, throwing her arms around him. They hugged each other close as both

laughed and cried. "I thought I would never see you again!"
Tears of happiness flooded her eyes.

"Nor I, you, my beloved sister," he answered. Remembering Deidre, he pushed her forward with gentle hands.
"Zerlina, this is Deidre."

The two women eyed each other and decided immediately
that they were to be friends. Zerlina held out her hand, clasping Deidre's hand warmly to demonstrate her welcome. "She
is beautiful, Wolfram. Never have I seen such eyes. Like the
flowers that bloom in the meadow."

Walking inside the house, they were met by a smiling blue-eyed young man a few years younger than Wolfram. His hair
was lighter than Wolfram's, his nose shorter, his build thinner, but except for those differences it was as if Deidre were
looking at Wolfram, so alike were they.

"Wolfram! By the fires of Muspell, how do you come to be
here, brother?" the young man asked, his face a mask of surprise.

Wolfram pounded his brother on the back. "It is a long
story, Warrick. I will tell you in time."

Coming quickly to his feet, a big-boned giant of a man with
flaming red hair and a thick red beard hastened toward them.
A scar along the left side of his cheek was all that marred his
rugged good looks. Deidre had no need to ask who this man
was, his facial features told her that he was Wolfram's father.

"Wolfram! By Odin's breath you are a sight for sore eyes. I
doubted that I would ere lay eyes upon you this side of
Valhalla." He enclosed his son in a bear hug, tears rolling
down his leathery face. They stood there clasped together for a
long while.

While the two men were thus embraced, Deidre looked
about her at the walls of the large room. Down the center of
the hall was a long hearth on a raised platform. Big pots hung
over the fire on chains from beams in the ceiling of the gabled
roof, much as in the small hut in Dubh-Linn. A loom and
several spindle whorls for the spinning of wool stood against
the farthest wall reminding Deidre of her home in Eire. On
either side of the long hall, indoor benches lined the walls
which appeared to be used for either sitting or sleeping. Toward the far wall was a chair, much higher than the benches
around it. It was heavily carved with geometric and floral
designs and forms which Deidre knew to be representations of

the gods. Several tables, which could be pushed aside to make
more room, stood heavily laden with food.

"And who might this be?" she heard a loud booming voice
say, breaking into her reverie. A large, bearlike hand grabbed
her shoulders and turned her around. She found herself looking into the patriarch's face. She judged him over fifty, yet
there was not a streak of gray in his mane of red hair.

"Deidre," Wolfram answered.

"Your wife? Your woman? Your slave? Which of these is
she?" Olaf the Red questioned.

Wolfram's eyes held a tinge of sadness. "I would that she be
my wife, but she is married by her Christian laws to another
and will not marry me," he answered.

"Ah-ha. She is your concubine then. Well, no matter."
Deidre felt shame at Olaf's words and tried to turn away, but
he had already entrapped her in his grasp. Now he put a hand
upon her belly, sliding downward to her hip. "She will be able
to bring forth many children for you. She has the hips of a
good breeder."

As if understanding Deidre's embarrassment, Zerlina
stepped hastily forward, water and towels in hand. "Father,
we have not greeted our guest properly," she scolded gently.

Deidre washed her face and hands of the night's grime and
smiled her thanks toward the red-haired woman. Wolfram,
too, cleansed himself, but Olaf was not to be silenced for long.

"It is good that you have taken this woman," he said.
"Your brother, bah! He has three wives and all three are barren. I am beginning to wonder if the fault is not with him. And
your younger brother also has no sons. He has not found a
woman enough to his liking, he says, to marry. Yet he has
spread his seed all over the village. I want grandsons, Wolfram. It is an old man's greatest desire."

Wolfram flashed Deidre a wicked grin. "We will see, my
father, if that wish cannot be fulfilled."

Deidre glanced away from him. All this talk of babies made
her suddenly realize her plight. If she could not marry
Wolfram, then any child she might carry would be a bastard
by the laws of her church. What was she to do? She loved
Wolfram and did not want to shun his bed, but could bring
shame upon an innocent baby born from her womb. If only
she could find a way to have her marriage annulled, to marry

Wolfram, then all would be well.

"I must see to it that I do not bear a child," she thought. It was said that if a woman was careful and judged her monthly time accurately, no child would be born.

Olaf took Deidre's elbow and led her to one of the tables. "When you bear a child, then you will marry my son. It will be good then. Odin has willed it. I know this in my heart." Olaf seemed faraway in thought for just a moment, murmuring, "Wolfram's mother was from across the seas, too. A Germanic woman with hair the color of honey. My Rolanda. She fought me at first but we soon had a deep love between us and in time she gave me a son. Wolfram. And you will give me a grandson. Then you will become my son's favored wife. This I know."

Deidre started to protest, but the look of happiness on the older man's face stilled her tongue.

"Where are you from, Raven?" he asked.

"My name is Deidre," she corrected him softly.

He shook his head. "No, with hair like yours I will call you Raven," he said with a laugh. "You will find that we Vikings always find nicknames for our people. Over there is Sweyn Forkbeard, next to him is Harald Longneck and so on. You will soon see how it is, Raven." He motioned for Wolfram to sit beside him, on the other side of Deidre. "Now, where is it that you are from, Raven? Britain?"

"The land of Eire," she responded.

"Ireland. So you are Irish. That is good. The Irish are a hearty race, the mixture of your blood with my son's will make for strong, healthy babies. Babies with red hair." He touched his own hair and laughed.

Olaf was interrupted by the sound of wood against wood as the door was slammed shut. There, with eyes blazing, stood a man dressed in all the Viking glory, complete with battle-axe in hand. Deidre did not have to guess who this was, her instincts whispered to her that here was Everard the Boar. He strode over toward Wolfram and stood toe to toe with him. He was shorter than Wolfram by a head's length, but made up for his lack of height in muscle and brawn. His light brown hair, hawklike nose, and proud bearing made Deidre think of a bird of prey.

"So, the wolf has returned to the door," Everard said.

Deidre's blood ran cold as she looked at the enmity in the man's eyes.

Wolfram felt anger boil in his veins. Here was the man who had sent him to the realms of Hel herself, sought his death, and yet until he had proof of the treacherous deed, he was helpless to act.

"Yes, I have returned," he said coldly. "I have brought much treasure for our father's storehouses with me."

The hulking hawk-nosed man noticed Deidre. He turned his head to appraise her as one would a finely wrought sword. "This treasure you speak of, does that include the woman?"

"No! The woman is mine," Wolfram thundered, tossing his thick mane of golden hair from his eyes as if daring his brother to say otherwise.

"Your wife?" Everard asked with a smirk.

"She is my woman," Wolfram responded. Deidre alone could tell what control he was managing and feared that at any moment his calm would be shattered.

As if trying to push the matter, to bring Wolfram to anger, Everard stepped toward Deidre, touching her blue-black hair.

"If this woman is not wife to Wolfram, I demand her for my own," Everard proclaimed, laughing. With a long stride he stepped toward his father as all eyes turned upon the older man.

"As eldest son, it is your right," Olaf said, turning to look upon Deidre. His stern expression reminded her that he was the leader of these people, the Jarl, his word law.

The thought of sharing a bed with Wolfram's fearsome brother was too much for Deidre to bear. She felt dizzy, as if the walls of the hall were closing in on her. Not wanting to faint she fought to steady herself, but to no avail. The world gradually went blank as she slumped to the floor.

3

Deidre regained consciousness slowly. Seeing the face of Zerlina swimming before her in a haze, feeling a cool cloth pressed to her forehead, she could hear Wolfram's sister's voice calling her name. Deidre struggled to get up but a gentle hand held her back.

"Wolfram," Deidre whispered.

"He is not here at the moment," Zerlina answered, her lovely face drawn down in a frown.

Again Deidre tried to sit up. "I don't know what is wrong," she said, embarrassed at having fainted in the hall in front of Wolfram's father and brothers. She did not wish to bring Wolfram shame.

Zerlina looked at her with affection and understanding. "Perhaps you are with child."

"No, that can't be," Deidre answered, refusing to let such a possibility enter her mind.

Wondering again where Wolfram was, she got up and went to look. She found him and Everard alone, locked together, rolling around the floor. "Oh no!" Deidre shrieked. "Stop them. Someone stop them."

Deidre tried to get to Wolfram, but Zerlina held her firmly by the shoulders. "It is well for them to get their aggression out in combat."

Everard's last words rang in Deidre's ears and a frightening thought entered her mind. She had heard of lands where it was the custom for the victor to be rewarded the woman he desired. Were they fighting over her?

Wolfram and Everard were both powerful men, with broad chests and muscles of iron. As they rolled over and over, each trying to pin the other down, Deidre sought Olaf, hoping that he would stop the fighting. But when he came, he merely looked upon the scene without expression.

Wolfram felt Everard's fist against his nose and winced as a burst of pain exploded through his head. Reaching up, he wiped the blood from his face with his hand. Years of anger welled up inside him. In retaliation he struck Everard hard across the face, his fury knowing no bounds. That his brother had sought to claim Deidre had been the final blow.

"I know what you did to me," he growled.

"Is that so? And just what was I supposed to have done?" Everard asked between punches.

"Don't play coy with me, brother," Wolfram returned, catching Everard by the foot and sending him sprawling to the ground. Now he stood straddling his brother. "I know what you did and I will see that you pay for your treachery." His eyes blazed his rage. Losing his balance for just a moment, he was shoved to the ground. Now it was Everard who had Wolfram at his mercy.

"You talk riddles," Everard said between clenched teeth as he watched Wolfram struggle to get up. "It is you who have wronged me, playing the favorite with our father!" He pounded Wolfram back down upon the hard earthen floor without mercy, causing Wolfram's ears to ring.

Pulling free of Zerlina's hands and running toward the man she loved, Deidre cried, "No! Sweet Jesus, no more of this!" Her head was swimming with the thought that Wolfram could not take much more of this abuse.

"Deidre!" Zerlina called out, but Deidre ignored the Viking woman.

Tearing at Everard's arms, Deidre sought to halt this assault. "Leave him alone. You will kill him!" she sobbed.

Olaf's angry shout rent the air. "Woman, leave them be. It is only right that this enmity be settled thusly." His bright red brows furrowed in a frown as Deidre stepped back, but not before her presence had been felt by both brothers. Everard let loose his grip, and Wolfram fell back upon the ground. He struggled to rise but could not. The blows upon his head had done their damage.

"Ha. It seems that I am victor," Everard crowed in his pride. "I am a fitting successor for my father." For the moment the danger was over for Wolfram, but nothing had really been settled between them. There would be another day to even the score.

Deidre again rushed toward Wolfram, gently wiping the blood from his face with the hem of her gown. She examined his nose. It was bleeding but not broken.

"I'm sorry I cried out as I did," she said softly, cradling his head in her lap. She feared that he would be angered with her, but instead he tried to smile at her.

"You do not understand our ways," he said, with labored breathing. "Soon you will know that here only the strongest survive. I should ask your forgiveness for being weak. A fine commander of a Viking ship I am."

"He is much heavier than you. It was not a fair fight," Deidre countered, glaring up at Everard who stood looking down at her.

"It is skill, not size which is important," Wolfram said weakly. He struggled to his feet as Deidre helped him up. Every muscle in his body ached, his head felt as if swords pierced through his skull, yet the greatest pain he would ever know would be if his father now chose to give Deidre to Everard. Had he brought her all the way from Ireland just to see her in the arms of his brother? No, he would never stand by and watch such a thing happen.

They stood clinging to each other, Deidre looking at Wolfram with eyes filled with pride and love. Whether he had won or lost he was still her beloved warrior.

Everard walked to his father. "The woman. What is your decision on her? I will leave it to you," he said with a grin, so sure of the answer.

Olaf looked first at one brother then at the other. Seeing the look of adoration in Deidre's eyes, he made his choice. "The woman is Wolfram's."

With an angry grunt Everard strode away, pausing only to say over his shoulder, "You have always favored him. No matter how I have tried to please you, it has always been Wolfram." With that said he slammed out of the door, leaving the hall in silence.

When at last the clash between the brothers was forgotten, the household sat down to the morning meal of *dagveror*. It was served later than usual today because of the ship's arrival.

Deidre joined the women at one end of the table while Wolfram sat among the men. A large boar roasted upon a spit on the fire. Deidre could smell the aroma of the succulent meat and cast her eyes in that direction. It had been a long journey and she was famished.

Befitting his rank, Olaf had many slaves. Several of these thralls were busily darting to and fro bringing loaves of flat bread from their baking spot upon the rocks of the fire to the guests at the table. There had been no thralls at the settlement at Dubh-Linn, but Wolfram had told her what to expect when they arrived at his home. It was the Viking way.

Zerlina introduced her to the women of Olaf's household. Adora, Zerlina's mother, was a woman of forty with the same abundant red-gold hair. Gerda, Everard's mother, a scowling, big-boned, plump brunette, soon made it clear that she considered Deidre to be an interloper and a nuisance of whom she wanted no part. Deidre made careful note to avoid this woman in the future.

"Do not feel hurt by Gerda's actions," Zerlina whispered in her ear. "She does not like any other woman, even my mother. Her beauty has long since faded, and she fears lest Olaf's eyes turn to a younger woman as many such men are wont to do."

"I'll remember your words," Deidre said softly. Looking at the women assembled, she wondered how many wives Olaf had. "Which one of the women is Wolfram's mother?" she asked, wondering why he had never spoken about her.

Zerlina smiled, "Warrick and I share the same mother with Wolfram. Wolfram's mother died the night he was born and my mother raised him as her own. Perhaps that is why I feel so much closer to Wolfram than to Everard or my sisters."

Olaf rapped sharply upon the table with his knife. It was a signal that the meal had officially begun. Zerlina whispered, "The patriarch also signals when the food is to be cleared away. Anyone who has not finished eating will find his food removed before his eyes. Therefore eat quickly."

Deidre found even morning mealtime to be a gay and noisy event with much laughter, boasting and storytelling. But remembering Zerlina's words to her, she ate hastily in silence. There was a great variety of food—chicken, goose, rabbit, fish, and boar as well as cheese and barley porridge. So intent upon eating was Deidre that she did not notice the eyes burning through her until Zerlina nudged her in the ribs.

"Beware of that one, Deidre," Zerlina cautioned.

Looking up, Deidre saw jealousy on a golden-haired young woman's face, and wondered at the envy in her eyes.

"She once loved Wolfram and he her, but she scorned his love to wed Everard. No doubt she thought it more suitable to her beauty to be the next Jarl's wife. She is Everard's first wife, Erika. The others are sitting across from you, the young woman with the red hair, and the auburn-haired beauty."

The thought that Wolfram had once loved another pained Deidre, and she once again cast eyes upon her rival. "Does . . . does she still care for Wolfram?" she asked.

Zerlina nodded her head. "Yes. I think perhaps she wonders if she chose the wrong brother. There are many who say that Wolfram will be Olaf's successor. Wolfram's mother was Olaf's first wife although Everard's mother conceived first."

Deidre fought against her own jealousy. One thing was certain: She would never let this woman, nor any other, take Wolfram from her. With her own eyes blazing, Deidre met the eyes of the blond-haired buxom beauty and knew that from henceforward, there would be war between them.

4

The waters of the fjord were calm, the sun a glow of fire in the sky as Wolfram and his father stood on the deck of the *Sea Wolf*. Olaf looked proudly upon his son as he heard the story of how Wolfram had escaped the Irish, walked all the way across Ireland to the settlement of Dubh-Linn, and saw there the building of his ship and the manning of his Viking crew. It had been five years since Olaf had seen his son. And while he had received word that Wolfram was alive and well, it pleased him to see just how well he had done for himself. Raiding the coasts of the land that had enslaved him, Wolfram had come home a rich man, turning adversity into triumph.

Wolfram's eyes were gentle, his voice a whisper as he talked about Deidre and her kindness to him. "She gave me a reason to live. I looked forward to her visits, though we could not understand each other's language at the time. Her gift to me was compassion."

Olaf shook his head thoughtfully. "So the Irish child, Raven, helped you to escape. Is that why you feel such a bond with her?"

"It is much deeper. I love her as I have never loved anything in my life before. She is everything I have ever wanted in a woman—brave, loving, beautiful. The sympathetic child and the woman who fought so bravely to come to her father's rescue have merged in my heart."

They walked slowly about the deck of the ship, Olaf examining the workmanship. He grunted his approval. "If you are as skilled in your ship building as you are in your choice of a woman, my son, then the rune stones must foretell good fortune for you. Your Deidre is lovely. Already I have taken her to my heart. She is like a rare jewel, that one. Be glad that you did not take the woman named Erika to wife. In their own ways the gods have favored you, despite the hardships you were forced to endure.''

Erika. The name had long been forced from his mind, the bitterness of her fickle heartlessness only a faded memory. Deidre surpassed Erika as the sun surpassed the moon in brightness. "I do not envy Everard. I only know that I will not let him touch my Deidre," Wolfram said, reaching out to grasp one of the oars of the ship. He wanted to tell his father of Everard's treachery, but held his tongue. Soon he would find the proof he needed of his brother's betrayal.

They talked about many things as each sought to enlighten the other about the years they had spent apart. Like Wolfram's mother, Olaf's third wife had died in childbirth bringing anguish to his heart. The child, a son, had also died.

"I thought that I had lost two sons, but Odin has brought back my second born," Olaf said. He grinned at Wolfram. "And perhaps soon I will have a grandson to replace the son I lost, eh?"

When the tour of the ship was over, Olaf took leave of his son while Wolfram stayed behind to check the ship's rigging. The *Sea Wolf* had sailed far, now it was time to rest. He looked about to make certain that all the cargo had been taken ashore and was relieved to find that it had been unloaded as planned. Sigurd had done well.

Anxious to return to Deidre, Wolfram turned around with the intention of going to the hall. But as he walked toward the stern of the boat a shadowy figure stepped in front of him.

"Wolfram!" breathed a soft husky voice he knew all too well. Erika stood before him, her long blonde hair unbound and falling to her waist. She looked at him with eyes that seemed to devour him, a smile upon her lips.

"So we meet again, Erika," he said coolly. "Where is your husband?"

Her full mouth trembled. "Drunk as usual," she answered. That Everard had fought in the hall to possess another woman made her seethe inside. How could he have humiliated her so in front of the entire hall? She would never forgive him. Her mind envisioned a hundred ways to seek revenge.

"Shouldn't you be at his side?" Wolfram asked sarcastically. He had no doubt as to what she was about. Erika was willful and loose in her morality. She had probably tired of

Everard and now wanted to resume their love affair. Once he would have been fooled by her, but no more. He had learned what true love was.

Slithering forward, Erika stood within an arm's length of the man whose bed she sought. Her eyes were moist with tears as she looked up at Wolfram. "I never should have married Everard," she whispered. "It was always you I loved!" She reached out to caress his chest boldly in a gesture which once would have sparked his desire. Wolfram removed her roving hands, casting her from him.

"You are my brother's wife. Do you forget the penalty for adultery?" This she-wolf was not worth dying for.

Erika looked hastily over her shoulder. It would be dangerous if they were caught together. They could both be punished. Everard was a possessive man and his resentment of his brother knew no bounds. She moved into the shadows.

"We won't be caught if we are careful," she whispered. She began to laugh. "You hate Everard and he hates you. What better revenge could you have upon him than to plant the seed of your child in his wife's belly? Think how you could laugh at him, raising your child as his own, watching your son become Jarl."

"If there is bitterness between Everard and me, do not think that I will trespass into his bed. I am a man of honor." He glared down at this woman he had once thought he loved. What kind of woman was she to betray her husband? He remembered how Deidre had fought against her love for him because of her vows of marriage to a man she did not love. The two women were as different as night and day.

Erika threw back her head and licked her lips in a gesture of passion. Shaking her thick golden hair she looked up at him coyly. "You love me still, I can see it in your eyes. Am I not worth risking punishment for?"

"What we had is dead."

"No!" Erika shook her head violently, denying this truth. She could not believe that he did not still desire her. "You are merely angered with me. I was a fool, I admit that now. Forgive me! My eyes were blinded to my love for you." Wolfram was handsome and strong, and he had been a virile lover. She longed for him now; somehow she had to rekindle his love. Her hands sought Wolfram's strong arms but he eluded her.

"I feel nothing for you, Erika," he answered, tonelessly. "My love belongs to another."

"Deidre is not one of us. You cannot love her! I have heard about Irish women and their chastity. You need a woman whose blood runs hot."

"This Irish woman is more of a woman than you will ever be, Erika." Turning his back upon her then, he walked away. Before he could move very far, Erika was upon him, clinging to him like one drowning in a stormy sea.

"No!" she cried out, "you must love me."

It was this embrace that met Deidre's eyes as she walked the path toward the ship. She had been anxious to find Wolfram and had remembered that he had said he would be at the dock with his father.

"Erika!" she gasped in surprise when she saw the two of them together.

Eyes flooded with tears, Deidre ran back in the direction of the hall. She was confused and deeply hurt. Had she but turned around to take another look she would have seen Wolfram push the woman's arms from around his neck.

"Are you mad?" Wolfram asked Erika in anger. "Did you not hear my words? I love another. Never more will I seek your favors."

"But I love you!"

Wolfram pushed Erika from him. "Leave me. I never want to talk of this again. Have the decency to honor your marriage vows or I swear *I* will see you punished for your adultery." With that he left the woman standing alone upon the deck of the mighty ship.

"You will be sorry you treated me this way," she murmured, as she watched him walk away. "I will make you rue the day you ever walked away from me." So vowing, the woman left the confines of the Viking ship.

5

Deidre lay on the lumpy straw mattress, staring at the walls of the small sleeping area. Built at right angles to the main hall, the bed closet was tiny, big enough only for a bed and space to walk around it. She looked at the thin door which led to the hall, longing for Wolfram to walk through the portal.

If only we were once again upon the shores of Dubh-Linn. We were so happy there, she thought. Now it seemed there were many obstacles to their happiness. Everard presented a threat. It was like having an axe poised above their heads. She could still see his leering face and closed her eyes to block out the sight, but she could not shut out the sight of Everard's wife in Wolfram's arms. Did he still love the woman?

He loves me. How could she doubt his love? Hadn't he shown that love over and over again in words and deeds. Just this day he had fought Everard for her. What more must he do to prove his love? And yet it was possible that he was torn between two loves. Hadn't she been torn, loving the blond-haired youth of her childhood, yet longing for the bearded Viking's touch? She had been caught between two flames, not knowing that they were one and the same. Could she ask him to forget so soon the love of his boyhood? No, it would take time.

Time, she reflected. Was there time? What if that scheming vixen trapped Wolfram, led him into danger? Deidre remembered well the penalty for adultery among Wolfram's people. She would not let such a thing happen to Wolfram. The blond vixen would not have a chance to work her treachery. Deidre would fight to keep Wolfram's love. Erika belonged to another man.

As I do, she thought suddenly. Spoken vows came back to haunt her in the silence of the room. That she could never be

Wolfram's wife, would never have the vows of a priest to bind their love, was like a thorn in her heart. She was tormented by her thoughts.

Hearing the sound of footsteps, Deidre stiffened. Was it Wolfram? She closed her eyes, feigning sleep, afraid to face him with her doubts.

"Deidre?" His voice was soft.

She longed to throw herself into his arms, tell him how much she loved him, but instead Deidre remained silent. There was another thought to torture her, the thought of bearing a child. What if Zerlina were right? Was she already carrying Wolfram's seed within her? The thought of holding Wolfram's child to her breast was a bittersweet desire.

"Sleep, little one. You are tired and so am I. We have had quite a journey," Wolfram whispered to her as he entered the small room. She felt him gently brush back the hair from her face in the gesture of affection she had grown to relish. The bed sagged with his weight as he eased himself gently next to her so as not to waken her.

Deidre feared that her lungs would burst from holding her breath. Her eyes ached with the longing to look upon him, but she kept still until she heard the familiar sounds of his heavy breathing, telling her that he was asleep. Now she regretted her silence. If ever she needed Wolfram's strong arms around her, it was now.

She thought of Erika and the pain she had brought Wolfram. Was it possible that she had misunderstood the embrace between the two? Wolfram had been gone a long time. Was it not natural for two childhood lovers to embrace upon his return?

I have let my own jealousy blind me, she thought in anguish. She turned toward him then to tell him how much she loved him, but she did not want to waken him from his sleep.

She watched him then, her eyes filled with softness and love. Love had brought her much happiness, but she sensed that it could bring her grief as well. Apart from him she would be incomplete, her heart as cold as the snow atop the mountains of the Northland.

"I love you, Viking," she said softly. "I did not know passion could be so . . . exhausting." She closed her eyes then, vowing to conquer this monster called jealousy, which had loomed in her heart today for the first time.

6

During the next few weeks Deidre came to know much about the strong clan of people who shared the blood and kinship of Wolfram. They were hard workers, although the hardest tasks were done by the slaves. There was always work to be done if one was to survive in this severe northern climate with its long winters. Viking life was rough, and there was little or no patience for weaklings. Deidre made up her mind that she would prove herself to be one of the strong.

Household tasks were fitted around the meal preparation twice daily, morning and night. Here in Skiringssal fish was the mainstay of the diet, eaten in some form at every meal. Grinding and baking was a daily chore, for unleavened barley bread needed to be eaten while it was hot or it would soon turn hard and stale. Flour was ground from a rotary hand quern, dough kneaded in a wooden trough and baked on the long-handled iron plates among the embers of an open fire. The women also hung herbs to dry, gathered wild plants to supplement the diet and wild honey to brew the beer and mead for the feasts, parties and evening meal.

As Deidre went about her chores, she often felt the eyes of Erika upon her, as if the woman had held hopes that she would somehow show herself to be unsuited to the Viking way of life. Erika frequently whispered to Gerda and the others, twittering behind her hand as if telling some secret. After such a conversation, Deidre was assigned the most unpleasant task of the day by Gerda, Olaf's first wife now and head woman of the household. Deidre held her head up proudly and finished every task without one word of complaint, trying to ignore the aching in her back, arms and legs at the end of the day.

Even though much of the cloth was purchased from merchant Vikings, spinning and weaving occupied several hours a day. It was here that Deidre felt at home, for in her father's lands, she had been well known for the beautiful cloth she had woven. She cut the cloth with small shears so that it could be sewn into garments with the needles carried in containers of hollow bird bones hung by small chains from the necks of the Viking women. Cloth was needed for many purposes besides clothing, such as blankets, wagon covers and sails for the Viking ships.

From a merchant from Frisia, Wolfram had purchased the finest woolen cloth from which Deidre made several garments to wear—long chemises, tunics and cloaks. Wolfram also gave her, much to Erika's envy, many fine silks from the East to be made into garments for special ceremonies and feasts. No other garment, however, would ever replace in her heart the blue silk dress he had given her in Dubh-Linn.

Deidre looked forward to the evening meal, though she often wished she could sit with Wolfram. She wondered why the men always sat together. She asked Zerlina one night.

"So that they might amuse themselves with ribald stories that our ears shouldn't hear," Zerlina whispered to Deidre with a smile. She had been kind to Deidre these past weeks when other women had been less so.

Deidre soon knew many of the Viking gods by name and their exploits. Odin was the supreme god, All Father, favored by the landowning jarls who thought of him as their special god. Odin, it was said, often disguised himself as a dark horseman wearing a large flowing cloak and a broad hat pulled down over his face. His horse Sleipnir had eight legs; his spear, Gungnir, never missed its mark; his hall Valhalla had six hundred and forty doors and a throne from which Odin could survey all creation. As the god of war it was Odin who directed battle and decided who would live and who would die. His attendants, the Valkyries, or warrior maidens as Zerlina called them, brought to Valhalla those who had died bravely.

Thor, the god of thunder and rain was the son of Odin and the god favored by the peasants. Thunder was caused by Thor driving a chariot drawn by goats across the sky. And lightning by his mighty hammer, which he used to slay his enemies. Every time there was a storm now Deidre could almost see the red-haired god at the reins of his chariot, so vivid had been the stories about Thor during those hours after dinner.

Freyr, that god of peace and fertility whose well-endowed statue had caused Deidre such embarrassment when first she had laid eyes upon it at the pagan ceremony in Dubh-Linn, was thought to be the dispenser of rain. He had a magic ship, which could be folded up like a tent, it was said, and carried in his pouch.

There was Loki, the mischief-making god—a shape changer and sky traveler—and his daughter Hel, ruler of the realm of the dead. Although the men of the hall did not fear an honorable death, Deidre found that many of them lived in fear that they would die ignoble deaths and be doomed to Hel's evil kingdom of the dead. She was said to be half alive and half decayed. Her face, neck, shoulders, breasts, arms and back were all of flesh, but from her hips down, every inch of Hel's skin looked shriveled like one who was dead. Deidre thought it no wonder that this goddess of the lower region's expression was always depicted as grim and gloomy.

The goddesses were of equal importance to the Vikings. Frigg, Odin's wife and first among goddesses, shared with Odin a knowledge of men's destinies. A maternal goddess and daughter of the Earth Mother, she was favored by Olaf's wives.

It was the goddess Freyja, however, who was Deidre's favorite. It was by her hand, Wolfram had vowed, that Deidre had been given to him. The goddess of love and fertility, she was always being pursued by giants and tricked by dwarfs so that she would bestow her favors upon them or marry them. It was said that she rode a chariot through the air drawn by cats and wore a magic cloak made of feathers, which enabled her to fly through the air like a bird. It was Freyja who accompanied Odin into battle for she had the right to bring back to her own hall half the warriors.

To the Vikings, the world was constantly being threatened by demons and monsters, unseen but still lurking about, Deidre supposed they were much like Satan and his evil angels. To ward off these evil creatures, many of the men and women wore amulets, grimly moustached human masks that they envisioned would act as their protector. Deidre wore a golden cross around her neck and more than one Viking had asked her if it was a symbol of Thor's hammer.

Deidre enjoyed the tales of the various gods and goddesses,

and on more than one occasion had been asked to tell stories from her Holy Book. She could well understand the Viking belief in giants, greedy dwarfs, and light and dark elves, for her people too had their ghosts, leprechauns and Daoine Sidhe or fairy people. It was difficult, however, for her to come to terms with the pagan sacrifices and rituals. She would seek out a quiet corner of the hall to say a prayer to her Christian God or the Holy Mother Mary.

Deidre saw very little of Wolfram during the day for he was busy working with the men. But at night alone with him in the sleeping chamber they shared, she gave of herself as she had never done before, almost as if to banish forever from his heart and mind the blonde-haired temptress who had been his first love. Secure in the warmth of Wolfram's arms, all differences between them were forgotten—religious beliefs, customs, misunderstandings—all vanished with his kisses.

"I knew the moment that I first saw you in your father's hall that I must claim you," he whispered one night as he let his eyes feast upon her naked loveliness. "You are mine, Deidre, until the day Ragnarok destroys the world."

His hands roamed over her as if asserting that claim, his lips were hard against her own. Deidre reached for him, holding tightly, longing to insure that they would always be together, though deep in her heart she feared that it would not always be so. How could she forget that she could never be his wife, would always be tied by her vows to another? And Wolfram, what would she do one day when the laws of his people demanded that he take a wife or perhaps several wives?

I will not think about it, she thought stubbornly, closing her eyes to block out the rest of the world. She breathed a sigh as Wolfram's lips traveled over her stomach, then returned to seize and explore the peaks of her breasts. Deidre entwined her fingers in his hair as his hands and lips sent shivers of yearning through her. He parted her legs gently and filled her with his love, bringing a wild burst of warmth and pleasure to them both.

"I love you," he whispered, gathering her close in his arms and burying his face in the softness of her hair.

"And I you," she murmured. For the moment her only world was Wolfram, bringing to her body the ultimate pleasure and to her heart the deepest love.

7

Deidre picked listlessly at the food on her plate as she sat across from Zerlina at the morning meal. For a week now she had been feeling sick in the mornings and the fear that she might be with child nagged at her thoughts. Twice now she had missed her monthly time, but had hoped that this was due to the strain of the ocean voyage and the hard work of the last few weeks.

"Deidre, is something the matter? You look so upset," Zerlina asked, reaching across the table to take Deidre's hand in hers.

"No. Nothing is wrong!" Deidre snapped, immediately regretting her harshness. Zerlina had been so kind to her she must not take her foul temper out on her. "I'm sorry, Zerlina."

"You hardly eat enough to keep a mouse alive. I worry about you." Zerlina left the table, taking a bowl with her and came back with a large helping of hot barley cereal. "Here, I put butter and cream on it. Eat it."

Deidre took a bite of the food, just to please Zerlina. "It is good . . ." she began but as a churning began in her stomach, she jumped up from her place at the table, clamping a hand over her mouth and ran from the room. She reached the outside just in time.

"Oh . . ." she groaned. She could hardly stand up, the nausea seemed to engulf her. If only these episodes of sickness would end.

She heard a voice calling to her as Zerlina came limping up to stand beside her. "Deidre." She held Deidre's hand and brushed the hair from her face as she bent over retching.

"I'm sorry. I don't know what is wrong with me," Deidre sobbed. She was embarrassed for Zerlina to see her weak like this. A Viking must be strong.

"I know what is wrong with you," Zerlina said with a smile. Leaving for just a moment, she returned with a dipper of cool water and pressed it to Deidre's lips. "You are with child, aren't you, Deidre?"

Deidre had refused to admit the truth to herself no matter how much her common sense had told her it was true, but now the truth was clearly written in Zerlina's eyes and she could hide from it no longer.

"I think so." She covered her face with her hands as all sorts of thoughts came to her mind. What cruel trick of fate had decreed that she should conceive now when she had been so happy, forcing the realities of the world from her mind? Now she must face the truth. She could never go back to her beloved Ireland again.

"It will be all right. Oh Deidre, I'm so happy for you. To bring forth life is the greatest of blessings." Zerlina held her in her arms until all the tears were spent.

"What am I going to do, Zerlina? What am I to do?"

"I will tell Olaf immediately," Zerlina said, breaking away. "He will be so pleased and so happy." The smile on her face was radiant.

Deidre shook her head violently. "No. You cannot tell him. Promise me, Zerlina. He cannot be happy to have a bastard grandchild. I will bring shame upon him and upon Wolfram." She thought of how it would be in Eire. There she would be shamed. It was as if the heathen gods in this cold land were scheming against her, taking away her happiness.

Zerlina led Deidre to an overturned barrel and bid her to sit down. "Olaf has many bastards himself and he is proud of every one of them. It is our way here for an important man to have several wives, as well as concubines."

"And you women tolerate this?"

"Yes, although I will not say that there are not times when there is jealousy. When a woman bears a child of such a union the man is proud. Although such a son may not become the next jarl, he is nevertheless given much love and a place of honor in his father's household. Then when he grows to manhood he is given his own hearth."

"My child would not be shunned?" Deidre knew that in her own land, such a thing would not be true. "If it were a son—?"

"You belong to Wolfram. His child would be given much love. You know Rorik?"

"Yes."

"He is one of my father's natural sons. There is not a finer man around than Rorik." She paused for a moment while Deidre sat deep in thought. The hope that now Deidre would be persuaded to marry her brother burned in her heart. It was right that they be married; they belonged together. Deidre did not belong with any other man. What a fine wife she would make for Wolfram, with all the honor of the first wife. "Does Wolfram know?"

Deidre shook her head. "No, I have not told him yet, but I will tonight." She stood up, anxious to be back at the hall before their absence was noticed.

"What of Olaf? He wants a grandchild more than anything in the world. He will hold you in great esteem."

"I will tell him in my own time, in my own way," Deidre answered. "Wolfram is the first one who should hear from my lips what our joining has created." She wondered what he would think about the coming baby, and knew that he would be proud.

They walked back to the hall in silence, each in their own musing. Zerlina had long ago given up hope of ever marrying and bearing her own child, for her twisted leg turned many away from asking her to be an honored wife. Now she looked upon this child that Deidre would bear with hope. It would bring her the greatest joy to hold a babe in her arms. Deidre was torn between happiness and sorrow, for loving Wolfram as she did how could she help but love the child of that love, and yet she wondered if her soul would be in peril. How she longed for the wisdom of her mother at this time, for Tara always gave her daughter added strength.

"But I will never see my mother again," Deidre whispered, the knowledge tearing at her heart. *My world will now be here with Wolfram,* she thought.

8

Deidre bent over the trough, forming the large roll of dough into small flat loaves to be baked for the evening meal. Behind her several of the female slaves stood beside the large soapstone cauldrons, boiling seawater to obtain salt. The steam from the pots made the air moist and muggy, and she brushed the perspiration from her temples with a flour smudged hand, leaving a white streak across her face.

"Deidre! Deidre! A ship! A ship!" Zerlina came through the door, her voice as excited as a child's. "Come, let us go down to the sea to greet them. We so seldom have visitors."

Hastily wiping the flour from her hands on her apron, Deidre followed Zerlina out the front door and down the steep narrow path. The sound of horns, the answering blasts, brightly colored sails billowing in the wind created a feeling of excitement. A pale mist softened the sharp outline of the mountains so that the scene before her appeared to be some mystical vision.

With Zerlina close beside her, Deidre watched as the Viking longship, with its oars spread out, moved up the fjord to the shore looking like a many-legged dragon. She remembered that day the *Sea Wolf* had been greeted on this same shore. Now she was one of the throng who stood about to greet the newcomers.

Deidre smiled as two young boys ran about the shore wielding their wooden swords and shields in mock battle. As the ship came closer the children stopped to gaze out at the sea, no doubt dreaming of sailing the seas themselves one day.

"Whose ship is that, Zerlina?" she asked. "Does it belong to one of Olaf's kinsmen?"

"I do not recognize the sails," Zerlina answered, crinkling

131

her eyes against the sun for a better look. "Perhaps it is a ship
in need of supplies and repair. In any instance, it is assured
that the hall will be filled tonight."

The two women watched as the ship was run ashore on the
beach, the crew carefully securing the ship then wading
through the water to unload the many casks and chests. Deidre
could see the familiar form of Wolfram striding toward one of
the men. A large man she had never seen before was slapping
Wolfram on the back, his loud voice floating in the breeze.

"I told you I would capture him for you!" the man said,
throwing back his head in a haughty gesture. "I give him to
you as a token of our friendship."

Wolfram's words were muffled, though he returned the
other man's gesture of friendship.

"Who is that man?" Deidre asked Zerlina.

"Can it be? Yes, it is. The man is Thorkill, one of Wolfram's childhood companions, a Viking of great renown and a
merchant of sorts."

Deidre wandered closer to where Wolfram and the man
stood. The ship was being unloaded, the chests being lugged
ashore and up the hill by the crewmen and some of the
stronger thralls. Other crewmen held their battle-axes and
swords in hand, looking fearsome in the light of the sun as
they climbed the steep incline of the mountain.

The ship had brought wealth from the north, it was
whispered, furs, whale ivory, oil and slaves—all of which
would be bartered.

Wolfram stood watching as the cargo was put ashore. From
what Diedre could hear of the conversation, the ship bound
for Skiringssal had been damaged in a storm, its sister ship lost
to the sea. The needed repairs to the ship were being discussed and it appeared that the visit would be a longer one
than planned.

The man named Thorkill motioned to several of his men.
"Bring the prisoner out!" he ordered. A tall, dirty figure was
led from the ship. Thorkill took Wolfram to where the prisoner stood.

"You can see for yourself that this is the man you sought."

The prisoner was ragged and filthy, his hair and beard
matted and long. His wrists were tied together and from his
neck collar a chain protruded so that he could be led. He

moved about slowly, his head held downward as if weeks of abuse had broken his spirit.

"How cruel!" Deidre murmured, feeling pity well up inside of her for this unknown man.

Wolfram strode forward, taking the prisoner's face in his hands and examining him as if he were a prized horse or cow.

"By Thor's hammer it is him," he remarked. He stepped back as the creature recovered his anger and lashed out at the Viking who stood before him.

"You will have to show him who is master, eh, Wolfram?" laughed Thorkill.

"Yes. I will wipe that look of defiance from his face." He raised his fist to the man. "I will teach you what it is like to be a slave."

An icy wave of intuition flooded Deidre. "No, it could not be true," she thought, yet Wolfram spoke to the man in Gaelic, not in his Nordic tongue.

"Take him to the slave quarters," Thorkill ordered his men. As the Viking turned around, Deidre could see that he was lacking one eye.

"I would rather die than live as a slave among heathens, you Viking dog. Kill me," the ragged, dark-haired captive snarled, tugging upon his bonds. Something about the voice was familiar to Deidre, and she hastened forward to get a better look at the man.

Stepping through the circle of men who guarded the prisoner, Deidre's eyes met the blue eyes of the bearded man as they focused in recognition of her. Her heart palpitated, she felt as if she could no longer breathe.

"Maddock! Maddock, is it you?" she exclaimed.

"Deidre," came the hoarse reply.

Deidre saw before her an Irishman, her kinsman. The same man who had enslaved Wolfram so many years ago. She watched helplessly, wordlessly as he was pushed up the hill to await the darkness of the wooden hut which would be his home.

9

Deidre threw herself at Wolfram, holding his arm tightly with her small hands. "No! Wolfram, do not do this," she pleaded.

He looked at her with a frown upon his handsome face. "I must," he said in a choked voice. He hated to cause her this pain but he could not appear the fool in front of Thorkill. The man had done him a favor by capturing his enemy. It was the supreme act of friendship among Vikings.

"Please!" Her grasp upon him tightened as her eyes met his. She read defiance there and fierce pride. "He is my kinsman."

"Do you have any idea what tortures I suffered at that man's hands?" he asked between clenched teeth, angered at her for causing a scene.

"Aye, I know well. I was there to see with my own eyes. I wept for you, I offered you comfort, but to give in to your vengeance, to enslave him, is to be no better than he."

Deidre felt hands tugging gently at her waist, pulling her away from Wolfram. "Calm yourself, Deidre," Zerlina whispered frantically in her ear. "It is not seemly for a woman to argue publicly with her man."

Wolfram's face was red with his anger. "Go back to the hall, woman," he said, "and do not interfere in a man's business." He coldly turned his back upon her, and in tears Deidre ran back to the large wooden building she now called home.

Sitting on a large rock behind the hall, Deidre gave vent to her tears of humiliation and sorrow. It was true what Wolfram had said. Maddock had been a cruel master. He had nearly starved Wolfram, he had beaten and taunted him unmercifully. She could understand how Wolfram could hate him and seek revenge, yet Maddock was an Irishman, the son of her father's cousin. How could she stand idly by and let him be enslaved?

So filled with confusion and misery was Deidre that she did not hear the footsteps of Erika coming up behind her until the woman's words cut through the silence. "What is wrong?" came the scathing voice. "Are you finding it too hard to be a Viking? Or is it that Wolfram has finally tired of you?"

Turning around, Deidre sought to brush the tears away from her cheeks. She would not let this woman see her tears. "You let your jealousy show, Erika. I came here to be alone with my thoughts."

"Ha! You think me a fool? You do not belong here. Your hair, your foolish accent, your silly Christian god, all proclaim that you are an outsider and not fit to be a Viking."

"I am as strong as you," Deidre replied. "I have worked hard these many weeks to learn your ways."

"And yet you scorn our gods, I can sense it every time you are forced to view one of our rituals. The shedding of animal blood shocks your cowardly Christian heart." She stood before Deidre like some angry pagan goddess. "Why don't you go back where you belong?"

"My place is here with Wolfram," Deidre answered softly. Quickly she walked into the hall away from the blonde woman's hateful words. In spite of their argument this afternoon, she loved Wolfram and would never give him up to this woman.

The hall was filled with the aroma of cooking food, tantalizing to all but Deidre. She watched as the thralls ran about lighting the soapstone oil lamps suspended from the ceiling with iron chains. The air rang with laughter and chatter. Already the throng of men from the ship were elbowing each other for a seat close to where Olaf sat in his high-backed chair. She could hear the boasting talk of exploits and of treasures brought back from across the seas.

Deidre looked about for Wolfram, but he was not in the hall. She wondered if he were still angry with her and regretted for just a moment that she had let her emotions get the best of her. She should have taken Wolfram aside, away from the presence of the man named Thorkill to speak with him, but the sight of her kinsman Maddock had been a shock to her.

As if her thoughts conjured him up, Wolfram strode through the door, his shoulders thrust back, his head held up with pride. Beside him walked Thorkill who appraised Deidre with his one eye as if she were an errant child. Wolfram walked toward the fire, bending over it and poking about in the flames as if at some invisible enemy. Deidre waited until Thorkill had taken his seat before she sought out Wolfram. She had to talk with him and soothe his anger.

Hearing footsteps behind him, Wolfram turned, his eyes filled with a mixture of anger and sorrow. Seeing that it was Deidre, he gestured for her to follow him to a far corner of the hall, away from the prying eyes of the others.

"Wolfram—" she began.

"I am Viking born, Deidre," he said icily, interrupting her. "I have told you that a Viking must be strong."

"And I am Irish, Viking. I cannot stand by meekly while you keep one of my kinsmen in bondage," she replied.

"Thorkill has bestowed upon me a great honor in capturing one of my enemies. I cannot insult him by refusing such a gift." He took hold of her shoulders, his eyes softening. "For the love you bear me, Deidre," he began, "try to understand our ways."

"By the love you bear me, Wolfram, please free him. You have said yourself that it is not fit for one man to own another. Do not let this stand as a wall between us." Her hands brushed his chest gently.

"Free him?"

"Yes, free him, to go back among his own kind as you have returned to your people."

"I did not bring the man here," he said, avoiding the subject. His mouth froze in the lines of a frown.

"But he has been given to you. Has the man not been punished enough?" Her lips trembled as they forced the words. "Please." She did not like to beg, but she would do so in order to free her kinsman.

For a moment Wolfram pondered the matter. He loved Deidre and did not want to cause her pain. And it was by her hand that he himself had been set free of his bondage. "Let me think about this matter," he said.

As if from out of the mists, Everard appeared behind them, his laugh loud and piercing. "You will think about freeing a slave just to please this woman," he taunted, loud enough for all to hear. "Wolfram, you have grown soft because of your fondness for this Irish concubine of yours. You think to gain her love by setting the prisoner free?"

"Shut up, Everard," Wolfram growled, reaching out to

strike his brother. Everard moved free of his brother's fist with the grace of a dancer.

"Soon you will be staying in the hall to do woman's work," Everard chortled. Quickly he moved back to his place at the table to avoid Wolfram's fiery anger, but the damage had been done with his tongue.

The tension was high in the room, the hall wrapped in a shroud of silence as all awaited Wolfram's words. "I will not free the Irish slave," he shouted.

Deidre watched sadly as Wolfram stalked away without a backward glance at her. He sat at the head table with Olaf, flanked by Thorkill on his right and Warrick on his left, his eyes refusing to meet hers. Deidre joined the other women feeling hurt and humiliated.

Wolfram lifted his drinking horn high. He drank more than usual, laughed more than usual at the ribald stories, even leering boldly at one of the slave girls. All in an effort to hide his shame at Everard's words and to prove his manhood. He would show Everard who was "soft" on the Irish woman. He would not even glance in her direction.

"What shall you do about my present to you?" Thorkill asked his friend boldly, his eyes darting to where Deidre sat.

"Make him work harder than he ever has in his life!" Wolfram answered gruffly.

"I say we should feed him to the wolves," Thorkill jested. Spearing a piece of beef with his knife he thrust it into his mouth. "Although as skinny as he is by now, even the wolves would likely scorn the Irish bastard!" he said with his mouth full.

Wolfram flinched at the man's words. He could feel Deidre's anger, without looking once at her face. He fought his own private demon, longing to quit this talk, yet knowing well that to force the issue would speak of his weakness.

I love Deidre. He thought to himself. *But I can let no one make a eunuch of me before my men, not even her.* Rising from the table he made his way to the keg of mead where he dipped his drinking horn again in the brew, letting the soothing beverage numb his senses. He did not even notice when the women retired early with the small children to leave the men alone at their drinking.

Wolfram's vision blurred, his head buzzed, as he continued at his drink. Never had he let his drinking get so out of hand before. Was it because for just a moment he had seen himself

through Deidre's eyes—a cruel, bitter, vengeful monster who
was in truth not any better than the man who even now was
locked in the darkness of Wolfram's prison? No! He would
not think these thoughts. He was right to keep the man imprisoned. It was the Viking way and he was a Viking.

Resting his head upon his arms, he closed his eyes against
the voices in his head and fell into a drunken slumber.

From her perch near the doorway to the hall, Deidre
watched Wolfram and her heart ached because of the bitterness between them. How could she have acted differently?

"He loves you, Deidre," a soft voice whispered. Turning
Deidre saw Zerlina standing behind her, holding an oil lamp in
her hands to chase away the darkness. "Never doubt that he
cares for you, for I know my brother well."

"He is angered by my words, though I did not mean to em-
barrass him. I could not stand by as if I were mute and watch
him give vent to his vengeance. Would he not have done the
same had it been one of his kinsmen imprisoned by my
people?" Her eyes were haunted by her unhappiness.

"He would have done as you did, Deidre, of that have no
doubt. I think deep down he knows that it took courage for
you to speak out as you did. It is just that to a Viking strength
is all important." She sat down beside Deidre on the hard
earthen floor. "It is Everard who has fanned the spark of con-
tention between you because of his own bitterness. He sensed
that Wolfram was tempted to do as you asked and set the Irish
prisoner free and used this as a means to shame Wolfram
before our father."

"I am sorry for that. Perhaps Wolfram would have set
Maddock free, but now he cannot. And I cannot share my bed
with a man who holds one of my kinsmen in bondage. I have
forgiven him much because of my love for him, but I cannot
forgive cruelty." She leaned against a wooden beam, longing
for the peaceful oblivion of sleep.

Zerlina put a hand on her shoulder. "Then may the gods aid
you both," she said softly. "Come, you need sleep this night.
Upon the morrow all will be well again and you can tell
Wolfram about the child that you carry." Helping Deidre to
her feet, Zerlina walked quietly down the hallway with Deidre
at her side to the bedchambers.

10

The sky was black as the full moon struggled against the cover of clouds that shrouded it from the earth below. Hiding in the safety of the night, a darkly clad woman stumbled about as she darted in and out among the rocks of the hillside. Shivering, she pulled her cloak about her shoulders as tightly as if it were Freyja's magic cloak. How she wished she could fly through the air now.

It was to free the Irishman that she had come. It was like a cankered sore that drove her on, though to do as she planned meant danger.

The woman's hair was bound securely beneath her head scarf, for she did not want to take the chance of being seen.

Hearing the chatter of several men she ducked back into the shadows, her heart lurching in her breast. She cursed them for being in her path, thinking quickly about what she would say were she to be found. Was there anyone who would guess her intent? No. She was safe enough. She would merely have to wait until the coast was clear again and hope that no eyes looked in her direction.

Fumbling with the keys at her breast she sought the one which would open the door to the treasure room. The captive would need weapons and gold pieces if he were to make good his escape.

She breathed in relief as the men, tired of their conversation, soon walked away. Climbing up the hill she stood in front of the door, her hands closing around the bolt as if it were a treasure. With all the strength born of her anger, she worked to slide the bolt free.

Slowly she opened the door, listening to the loud snores of

the man inside. She was thankful now that she had learned a few words of Gaelic from the merchants who had touched upon the shores.

"Wake up!" she hissed. "You must hurry." With a bold shove she wakened the captive just as the moon finally broke free of the clouds.

"Who are you?" the Irishman asked. He had never seen this woman before.

"It does not matter. I bring you freedom," she replied haughtily.

"Why? You are Viking by your accent. Why would you seek to aid me?" The man stood on shaky legs, a feeling of foreboding overwhelming his senses. Was this a trap? Did they seek to end his life?

"I have my reasons. Now come. Do you want freedom or to stay?" She worked at the chains that bound him, unlocking them with the key which she knew to be the right one. "I will bring weapons and enough gold for you to travel far."

Helping the man to walk, cringing from his filthy rags, she led him down the hillside. More than once the weight of the man pulled her to the ground, and she shrieked in fury as she felt the stones cut into her flesh.

"Go to the docks," she ordered in her halting Gaelic. "I will bring you sword, horse, and point you in direction that will bring you to another village. There you must seek out one named Thurston who will help you return to Ireland."

The man searched her face, shrinking back as he saw the hatred clearly written there. "You do not do this for love of me or my people," he said softly. Her answer was only a smile.

It is to rid myself once and for all of a cursed girl with raven hair, she thought to herself. What better way was there to turn Wolfram against the Irish beauty? He would have no doubt as to her guilt for who else but the Irish woman would seek to free her captive kinsman? She laughed. Soon she would have what she wanted, and there would be no one who would ever perceive that it was her hand that had done the deed.

Running toward the treasure storehouses, she fled past a startled guard who tried to see her more clearly. It was the same woman he had seen upon the hill at the slave's quarters. What was she up to? Shaking his head he strode toward the hall. Perhaps it was only to meet a lover that the woman had come into the night.

"And yet her eyes . . ." He shivered. They had been almost unearthly, demonic as she had run past him. "May the gods be with me," he intoned, clinging to his amulet. With long powerful strides he walked through the door.

11

Wolfram awoke as he heard the faint stirrings of the slaves as they went about the morning's daily chores. His temples throbbed as if all the Valkyries of Valhalla were riding through his head. In agony he rose from the table, stumbling over the inert form of Thorkill as he did so. The hall was strewn with the drunken bodies of Thorkill's men, though none of Wolfram's men were in sight. He feared that he would be sick and fought against the bile that rose in his throat. Now he remembered why he seldom drank to excess.

Quickly he took himself to the out-of-doors, where a breath of the fresh morning air acted as a potion to revive him. He thought of Deidre. This was the first time since they had come to Skiringssal that they had slept apart.

"Odin curse that Irishman. First he enslaves me and now he is the cause of tearing Deidre from my arms," he swore, hitting his open palm with his fist. But he knew in his heart that it was not the Irishman who was to blame. It was his pride, his stubbornness. If not for that he would have surely granted her request. He had no need for slaves, in fact loathed the practice of keeping others in bondage.

On wobbly legs he made his way to the sleeping area. Deidre lay fast asleep, curled up like an innocent child. Her long silken hair flowed upon the pillow like the morning tide upon the rocks. The anger between them tore at his heart. He could not blame her for her feelings, yet he could not and would not back down and appear to be weak. He admired her spirit but in this he had to remain strong.

"Is there not a way?" he whispered. There was only one way for a slave to gain his release, to kill an enemy of the jarl's land or to show skill in battle. Would it not be wise to do such a thing? Surely this was the answer. He would not be showing weakness and Deidre's kinsman would have a chance to earn his freedom.

For a long while he gazed down at her in the early morning light, at her curves, her soft breasts rising like the mountains near the fjord. Her cheeks were red with weeping, and he longed to reach out and soothe her sadness. How could he ever forget the feel of her in his arms?

"Deidre," he whispered. "Deidre, wake up." He bent down to gather her in his arms, feeling her stiffen as she opened her eyes and looked at him.

"Wolfram," she breathed.

"No more harsh words between us, Deidre," he said softly. "I have thought of a way to melt this wall we have built." He explained it all to her then, holding her close. She was overwhelmed by the feelings his nearness always brought.

"You would do that?" she exclaimed, remembering Zerlina's words to her. "Give him a chance to win his freedom?"

"Yes." He reached down to slide her chemise from her shoulders. "Did you miss me?" he teased, bending down to kiss her exposed breast.

A ripple of delight surged through her, yet she fought for control. "Perhaps," she said with a smile. She started to tell him about the baby, but before she could speak, he kissed her.

He gloried in the touch of her, the smell of her, the sight of her. Why was it that whenever he was near her he forgot all else? Slowly he slid her chemise from her body.

"Wolfram!" It was Thorkill who had barged into the sleeping chamber. Deidre hastened to cover herself, angry at the daring of the Viking to burst into the room without knocking.

"What is it?" Wolfram asked in fury. "It had better be a matter of great urgency for you to barge into my bedroom." He stood up, purposely blocking Deidre from the other man's sight so that she could rearrange her garments.

"The Irish captive."

"Yes?" Wolfram feared that the man was dead.

"He is gone! Did you free him?"

Wolfram shook his head. "Somehow he must have escaped. The man must have been stronger than we imagined."

"So strong that he could unbolt the door from the outside? That would take magic, my friend." His eyes turned toward Deidre, accusing her without saying the words.

"The door was unbolted?" Wolfram asked in disbelief.

"Yes. It looks like the Irish woman has had her way after all." This time there could be no misunderstanding about what he meant. He was saying clearly that it had been Deidre who had freed the man. Who else would do such a thing?

"She would not—" Wolfram began, anxious to believe Deidre's innocence.

"The guard told me that last night he saw a woman near the captive's prison. Who else would have reason to set the man free but his kinswoman? Who?"

"No!" The sob tore from Deidre's throat. She stood up to face her accuser. She threw herself against Wolfram, clinging to him in an effort to force such a thought from his mind. She felt his body stiffen as his arms pushed her body away from him. The tone of his voice, the look in his eyes was not to be borne.

"How could you?" he asked.

"I did not. It was not I. Believe me, Wolfram." Tears brimmed her eyes.

"And can you say that you are sorry that one has escaped?" Thorkill asked with malice.

"I am not sorry, but it was not by my hand that he was freed. I would not so betray Wolfram."

Wolfram faced her then with such fury in his eyes that Deidre stepped away from him. "You lie. You are no better than Erika. Be gone from my sight. I am afraid of what I might do to you."

Deidre felt numbed by her grief. The evidence was against her. Who would believe that she had not done the deed? She feared that she would crumple in a heap before these two men, yet somehow her strength aided her as she walked out the door. Turning she whispered, "It is as I have said, Wolfram." With that she was gone.

Deidre stood alone in the great hall except for the slaves milling about, cleaning up the overturned chairs and benches, the discarded flagons, and wiping the spilled mead from the floor. Thorkill and his men had left the large room in a clutter in their drunken frenzy. She bent down and picked up the mug which Wolfram had held, tears blurring her eyes.

"Why does he not believe me?" she mourned. It was as if she were dead inside, moving about the hall like a soulless being.

She walked toward the sunken trough in the middle of the hall where the logs from the fire sputtered and burned low. A feeling of anguish overcame her as if the very walls mocked her, telling her she did not belong here. All about, the carved figures seemed to be staring at her from the iron grates of the fire to the high vaulted roof of the hall. The Vikings were fond of their carvings.

From the corner of her eye, Deidre had watched as Wolfram had swept through the thick wooden door, following Thorkill to see the proof of her guilt. How many words must she speak to refute the evidence? How would she ever remove the weight from her shoulders?

"Who would seek to free Maddock?" she wondered. "Was it perhaps someone seeking to keep the man as his own slave? Had Maddock escaped one prison only to be bound to another? Or was the reason a more sinister one? What of Thorkill? What did she know of that man? Had he given the slave to Wolfram only to regret that action. Had he sought to reclaim the slave and then placed the blame upon Deidre? Was it one of the female slaves who had set her kinsman free?

She seemed not to notice as the chatter of voices echoed through the hall announcing that the others were out of their beds and ready for the morning meal; nor did she hear the gasp as the others noticed Wolfram standing behind her, his hands upon his hips, his mouth curled in a frown. Only when his voice cut through the smoke-filled air did she turn from her musing.

"So, not only do you disobey, but you seek to steal from me as well," Wolfram rasped. Behind him Thorkill glared at her, mimicking Wolfram's stance.

"What are you talking about?" she gasped, his words like a blow to her belly.

"The storehouse, woman," Thorkill shouted. "It was entered during the night, a sword and battle-axe taken as well as these." He threw a handful of golden trinkets at her feet. "Your kinsman left a trail of them to mark the path from the door. You took these to give to him!"

Deidre's eyes widened in horror. "No. I could never steal from you. How could you think I would do such a thing?" Her eyes met Wolfram's, but she found no solace in those angry blue pools which stared back at her. She wanted to wake up from this nightmare and find herself safely in his arms again.

Her entire world was being tumbled upside down, and she could do naught to stop the onslaught.

"No, Wolfram. Deidre was with me last night." Zerlina hobbled forward to stand beside her brother.

"And were you with her the entire night through?"

"No, but I know that you are wrong and foolish to act as you do now." She looked at Deidre with sympathy in her eyes and whispered to her that she would stand by her. "Tell him about the child," her lips mouthed silently.

"Zerlina is right," came a voice behind Deidre. "At least give the Irish woman a chance to explain." Wolfram's younger brother Warrick brushed by Deidre to shield her from his brother's wrath. Wolfram clenched his fists, fighting to maintain his self-control. The penalty for stealing was to be hung or at the very least to be beaten and banished. He could do neither of these things to Deidre and continue to live upon the earth, but neither could he let her crime go unpunished. He strode forward raising his hand to strike her, but her violet eyes held such anguish that he quickly lowered it again. He could not harm her, that he knew.

"Take her to the storehouse until I decide her punishment," he said sadly. "Lock her in the darkness in that same room she thought fit to enter." He hid his tenderness for her behind an impassive mask as he pushed her ahead of him. Two of the Viking men led her away.

"Wolfram," she whimpered, mortified with shame to be dragged out of the hall like some criminal. All eyes watched her go in silence.

Her punishment hung like a dark shroud before Wolfram's eyes. He wished now that he had been the one to free the Irish dog who had imprisoned him, for then he would not feel this sword thrust to his heart.

"If you do this, all love I have for you will die, my bitterness will poison it," she sobbed, fighting the hands which held her.

I'm sorry. I'm sorry, my love, his heart cried out, but his words did not betray such feelings. "I cannot undo what has been done," he said solemnly and stood and watched the light go out of his world.

12

Deidre paced back and forth in the small confines of the storehouse, tripping every so often over some cold treasure and losing her balance. Fumbling around in the dark, she felt the cold metal of an iron sword, as cold as Wolfram's heart. She tried to adjust her eyes to the darkness, searching about for any familiar object, fearful of this blackness they had thrust her into.

"What will happen to me now?" she cried. She had gone beyond anger now, feeling only the darkest despair. She could not believe what had happened, nor Wolfram's rejection of her. How could she tell him about the baby now?

Her fingers reached out to touch the shapes and textures of her surroundings. It was strange how her sense of touch took over for the missing sense of sight. She felt the sharp edge of a battle-axe and drew back her hand. Crawling on hands and knees she soon found what she sought, a pile of furs and soft stitched tapestries which would be her bed. Trembling, she pulled one of the tapestries over her body and wondered if it was Wolfram's intent to leave her in this prison until she died.

Tell him about the baby, a voice whispered inside her. Would Wolfram keep her here if he knew about the child growing within her? No, he would not. But Deidre's pride would not let her call out to him. If he loved her he would come to take her away from this darkness and humiliation.

Wolfram walked back and forth in his bedchamber like a trapped bear in a cage. His eyes stared at the bed, remembering the nights he had spent with Deidre in his arms. How he ached to hold her now. It took all of his self-control not to run to where she was imprisoned and gather her in his arms, but

147

each time he moved in that direction he was stopped by his stubborn pride.

"Deidre! Deidre!" he breathed. It was a futile cry, drowning in the mists of Asgard, the home of the gods.

A voice deep within Wolfram shouted to him that he had lost a treasure more precious to him than all the treasures in the storeroom. Even so he refused to listen to the pleading of his heart.

At last he left the bedchamber to roam aimlessly about the thin, dirt-floored hallways between the sleeping closets. Passing Zerlina's chamber he heard her soft sobbing and wondered if it was for the Irish girl that she shed her tears. Ah, sweet Zerlina, always taking upon her frail shoulders the burdens of those she loved.

Wolfram started to enter the chamber to comfort his sister, but the fear that her gentle ways might sway him from his purpose made him pass by her door.

The hall rumbled with the sound of laughter as Wolfram stepped into the large room. Thorkill and his men were enjoying fully the hospitality of their hosts, as well they should for it was the Viking way. For a moment Wolfram felt angered, as if it were Thorkill's fault for all that had happened. Had he never come here and brought the Irish captive, Deidre would still be safe within this very hall. He shook the thoughts from his head. No, the fault was Deidre's.

Wolfram threw another log on the fire, staring at the flickering flames. How could she have acted so foolishly in freeing her kinsman? Did she not know how angered he would be, how he would be forced to punish her for such disobedience? He had been much too lenient with her because he loved her and wanted to win her heart.

"And now to find that the storehouses have been robbed as well, weapons and golden pieces missing, is the final betrayal. After all the gifts I have given to her how could she steal from me?"

He looked up to see Warrick and Everard staring at him and he returned their stare with blazing eyes. Olaf, too, looked upon his son as he entered the hall, though his look was one of anger.

"What is this I hear, that you have ordered Raven to be locked in the storehouse as punishment?" he thundered.

"It is true," Wolfram answered, staring furiously at his

father. "She disobeyed me, freed one of my slaves and robbed that very storehouse, no doubt to send her kinsman back to Ireland."

"And you have proof that it was your Deidre who did these things?" Olaf asked, standing with his arms folded across his chest.

"What more proof do I need? A woman was seen near the cell where the prisoner was lodged. The weapons are gone." His father's interference goaded him to more anger. "These things were not hers to give."

Olaf shook his head. "You have much to learn, my son. Let us hope that you do not learn too late." He reached out to take a loaf of the bread baking among the embers, juggling it in his calloused fingers until it was cool enough to eat. "What did Deidre say to all this?"

"She vows her innocence."

"And you do not believe her word?"

Before Wolfram could answer, Warrick had bounded forward with a smile. "Wolfram is as always stubborn. If such a beauty belonged to me, I would not wish to be parted from her. How can he blame her for feeling sympathy for one of her own? Wolfram himself would have done the same."

"But I would not have lied about it. Perhaps that is what wounds me the deepest, that she would not tell me the truth. After all we have shared, to have lied to me." Wolfram tossed the contents of the cup he was drinking into the fire, sending up a blaze among the flames to match the one in his heart.

"She would have been a fool to have admitted such. The woman is no fool. She must have known well that you would punish her." Again it was Warrick who spoke.

"You should sell her," Everard said with a smirk. "That is what I would do. Make her take the place of the slave that you lost."

Wolfram blanched at his brother's words. No matter how angry he was with Deidre he would never do such a thing. Life without her was too lonely. This conflict between them tore at his heart.

"Silence! All of you," Olaf thundered, causing the slaves to stop their toiling and look at him. "You are all assuming that the Irish woman is guilty. I say that such has not been proven. If she were a male, she would be allowed the trial by combat to prove her words to be true. We Vikings pride ourselves on the fact that our women are strong, and that unlike the foolish Christians we hold them to be our equals in matters of the law. Yet just because Raven is a woman, you assume that she is guilty. What justice is there in that? That is not our way.''

Wolfram stiffened at Olaf's words, knowing that his father spoke the truth. Had he been unfair to Deidre? Even Everard could not be punished for his deed because Wolfram had not been able to gather proof of his treachery.

"I did what I had to do," he whispered, averting his eyes.

"And do you treasure your friendship for Thorkill greater than your love for Deidre? Is it more important to save face with this man than to learn the truth?"

Wolfram put back his head and gave vent to his anguish in a low growl of sorrow, "Nooooo." Didn't his father know the turmoil he had suffered these last few hours? He had longed to take Deidre away from these shores to sail the ocean just the two of them, to leave family and friends to insure that he would not have to imprison her, but he could not. His honor was at stake, his reputation, all that a man had upon his death.

Wolfram felt his father's hands upon his shoulders and looked into those eyes filled with wisdom and compassion. "Go to her, Wolfram, before it is too late. We will decide her guilt or innocence at the Thing. Until then, set her free."

Wolfram broke free from his father, tortured by his emotions. Olaf watched him stride away. He looked upon his son's back, those slumped shoulders, and knew that he had been right about how much Wolfram loved the dark-haired woman.

"As much as I loved your mother," Olaf whispered, lifting his eyes to Odin, hoping that Wolfram would not lose the woman he loved, as he had lost the love of his life.

13

Wolfram made his way to the storehouse, clutching the keys tightly in his hand. He felt as if the Midgard serpent Jormungand was gnawing at his brain, tormenting him. He wanted so much to believe that Deidre was innocent, but there were many who claimed that she lied. The guard, and Gerda and Erika too claimed to have seen her that night headed for the storehouse. The evidence was against her.

Opening the door, Wolfram searched about the room for Deidre. Where was she? He feared for just one moment that she, too, had escaped from this place to join her kinsman, but then he saw her in the far corner, curled upon a pile of furs. She looked so fragile, so beguiling, so innocent, that the very sight of her sent fire coursing through his veins. He had missed her; it was a simple fact. Even one night had been an eternity of loneliness without her.

"Deidre," he called softly.

She turned slowly and for one fleeting moment their eyes met and held in the torchlight. Her breath stopped as she recognized the look in his eyes. He still doubted her; it was plain to see by the stern line of his mouth. And she had thought that his coming here meant that he finally realized she was telling the truth.

"Why are you here?" she asked in a whisper, turning away from him. She felt like a caged animal, all her dignity vanished.

"My father has demanded that I release you," he answered.

"Your father," she replied, feeling as if a part of her had died. It should have been Wolfram who had sought to free her. "At least *he* does not doubt me." She closed her eyes.

When she opened them again she saw Wolfram bending over her.

"Are you ill?" he asked, thrusting the torchlight in front of her eyes. Deidre shrank back at the glare of the light. "You do not look well."

"I do not feel well," she answered crisply. "Being locked in a dark, damp room is not a way to bring health to the body."

Wolfram ached to touch her, to comfort her. He could see the full swell of her breasts and remembered how soft her skin was to his touch. Moving toward her he could smell the scent of her hair, an enchanting smell from the spices in the storehouse.

"Deidre . . ." he began, reaching out to her.

She pulled away from his touch as if it were loathsome to her. She spoke only three words. "Loving is trusting." Deidre was torn in two by his doubts. "Everything I have said is the truth, Wolfram."

He wanted nothing more than to take her in his arms, to tell her that he did believe her, but his doubts weighed heavily on his mind and his silence told of his thoughts.

"If you do not believe me, why do you not leave me here, Wolfram," she said coldly.

"Olaf the Red has said that you will be free to move about the hall until you are judged innocent or guilty." His words turned her blood to ice. "Come." He took her hand and helped her to her feet. The brief touching of their hands brought forth a spark between them and once again their eyes met, but Deidre broke away.

"Do you not wonder if I did this thing, why I did not run away, too? Have you asked yourself that, Wolfram?"

"Because you vowed before your God that you would not run away from me again," he replied without really thinking. His words were like a knife to her heart.

Deidre ran to the door. Stepping outside she looked at the bright rainbow of colors in the sky. The northern lights. It was as if God's very hand had painted the sky with brilliant hues. "In spite of these many lights you can still be blind," she said sadly beneath her breath. She ran all the way to the hall, then nearly bumped headlong into Erika who laughed beneath her breath and looked upon Deidre with her piercing blue eyes as if to tell her again that she should go back to the Land of Eire where she belonged.

But I will not go back! she swore to herself. *I will prove before all that I am not guilty. No matter what I must do I will prove once and for all that I am strong.* Touching her stomach, feeling strength from the life inside her, Deidre made her way to the bedchamber she shared with Wolfram to gather up her things. She would move to another sleeping closet until things were better between them. "*I* would have believed *you*," she whispered in reproach, fighting the tears which misted her eyes.

14

Wolfram brushed the damp hair out of his eyes and looked up at the bright sun as it faded in the horizon. The days were becoming longer and longer now as summer loomed in the air of the Northland. The sound of hammering echoed through the forest as Wolfram, Thorkill and Thorkill's men worked at the edge of the woods to cut and carve the necessary wood to repair the ship. As he had many times before, Wolfram thought of Deidre. They had hardly spoken since he had released her from the storehouse several days ago. Her eyes damned him whenever she looked upon him. He wondered what she was doing at this very minute. Was she repairing the sails in the hall with the other women, or at her spinning?

"Ah, my friend, it appears that with your help we will soon be setting out again," Thorkill said. He sat squatted beside Wolfram, busy at work with his chisel, carving a groove in a piece of the wood. For several days now he and Wolfram had labored to repair the damage wrought to the ship by the storm. The planking on Thorkill's ship had to be replaced as well as the rudder and the sails. Two of Thorkill's oars had been damaged, nearly broken in two by the savage waves and these needed to be replaced.

"Yes, soon you will feel the wind in your face again and the rolling ship beneath your feet." Wolfram gazed down the hill at the sea. How he, too, loved the taste of salt in the air, the excitement of sea-roving, but as much as he loved his ship it was Deidre that was his life now. How could he live if she were no longer by his side?

Thorkill notched a stick as he had at the end of each day's work to mark off another day. Slowly the ship was regaining its former glory.

The clouds floated in the air, forming dark shapes like the elves of Svartalfheim, and Thorkill rose to his feet. "I think I will stop for now," he said. "Will you join me in the hall for a drink of mead?"

Wolfram shook his head, "no." Since this rift between himself and Deidre he could not bear to spend much time in the hall, fearing that he would see her and feel again the aching in his heart.

Is my father right? Could it be that I have accused her unjustly? The thought tormented his mind. Wolfram hit the wood with his hammer, trying desperately to forget, and issued a curse when his tool missed its mark and injured his finger. The hammer flew from his hand, and he bent down to retrieve it. Just then his ears perceived the sound of metal striking wood above his head. "What in Hel . . .?"

He stood back up and looked in the direction of the noise. There, stuck in the trunk of a tree was an axe, embedded where Wolfram had stood only a moment before. Had he not bent down to pick up his hammer, he would have had his skull cleaved in two.

Darting in and out of the trees, he ran in the direction from which the axe had come, but there was no one in sight.

"Thorkill. Thorkill," he called, but there was no answer. He was alone in the woods. He had no doubt for a moment that someone had tried to kill him. A thrown axe could be no accident. It had been deliberate and he knew who had reason to do such a thing. Everard. Who else would want to see him dead? Who had sold him into slavery?

In two strides he reached the axe, turning it over in his hands as soon as he had pulled it from the tree. He had proof now that Everard had done the deed for this was his brother's weapon. He recognized the carvings on the handle.

"By Thor's hammer I will see him punished for this," he swore. Hearing a rustling sound behind him he gripped the handle of the axe, prepared to do battle. "So you come to finish me off," he said whirling around, but it was not Everard who stood behind him, but Warrick.

"I heard you shout, Wolfram," his younger brother said in alarm. "What has happened?"

Wolfram eyed this brother at whose mother's side he had been reared. He was relieved to see him, yet realized that it was time for Everard's treachery to come to light. He needed someone to confide in, particularly now that Deidre was not by his side to soothe his raging temper.

"It seems that someone wishes me dead," Wolfram said icily. He thrust the axe into Warrick's hands. "This axe was aimed at my head."

"Aimed at your head?" Warrick's eyes were wide with disbelief.

"Had I not ducked to retrieve my hammer I would not be standing before you now, but in Odin's mighty hall among those gone from this world. How foolish was I to put his treachery out of my thoughts." Taking the axe, Wolfram heaved it angrily, sending it back to its target in the tree trunk.

"Who? What? Tell me what is going on," Warrick exclaimed.

Wolfram motioned for Warrick to sit beside him on the grass, and told him of his suspicions starting with his kidnapping five years before.

"No doubt Everard fears that Father will entrust me with the jarldom upon his death," Wolfram murmured. "With me safely out of the way, he will easily take control."

Warrick shook his head. "I cannot believe that he would do such a thing. He is eldest. He will be next jarl. Why would he endanger his honor? Risk the wrath of the gods? You must be wrong in what you suppose, brother."

"The evidence is all too clear. Eric told me that it was by my brother's hand that I became a slave." He pointed toward the axe. "That too proves him to be guilty."

Warrick clenched his fists. "If what you say is true, then Everard must be punished for what he has done. We must tell Father."

Wolfram put a hand on his younger brother's arm as he began to rise to his feet. "No. We must gather proof. We cannot tell Father until the evidence is overwhelmingly against Everard. There are no witnesses, for Eric Haraldsson is far away from these shores. It will be only his word against mine."

Warrick's eyes blazed fury. "Then we will find a way to see that he is punished for his betrayal. Until then, take care, brother." With these words, Warrick left Wolfram alone with his thoughts in the gray haze of the setting sun.

15

Deidre spent more time out of doors as the days passed by, enjoying her freedom. Listening to the song of the birds, watching them in their flight, and breathing in the fragrant smell of the flowers and fresh scent of the trees, made her realize more than ever before what a precious gift life was. If only Wolfram believed in her, her happiness would have been complete.

"Deidre." The voice of Zerlina called to her from afar.

Deidre got up from the log she was sitting on near the grove of trees behind the hall, cupped her hands to her mouth and called back. "Over here!"

Zerlina motioned to her and Deidre hastened toward her, feeling carefree as her unbound hair blew in the breeze. "What is it, Zerlina?" she asked upon reaching her red-headed friend.

"We are going on a journey," Zerlina answered, averting her eyes. "Collect your belongings together, we leave today."

"A journey?" The thought came to Deidre's mind that perhaps she was to be sent back to her people "What is it, Zerlina? Tell me what is happening."

"We are to attend the "thing." It is our meeting in which your fate will be decided once and for all. Olaf has said that this must be so." Zerlina's eyes were pleading. "For the last time, I beg you, Deidre. Tell Wolfram about the child that you carry. It will spare you all of this."

Deidre remembered hearing of such an assembly of free men and now tried hard to remember all the "man talk" from the hall. It was there that the people would gather to hear laws proclaimed, to lodge suits against trangressors, to worship gods, display skills and even to buy and sell. There had been a meeting of householders under Olaf's jurisdiction a few days after she had arrived upon these shores. The "thing" would be much the same only on a grander scale.

"It is here that I will prove my innocence, is that not so?" Zerlina nodded her head, "yes."

"Olaf believes that you speak true and has insisted that you be given this chance, much as our warriors prove themselves by combat." She touched Deidre's arm. "You cannot go through with this, Deidre. If you but ask it of Wolfram, tell him about the baby, he will spare you. You have no idea what will be asked of you."

For a moment fear of the unknown flashed through Deidre, but she fought against it, throwing back her shoulders and holding up her head. "Let us go to this meeting of yours, this gathering. I am anxious to prove myself innocent." In truth these last few days nearly all the members of the hall shunned her as if she were a leper.

Returning to the hall with Zerlina, Deidre gathered her gowns together and tied them in her cloak. Olaf had given her several necklaces as a token of his affection for her, and Wolfram had given her gold and silver arm bracelets. She put these in a small sack along with her brooches and other jewelry. The brooch which Wolfram had given her so long ago remained upon her breast. She took two pairs of leather shoes, one of thick leather in case the days held rain and two cloaks, one made of fur in case the nights were chilly.

Zerlina, Deidre, Adora, Gerda, and the rest of the household women gathered together the baking pans, wooden bowls and spoons, buckets, and several iron cauldrons which would be suspended over cooking fires by a tripod. Even far away from the hall, there would still be cooking to be done.

Stepping outside, Deidre could see several ornately decorated and carved wagons which would take them to their destination. Looking closely she could see that the wagons were carved with faces and images of the deities. She shuddered at the sight of the grinning heads carved near the cradles of these wagons. Were these the trolls and dwarfs and dark elves she had heard Wolfram's people talk about?

"Come on, I'll help you into the wagon," Warrick invited, putting his arms around Deidre's waist. His eyes held kindness for her as he smiled. "My brother is a fool," he said, "but no matter what happens I will be your friend."

He was so like Wolfram in appearance that it pained

Deidre's heart to look at him, yet she returned his smile. "I have need of friends."

Deidre looked up and could see Wolfram staring at her for just an instant, then he glanced away. Deidre saw him join Everard, Olaf, and the other men who would ride on horseback beside the four wagons. Zerlina, Deidre, Adora and Gerda would ride in one wagon, Erika and Everard's other two wives in another. The remaining two wagons would be shared by the other women of importance in the household. The female and male thralls would have to walk the entire journey. Deidre pitied them their bondage; it was a hard life to be a slave.

When all preparations had been completed, they set out upon their journey. Deidre could see that the men of the household were decked out in their finery: cloaks billowing out behind them as they rode, bright ribbons or hlaǒ worn tied around their foreheads, arms bedecked with bracelets as they held their weapons in their hands. Deidre wondered if it would not be uncomfortable to have to carry spear, shield, battle-axe or sword while riding. She supposed that indeed it would be, but knew how important it was to the men of Olaf's household to arrive in style at the gathering.

Looking over at Erika, she was not surprised to see the woman adorned in all her finest jewelry, bracelets covering every inch of her arms. Erika had chosen a brightly colored gown of scarlet and rode with her nose in the air as if she and not Olaf were the Jarl.

Deidre had chosen a plain dun-colored gown to wear over her yellow, pleated chemise, and a cloak of dark brown. One bracelet, an amber necklace and her beloved brooch with its matching twin were all the jewelry she wore. "I did not dress as fine as Erika," Deidre said to Zerlina. "I will look like a pigeon compared to a peacock."

Zerlina looked upon Erika and snorted in disgust, "You would look more beautiful than that one in a coarse woven sack without any jewelry on at all." Zerlina met Erika's eyes with a disdainful look. "Your beauty surpasses hers. She reminds me of the strutting birds of the East my brother told me of seeing on one of his journeys."

As the party traveled along they were joined by others. From impoverished peasants to tradesmen and artisans, from wealthy Viking raiders to the heavy-laden thralls, all joined in to go to the "thing." Through dense forests and low-lying fields and meadows they rode through the daylight hours.

When Deidre thought that her aching bottom could stand the wagon no more, they finally arrived at their journey's end. Olaf, Everard, Wolfram, Warrick and the others erected rough tents of wool and laid down piles of fur for sleeping pallets. Men took up their drinking horns, toasting each other boldly with their mead and ale, the women too sharing in the drinking. Stories abounded as the sagas were told and retold.

Deidre heard again of Yggdrasill, the gigantic ash tree which the Vikings thought supported the nine worlds. It was said that its branches reached the sky; its roots touched Asgard, the home of the gods; Midgard, the home of mortals; and even the darkness of Hel.

Zerlina told a story too about how Freyja was once the wife of Odin. A very vain goddess, he deserted her for the goddess Frigga because Freyja loved finery more than her husband. As she told the tale she looked at Erika, and Deidre had to suppress a giggle or two as others in the party looked Erika's way also. Deidre knew that from that moment on she would never be able to look upon Erika's face without thinking of this story.

Although the night was bright with a rosy glow from the midnight sun, fires were lit as the company filled their stomachs with pork and mutton and various vegetables which bubbled from the cauldrons over the fire. Fish and meat were baked in holes in the ground covered with heated stones, and the aroma made Deidre realize that she was hungry from the journey. She ate a goodly share of the mutton and vegetables which Zerlina had brought to her.

"I think I will stay up all night," Deidre said with a laugh. She wondered if she would be able to sleep a wink. In the house of wood there were shutters to block out the eternal light of the summer sky, but here there would be no such shelter. The apprehension of what she faced at this assembly also wore on her mind.

Like a hovering mother, however, Zerlina pointed to Deidre's sleeping pallet and motioned for her to lie down. "A woman with child needs her sleep," she scolded gently. "Besides, you do not want to fall asleep during the assembly."

It was then that Warrick entered the crude shelter, and Deidre wondered if he had heard Zerlina speak about the child she carried. He made no mention of that fact but instead was lost in his own thoughts.

"You heard that someone tried to kill Wolfram in the forest?" he said. Deidre nodded. Indeed she had heard the story and had feared for Wolfram's life ever since.

"No one has tried to harm him again, have they?" she asked fearfully.

"No. But I intend to see that no one does. I intend to demand tomorrow that Everard be put to the test," he said in a whisper.

"Be put to the test?" Deidre asked.

"The trial by ordeal. I know he is guilty. It is about time he were brought down for his wrong-doing."

Remembering her own plight, her own innocence, Deidre wondered if by chance Everard too had been wrongly accused. "Do not do such a thing," she pleaded softly. "It will only start trouble."

Warrick looked at her and laughed. It was a laugh which sounded evil and full of hatred, and for just a moment Deidre feared him. But he soon was smiling again, and Deidre's fears fled.

"Don't do this, Warrick," she said again. I fear that great trouble will come of it."

He gently kissed her forehead. "A man must do what he must do." He walked to the entrance of the tent, then looked back at her. "As to you, dear beauty, I wish the gods be with you tomorrow to prove your innocence and take away all your pain."

Deidre tossed and turned upon her bed of furs, pondering his words. Why did she have this strange foreboding in her soul?

When at last she fell asleep, it was with Wolfram's name upon her lips.

16

Deidre woke the next morning to the sound of laughter. Looking outside the confines of her shelter, she saw that during the night many others had arrived, their small camps sprinkled about the hillside like the leaves of autumn. She could see the familiar forms of Helga, Signy, Hildegard, Rorik, Roland and Sigurd among the crowd and felt excitement surge through her upon seeing them again. It had been so long.

Jumping up from her bed, hastening to dress and comb her hair, she hurried outside to greet them. Greeting Signy and Roland first, she noticed that Signy was big with child, her ample form proof of Roland's virility, or so he said.

Roland looked at Deidre, his eyes appraising her. "How goes it with you and Wolfram?" he asked. "I thought to see you big with child too by now."

Deidre could not control the blush which spread over her face. She longed to confide in him, to tell him of her estrangement from Wolfram, but she could not utter the words. Instead, she told him simply, "Wolfram and I have parted for the moment."

Signy clucked her tongue sympathetically, hearing the story of what had happened. "It must have been the evil Loki who did such a thing," she said. Signy thought that the gods controlled every event in a man's and woman's life.

Holding tightly to each other's hands, Rorik and Helga came up beside Deidre. Seeing them so inseparable, Deidre wondered if perhaps a wedding would soon be in order.

"Where is Wolfram?" Rorik asked. "I was going to ask him when we would next go *a viking*. Too long have we been upon these shores." Deidre watched as he sought Wolfram out. He was in a jolly mood. But shortly the laughter died upon his lips, and Deidre supposed that Wolfram had told his friend about his brush with death. "Has Sigurd heard the news yet?" she heard Rorik ask.

She watched as Rorik ran to fetch Sigurd, bringing him over to where Wolfram stood. Sigurd, Wolfram's best friend, looked angry. He was scowling as he said, "I want to know who did such a thing." She watched as Wolfram, Rorik and Sigurd discussed the matter. The three men then parted and Sigurd walked briskly toward her.

"Was it Everard who threatened Wolfram's life?" he asked her with a frown.

"I don't know. I have heard talk, and Wolfram and his brother have come to blows," she answered truthfully.

"I'd like to battle him myself!" Sigurd said angrily. He stood in silence for a long time, deep in thought and Deidre could see that his eyes suddenly softened as Zerlina came up behind her.

"Hello, Zerlina." Sigurd greeted her with a smile which made his hard chiseled features become mellow.

"Hello, Sigurd," Zerlina answered, twisting her hands in front of her timidly. Did Deidre imagine it or were there tears in Zerlina's eyes?

"How have you been, Zerlina?" Sigurd asked softly. His eyes roved over Wolfram's sister as if wishing to memorize every curve and hollow for the moments when he was away from her.

"I have been fine, Sigurd." Her voice was stiff, but her eyes told of her feelings, no matter how hard she tried to hide them.

"Why, they are in love with each other," Deidre thought with surprise as she looked from one to the other. The idea delighted her, yet she sensed that something was very wrong between the two of them. Something that words alone could not erase. She wanted to ask Zerlina so many questions, but now was not the time.

As the sounding of a horn rent the air, the jarls and their bondi began to assemble. Had Olaf been able to find any witnesses who would testify in her behalf, Deidre wondered? What would she do if there were none to come to her defense? For some reason she had the feeling that Zerlina had not told her all, for fear of frightening her.

"I must go," Sigurd said as he hurried toward the assembly.

Zerlina's eyes followed Sigurd as he strode away. Deidre felt a wave of pity for the lame girl wash over her. All the happiness in the world should have been Zerlina's due, she was so good and lovely and yet she was unhappy. Deidre sensed that it was because of Sigurd. She was tempted to ask Wolfram's sister the reason for her sadness, but was interrupted in her thoughts by the sounding of a horn again.

"It will be a long time before this meeting is over," Zerlina murmured. "Did you eat, Deidre?"

Deidre shook her head, wishing now that she had taken time for *dagveror*. Already she was hungry. By tonight she would be starving. As if reading her thoughts, Zerlina pulled a piece of bread and an apple from a small pouch at her side.

"For you, little mother," she said with a sad smile, then pleaded again, "Please tell Wolfram about the child. It will spare you so much pain."

Deidre was stubborn in her pride. "No, I will not use the child. What will be, will be. I am innocent."

"Then I hope that the truth is made evident, for I would not wish you to suffer a trial by ordeal." Zerlina's eyes grew wide in her pale face.

A shudder ran through Deidre's body at the thought of such a thing. So that was what would happen if there were none found to speak in her behalf. She whispered a prayer under her breath that all would be well.

Deidre ate in a hurry and then she and Zerlina joined the throng. A large tent had been erected at the foot of the hill and there the chieftains and jarls sat in wooden chairs brought from their halls. On the hillside, the bondi gathered together, arranging themselves according to which jarl they served. Behind them in their ragged garments, their heads closely cropped to identify them as slaves, stood the thralls.

As a white-haired old man stepped forward, Zerlina whispered that he was the lawgiver. After he finished reciting aloud the Viking law and traditions as was customary, a rumbling undercurrent of voices blew in the wind from the hillside where the onlookers stood. Giving them a stern look, the lawgiver motioned to a tall man who again raised a horn to his lips, after which there was silence once more.

Zerlina told Deidre that under Viking law, a jarl or bondi charged with a crime such as theft or murder would be brought before a court of judges made up of his peers. The ac-

cused could either plead innocent or guilty. If he pleaded innocent he could call witnesses to testify to the facts of his honesty
and good character as well as to his innocence, or he could demand a trial by ordeal.

The meeting began. Minor crimes were first. A bondi was
charged with cutting down a tree. His punishment was to help
the landowner plant a new orchard of trees. The assembly was
reminded that only landowners could cut down trees, but
chastised landowners to do so sparingly as trees were more important than gold in the Northland. Another bondi was
charged with killing a thrall, a minor offense among the Vikings who considered these slaves to be little more than farm
animals, fit mostly to spread dung in the field or toil over the
hot fires in the kitchen and bathhouses. Under Viking law, a
master could put an aged slave to death as one would an old
dog, but to kill another man's property was a crime. The
bondi was ordered to take the thrall's place for a time not to
exceed one month.

As each sentence was passed and each decision made, the
assembled peoples showed their agreement with the decision
by striking their shields or rattling their spears. Zerlina called
this "grasping of weapons." Deidre found the noise unpleasant and put her hands over her ears to block out the sound.

The baser crimes were judged next. Zerlina whispered in
Deidre's ear that harsh punishments were used to keep order
and peace among men who were hardened by their struggle
with nature. Only upon the sea did the Northmen take the law
into their own hands. Upon the ocean there was no law but
victory and no punishment but defeat.

Indeed many of the punishments seemed severe. A woman
found to have committed thievery was sentenced to slavery as
was a man who was a debtor. Several insurrectionists were
ordered to have their hands struck from their arms and this
penalty was carried out before the throng. Deidre turned her
head away to keep from getting sick, but still stood bravely by
to watch the other proceedings.

A woman and man were brought before the crowd and
charged with adultery. The woman's husband had found the
two together in his bed when he had returned unexpectedly
from a voyage. Although it was within his rights to kill a man
found with his wife, he had elected to have the matter settled
before the assembly. The guilty pair were ordered to be

hanged from the nearest tree so that both would be punished equally. Deidre sought Erika's face to see how she responded to this punishment, which might well be her own should she share the bed of her husband's brother.

Deidre had heard whispers about the *wergild*, the monetary levy imposed on wrongdoers to compensate those they wronged. Although in the land of Eire they had meetings of the clans and tribes, much the same as these meetings, the Irish often resorted to blood feuds or violence to settle their differences. We could learn much about law and order from this Northland custom of *wergild*, she thought.

"And will I pay a *wergild*?" she asked Zerlina.

Zerlina shook her head. "No, that is for murder or bodily injury." She feared that Deidre would ask the question that she did not want to answer. How could she tell her that the punishment for stealing could be hanging or banishment if she were found guilty. But that would never happen, for Zerlina would tell Wolfram about the child first and he would insist that Deidre's life be spared.

Thinking to herself that if the punishment for murder was to pay a wergild, then her own punishment, if found guilty, would be much less severe, Deidre breathed freely.

"I'm tired, Zerlina," she whispered after the proceedings had taken much of the morning. It looked as if they would continue well into the early evening hours.

Zerlina spread her cloak upon the ground and offered Deidre a seat. A forest of bodies hid the goings on from Deidre's eyes, but she did not care. This matter of punishings was not to her liking, though she had to admit that most of the judgments were fair. At least here there would not be those who would take the law into their own hands.

Wishing that she could find some shade, Deidre closed her eyes to the bright noon sun. She could hear the murmur of the crowd as three murderers stood before the judges. They were ordered to pay the victim's family *a wergild,* the estimated value of the dead person's worth. Since one of the victims had been a poor bondi, the payment was minimal: but a rich bondi had brought *a wergild* of several pieces of silver, two pigs, four sheep and three cows. A man found guilty of wounding another man in a brawl was ordered to make "bone payment" to the victim in the form of enough silver to pay for the treatment of his wounds.

Lying back upon Zerlina's cloak and looking up at the sky, Deidre tried to put thoughts of her own ordeal out of her mind. All of a sudden she heard a familiar voice—that of Warrick—accusing Everard Olafsson of trying to murder his brother, Wolfram.

Deidre rose to her feet so quickly that she nearly passed out. Grasping Zerlina's hand, she held on tightly as Everard was brought before the assembly to face the charges brought against him.

"I am innocent of this wrongful charge," his low voice growled. "There is one who seeks to strip that which is rightfully mine from me." His eyes roamed to where Wolfram stood. No doubt he thought that Warrick and Wolfram had conspired together, but Deidre knew it to be Warrick's doing.

If Everard had hated Wolfram before, he loathed him now. Wolfram could see the anger in his brother's eyes, but he answered that fury with a blaze from his own eyes. Though he was angered that Warrick had taken matters into his own hands in bringing the charge against Everard, he steeled his mind to prove that his elder brother was guilty.

Everard stepped forward so that the assembled throng could look upon his face. "I demand a trial by combat," he said. "Let it be proven before all this assembly that I am innocent of this accusation." His eyes looked into those of his father, standing with his hair flaming in the sunlight, glowering with rage to be so embarrassed before the gathering of the assembly.

Deidre was appalled when several men placed wagers upon this test of strength and truth. She longed to rush to Olaf, to plead with him to stop this battle, but she knew that to do so would cause not only Wolfram's anger, but Olaf's as well. Even if he no longer loved her, she still cared for him and carried his child. Thus she stood watching as the two men chose swords as their weapons. Deidre whispered a frantic prayer that when this day was ended, Wolfram would still be among the living.

The swords glowed in the sun, their engraved and jeweled hilts casting bright lights from afar. Wolfram inspected his carefully, satisfied that it was exactly like that which Everard held.

The lawgiver set forth the terms of the combat. "This fight will last only until one of these two mighty warriors is wounded," he said. Deidre gave a gasp of relief at his words, but the crowd roared their disapproval loudly, thirsting for the sight of blood. All commotion ceased, however, as Everard raised his sword.

"I will show you to be a liar this day," he swore loudly before all. He grinned fiercely, certain that he would be the victor.

The lawgiver stepped forward. "By mighty Thor, we begin this combat," he shouted, bringing his hand downward to begin the fighting and then stepping back to safety. Deidre's hands were cold, her heart lurching in her breast at the sight of the hulking Everard circling Wolfram like a skulking lion.

Wolfram moved with silent grace, like a hunter. The Viking throng elbowed each other to get a better view of the happenings, the crowd becoming silent as Everard lunged swiftly like a striking reptile. Wolfram danced aside, unscathed by his brother's sword.

"You may have escaped me once, but you will not do so again," Everard threatened between clenched teeth. He struck again, this blow being parried by Wolfram's blade. Again and again the sound of iron on iron sounded on the hillside along with the voices of the Vikings calling loudly to the fighter they favored. Perspiration rolled down Wolfram's face. Gazing at his brother he saw the eyes narrowed with hatred.

"I feel as much loathing for you as you do me, brother," Wolfram growled. His thrust missed Everard only by a wolf's tooth.

As the sun rose high in the sky, the two brothers strained together, each holding his own. From her site upon the hillside, Deidre stood as still as a statue, afraid to look and yet afraid not to see all that was happening.

"Oh, Wolfram, Wolfram, my heart is with you. May the Lord be with you," she whispered. Even though these last several days had split them apart, she loved him and had already forgiven him for locking her in the storehouse, for doubting her. After all, even she had to admit that the evidence was against her.

The veins swelled in Everard's throat as he made a sudden lunge for Wolfram. Wolfram felt the blade just brush his ear. He leaped forward, aiming a blow to Everard's arm, but as he moved his foot caught in a small rodent hole and he fell to the earth with a thud. The air was silent as the assembly watched.

Everard moved in to take quick advantage of his good fortune. A sob escaped Deidre as she saw him thrust with his blade. "Wolfram!" she gasped, covering her eyes. When she looked up again Wolfram's arm dripped blood. Everard's sword had made its mark. Quickly the lawgiver stepped between the two brothers.

"The decision has been made," he said. The sound of sword against shield sounded and cheers were brought forth as loud as Thor's thunder, for the crowd had decided that Everard had been proven innocent this day. It had been so proved by the might of Thor.

Deidre felt a hand on her arm and looked up to see Zerlina looking at her. "And so the matter is at rest, at least for the moment," she murmured. Seeing Deidre's fear written clearly in her eyes she added, "Wolfram is all right. The wound is not deep. My mother will see to his care. It is you whom I worry about now, for soon it will be time to prove your innocence."

17

Zerlina's words came true sooner than either she or Deidre had feared. Deidre was pushed forward by a Viking she did not know to hear the charges against her.

Wolfram had seen little of Deidre before they set off upon the journey to the assembly, but he had tried with all his power to find any witnesses who could attest to her innocence. So far he found only those who felt her guilty, and Wolfram had become even more convinced that it had been by Deidre's hand that Maddock had escaped. Even so he would do all within his power to see that her punishment was minimal.

At the sight of Wolfram's wound Deidre forgot for the moment her own plight, but when the lawgiver stepped forward, her fears returned.

"Since no witnesses have spoken for you, it has been determined that you be given the chance to prove your innocence by ordeal," he said loudly for all to hear.

"No!" Wolfram stepped forward, holding Deidre's eyes with his own. He could not bear to see her suffer the hot stones. Blood seeped from the linen around his wound, and he winced at the pain his movement had caused.

"It has been decided," the lawgiver said beneath his breath angrily.

"I will be brave no matter what the punishment may be," Deidre vowed beneath her breath.
breath.

"Do you wish to avoid this trial?" the lawgiver asked Deidre, unnerved by Wolfram's actions. Seeing the scorn in the lawgiver's eyes, Wolfram stepped back.

Deidre knew in her heart that this was the only way. She was not guilty; surely if she had faith it would be proven. Out of

170

the corner of her eye she saw Wolfram step forward, only to
be intercepted by Olaf. She heard him arguing with his father,
telling him to stop the ordeal, but Olaf argued that it was
Deidre's right. Matters had progressed too far for them to
back out now.

"Do you wish a trial by ordeal?" the lawgiver repeated, ir-
ritated by the disturbance.

"Yes," Deidre said with conviction. "Let it be proven that I
am innocent of these charges. I did not release my kinsman
from his bondage though I abhorred his being made a slave.
Nor did I open Wolfram Olafsson's storehouse. Let it be so
proven this day." She managed to talk in a calm, clear voice
despite the trembling of her hands.

"Since this is the day of Odin, god of wisdom, so be it,"
ordered the lawgiver. He commanded that several stones be
cast into the fire. Deidre flinched as she imagined the agony
they would cause. Her eyes darted again and again to the fire.

When the stones were red hot, they were picked up with a
long metal spoon to be thrust into Deidre's hand. Deidre
winced, clenching her jaw tightly to keep from crying out
aloud. Wolfram felt as if the stones were being placed into his
own hand, so deep was his grief.

"How could I have let her suffer so," he moaned, feeling
anger at himself for his foolish pride well up like the ocean's
tide. He would never be able to make up for the pain she
was now suffering, he thought.

The stones were left in Deidre's hand for only a short,
dreadful moment, yet the moment seemed like eternity. When
they were removed and her hand bandaged, she was sent from
the front of the crowd to return to their presence again on
Saturday when the judges would reconvene to look at her.
Their decision would be based not upon whether her hand was
burned, which it would of course be, but rather on the severity
and cleanliness of that burn. If clean, she would be deemed innocent, if festering, she would be pronounced guilty and her
sentence given.

"Deidre!" Wolfram cried, rushing forward with the intention of begging her forgiveness. But his way was blocked by
the crowd, and he could only watch in helpless desperation as
she was taken away. "I have lost her," he whispered. The
words were a torture to his soul.

18

Deidre stood beside Zerlina in the small confines of the tent as Wolfram's sister dipped Deidre's pained hand over and over into a large bowl filled with icy water. One of the thralls had been sent in secret to fetch some snow from the peaks of the mountains.

"This will take away the pain, though I regret that I cannot use any herbs upon your wound," Zerlina whispered. "It is forbidden."

Deidre was amazed at how the chilled water took away the stabbing pain as if by magic. *Yet it is my heart that pains me more,* she thought. She had heard Wolfram's cry to her and had seen the anguish in his eyes. Would they now be able to give vent to their love again?

As if reading her thoughts Zerlina said softly, "Wolfram was ready to run forward and carry you away with him to save you from this. Do not blame him in your heart for what has happened. Although he loves you, he must always bear in mind that his men must always think him to be strong. Had it been another who had been accused of freeing a slave and stealing, the punishment would have been far worse."

"I know," Deidre replied with a sad smile. "I only regret that your brother did not trust my word and would not listen to my pleas." She sighed. "Well, perhaps now he will believe that I am not guilty." Deidre looked at her hand. It was sore and red but by whatever power there be, it was not seriously burned. She knew in her heart that there would be no festering. Before all she would be deemed innocent. "Wolfram's wound. It is not serious?" Deidre asked then, remembering that she was not the only one to have suffered pain this day.

"No, only a flesh wound. He was very fortunate. I witnessed one such combat in which both fighters were wounded unto death."

"I wish I could go to him," Deidre sighed.

"But you cannot. It would be unseemly until you are judged to be free of the charges brought against you." Carefully Zerlina bound Deidre's hand then looked into her eyes. "You must tell him about the baby when you do see him. There is no reason to keep silent. It will form a bond between you that can never more be broken. You and Wolfram will forget all about this day and think only of the child your love has brought forth."

Deidre started to speak but her words were stopped by the sight of Olaf himself pushing through the small opening in the tent. He came forward and gave her a resounding slap upon the back as if she had been a man.

"You make me proud, Raven," he thundered. "Never have I seen such bravery. To have uttered no plea for mercy, to have borne the pain without tears, to have stood silent without uttering a whimper, all make me salute you, woman. No Viking warrior has ever acted any more fearlessly. You may not be Viking born, but you are a true Viking nonetheless." He reached for her hand, unwound the bandage Zerlina had wound so tightly only moments before and examined the wound carefully. "It is as I thought. When Saturday arrives it will be seen by all that what I have always suspected is true. It was as you said, Raven. I do not know by whose hand the Irish slave was freed, but it was not by your hand that such a thing was done."

Zerlina stepped forward to bandage Deidre's hand again. "It was my father who ordered that you stand before the throng at the assembly, not Wolfram. He wanted all to see that you were innocent, Deidre."

"A man can proclaim his innocence by combat, I wanted you to have a chance to prove your word to be true also, though I knew that you would suffer some pain. It was not seemly that you should be locked away, your guilt already judged." He strode back and forth across the shelter, his head bent slightly so that he would not brush the top and send the structure tumbling down. "My son has been foolish. Perhaps it is because he loves you overmuch, and fears to show his weakness for you before the others."

"I only wish I knew who had done the deed of which I was

accused," Deidre exclaimed. "Who would act the coward and not come forth when I was wrongly accused?"

Olaf looked at her, his bright red eyebrows furled. "Perhaps we will never know. It is Odin's will." He left the tent then, turning around only to offer Deidre a smile.

"Perhaps it *is* Odin's will," she murmured. Despite all that had happened, she smiled. Olaf had called her Viking, had thought her brave. In front of all, Deidre had proven more than her innocence this day.

19

It was as Olaf had said. Before all Deidre's hand was un-
wrapped and her innocence proclaimed, but her joy was
marred by the anger she saw written in Everard's face and by
his angry words as he brushed by Wolfram.

"I will never forget nor forgive you for this," he had hissed.
"With every ounce of my strength I will see that you pay for
all that you have done." Despite Everard's proven innocence,
he had yet to forgive his brother.

It was a solemn journey back from the assembly. Everard
and Olaf had ridden back together earlier in the day. Only
Wolfram and Warrick accompanied the women back to the
hall and both had ridden in silence, although Wolfram's eyes
had strayed in Deidre's direction more than once during the
journey. Touching her stomach and the child which grew
there, the fruit of their love, Deidre wondered what Wolfram
would think about the baby.

When they arrived back at the hall Deidre looked for
Wolfram but he had disappeared. Disappointed, she went to
their small room and sought the comfort of the soft, warm
bed. It was good to be home again after the long tedious
journey.

Burrowing deep amid the woolen blankets of the bed, she
thought again about the life within her. If at first she had not
wanted this child, she loved it now, more so with each passing
day. A life. She was giving life to another being. It was a wondrous thing. So thinking she fell into a deep sleep.

Wolfram came to the door of the sleeping chamber, tormented by his thoughts and feelings. "How she must hate me
for all I put her through. If only I had believed her when she
vowed her innocence, but this stubborn pride of mine goaded

me into losing that which I hold more precious than all else in this life." He turned to leave, but as he did, he knocked over the small bowl of burning oil, sending it crashing to the dirt floor. With an oath he bent to retrieve it, beating the burning flames out with his hands.

Deidre awoke with a start. "Who is there?" she breathed. Wolfram stood up, clutching at his burned hand. "Wolfram!" Rising from the bed she quickly went in search of something that would heal the burn and returned with an ointment of onions, which she spread upon his hand.

"The burn is not severe," she said at last.

"Though I wish it were. Odin has punished me this day, he has made me feel your pain." He turned away from her. "Can you ever forgive me, Deidre?"

"I already have, Wolfram," she whispered gently.

He turned around, his eyes haunted. "I don't know if I can forgive myself. I have been a stubborn fool."

He gathered her close in his arms and she clung to him as he cradled her to his chest, as if he could erase the pain in her heart with his tenderness. She kissed his mouth with a fierceness which spoke of her love.

At last he stepped away from her. "Let there never be any other misunderstandings between us. Love me, Deidre, as I love you."

She did not want to reproach him but only whispered. "One cannot have love without trust, Wolfram. By the love you bear me, never doubt me again."

"Never. You are like my heart. Without you I cannot live. I have never loved anything as much as I love you." Forgetful of his own pain, he gently took her injured hand in his own, as if by joining their wounds they would be healed. She reached up and ran her fingers through his hair. How long she had wanted to do that.

"There is something I must tell you, Wolfram," she whispered. "I carry your child."

"My child! Deidre, why did you not tell me? I would never have allowed you to go through the trial by ordeal had I known," he exclaimed.

"That is why I did not tell you," she answered. "If I had not been proven innocent by your ways there would always have been a wall between us." He started to protest but knew that she spoke the truth.

"Ah, Deidre, Deidre, Deidre," he murmured, burying his face in her hair to breathe in her sweet fragrance. A loud knock at the door interrupted them. "Who is it?" he asked gruffly.

"It is only I," came a voice. He recognized that voice. It was his father's thrall, a meek little old man who was approaching his declining years.

"What is it Medwin?" Wolfram barked.

"Your father," came the voice. "He has been injured and calls for you. Come. He is at the standing stones behind the barns. Hurry!"

"My father? Injured?" Wolfram's face turned a deathly pale as he rushed to the door and yanked it open, but the thrall was already gone, the hallway empty. He swore beneath his breath, then turned to Deidre. "Wait here for me. I will be back as soon as I find out what this is all about." He kissed her quickly on the lips and turned to leave, but she reached out to stop him.

"I will go with you," she said.

"No, I must go alone." The look in his eye told her that he would not listen to any arguments. "Go to Zerlina and tell her what has happened. Gather up what healing supplies you can, so that when I bring him back we will be able to help him."

Wolfram ran from the large house into the cool of the morning air. Going to the stables, he mounted a horse, then rode past the barns, past the outhouses to where the grave mounds of the dead of his family lay in their eternal slumber. It was a great distance from the main house and he paused, looking about him. He could see no sign of anyone nearby.

A voice whispered to him to be cautious, yet he took no heed, thinking only of his father's plight. He wondered how Medwin had known and reasoned that they must have been together, perhaps visiting one of the graves to pay homage when some accident befell.

Guiding his horse to the edge of the cliff he called to his father, his voice lost in the wind. There was no answer. He weaved in and out among the trees, searching, looking. He could find no sign of his father and a great fear overtook him as the thought flashed through his mind that perhaps his father had fallen from the cliff. From such a height it was more than likely that the older man would have suffered a mortal injury. He seemd to hear a cry for help and breathed a sigh of relief. At least his father was alive.

"Father! Father!" he shouted, jumping from the horse. Descending the face of the cliff, hanging on to the rocks and shrubs, he climbed down, his eyes straining to the cliff's bottom, his ears listening for any further cry of anguish. Hearing a noise at the back of him, he turned, but was suddenly struck from behind.

Flames of fire, then darkness exploded before Wolfram's eyes as he fell downward, reaching out his hand to grasp the blackness. A loud mocking laughter sounded in his ears as he plunged down, down, down.

20

Deidre ran from room to room calling out to Zerlina, feeling panic rise within her. At last the red-haired woman came in from outside with a bucket of milk in her hands.

"What is it, Deidre? Why do you seek me out this early in the morning?"

"It's your father, Zerlina. Wolfram has gone to help him. He bid me to find you and ready ourselves lest Olaf is seriously injured." Deidre was breathless from her haste.

"My father? I don't understand, Deidre. What are you saying?"

Deidre realized that she was speaking so fast with her heavy accent that Zerlina could not comprehend all her words. Here and there she had lapsed into a Gaelic word or two.

"Your father's thrall Medwin came to the sleeping chamber a little while ago," she said slowly. "He told Wolfram that your father had been injured and was asking for him. Wolfram has gone to find Olaf. He told me to seek you out and prepare ourselves."

Zerlina's eyes opened wide and she grabbed Deidre's arm. "My father is here, Deidre. In the hall. I just spoke to him a few minutes ago before I went about my milking. What fantasy is this that Medwin has conjured up?"

"Olaf is here?" Deidre's voice was barely more than a whisper.

"Come, I will show you." Zerlina started toward the great hall, but Deidre stopped her.

"Something is terribly wrong. Wolfram may be in great danger. Hurry. We must go after him before it is too late."

"You fear for his life?"

"Yes!"

179

Zerlina shuffled after Deidre, trying with all her might to keep up, but her foot was a great impediment to her running. "You go on ahead. I will catch up with you." She winced in pain as she pushed herself forward in a futile effort to match Deidre's strides. Although she felt pity for the crippled woman, Deidre did as she asked, reaching Olaf and pouring out her story to him. He scratched his full red beard and creased his brow.

"We will go and find out what goes on here," he finally said, taking Deidre by the hand and motioning to Zerlina to come with them.

Olaf guided them to the stables where the thralls bridled three horses for Olaf and the women. Zerlina sprang upon her horse's back as easily as if she were one of the fairy folk Deidre's people told about, and Deidre did the same. Olaf needed a hand up from his thralls for his girth did much to hinder his grace.

Upon her horse's back, Zerlina became as one with her fine stallion, surpassing both Deidre and Olaf in speed and horsemanship. Galloping like the wind they passed the barns and rode onward to the grave mounds.

"Father, look. Over there!" Zerlina shouted. Deidre and Olaf could see the shape of what looked to be a large sack, hidden partway behind a bush. As they rode closer they discovered that it was a body. Deidre's heart nearly stopped, fearing lest it be Wolfram, but the form was covered in dark brown while Wolfram had been wearing a dun-colored tunic.

Zerlina rode close to take a look at the body. "It's Medwin!" she cried. "He has been stabbed in the back." Sliding from her horse, she bent to examine the white-haired slave. "He's dead."

Somehow Deidre knew that he would be. No doubt the act had been done to silence him. What if Wolfram had suffered the same fate? The very thought of him lying dead somewhere was more than she could bear. Heedless of the dangers of riding at such a furious pace, forgetful of Olaf and Zerlina, Deidre pressed her horse ahead to where she could see a large upright stone.

"The standing stone," she exclaimed, remembering Medwin's words to Wolfram. She called Wolfram's name, but there was no answer. Riding in circles, scanning the rocky ground, she searched for any sign of Wolfram and remembered with fear that he was weaponless. He had not even taken a table knife with him. His father's welfare had banished all other thoughts from his mind.

"If only I had gone with him." It was a torture to her soul to speak of what might have been, she only knew that she had to find him alive.

Hearing the sound of horses' hooves, Deidre looked behind her to see Olaf and his daughter riding up to her. "You have not found him," Olaf stated, looking at Deidre's haggard face.

"No. He is not here." Deidre did not know exactly what inner voice called to her at that moment, nor in days to come would she be able to explain, but suddenly she felt compelled to ride to the cliff's edge.

"Come back. Your horse will stumble upon the rocks," Olaf warned. He could not let her come to harm, but before he reached her he heard her cry.

"Wolfram!" Her voice was a wail as she spotted his battered body amid the stones near the bottom of the rocky headland. Hysterical in her grief, she sought to run to him, but Olaf held her firm. Were she to fall, it might mean her death.

"He could not have survived such an accident. He is dead, my Raven," Olaf said. "May Odin guard him now." His flaming red head bent in silent grief for the son he so loved.

"He cannot be dead," Zerlina sobbed, closing her eyes to the tears which spilled from her large blue eyes.

Deidre fought the arms which held her. "Let me go to him! Please, let me go." In her sorrow she was unusually strong and pulled away from Olaf's arms. "We can't just leave him there," she shouted. "I must be with him. He would do the same for me."

"No, Raven. It could mean your death if you were to stumble. My son would not want you to risk death for him. Come, we will go back. I will bring my thralls and sons to carry him up the cliff." He reached out to grab her but caught instead only the sleeve of her gown.

Deidre ran to the cliff's edge. "He cannot be dead." With a hasty prayer to God, she started the downward climb.

"Foolish woman!" Olaf roared, yet he had to admire her courage.

Grasping at the bushes which grew along the mountainside, struggling against the heavy linen skirts of her gown, Deidre began her descent. More than once her footing slipped and she thought that she would plunge to her death. Her hands were blistered, her arms scraped and raw from the rocks. When at last she was at the side of the man she loved, she bent her ear to his chest.

"Wolfram!" she sobbed as if willing him to live. There was a faint flutter, a heartbeat. Wolfram was alive, but for how long. Frantically she ran her fingers over his body to inspect his injuries. His arm was broken, he was bleeding, his breathing was shallow. A large lump at the back of his head explained his unconsciousness, but there was no sword wound as Deidre had suspected. Could Wolfram then just have fallen down the mountainside?

"Oh, Wolfram, my love, my life, you are still with us. You live. My God and your gods have been kind to us this day," she whispered. Rising to her feet, she yelled up at Olaf who lay upon his belly looking down at her. "Wolfram is alive!"

"Alive? Odin be praised," he yelled.

"I think perhaps he started down the mountain when he slipped," Deidre exclaimed.

Olaf stood up. "Stay where you are with my son. There is a pathway which leads down to the bottom of the steep incline. I am not as graceful as you, Raven. Zerlina and I will join you in a moment with the horses so that we may take my son back to the hall."

Deidre bent over Wolfram, smoothing back the hair from his face and crooning to him while she waited for Olaf. He soon reached her, picking his son up in his arms and carefully placing him over the horse's back. The upward climb was slower and still steep and rocky, but certainly a much easier climb than it would have been to try and return up the side of the mountain.

At the top of the cliff, Olaf set Wolfram down. Deidre again wrapped him in the softness of her arms for just a moment, then tearing a strip of cloth from the hem of her gown and dipping it in a cool mountain spring, she applied it to his head.

Wolfram's eyes flickered for just a moment and he moaned, but his eyes remained closed. He was still unconscious, but Deidre was warmed by the hope that now he would recover.

"Let's take him home, Olaf," she said softly.

21

The sound of Wolfram's moaning woke Deidre from her sound sleep. She had kept a constant vigil over him for the last few days and nights and had finally given into her exhaustion. She had packed snow on his head wound, set the bones of his arm back in place, wrapped a linen cloth tightly around his injured arm and spread a sticky paste over the cloth which would harden to a rocklike strength. It was, however, his internal organs and head wound which worried her. Wolfram still had not regained his senses. Deidre had seen those with injuries such as his who either never woke again or awakened only to be lost to their memories. Loving him as she did, Deidre wished that she could change places with him to take upon herself his pain.

"How is he?" The voice was Warrick's.

"He is still in his deep slumber," she answered, looking up into the face which so reminded her of Wolfram's. Warrick had been such a help to her these few days, constantly staying by her side, bringing her food, holding her hand. Without him she might not have had the strength to keep on with her vigil. Wolfram's other brother, on the other hand, had kept from the hall as if to admit his guilt.

Warrick's eyes met Deidre's. "How did this happen, Deidre? I have heard rumblings in the hall but I want to hear it from your own lips."

"I don't know for certain, but I feel that Everard tried to kill Wolfram," she replied, rising from her perch beside the wounded man.

Warrick clenched his fists. "Oh that I could avenge my brother. Everard must be punished for what he has done."

Deidre gently touched his shoulder. "There is no proof that

Everard is guilty. Besides, he was proven innocent by the ordeal of combat. Who would fault him now?''

"Then we must gather some proof. He may try again to harm Wolfram." He clenched his fists in anger.

Warrick was so kind, so gentle, that it hurt Deidre's heart to see him so upset. She feared that he might seek out his oldest brother and if that were to happen the slender Warrick would be no match for the hulking Everard. Hadn't even Wolfram been bested by him twice?

"Do what you must," she said, "but promise me that you will not come to blows with Everard. I have one son of Olaf to tend, I do not want to see another at his side."

He stood silent for a moment, then smiled at her. "I promise," he said, leaving her alone with Wolfram once again.

Deidre bent over Wolfram to press a cool hand against his brow. There did not seem to be any sign of a fever and for this she thanked God. It was usually infection which claimed the lives of those who had been injured.

Deidre spoke softly in Wolfram's ear and he groaned in his sleep. The touch of her hand and the gentle words which she spoke seemed to soothe him and banish the pain from his senses, but she wondered what dreams swam about in his mind.

Deidre held him close against her and closed her eyes. "Wolfram, come back to me," she whispered.

Huddled close to her warmth, Wolfram was still engulfed in the cruel, cold world of unconsciousness, hearing the whispers of voices. It was as if he were between sleep and wakefulness, in a dreamless world of mist, fighting so hard to escape. He wanted to return to the world but could not. He moved his lips but no sound came out.

Deidre pulled him to her breast, kissing his brow and murmuring words of love to calm him.

"Well, so it is the foreign girl who tends her fallen lover," hissed a voice from the doorway. Erika stood behind her, flashing venom in her eyes.

"Yes, I care for him. I would do anything to ease his pain. I love him," Deidre answered, meeting the other woman's eyes.

"You could not love him half as much as I do," Erika said. "Nor could he love you half as much as he once loved me. If not for my father, we would now be husband and wife."

Deidre remembered what Zerlina had told her about this woman, that she had married Everard thinking that he would be the next jarl. "Was it not perhaps your ambition which led you to Everard?" she asked sweetly. She would not let this Viking woman unnerve her.

"Not ambition, but my love for Wolfram," Erika stated. Her voice was stern and echoed her dislike for the woman who had now found favor with Wolfram. How it angered her that in spite of all she had done, the Irish woman was still Wolfram's lover.

Deidre left Wolfram's side to stand eye to eye with Erika. "It seems a strange sort of love to marry another man."

"Nevertheless it is true. It was because of my father. You do not know our Viking ways. Parents often arrange marriages."

"Yet Zerlina has told me that a free woman can veto such an arrangement." Deidre would not let this blonde bitch have the last word.

"Zerlina. A fine one to talk about marriage customs. She with her crippled leg. No man has asked for her." She walked about Deidre with a smile of triumph on her face. "It is also true that if a woman marries against the will of her parents, her husband can be declared outlaw and can be legally slain by her relatives. Has Zerlina also told you about this Viking custom?" Deidre's shocked look told her that the sister to Wolfram had not. "It was from this that I shielded Wolfram, for my father swore that if I wed with him, he would strike him down. I married a man I did not love to save the man I did love."

That this woman could stand before her lying so boldly appalled Deidre. She turned away, but Erika caught her by the arm, hurting her. "He only sought your bed because he thought that I was gone from him."

Remembering her own words to Wolfram, words about trusting and love, she was confident that this was not true and was not afraid to speak out. "Wolfram loves me. No amount of words can ever make me think differently."

Erika's eyes squinted in her anger, distorting her face into an ugly mask. "What will it take to chase you from this hall?" she hissed. "I have done everything I know how . . ." She caught herself in time before she spoke too much.

Deidre was too concerned about Wolfram's health to notice

the look upon Erika's face or to hear her last words. With quiet dignity she said merely, "Please leave us alone now. I must tend to Wolfram."

Erika laughed. "I will leave now, but there will come a time when I will never leave Wolfram again." Sweeping past Deidre with her head held high like a Viking princess, she slammed the door behind her.

22

The days passed slowly for Deidre and the nights seemed to crawl along with the pace of a snail, and still Wolfram did not regain consciousness. His face was pale, his body wasted, and Deidre began to fear for his life. If not for the slight movement of his breathing, she would have thought him dead.

Deidre frantically searched his face for any sign of consciousness, of awareness, but always it was the same. Wolfram was still a prisoner of his dark world.

Leaving his side only long enough to eat, Deidre was aware of Erika's eyes upon her. She always seemed to be watching with a smile upon her face, as if she were the victor, but much to Deidre's relief she didn't return to the room where Wolfram lay.

Everard too watched Deidre but there was no smile upon his face. She wondered what thoughts were going through his head as his brother lay near death. Was he in any way remorseful for the evil he had done. Or was he feeling instead relief that his treachery would perhaps never be discovered?

Deidre's vigil was taking a toll upon her health. Her eyes were puffy and underlined with dark circles, her face wane, her once bright smile gone. She watched and waited but Wolfram would not respond.

"So handsome," she said softly to his sleeping form, "even in your long sleep." How long could he remain in his dazed condition without eating, without waking? She knew that she would have to do something soon or pray for a miracle.

Kneeling beside Wolfram, her hands clasped in prayer, she called upon her God. "Please don't take him from me, Lord," she sobbed. "It is I who am the sinner, not he. I am the one who has betrayed my Christian vows. Punish me if you must for what we have done, but please bring him back to his loved ones." She stayed upon her knees for a long time, looking up as she heard Zerlina enter the room.

"Deidre, you push yourself beyond endurance. Why don't you rest and let me take your place," she pleaded.

Deidre shook her head stubbornly. "No, I must stay with him and give him all of my strength."

Zerlina touched her shoulder. "Stay by his side then, but at least get some sleep. It will do Wolfram no good if your health is taken away. You must think of the babe now." Zerlina put her strong arms around Deidre and forced her to lay down upon the pallet which had been her bed for the long nights and days at Wolfram's side. Singing to her softly, she soon lulled the exhausted Deidre to her slumber and then took her turn at her brother's side.

"You have always listened to my words, Wolfram," she whispered in his ear. "Even as children you did as I bid you. Hear me now. Do not let your enemies triumph over you. Wake, Wolfram. You have so much to live for and so many who love you."

"Yes, many who love you, my son," echoed a voice behind her. It was their father who stood in the doorway to the tiny room, watching his son with stricken eyes. His sorrow turned to sudden anger as he looked upon his son's pale face. "I want to know who has done this to my son."

Zerlina sighed. "Only the gods know, Father." She had heard talk about Everard's treachery, but was wise enough to know that things were not always as they seemed to be and so she kept silent on the matter.

"I will find out," Olaf swore. "And when I do, woe be to the man or woman who brought this house to sadness." He looked down at the sleeping Deidre. Loyalty, strength, beauty and grace were in this Irish woman. She had stayed by his son's side these many days with never a thought for herself.

Seeing the tenderness in his eyes, Zerlina whispered, "I love her too, Father. Wolfram told me once that Freyja had given her to him. Perhaps then it is to Freyja that I must go to seek happiness for Deidre and my brother."

"We must ask the help of all the gods," Olaf responded, his eyes warm as they fell upon Deidre's face. "Raven, I make you this promise. As you have proven yourself to me, so shall

I prove myself to you. As long as I am alive you will enjoy a high place in this family whether my son lives or not. And I further promise to go to the realm of Niflheim, of the very dead to see that the villain of this foul deed is punished." With this said, Olaf turned and left the room.

Zerlina touched her brother's forehead to wipe the perspiration from his head and found his skin hot to her touch. In desperation she struggled to get him to drink the water she held to his lips, but it was an impossible task. At last she sat down and put her face in her hands, awaiting the inevitable.

Deidre slept for several hours as the days and nights of worry finally caught up with her. When at last she awoke, she found Zerlina looking down at her and was reminded of her mother in Ireland. Both were wise and gentle.

"How is Wolfram?" Deidre asked, rising to her feet and taking her place beside him.

"I fear that he has caught a fever. His skin is burning. I have tried without success to get him to drink water, for without water, there is little hope of surviving. We must face the truth, Deidre."

Deidre put her hand against his face, recoiling in alarm at the feel of his skin. He was turning with fever as Zerlina said.

"Dear God, no!" she screamed. It was as if her greatest fear were materializing like some evil giant to stand sway over their happiness. "It's my fault. I should never have left his side."

"It is not your fault! If you want to blame anyone, blame me. I should have discovered his condition sooner." Zerlina moved toward the door. "I will bring my mother. Perhaps there is something she can do."

Adora returned with Zerlina and together the three women began a vigil which was to last the rest of the day. By midnight Wolfram's condition had worsened. He twisted and turned on the bed, lost in his own frantic dreams. It was a torture for Deidre to watch him, helpless to do anything to chase away the demons that pursued him. His body was like a raging fire.

"He is going to die," Adora sobbed.

"No. He will not die," Deidre cried. She would not give up. Not while there was breath in her body. A story her mother had once told her about how Deidre, as a child, had been ravaged by a fever and nearly given up for dead, came to Deidre's mind.

"Help me take off his clothes," Deidre ordered. Wolfram was swatched in his heavy linen tunic and covered with a blanket.

"Are you out of your mind?" Adora asked, looking at Deidre as if she believed it to be true. Never had she heard such foolishness.

"Do as she says, Mother. Deidre would not harm Wolfram. He will die unless we do something. We must trust her in this." Zerlina and Adora stripped Wolfram until he was naked as an infant and covered him with a thin linen blanket. Deidre sponged him with tepid water, letting the water evaporate. All through the night until daybreak she kept up this treatment.

At last Wolfram's breathing seemed easier, his flesh was cool to the touch. Only then did Zerlina and her mother leave the room.

"If only I could waken tomorrow and find that this has all been a nightmare." She brushed his blond hair back from his face and kissed him gently on the lips.

Wolfram could feel the warmth next to him. He murmured and his eyes fluttered as he fought to awaken, yet a part of him wanted to remain like this in his warm womblike state where there was no fear, no pain. It was as if he were watching his own body, observing another young man fighting his way through a long tunnel of darkness. He was moving toward a tiny speck of brightness and reached out his hand, groping. He touched the softness of skin and grasped at it, holding tight as if he were drowning, clutching a log.

Deidre held on to Wolfram's hand, calling out his name. She saw his eyes flutter open, found herself looking into their bright blue depths. She drew him closer to her.

"Wolfram. Thank God." She touched his face, running her fingers over his nose, his chin, his lips. She smiled at him, her violent eyes looking deeply into the sea blue of his own.

"Deidre," he mumbled. "Where am I?" His eyes darted back and forth as he held on to her hand. The vigil was over. Wolfram had come back to her.

23

Deidre sat by the fire in the great hall, looking into the flames. It had been several days now since Wolfram had opened his eyes. She tried to concentrate on her weaving, but the threads got tangled as she stared across the room to where Wolfram sat playing a board game with Olaf by the light of an oil lamp. It was a game called *hnefatafl* and entailed a set of glass game pieces being moved across the wooden board in the manner of a Viking jarl and his men. Each player had to defend his men from attacking forces. From time to time Wolfram would catch Deidre looking at him and smile. Both longed for the time when he was recovered enough for them to make love.

One of the dogs of the hall nuzzled Deidre's hand, wishing to be petted and she put down her weaving to do so. The dog was Warrick's and she knew that the master would not be far away.

"So my brother is his old self again," she heard him say as he took a seat beside her. "No thanks to Everard. If it were up to me, we would have another trial by ordeal and soon put the matter to rest!"

"Your father has forbidden such a thing," she answered, feeling as Warrick did but wishing to keep the peace. There had been enough tragedy already.

"Father is an old fool!" Warrick answered, in a display of anger that Deidre had seldom witnessed. She was touched at the apparent loyalty displayed by Warrick for Wolfram. No doubt growing up together had strengthened their bond.

Deidre put her hand upon his shoulder to quiet him. "Your father does what he thinks is best." Warrick ignored her soft words. Giving his father a dour look he strode from the hall, followed by the large hound.

Wolfram's gradual recovery had brought with it a renewed sense of pleasure with his life. "My two great loves," he said beneath his breath, "Deidre and the sea." And soon there would be a child. He felt a surge of pride, love, and determination that Deidre would be his wife. He would talk with his father. Perhaps Olaf could persuade the dark-haired beauty of the wisdom of forgetting the vows spoken across the sea. Just then Everard entered the hall and approached him. Wolfram knew that he must speak with him.

"It is time we talk, brother," he said, drawing Everard aside when he came near. Everard might envy him, might have a foul temper and a sharp tongue, but Wolfram had begun to doubt that Everard had been the one who had tried to harm him. The action seemed too obvious.

"Yes, it is time," Everard answered. Gone now were his malice and his anger.

"Did you plot to have me sold into bondage?" he asked. The question was to the point, without guile and he feared that Everard's temper would flare, but it did not.

"No! I am innocent of such treachery. Though it pains me to think that you would wonder such a thing about me." He looked directly into Wolfram's eyes. "We have had anger between us, but always there has been honor."

Eric Haraldsson's face came to Wolfram's mind. His voice had been sincere when he had named Wolfram's brother as the one who had plotted to have him sold as a thrall. "It is only because another accused you that I thought you guilty of the deed."

"I would like to avenge my honor on this liar," Evarard vowed, his jaw clenched in fury. There was a long silence. Suddenly he held Wolfram in a large bear-hold grip, but this time it was not a wrestling hold, but a gesture of affection. "It is time all the bad blood between us was ended. I will need your support when I am one day named as the next jarl."

"And you will have it," Wolfram affirmed, hugging his brother back.

Deidre could see the smile on Olaf's face as he watched his sons embraced in friendship. His face twitched in mirth, sending the scar on his face in motion as if in a dance.

"Come, we will have merrymaking this night to celebrate," Olaf laughed in his booming voice.

Wolfram's eyes met Deidre's. "There is something else that

we celebrate," he whispered softly in her ear. "It is time father knew."

The look between the two lovers was not unnoticed by Olaf. "I thought you would not keep that one from your bed much longer," he said with a smile, causing Deidre to blush.

Deidre stepped forward. Now that it was time to tell this red-haired Viking, she was suddenly shy.

"Well, speak up, Raven. What is it that you have to tell me. Do not fear my anger. Have I not proven to be your friend?" He took her hand in his great paw-like hand and looked upon her with kind blue eyes, so like Wolfram's own. His heavy brows were drawn together in a worried frown. "She is not ailing, is she?" he asked of Wolfram as Deidre remained silent. "She does not long to return to her home across the seas?" He loved Raven like a daughter and knew that it would break his heart if she did not want to stay with his son. His eyes could not have deceived him that these two were in love.

"I am with child," Deidre said so softly that Olaf could barely hear her and at first didn't understand.

"Did I hear you right?" Olaf asked as the words finally made sense to him. "You are carrying my grandchild?" Deidre nodded. "*Ahhhhhhhhhh!*" His loud cry of joy pierced the air causing all eyes to look upon him. He picked Deidre up in his arms and swung her about. Never had he felt such joy. He had wanted such a thing to happen since he had first laid eyes upon the Irish woman.

Gently he set her down, heedful lest he injure her. He had not meant to get so carried away.

"A baby. A grandchild," he babbled. He motioned for the crowd of onlookers to go back to the hall where he announced the news proudly, though most had heard his shouts of happiness and had guessed at the cause.

Deidre could feel Erika's jealous eyes upon her, but no one could spoil this moment. It was right that Olaf knew.

"There must be a wedding in this household," Olaf announced, holding Deidre's hand in his left hand and Wolfram's hand in his right. He joined the two hands of the lovers together. "I will not have my grandchild proclaimed a bastard for he will one day be a jarl."

Deidre pulled her hand away. "I cannot marry Wolfram," she said for the hundredth time since coming to the Northland.

"Bah!" Olaf said in annoyance. "I do not recognize your foolish Christian customs. I have given you your way, but now with the child coming I will do so no more. You will wed my son before the leaves of autumn fall from the trees. The gods have willed that it be so."

Deidre did not know what to say, but common sense took hold of her. She loved Wolfram, was carrying his baby, and she did not want her child to be illegitimate. If a man could have more than one wife in this country, then perhaps she need not feel too guilty about having more than one husband. "Phelan is in Eire and I am here."

"God forgive me for what I am about to do," she whispered, for she would wed Wolfram by his pagan laws and rituals and pray to her God to be merciful to her for making such a decision.

Sitting beside Wolfram at the large table, she met Zerlina's eyes and smiled. Now Zerlina would truly be her sister.

"And I will do everything in my power to see that before the winter snows fall she will be as happy with Sigurd as I am with Wolfram," she vowed silently.

The table was spread with the tablecloth as usual and the mead flowed freely in celebration of the coming event.

Warrick took a seat across the table from Deidre and she looked up and smiled at him, but he did not return that smile. For a long moment there was silence between them, a silence that Deidre did not understand. He seemed upset about something. What? Did he still suspect Everard? Was he angered by the fact that Wolfram had made peace with his brother? At last she could stand his scowls no longer.

"Warrick, what is it? Why do you frown?"

Although her voice was soft and gentle it seemed to startle him. For just a moment he seemed disoriented, at a loss for words, mumbling only, "the baby."

"I am happy. I want you to be happy for me." She reached out and brushed his hand with affection and this time was rewarded by his slight smile.

"I am happy for you Deidre, it's just that you . . . didn't tell me. I . . . I didn't know."

"Only Zerlina knew. Even Wolfram did not know."

"Wolfram," he repeated tonelessly, then looked up at her. "I hope that it will be a girl. One as lovely as you." Suddenly his smile was brighter, like the Warrick Deidre was used to.

"You never have told me how you and Wolfram met," he said, making pleasant conversation.

She told him the story. "He and his men raided my father's hall on the day of my wedding," she answered. "He claimed me and was about to force himself upon me when he saw this brooch." She touched it lightly as if with reverence.

"The brooch?" He had often noticed her wearing it.

"Yes. While he was enslaved I befriended him and he gave this to me. When he saw it, he remembered that I had been kind to him and made a vow not to harm me or my family."

"And yet he carried you away from your husband and family. It is not like Wolfram to break a vow."

"He did not. One of my own countrymen betrayed us to Wolfram's Vikings. I was trying to find out his identity when I was forced to hide in a barrel to escape being noticed. Wolfram found me aboard the *Sea Wolf,* and you know the rest." Her eyes strayed to Wolfram and caressed him gently, then she turned back to Warrick.

Warrick shook his head. "Your husband would most likely give a king's ransom for you. I am glad that he does not know where you are."

"Yes," she sighed. "Munster is nearly a whole world away from this land of fire and ice."

"Munster? I've not heard of it. Is it a beautiful country, Deidre?"

"Yes, Warrick. Green and golden with the mists of rain bringing all colors to the sky in a rainbow. When I was a child I always sought to find the end of that rainbow."

Warrick's thoughts seemed far away. "Perhaps someday I will see this Ireland of yours," he said.

"Perhaps," Deidre returned. She remembered her family and wondered if Bridget had ever recovered from the shock of Ian's death. Was her mother well? Did she ever think of Deidre? Did they think her dead? What of Brian and Colin, and her father? There were so many questions.

Feeling Wolfram's hand grasp hers under the table, Deidre was returned to the present. Finally they would be joined together in marriage, and if it was not as binding as the words spoken by a priest, well so be it. Deidre knew that their love bound them together, and that was all that mattered. Soon there would be a child of that love. She was content.

24

Through the dusk to early dawn the midnight sun loomed upon the horizon like a ball of fire. Wolfram had not exaggerated when he had spoken about the summer months in this northland, but soon the never ending lights would start to diminish as winter approached. Deidre lay by Wolfram's side in the early hours of the morning.

"Have I told you lately how much I love you, woman?" he asked softly.

"Not lately," she answered. His face was etched with desire and she realized that her presence next to him had aroused him.

"Then I am telling you now." He swept her up into his arms and rolled her over on top of him. "I love you. I love you. I love you. I thank the gods that you are mine. And now you carry my child. I am a happy man." His hands tangled in her hair as he kissed her, his lips drinking deeply of her very soul. The kiss was long, satisfying to them both, an unspoken affirmation of their love.

He ran his hands along the softness of her curves. How he loved the smooth soft skin of her body. Deidre's arms encircled his neck. "Hold me tight, Wolfram. Don't ever let me go." Her senses were roused and she felt a wanton urge to abandon herself to this flood of ecstasy his nearness brought forth.

"Nothing this side of Hel will ever part us again," he breathed. His mouth trailed down the softness of her skin, nibbling gently at her throat and she gasped in delight, molding herself tightly to the warm, hard length of his manhood.

Cupping her breasts, rubbing his fingers over the straining peaks, he could feel the change in her body that the baby had wrought and it excited him. His woman. His child. Deidre felt his lips sweep across her stomach in reverence to the life she carried within her, felt his tongue explore her in places that no one else had ever touched. She gave herself up to his touch, straining against him. Her head spun wildly as she clung to him.

Usually shy and undemanding, Deidre now became bolder, longing to bring him pleasure and in turn fulfill her own desires. Now it was her hands which caressed him, her lips which sought his mouth. Running her hand down his flat stomach she stroked the bulge of his manhood, hearing his gasp of pleasure as she traced the length of him with her fingers, working magic upon that throbbing maleness which gave her so much delight. His flesh burned to the flame of her caress.

"You belong to me, only to me," he whispered, stroking her midnight black hair as it flowed freely beneath his fingers like the rippling tide. "Even when you were gone from me you haunted me," he breathed. "A raven-haired goddess who invaded my every dream. By morning you would disappear, leaving me saddened, but tonight and forevermore you will not leave, you will stay in my arms."

"Yes, I will stay. Always." Her arms fastened around his neck, drawing him ever nearer. Again and again his lips met hers, searing, burning, caressing her hair, her throat, the swollen peaks of her breasts. His hands brought her the deepest pleasure as he found her secret place and Deidre was engulfed by waves of sensation.

Again she whispered, "Love me." His body covered hers now, their arms and legs entwining like the roots of the tree of life, the axis of the three levels of the nine worlds of Wolfram's belief. Deidre could feel the strength of his muscled arms as they wrapped around her, his broad, lightly furred chest pressed against her enlarged breasts, his firm flat belly straining against her own. She marveled at how right it felt to be so entwined. Opening herself up to him, she heard him groan as he entered her. Then, holding himself back, giving her pleasure as he filled her sheath with his pulsating sword, he took Deidre to the heights of ecstasy she had longed for.

In that moment they were joined as one, offering to each other their very souls. The world seemed to quake beneath them as they moved, rising and falling like ocean waves. His face was etched in passion as an explosion of pleasure flooded through them. Wolfram cried out Deidre's name over and over as the storm washed through them both.

With a deep sigh she snuggled against him. His hands still held her tightly as if afraid to let her go, afraid that she might somehow disappear. Smiling, Deidre held onto him, too, drifting off into a contented slumber in the aftermath of their lovemaking as words of love were whispered softly in her ear.

25

Deidre took up her linen chemise and a linen towel and headed for the bathhouse as she had every Saturday since Wolfram had first brought her here. Saturday was the Viking ritual day of bathing. She smiled now as she remembered how her people of Eire and the priests had always called the Northmen unwashed heathens. How false that statement was. Among the Vikings she had found cleanliness was expected.

"Shall I walk with you to the bathhouse?" she heard Zerlina say.

"Yes, I should like that," Deidre replied and then confided, "I am starting to swell with the child. I have never really become used to this bathing of women together. I wish that I could bathe alone."

"You are lovely, Deidre. Motherhood will make you even more beautiful. And soon you will be the honored first wife of my brother. All the women have birthed children themselves except for Erika and myself. Your belly will not offend them. To grow life within is the most joyous of honors," Zerlina reassured her as they walked along the path to the bathhouse.

"It is just that Erika looks at me with such hateful eyes." It seemed that every time Deidre looked around Erika was watching her. Erika's body was large-boned, her breasts jutting out like mountains, her hips full and rounded. She carried her voluptuous body well upon her tall frame. Deidre, on the other hand, was slimmer with darker coloring. Her waist, once small, was beginning to thicken, her breasts growing larger as her pregnancy advanced.

Zerlina stopped walking. "Erika stares at you because she is jealous of your beauty. Until you came she was the most beautiful one here. She will be green as the spruce trees with

199

her envy when you are Wolfram's wife and bear him his child.
Her barren body has brought forth no fruit for Everard."

They walked beyond where the outhouses were, past the fire
pit where refuse was burned, and came at last to the bathhouse. Before they entered, however, Deidre took Zerlina
aside, asking her the question which had plagued her mind for
quite awhile.

"Zerlina, at the assembly I heard you talking to Sigurd. Do
you love him?" The question was blunt and Deidre was afraid
that Zerlina would be offended by her bold manner, but
Zerlina only smiled sadly.

"Yes, I love him. Perhaps I always will."

"Then why are you not together?"

Zerlina bit her lip to keep from crying. Her eyes strayed
down to her twisted foot. "I would not give him half a
woman. A Viking prides himself on strength and beauty of
body."

"But you are beautiful, Zerlina. I think you are much more
beautiful than Erika, or any of the others. Your hair shines
with flames in the sun, your eyes are the blue of the sea, your
features perfect. But what is most important is that you are
beautiful inside."

Zerlina tried to smile through her tears. "But my leg is
twisted and ugly and it is by the body that a man judges his
woman. I could not bear for Sigurd to see me unclothed."

Deidre had seen Zerlina naked during this ritual of the bath
and she had not thought her ugly at all. It was true that her
foot was twisted, her left leg slightly smaller than the other,
but her figure was perfect with high, firm breasts, slim hips
and a waist a man could span with his hands. Was it because
of Erika's taunts that Zerlina thought herself ugly? Deidre
thought perhaps it was and cursed the cruelty of the blonde
bitch.

"In all ways you are beautiful, Zerlina," Deidre whispered.
"How I wish that you could be as happy as I am, that you
could marry Sigurd."

Tears were now flowing down Zerlina's cheeks. "Sigurd has
not asked for me. Nor would he unless out of friendship that
he bears for Wolfram and pity for me. Let us speak no more
about it."

Together they stepped inside the bathhouse where the
cauldrons of water boiled over the fire and brought forth a

sauna. The men had already had their baths and were now out and about beyond the confines of the steaming room.

Erika and the others sat in a giant tub in the middle of the small room. Deidre could hear Erika's throaty laughter as they stepped inside, and felt the urge to flee from those blue eyes which she knew would soon turn upon her. Zerlina's hand upon her shoulder soothed away her fears.

Deidre stepped out of her garments, placing a hand upon her stomach, ripe with the fruit of Wolfram's child. Hearing the sound of skin striking skin, she looked around to see Erika strike one of the thrall women.

"Stupid fool, you have nearly scalded me," Erika hissed.

Deidre tried hard to see what was going on, but the smoke and steam merged together to sting her eyes and make clear vision difficult. No doubt the slave girl had accidentally poured some of the water meant to refresh the bath upon Erika's sensitive skin. She too must have been blinded by the smoke and the steam. Deidre felt a twinge of pity for the thrall and anger at Erika.

Ignoring Erika's harshness with the slave girl, the other women chatted on about womanly things—their children, baking bread, chores that needed to be done, and most of all about the treasures they possessed. Deidre had learned that the position of women was higher here than in Christian lands. A woman was not, like Eve, the mother of sin, as the priests taught, but the mother of strong, brave man brought forth from their loins. A woman had one-third right to her husband's wealth and after twenty years of marriage, one-half of his wealth which she shared among his other wives if there were more than one. She was consulted by the husband in business arrangements and was the hostess in the home, mingling freely with the men.

As Deidre suspected, Erika's eyes turned at once to her as she took her place amid the women. Her eyes were cold and penetrating, as if to strip Deidre's very soul from her. At last Deidre could not stand it. In her frustration she forgot for a moment to speak in the Nordic tongue and asked of Erika in Gaelic, "Why do you look at me as you do?" She started to ask the question again in Erika's language, but before she could do so Erika, also angered, answered her.

"Look at you—?" She stopped abruptly as she realized that she too was talking in Gaelic and cursed herself for her foolishness as all eyes turned to stare at her in surprise.

"How do you know Deidre's language?" Zerlina asked suspiciously. "You have never mentioned that you could speak other than our own tongue."

Erika sank lower in the tub in an effort to hide from Zerlina's searching eyes and from the eyes now turned her way. "A merchant taught me a few words," she answered now in her own tongue. In an effort to change the subject she looked toward Deidre, anxious to turn the attention once more to the foreigner. "You have put on more than a little weight," she gloated.

"Yes, she has become a bit plump," Gerda said snidely, looking with envy upon Deidre's rounded breasts and wishing her own were as firm.

Adora smiled at Deidre, offering her a gesture of friendship for the first time. "I have borne two children of my own and I know well the signs. Deidre carries within her Wolfram's son."

"A son?" Erika's smile faded and in its place was a scowl. "How do we know that the child is of Wolfram's seed?"

Zerlina could stay quiet no longer. Rising from the tub, she turned to Erika. "Your jealousy has made your tongue flap in your head. You are cruel and vicious. I wonder just how far your hatred will lead you."

"What do you mean?" Erika asked, her face a mask of apprehension.

"You know well what I mean," Zerlina answered. "From the first you have resented Deidre. It was your words, your lies, which condemned Deidre in Wolfram's eyes. No doubt Gerda echoed your own tattlings in an effort to cause mischief. But it is all too clear now. If only I had realized before, I could have saved Deidre much pain."

Deidre, watching the confrontation between the two women, gasped as she too realized the truth. "It was Erika."

"Yes," Zerlina answered.

It took all Deidre's self-control not to strike the other woman. "I see it clearly now. You were the one who freed my kinsman."

Erika's eyes told the truth of Deidre's accusation, though her words denied it. "No. You are besieged by demons of the mind to even say such a thing. I will have you punished for this." She grabbed at Deidre before she could stand up, dragging her under the water as they grappled, all anger between them at the boiling point. Deidre felt the water fill her lungs and choked, fighting frantically to lift her head above the water, kicking out with her foot as she did so. As she managed to struggle to the surface, she threw herself upon the other woman, heedless of the arms which sought to disentangle her from Erika's body. She thought only of the misery this blonde woman had caused her since the first day she had arrived. She felt a sharp pain as Erika caught a fistful of her dark tresses and yanked savagely. In retaliation Deidre lunged forward.

"No, Deidre, the baby," Zerlina cried, stepping in between the two women. "You cannot endanger yourself, though I would love to see you triumph over this she-wolf."

"She is the one. She freed my kinsman, knowing that I would bear the blame," Deidre panted, her eyes blazing anger. Her anger cooled as she realized that few would believe that Everard's wife had done the deed. To accuse the woman would start anew the resentment between Wolfram and his brother and perhaps cause more fighting. She must think of Wolfram and the child. The deed was done.

As if reading her mind, Erika smiled. "Do you challenge me, Irish woman?" She stepped forward menacingly, but Zerlina again came between the two women.

"The gods know of your guilt, Erika. You will have to live with that." She turned once more to Deidre. "No doubt she would gloat to cause you to lose the child, but such a one as she is not worth the effort for you to raise your little finger. Come, we will leave this place. The truth has been told this day."

The other women looked at Erika and then at Deidre and then back to Erika again. They too sensed that the blonde woman had done the deed and their faces, mirrored their suspicions. Guilt for their own treatment of Deidre came to their minds.

Without even bothering to towel themselves dry, Deidre and Zerlina dressed in their chemises and left the bathhouse. Zerlina guided Deidre back to the house.

"You have won a victory today, Deidre," Zerlina whispered. Deidre smiled, knowing in her heart that Wolfram's sister's words were true.

26

From miles around the guests came for the wedding of Olaf the Red's son and the beauty from the land of Ireland. For an entire week before the actual ceremony there was feasting and drinking. Deidre remembered another wedding, one that now seemed long ago, but this time she was not a virginal maiden, and the man she was to wed was the man of her choice.

She related the story of that other wedding to Zerlina and remarked with a smile that the men of her father's hall had been fond of their mead also. "Perhaps men round the world are the same after all," she mused. "They love their fighting first, their ale second, and their wives more than anything in the world, except for the other two."

All of the women of the household took part in the planning of the wedding, including the lusty Erika, but Deidre was not allowed to lift a finger. Her only duty was to look beautiful for her bridegroom.

Adora's skilled fingers would make Deidre's wedding gown as well as the sleeping gown to be worn in the bridal chamber on her wedding night. Wolfram joked that Adora was wasting her time in sewing the nightgown for it would soon be removed, he said with a wink.

When the nightgown was finished, Deidre gasped at the beauty of the garment. Of the sheerest silk, a fabric which Olaf had brought back from the Orient, it looked like the gowns of the fairy-folk.

"It is made from the cocoons of tiny wormlike creatures who spin the cloth by the order of the gods," Adora informed her with a smile. The color was of an aqua that matched the sea.

The bridal gown was also of silk, embroidered with colorful threads at the hem and upon the bodice, the swirls of color emphasizing Deidre's breasts. Brightly colored ribbons, woven upon the ribbon looms by Olaf's wives, decorated the sleeves, hanging down from the shoulders of the garment so that they would billow in the breeze.

When at last the day of the ceremony dawned, Deidre was nervous and ready to cry at the least provocation. If not for Zerlina's glowing smile and strong arm, she knew that she would surely have fallen to pieces.

After a simple morning meal of cereal and fruit, Deidre proceeded to the bathhouse with Zerlina and two female thralls. They bathed her, washed her long raven-black hair, anointed her with fragrant oils and chanted incantations over her. To pacify her own God and ascertain that he would not be angry with her for joining in such pagan customs, Deidre closed her eyes and made the sign of the cross. Leaning back in the tub, she lost all her fears as the warmth of the water caressed her.

"At last we will belong to each other in the eyes of your people and by your laws, Wolfram," she sighed, giving herself up to her dreams.

Stepping out of the water, Deidre found a fire kindled and remembered that fire as well as water was a purifier. She stood before the blazing flames as the two slave women toweled her dry and then brushed her hair until it gleamed with blue-black highlights. Today Deidre would wear her hair hanging down her back, its midnight waves gathered within a gold circlet. But after today she would have to wear it in a bun, covered with a kerchief while she worked among the other wives in the hall. Married women hid their hair. Only when they were alone at night would Wolfram be allowed to glory in the wonder of her tresses. She would not be like Erika, flaunting herself before the men of the hall. She would be a proper Viking wife, for there was only one man she wanted to please and that was Wolfram. Only at festivals would she wear her hair unbound.

Wolfram, anxious to see Deidre, stuck his head inside the bathhouse and was issued a stern reprimand by Zerlina. "Wolfram, I hate to be discourteous, dear brother," she said, "but you must leave." She slipped a robe over Deidre's form.

Wolfram threw up his hands in mock anger, "Ah, to be

thrown like a dog out into the cold by my own sister." He winked at Deidre over his shoulder. "Make haste with my future bride's preparations. I do not like to be parted from her for long."

Walking back to the hall Deidre saw Warrick standing outside the main entrance and she smiled at him, anxious to share her joy with those she loved, but he did not return her smile. His eyes were moody, his mouth set in a scowl. She wondered at the cause of his foul mood. Usually Warrick was so cheerful, but lately he seemed changed, different somehow. Pacing up and down, he seemed to be obviously agitated.

"Warrick, have I offended you in some way?" The thought bothered her, for she felt that Warrick had always been her friend. Even when Wolfram had doubted her innocence in the matter of Maddock, Warrick had stood by her.

He stopped his pacing and his eyes swept over her. "You are beautiful. Beautiful," he breathed. "You are like a rare jewel. Small, graceful, dark of hair. You should be a Viking queen!"

She laughed softly, relieved that his mood had not been her doing and overwhelmed by his compliment. "I will be content to be Wolfram's wife."

"Wolfram. Wolfram. He is not good enough for you! You deserve far better than he." His jaw was clenched as if in defiance.

"Wolfram is the man I love. You know that Warrick." Deidre was totally bewildered by Warrick's behavior and was a little relieved to see the throng of women come and sweep her away. "The goddess Freyja herself could not be as lovely as you," one of them whispered in her awe. Deidre followed them to her bedchamber and there a soft pleated silk chemise was slipped over her head. Over the chemise the wedding gown was draped, two large brooches holding the loops of the gown at the shoulders. The short sleeves of the chemise peeked out from under the gown. Around her neck Deidre wore the amber necklace which was one of her prized possessions.

Securing a golden chain from which many keys hung, Zerlina whispered, "Your badge of honorable wifehood." The keys were those to Wolfram's storehouses and wine cellars and for a brief moment Deidre remembered being locked within those walls. She shook her head to chase away all the unpleasant memories; only contentment awaited her now.

The chain of keys was suspended from the oval brooch Wolfram had given her when she was just a child. Three other chains were hung upon the gown holding a knife, scissors and a container for needles. Deidre had often noticed the same kind of chains upon the married women of the hall. Now having this token of her married state upon her made her smile. She felt as if she truly belonged.

Deidre made an impressive figure striding along in her long flowing dress, the hem of the dress sweeping the floor, the ribbons at her sleeves floating behind her. Wolfram's eyes swept over her, taking in her beauty.

"I never realized just how truly beautiful you were until this moment," he said. He too looked splendid in a blue tunic embroidered with gold. A finely wrought belt emphasized his trim waist. Instead of the tight trousers he usually wore, Wolfram had on very full trousers, gathered at the knee.

"Ah, had I seen her first and did not already have two wives to nag at me," Olaf teased coming up behind. He put his arms around Deidre and kissed her on the lips. His beard and moustache tickled her nose and she fought to keep from sneezing.

"I am to be the one to escort you to the waiting *skuldelev*," Olaf said proudly. He took her arm and led her down the rocky path to the shore where a small boat decorated with ribbons and all manner of brightly colored banners awaited. Four thralls sat upon chests to work the oars. Kissing her gently upon the forehead, Olaf took his leave of her to meet her farther down the shoreline where both he and Wolfram would be waiting to walk together to where the ceremony would be held.

The breeze was cool and crisp, whipping Deidre's hair around her face as the small ship moved up the shoreline. She could see the throng of well-wishers watching her from the rocky beach and she held her head up proudly. From the crowd came the whispers that she looked like a goddess as she floated along the fjord in her silken gown.

At last the ship reached its destination and Deidre stepped upon dry land once more to grasp Wolfram's outstretched hands. The wedding ceremony was to be out of doors, on the hillside overlooking the ocean. Many festivals and ceremonies were attended to there, and Deidre had been there once before when Olaf had made a sacrifice to Thor. Now carrying branches in their hands to portray fertility—Wolfram a branch of the ash tree, the symbol of man, and Deidre the branch of the elm, to signify her womanhood—they walked up the mountainside.

Beneath the branches of a tree, Olaf recited the vows. It was his right as the patriarch and priest of the family. Wolfram and Deidre repeated after him and the thought ran through Deidre's mind that in some ways this ceremony was not all so different from the Christian rites. Just as she had done before Father Finian, Deidre now drank from a goblet of wine which was then passed to Wolfram and she thought of Phelan. What would he think if he knew that his wife was now being joined to another?

"May Thor smile upon you always and bring many children to your hearth," Olaf intoned. Deidre blushed, remembering that she was already with child.

Wolfram held out three rings to Deidre and slipped them upon her fingers. "Three rings means that I am a very rich man," he said softly. "But never have I been richer than at this moment when I have before me my greatest treasure, my wife."

Deidre's eyes were filled with her love as he bent to kiss her before the assembled crowd. Picking her up in his arms as if to carry her back toward the hall, he whispered to Deidre that this was the sign that he had claimed her for his mate for life. After carrying her a short distance he set her back down and they watched the rest of the ceremony apart from the others.

Animal sacrifices were made then, and Wolfram and Deidre ran back toward the hall amid cheers and ribald comments. Sitting in two large chairs, Deidre and Wolfram held court as if they were royalty, accepting words of congratulations and hugs and kisses from those who wished to share their joy. There was singing and dancing and general merrymaking.

Wolfram joined in the singing and Deidre was surprised by his fine voice, never had she heard him sing before. It was a love song that he sang, written just for her.

When at last the married couple was escorted to their sleeping chamber, Wolfram turned upon the throng with mock anger. "Out! Everybody out," he said with a grin. No doubt every man there envied him this night.

"And so we are finally alone," Deidre said softly. "No one will ever be able to part us again. Never in this world." She reached up and wound her arms around Wolfram's neck, bringing his lips down to hers.

When Wolfram's lips finally drew away from the softness of his wife's mouth, he took her hand and led her gently toward the bed. It had been so long since he had first claimed her and now at last she belonged to him. The words sang in his heart. Deidre was his wife! *I will take no other.*

The bed dipped with Wolfram's weight as he knelt beside the woman he so loved. He could smell the exotic fragrance of her body; it engulfed him like a cloud.

"You carry my child," he murmured, touching the swell of her belly with gentle and reverent hands.

"Does that please you, Viking?" she asked in a voice which was barely a whisper.

"It pleases me more than anything in this life!"

"And do you hope for a son?" she teased.

"A son would make me happy as would a daughter who looked just like her mother." He uncovered her shoulders and planted a kiss on the softness of the skin there. His mouth ran the length of her bare arm, kissing at last the tips of her beringed fingers.

Wolfram worshiped his wife with eyes and hands and lips, undressing her ever so slowly and savoring her beauty. If it was possible, she was even more beautiful tonight. He touched the swell of her breasts and Deidre moved closer to him, shuddering as he caressed the peaks with gentle fingers. She reached up to tug at his tunic, longing to feel his bare chest next to her skin.

"I feel as if this were our first time together," Wolfram breathed, reaching up and helping her undress him. At long last her wish was fulfilled as he covered Deidre with his strong muscular body, making certain that he did not crush her beneath him. Wolfram was all tenderness and gentle love.

Deidre ran her fingers over the hardness of his chest with its golden thatch of hair, wanting to bring him the same quiver of fire that she felt.

"Oh yes," Wolfram breathed. He bent his head and gently traced the outline of her nipple with his tongue.

Deidre grew bolder as the fires of her passion leaped within her blood. Taking Wolfram's manhood in her trembling fingers, she touched the length of that shaft, unleashing all the power and virility of his flesh.

When at last they were joined together, Deidre arched her back against the pleasure of his entry. There was only this moment, this man and her overpowering love. This was what she had always imagined her wedding night would be like, and she knew in her heart that no longer would she think about her vows to her Irish Phelan. Wolfram was truly her husband for as long as they both breathed the air of life.

27

Autumn came to the Northland with its blaze of greens, reds, golds and browns as the days of summer were laid to rest. The household of Olaf the Red prepared for the festival of the Autumn Equinox, the last festival before the winter snows began.

A thick cloud of smoke hung over the hall from the large hearth fire as the women prepared the evening meal. They chattered away about all that must be done to prepare for the winter. There would be the drying and salting of the food, the pickling of the herring and the storage of the grain in the big barns. And there was another topic of conversation, Deidre's baby. Adora had calculated from the Irish woman's symptoms that the child would be born with the first snows of the winter.

"I say it will be a girl," Gerda stated with a smile. "You can see how she swells in the belly, carrying the child high in her womb. It is the sign of a female child."

Adora would have no part of that statement. "It will be a male child, a son for Wolfram to carry on the line of Olaf. Deidre's belly is big to be sure, but that is because the baby will be a big, strong boy!"

Deidre ignored the bantering with a contented smile. No matter what sex the child had, she would love it because it was part of Wolfram, and he would love it because it was part of her. In truth they had been happy these months. Both of them worked hard during the day, she with the women and he hunting the meat and gathering the grain which would feed the family throughout the long winter months. But the nights were filled with their love.

Erika continued to fume inside as she witnessed Deidre's

contentment. Month after month Erika had watched for the signs which would tell of her own impending motherhood, but those signs never came and she had remained barren.

"It does not matter if the child be male or female," she said with a smirk. "If it is an unhealthy child or deformed in any way it will soon meet its end."

Deidre was slicing one of the fish to ready it for dunking in the brine and nearly cut herself as she heard Erika's words. She turned her eyes upon Zerlina.

"What is she talking about?" she asked. She knew of Erika's jealousy, but surely even Erika could not bring herself to harm an innocent babe.

"Do not listen to her," Zerlina snapped, remembering that if not for Olaf's mercy she would never have lived past her birth day.

Deidre returned to her pickling, but she could feel the tension in the air.

"Shouldn't we tell her?" Adora's soft voice whispered.

"Of course we should tell her!" Erika piped up. She stood with her hands upon her ample hips looking down at Deidre as she squatted upon the ground. "It is a Viking custom that unwanted children or babies who are deformed in any way be left out of doors to die!"

"Left out of doors . . .?" Deidre questioned.

"Killing malformed infants by leaving them out in the cold of winter alone," Erika snorted. The look of horror in Deidre's eyes was a balm to her soul. Let the chit spend her sleepless nights worrying about her unborn child.

Zerlina spilled the pail of milk she held in her hands upon Erika's gown. "Oh, I'm sorry, Erika. How clumsy of me." She watched in amusement as Erika rushed off to dry herself.

"Zerlina, is it true what she says?" Deidre asked with wide eyes.

"Not always. I am living proof of that. Olaf was kind to my mother and allowed me to live, for which I will always love him and be grateful to him for. Deidre, you must realize that in this land only the strong survive. It is the way of life. If a child has a severe deformity, or is small and unhealthy, it is often deserted. But if its father claims it and wishes it to live, then that child once accepted receives love, honor and discipline from the family members."

"And my child. What if—?"

"Your child will be strong and beautiful. How else could it be when it has been created by such as you and Wolfram? A child of such love will be perfect." Zerlina picked up another pail of milk and began her cheese making, cursing once again the thoughtless tongue of Erika.

Deidre felt the walls closing in on her; she had to get away from the smoke and noise of the room. Throwing the fish back in their pail, she rose to her feet and stepped out of doors. The trees seemed to be reaching out to the sky in prayer as they shed their leaves, and Deidre was once again reminded that she was in a pagan land. A stranger after all to the ways of the Northmen. A shudder ran up her spine as she thought about what might happen to her child.

"No!" she cried, covering her mouth with her hand. "Wolfram would never allow such a thing to happen." She breathed in the fragrance of the falling leaves and the salt air as she walked along and tried to calm herself. She must not let Erika upset her this way. No doubt that is exactly what the woman had planned. She would be strong. She would be a Viking.

Deidre looked about her, suddenly afraid that she had lost her way. She had been a fool to come so far without another to guide her. A crackling of the dead leaves behind her caused her to turn around with a start.

"Who's there?" she asked. There was no answer, but again she heard the sound. Was it a large animal, a bear or a wolf perhaps? Deidre grabbed for the scissors which hung around her neck, her only means of protection. She could almost feel the eyes upon the back of her neck and sensed that whatever was out there was human and not animal.

"Why do you not answer me?" Deidre asked in a voice which quaked with her fear. She walked along again and it was as if the footsteps behind her echoed her own.

Blind fear took hold of Deidre then as she remembered what had happened once before. Was this the same hunter who had stalked Wolfram?

"I have to hide!" she told herself as she broke into a run. Her legs were trembling yet she managed to flee in spite of the long skirts which clung to her ankles. She stopped for only a moment and could hear the footsteps no longer and breathed a sigh of relief. But yet again she heard the crackle in the undergrowth, coming closer and closer.

Once more Deidre took to her heels seeing a figure up ahead of her. The man was walking along in an easy gait as if he had all the time in the world to arrive at his destination. The blond hair streaked with gray, the set of his shoulders told Deidre of his identity.

"Sigurd!" Never had she been so glad to see another human being. She ran toward him, tripping in her haste once or twice, always getting back on her feet. Sigurd lived far to the north in another village. Oh, how she had missed him.

"Deidre? What are you doing out here?" He was astounded to see her out so far from the family's house.

She threw herself into his protective arms. "I'm so glad to see you. So glad." She told him of her fears and he listened sympathetically, patting her hand and wiping away a tear or two. "Perhaps it was a deer that you heard," he suggested, not wanting her to succumb to panic.

"No, no, it was a person, I know it," she whispered, finally getting a hold on her emotions. She rose to her feet and thrust her chin up proudly. Sigurd must not think her a coward. "But I am not afraid."

It was then that Sigurd's eyes took in her bulging frame. It had been a long time since he had seen her, since the assembly. "So Wolfram has finally planted his seed. It is about time."

Deidre blushed under his scrutinizing gaze. "We are wed," she said proudly, telling him all about what had happened since she had seen him at the "thing."

"I'm happy for you, Deidre." He smiled. "How I wish that I could have been there, but farming ties one to the land. Sometimes I wish I were in Dubh-Linn again. Life was so simple there."

At the mention of the settlement Deidre's eyes clouded. Even though she was blissfully happy with Wolfram, there were still times when she thought about Eire, when she longed to see her family again.

"I am anxious to go out on the sea again," Sigurd whispered as much to himself as to her.

Deidre sensed a feeling of loneliness and isolation about him. Putting a hand on his shoulder she whispered, "Zerlina has been very kind to me, a true sister."

He looked at her with a face full of mixed emotions. "How is Zerlina?" he asked.

"Lonely. I think she pines for you."

Sigurd looked away, afraid to show his weakness for any woman. "She has her family around her. How can she be lonely?"

"A woman can be lonely amid a whole crowd of loved ones if the man she loves is not with her. And on the other hand, if she is without her loved ones and with the man she loves, then her world is full."

"Zerlina does not love me," he said.

"Yes, she does. How can you doubt it?"

Sigurd frowned. "I'm not good enough for her. She is the daughter of a *jarl* and I am *nobody*. I have nothing to give her. She would be better off with somebody else."

Deidre gave a sigh of frustration. "Men can be so foolish in their pride at times," she said. The two of them started walking toward the hall. She would bring up the subject again another time.

"What brings you our way, Sigurd?" Deidre asked.

"To fetch Wolfram. I have heard of a huge hoard of treasure upon the island to the south. It is time we went sailing once more, before the snows set in." He kicked at a pebble in his path, no doubt still thinking of his impossible love for the Jarl's daughter.

Deidre stopped in her tracks. "I don't want Wolfram to go, Sigurd. Take another in his place. Something might happen to him. Please."

But Sigurd insisted. "Nothing will happen to him, Deidre. Besides Wolfram is our leader. No one else can guide the *Sea-Wolf*."

Deidre felt fear spread through her, but she did not press the matter. Tonight when she and Wolfram were alone she would beg him not to go. She needed him now; the baby would need him.

They made their way to the great hall where Sigurd could smell the feast being prepared. He sniffed the air and licked his lips.

"Stay for the feast, Sigurd!" Deidre said with a laugh. "It will be well to have your company among us." *And it will be well to have you near Zerlina too,* she thought with a smile. Tonight she would do all within her power to bring these two stubborn lovers together.

28

There was a chill in the air the night of the Autumn Equinox feast. A chill which told of the approaching winter. Deidre pulled her cloak snugly against her body in an effort to ward off the cold and stepped closer to the fire. She could see Sigurd and Wolfram huddled close together, their faces glowing with the excitement of going to sea again and it was all she could do not to run to her husband and beg him to stay behind.

Later. I will wait until we are alone, she vowed.

Warrick walked about the hall, refilling the drinking horns of the men which were being used this night. The horns were elaborately ornamented and more than one brawny man soon found that the first trickle could often become a sudden tidal wave of the brew.

"Drinking from these ceremonial cattle horns is an art that is not quickly mastered," Warrick said with a laugh as one young man found his mead upon his lap. Warrick was in a better mood tonight than Deidre had seen him in recently. No doubt the festival had lightened his humor. Since the marriage ceremony, Warrick had kept aloof of Deidre and though she had sought to keep his bond of friendship, their relationship had noticeably changed.

Zerlina came to Deidre's side, as usual concerned about her health and that of the baby's. As she looked about at the men and their drinking horns she laughed and explained. "The men see the horns as a test. They cannot put them down until they are emptied, so a man must have a strong stomach and head to match, ere he will soon find himself the object of scorn. At times I am surprised at how like little children these strong Vikings are."

Deidre laughed. She had often thought the same thing her-

216

self. Her mood sobered as she noticed that Sigurd and Wolfram were still at their talk. "No one would ever mistake those two for children," she said, taking note of how Zerlina's eyes were riveted upon Sigurd's strong manly form.

"Come," Deidre said, taking Zerlina's hand and pulling her toward where Wolfram and Sigurd stood. "We must greet Sigurd properly as a guest in our house." She could feel Zerlina try to pull away, but being the stronger of the two she managed to draw Wolfram's sister to a spot in front of Sigurd. With a knowing wink at Wolfram, Deidre led him away, leaving Zerlina and Sigurd alone.

"I'm glad that you could come to the feast," Zerlina said somewhat stiffly, feeling awkward to have been so obviously foisted upon Sigurd. She would have been angry if she had not known of Deidre's good intentions.

Sigurd grinned then. "It seems there is matchmaking afoot. But I don't mind, for I can't imagine a woman I would rather have at my side."

Zerlina smiled then, a radiant smile which emphasized her loveliness. "Do you remember the feast of the Autumn Equinox seven cycles of the sun ago?" she asked. The years seemed to melt away and she felt a child again.

"How could I forget. A freckle-faced beauty who followed Wolfram and me everywhere."

"I am not a beauty," she whispered.

"I think that you are. Your hair is as red and glowing as the flames of a fire, your eyes sparkle like the stars . . ." Embarrassed then by this effusive emotion he said a little awkwardly, "but I miss those freckles. Where did they go?"

"I begged Freyja to take them from me," she laughed. "I hated every one." There was a long silence between them until at last Zerlina looked up. "But if you miss them, then I wish that I could have them back."

Sigurd reached out and gently touched her face. "So many years have passed since those days. Where have they gone?"

Zerlina's eyes softened with her love. "I thought you the most magnificent of warriors. How I wished that I had been born a male child so that I could be as you were."

Sigurd chuckled. "I for one am glad that you were not." Putting his arm around her waist he led her out of doors. They looked off to the north to see the splendid glow of colors, the northern lights. There beneath the radiance of the skies,

Sigurd gently kissed Zerlina, forgetting for the moment that
she was a jarl's daughter and he only a peasant Viking.

"I have wanted to do this since the blossom of womanhood
touched your cheeks," he whispered. "Beautiful Zerlina. How
I wish I had the sun and the moon to offer you." His hands
removed the kerchief she wore tonight around her head and he
ran his fingers through the silken strands of her hair. He
started to kiss her again, but the glow of the rainbow lights
caught the gleam of her knife hanging from the chain at her
waist—the badge of her mark as a jarl's daughter. It was a
reminder to him then of all she was and of all that he was not.
Sigurd stepped away from her as if she had slapped him.

"What is it Sigurd?" Zerlina asked, feeling hurt by the cold
look in his eyes. He had returned to his distant manner with
her and she wondered why.

"Let's get back to the hall," he said, fighting the beating of
his heart and the urge he had to reach out and gather her into
his arms.

Inside the feast was progressing with dance and song. With
a toss of her head and a smile in his direction, Erika soon had
Sigurd on her arm as they joined in the dancing. Zerlina
watched the two of them, mindful that her personal affliction
would never allow her to share with Sigurd such pleasure.
How else would she handicap him if they were together? As
Sigurd flung Erika high in the air with a thundering laugh,
Zerlina fled the room and ran to her bedchamber. She knew
now that their relationship could never be. Yet for one shining
moment this night she had been happy, had felt the kiss of a
man upon her lips, and had known what love was.

"Oh, Sigurd, how I love you," she said aloud, and with
sadness closed her eyes.

Deidre had watched with pleasure as Sigurd and Zerlina had
slipped outside. Now she was angry as Erika threw herself at
Sigurd, no doubt to get back at Zerlina. Men could be so
stupid at times, she thought.

"I thought your friend knew the value of treasure. I see now
that he is fooled by iron and gilt," she said to Wolfram. Turning to follow Zerlina to her chamber, she was halted by
Wolfram's hand upon her arm.

"Leave her, Deidre. Zerlina must come to terms with this
alone."

Deidre started to reply, but the sound of Warrick's lusty

laughter came to her ears. With a hearty pound on Wolfram's back he offered a toast.

"So, is it true that you are to go to sea again?" he asked Wolfram with a raised brow. At Wolfram's nod he chuckled. "Long have I waited for the chance to sail with you, Wolfram. What say you to all of Olaf's sons setting forth together? I have enough friends to gather for the crew. Perhaps you would let me take command . . ."

"I intend to command the *Sea Wolf*, Warrick," Wolfram answered. "But come along if you like."

"How about you, Everard?" Warrick shouted across the room to his scowling brother. "Shall we make it a three-some?"

With his eyes burning into his wife's gyrating figure, Everard grunted a hasty "no." It would not be wise to leave Erika unattended to.

The brothers talked, making preparations for the journey while Deidre stood listening in silence, jealous of her husband's other love, the sea. It was as if she had suddenly become invisible to Wolfram's eyes as he chattered on, and in frustration Deidre left his side.

The feast lasted well into the night with drinking and story-telling. Here and there a brawl broke out as the men imbibed too much of their ale and mead. Anxious to be alone with her husband, Deidre felt as if the night would never end.

"You have not enjoyed the feast." It was Wolfram's voice in her ear.

"I am tired, that is all," Deidre replied. She fought against the tears which threatened to spill. She was always so close to tears these days and wondered why. It had never been her way before to be moody.

Wolfram lifted Deidre up in his arms, cradling her against his chest and carried her to their bed chamber. All else was forgotten but the touching of their bodies.

"I never get enough of you, little one," Wolfram breathed against her hair. "You are in my blood, in my heart, and in my soul for as long as I live." He kissed her hair and then covered her mouth with his own.

Deidre clung to him, never wanting to let him go. "Don't go to sea, Wolfram," she whispered. "Stay here. I need you so. If anything were to happen to you I think I would die."

Wolfram silenced Deidre's words with his fingers. "Nothing will happen to me, little one. The voyage is a short one. I will only be gone a few days. If it will make you feel more protected, I will leave one of the others here to watch over you. I will leave Sigurd behind. I know that I can trust him to take care of you."

Deidre started to protest, to tell him that it was he that she needed and not Sigurd, but Wolfram's lips muffled her words. His body sought hers in a frantic passion and all else was banished from the night but the sounds of their pleasure.

29

The *Sea Wolf* sailed three days later, her red and white sails billowing with the autumn winds. From his place at the prow, Wolfram watched the dark-haired figure of his wife grow smaller and smaller. He had not lied to her when he had said that she was in his blood. He had always relished his trips to sea, but this time he would count the days until she was in his arms again.

The sea was dark as they sailed, but the northern sky was bright and luminous, deceiving with its light for it was a cold wind which puffed at the sails.

Wolfram scanned the horizon for any sign of this island he had heard about, but saw instead only an endless expanse of blue. It was Warrick who had chosen this course and Wolfram had given in to his younger brother, amused at his enthusiasm. Now he had second thoughts about having allowed a novice to guide them, brother or not.

It was an untried crew, nearly two-thirds of it men that Warrick had procured and because it was to have been a voyage of only a few days, again Wolfram had let his brother have his way. Now he regretted his foolishness.

Sigurd had stayed behind, much to his disappointment at being left to tend the women, but always one to obey Wolfram's orders, and Rorik too was absent from this short journey. There were few of the men that Wolfram really trusted aboard. Wolfram had only Roland to share his misgivings with and Roland too had begin to wonder if they should not turn back.

"We should be sailing south, not north at this time of

year," Roland grumbled. "We will run into floating ice if we continue on this path."

Overhearing his words, Warrick came up behind them. He had been edgy and quick to anger since they had sailed. It was as if Wolfram was seeing a different side to his usually smiling and docile brother. Did he really know Warrick as well as he had thought? Without knowing why, Wolfram felt a flicker of apprehension.

"I have set the course, bondi," Warrick snapped.

"We should be going south."

"You dare to question me, Roland? I tell you I know where I lead you. I have chosen this route because it's the shortest one." His voice was nearly a shriek.

"And I tell you that it is folly to sail where you lead us so close to the winter months." Roland had begun to mistrust Warrick, this Wolfram could plainly see.

Roland is not blinded by a brother's love, Wolfram thought. Something in the gleam of Warrick's eyes seemed to hint at irrationality and he knew suddenly that brother or not, he was unfit to guide the ship. Why was he so stubborn? What was he up to?

"When we return back to our father's hall with more gold than we can carry, you will be singing a different tune," Warrick snarled back, turning on his heel and stalking away.

There was no moon that night nor stars to guide them. Roland hung the lamps filled with whale oil about the deck and Wolfram brought out the sunstone to guide them. When held at right angles to the plane of light from the sun, the mineral crystal changed from yellow to dark blue so that a navigator in mid-ocean could locate the exact position of the sun and thus calculate the ship's position.

The men loyal to Wolfram began to mutter to themselves about the bad omens of the journey. It was as if even the god, Thor, was against them.

Wolfram felt the chill arctic wind upon his face, saw the floating cakes of ice reflecting in the lanterns of the ship and quickly gave the order to turn back. He could not, nor would not put his men in danger. Warrick would just have to understand. He, Wolfram, made the final decisions.

He sought out Warrick to tell him of his decision and it was then that he knew something was terribly wrong with his brother. Gone now was any resemblance to the brother Wolfram had known and loved.

"You can't turn back. You can't. I won't let you!" Warrick shouted.

"I already have given the order. We are traveling south." He fought against his temper. It was his fault that things had gone so far. He should never have let another influence his decisions. Trust was a delicate thing.

Warrick's eyes scanned the sea. "No. No," he shouted. He could not let his plans come to naught. Not now when he was so close to victory. He had Wolfram right in the palm of his hand. His brother would not escape him this time. He laughed to think of how he had so skillfully turned Everard against Wolfram and Wolfram against Everard. He would outwit Wolfram again.

"I told you when we sailed that it would be I who would command this ship. The *Sea Wolf* is mine, Warrick, and I will have the say in which direction we go. I cannot let you risk the lives of these men for some hare-brained quest for gold." He turned his back, trying to control his temper, his anger at himself, but Warrick reached out to grab him.

"Please, Wolfram. Trust me in this." Again he was the smiling, obsequious one. He had to stall for time until they met the other ship. The Danish ship. Wolfram would find himself enslaved again, but this time there would be no Irish girl to help him escape. The Danes were to be waiting with their ship to take Wolfram and his followers to the slave markets of the East. Sigurd's desire to go to sea had fit very well into Warrick's plans.

Wolfram shrugged off his brother's grasp. There was no doubt now in his mind that something was terribly wrong. There was something more to this than treasure, his instinct told him.

"We have turned back. It is I who make the decisions, Warrick. Not you."

A piercing laugh escaped from Warrick's throat. "Think again, Wolfram. I have only to contradict your order. These are my men, not yours. They will do as I command them."

Wolfram gasped. "That laugh!" He recognized it from the night at the cliff. How could he ever forget that sound? His blood ran cold, as cold as the Arctic seas. "You!" he said.

"Yes, it was I," Warrick answered, feeling secure in confronting Wolfram now. There was no escape. He needed to pretend no longer that he loved his brother. His eyes were filled with bitterness and hatred. "I tried to kill you."

"But why? Why?" Wolfram tried hard to understand such treachery, but found that he could not.

"Why? Think, Wolfram," Warrick's voice was scathing. *"I want to be Jarl.* It is as simple as that."

"You. Jarl?"

"I am a third son. What will I inherit? Everard is the oldest and *you* are the favorite of my father. Did you think that I would be content to sit and wait forever?"

"But we grew up together at your mother's knee. She took me in as her own child, indeed I felt as if you were my full-blooded brother."

"And how I hated you for that. It was not bad enough that I had to share my father's love, I had to share my mother's love as well. It was always as if I were invisible. Zerlina with her affliction got more attention than I did." Warrick tugged at the neck of his tunic as if suddenly fearing that he might suffocate.

Wolfram's eyes held no pity. Years of pain and degradation could not yet be forgotten. "And do you plan to kill me?"

Warrick laughed, remembering how Eric Haraldsson had unwittingly helped him. He had spoken the truth when he had the Danes. It is there we go, to meet them."

"You hate me that much?"

"Yes. I have always hated you. How it made me sick to have to play the loving brother."

Wolfram clenched his jaw, controlling his temper as best he could. "And you played your part well. All the while I thought it was Everard."

Warrick laughed, remembering how Eric Haraldsson had unwittingly helped him. He had spoken the truth when he had told Wolfram that his brother had been responsible for sending him into slavery. He had just forgotten to say *which* brother.

Wolfram glanced about him, wondering how many of these men would fight on his side. He stalled for time. "And Deidre. What of her?"

"When you are gone she will turn to me. She has always

been meant for me. I knew that the very first time I saw her. She is mine! While you toil in slavery she will be my Viking Queen.''

Wolfram could control his anger no longer. "Then you had best kill me right now, Warrick, for I will never live one moment again as a slave!" With that Wolfram leaped upon his brother, pushing him to the ground. Over and over they rolled as havoc erupted among the men. Wolfram looked at Warrick's face, so close to his, the features so like his own. Could he kill his brother, no matter what he had done? No, he could not.

Warrick's eyes were dark with hatred. "I would not find a greater pleasure on this earth than cutting your throat right now, but you have not the guts to strike me down. Your love for the Irish wench has made you soft."

Wolfram's hands were at Warrick's throat. It would be so easy to kill him now, but murder was not a thing Wolfram could do. Warrick, however, did not share his brother's compassion. Taking advantage of Wolfram's loosening hands, Warrick brought up both arms and broke his hold. Throwing a blow to Wolfram's jaw he sent his brother sprawling.

"Kill them. Kill them all!" he shouted to his followers. Warrick's foot caught Wolfram in the chest just as he stood up and Wolfram was thrown over the side of the ship.

The ice-cold sea took Wolfram's breath away as he hit the waters. He heard a roaring in his ears as the ocean closed about his head. He felt as if his lungs would burst, but he could not let the seawater fill his lungs. The burning in his chest was unbearable, he felt as if he would die at that moment but the sight of Deidre's face before him gave him courage.

Odin, save me! he thought. But the old gods had deserted him. He reached out his hand to Aegir, god of the sea, but that god did not heed him.

Pushing with all his might against his watery grave, Wolfram broke the surface. Air filled his lungs again and he knew the breath of life. He could see the lights of the ship looking like the eyes of some gigantic sea monster, could hear the cries of his men. Was it the mist of the sea that he felt spring to his eyes or his tears?

"May God have mercy upon their souls," he intoned, repeating the words he had heard Deidre say. If his own gods would not help them, perhaps the Christian God would find it in his mercy to do so.

Wolfram felt the tide carrying him toward the shore and looked back at his ship once more. The screams had ceased and the agony of the dying was over. He was alone in the endless sea with no hope of being rescued. Warrick had been the victor after all.

Alone, awaiting his death, Wolfram whispered the name that came to his lips, the word branded upon his heart, "Deidre."

30

Deidre sat at her loom weaving threads of wool. Wolfram had been gone four days now, but it seemed a lifetime. She had never before realized just how cold the nights could be without his love to shield her.

She looked across the room where Sigurd sat. He had been her only comfort during those days of her husband's absence. His vivid tales about his adventures with Wolfram made her feel as though Wolfram were there with them. Rising from the bench where she sat, Deidre went to Sigurd and touched his shoulder.

"Why so glum, Sigurd?" she asked. "Are you still angry with Wolfram for asking you to stay behind while he sailed with Warrick? It is because he trusts you so that he bid you stay."

Sigurd avoided her eyes, fearful that she would be able to read his real reasons for unhappiness: his love for Zerlina. It was torture being in the same house with her, having given into his heart that one time. He must never allow it to happen again for it would be cruel to prolong an involvement that could never be permanent.

"Is it because you were asked to stay?" Deidre repeated. Sigurd was so deep within his own world that he had not heard her words.

Sigurd shook his mane of hair. "No, I am not angry."

Deidre's tone lightened then and she teased, "Zerlina has kept to her room since you have been with us. Could her absence from the hall be the reason for your unhappiness?"

Sigurd put his chin upon his hands. He wanted to confide his feelings to someone. It was tearing him apart inside to love Zerlina so and yet not be able to claim her. Since the night he

227

had kissed her she truly had acted as if he were an evil troll.

"It is because of me that she stays to herself. I offended her on the night of the feast," Sigurd finally said.

"Offended her. How?"

"I kissed her. I am not fit to touch one such as she." Again before his eyes was the knife she wore, her badge of rank. But it was more than that. Zerlina was gentle and loving and a lady. Sigurd was suddenly ashamed at the remembrance of all the women he had forced himself upon after a raid. What would Zerlina think of him were she to know of his lusty actions? Would she then think him to be the brave warrior?

"It is not because of your kiss that she weeps alone at night in her room," Deidre scolded, "but because you so heartlessly reminded her of that which she had no doubt forgotten there in the moonlight."

"She weeps?" The thought of Zerlina crying unnerved him.

"Aye, she sheds her tears because she thinks you kissed her out of pity. She told me this herself. It no doubt wounded her deeply to see you cavorting with Erika as you did."

"Erika? She means naught to me. Odin's tears, I don't understand the ways of women!" He got up from his bench and strode around the room. "Why can't she see that what I do is for her own good, because I love her. Freyr himself knows how much I long to make love to her, but I would not shame her."

"There is no shame in love, Sigurd. I think perhaps what shames her is the fear that you find her less than a woman. She has told me so herself."

"Less than a woman? She is everything a man could ever want!" Sigurd was completely baffled by Deidre's words, but a sudden thought came to him. "Is it because of her leg?"

Deidre nodded. "She feels that you pity her."

"I love her. I feel no pity for her. Pity is for those who have no hope and for the weak. Zerlina is like the amber we Vikings treasure so dearly. Strong on the outside, pleasing to the eye, radiating with warmth, she is a treasure worth claiming."

"And yet you have not claimed her. Oh, Sigurd, my proud foolish friend, it is you who have put up the barriers around your love for her. Look at Wolfram and I. More than an ocean separated us and yet we could not deny our love. Don't wait until it is too late for you to share the happiness you both want. Reach out and grab your joy like a star from the sky."

Sigurd smiled at Deidre's words. She was a brave one to call him foolish and risk his temper. He started to tell her how much he admired her and that he would do as she told him, but it was at that moment that the door opened, letting in the chill wind. Standing before them, haggard and drawn, was Warrick.

"Warrick!" Deidre cried. All thoughts of Zerlina and Sigurd flew from her mind as she rushed to Warrick's side. Her eyes searched the doorway for Wolfram but saw only a few of Warrick's men standing there.

"The Danes. They fell upon us. Like foul, evil giants they crushed us." Warrick slumped in Olaf's great carved chair and put his head in his hands.

"Where is Wolfram?" Deidre shouted, trying to control her hysteria as she cast her eyes again to the open doorway.

"He fought them bravely. No man could have done more, but we were outnumbered." Warrick's eyes looked past her, his jaw held rigid.

"Where is he? Where is my husband?" Deidre reached out and grabbed at Warrick's tunic. It was splattered with blood and she shrank back from him.

"The Danes? It was the Danes who attacked you? Why? We have no quarrel with them," Sigurd said, shaking his head in bewilderment. It was true that in the land of Eire there was often fighting between Danes and Norwegians. But not here on these shores.

"Perhaps they thought we were loaded with treasure," Warrick replied.

Deidre ran to the door calling Wolfram's name, but there was no answer. "Why won't you tell me where my Wolfram is?" she cried, then started to rush down the pathway to where the ships were docked, but Sigurd blocked her way. He had read in Warrick's eyes that Wolfram was not with them. It tore at his soul that he had not been there beside his friend to fight to the end. "Come inside, Deidre," he said tonelessly.

Zerlina and Olaf had joined the throng in the great hall. They too demanded to know where Wolfram was, but Warrick held his peace, relishing the attention he was now being offered.

"Is our brother wounded, Warrick?" Zerlina cried out. Her eyes met Sigurd's and he could see that they were red from crying. He moved toward her but she moved away, standing behind her father as if Olaf could shield her from pain.

Warrick still did not answer, fearful lest someone see into his black heart. He started to leave the hall but Deidre was upon him before he could take more than a few steps.

"Take me to Wolfram!" she sobbed. "I have to be with him. If he is wounded, I will tend him. Please. He is my husband. I have the right. I carry his child. You cannot keep me from his side."

"Wolfram is dead, Deidre. I thought to spare you this sad news until the morrow, but you force my hand. Wolfram is dead. The Danes murdered him!"

"I had feared as much," Sigurd said softly. "I should have been with him. I should have died by his side."

Deidre could not speak. Her eyes merely stared up at Warrick's face. It was as if she could not utter a sound. Her mouth formed the words. "No!"

"I will avenge my son," Olaf growled. "We will set out at dawn tomorrow and follow the Danes to the end of the earth if need be."

"Where is Wolfram's body, Warrick? We must prepare it for burial." Zerlina's voice shook, her hands trembled, yet as much as her heart was breaking she thought of Deidre and sought her out. Her arms wrapped around her sister-in-law, bringing her comfort.

"Wolfram fell overboard during the fighting. His body was given a watery grave." He looked away from Zerlina's searching eyes, remembering the look upon Wolfram's face when he had proclaimed him traitor.

Deidre found her voice. "Wolfram is not dead," she determined. The fact that there was no body gave her hope.

"I say that he is. I saw him fall," Warrick answered softly. Now Deidre would turn to him again. It would be like it was before. She was no longer a wife. Wolfram was dead. Someday Warrick would make her a Viking queen. It was her destiny.

Deidre closed her eyes. It was the same intuition she had now that she had had the night upon the cliffs. Wolfram was not dead, she could not believe Warrick's words. "Wolfram is alive. I feel it. If he were dead I would know it. We must find him."

Olaf stepped forward, fearful of Deidre's pale face. "You are overwrought, my child," he said gently. "Rest. Tomorrow we will think again about this matter."

"No, we must find Wolfram. You must set sail at once and find him. He is alive." Her eyes darted back and forth among the assembled Vikings, but none offered to set out on the search. Warrick's men knew all too well the real fate of Wolfram the Bold. There was no way he could have survived.

Sigurd stepped forward. "He cannot be alive, Deidre. If there was any chance that Wolfram was alive I would go to the realm of Niflheim itself to fetch him."

Olaf remembered how Deidre had insisted that Wolfram lived after his fall from the cliff, how he himself had doubted. But this was different; no one could survive all alone in the icy sea. His son was dead. Gathering Deidre up in his arms, he took his weeping daughter-in-law to her sleeping chamber then sought the solace of his own to cry for his son.

31

Deidre spent the next few days in a haze of grief. She had no awareness of time nor of those about her. She tried to eat but the food choked her and so she instead cast it aside.

Olaf had gone out in his own ship to search for the Danes who had murdered his son, but he had found no trace of them. No doubt after the winter snows had melted he would even the score for the treachery of their act.

Deidre knew that she had to accept the truth—that Wolfram was gone—but she could not still the voice deep inside her which whispered that Wolfram lived. Perhaps it was his soul that called to her, and at those times she wished to join him in death. But the thought of their child growing deep within her womb gave her reason to live.

So it was that after the fifth day, Deidre began to eat again and gather her strength. Zerlina took her place beside Deidre and together they wiped away their tears.

"If only he had listened to me. I did not want him to go, Zerlina. If only I had held him to me."

"We can torture ourselves with those thoughts, Deidre," Zerlina said gently. "But we cannot change the past, though we might well wish to do so."

"I will always remember his love," Deidre cried softly. She knew it would be a long time before her tears were dried, and the ache in her heart a long time healing.

Several miles from where Deidre lay, in a small hut on an island in the Norwegian Sea, a man slept the deep sleep of the fevered. The sound of his moaning woke the hermit from his sleep, and he rose to his feet to care for the injured one. He had fished him from the sea, like a mermaid of legend or some frozen god of the waters. Now he kept a vigil over the man and prayed for his soul and his life.

"Who are you?" asked the short, bearded, paunchy fur-bedecked man. He smiled to himself to think that he waited for an answer. He had been alone too long and now the presence of another human being had addled his mind.

The hermit reached out a hand and touched the forehead of the sleeping man. It was no longer feverish. That was a good sign. Soon the man would awaken and then he could put an end to his wondering.

"God have mercy on their souls," the moaning man mumbled. He seemed to be caught deep within the clutches of a nightmare, thrashing and fighting with someone in his land of dreams. "No. No. I can't kill him. He is my brother."

The hermit looked down upon the man. He had the bearing of a warrior and yet he had called out for the God the hermit had once served. What manner of man was this before him? He was handsome once he was washed clean of the grime which had originally covered him.

"Who are you?" the hermit asked again. Was this man sent to torture him, to make him think about things he had wanted to forget?

A scream tore from the lips of the unconscious man as he began to fight the thin linen sheet which covered him. No doubt he thought it the ocean's depths.

The hermit turned his eyes upward and mouthed words which had nearly been forgotten these many years. Perhaps now his prayers would bring God's help to the man lying before him.

"It's all right," he said to the man on the straw-covered bed. "You're safe here." Taking a place by the sleeping man's side he closed his eyes and waited for the morning to come.

32

Zerlina stood outside the door of the hall watching as the autumn leaves fell to the ground. "Wolfram," she whispered. She felt such pity for Deidre. She had lost so much. Somehow it seemed that the gods had been cruel in not sparing her brother's life. He had so much to live for. Why had he not been spared?

"Zerlina." It was Sigurd's voice that called to her. Turning around she read the sadness in his eyes. He too had loved her brother.

"Oh, Sigurd!" Zerlina sobbed. She looked so lovely, so fragile in her grief that immediately Sigurd put his arms around her and held her tightly against him.

"Go ahead and cry, Zerlina. Get out your grief with your tears. I cry for him, too. Wolfram was a great man. He will be missed by all. Damn the Danes and their treachery!" He stroked her hair like a child's and brushed away her tears and together they walked out in the chill air of the autumn night.

"Deidre pleaded with him not to go, but he would not listen. How I wish I had joined her in her pleas, perhaps then my brother would be with us in the hall this very night."

"It should have been I who sailed with him, not Warrick. Warrick is but a pup. What could he have known about fighting Danes? How could I have been so stupid as to let Wolfram leave me behind?" Sigurd closed his eyes and clenched his jaw. Could he ever forgive himself for not being by his friend's side? If Wolfram was to die, he too should have met death by his side.

Zerlina felt Sigurd's pain and reached up to touch his face. His skin felt hard and cool against her hand. Gently she traced the faint lines of a scar near his ear. Her touch stirred Sigurd, sparked his desire for her.

"We should go inside, Zerlina," he said brusquely, pulling away from her. He cursed himself for the thoughts running inside his head. He wanted to crush her to him, cover her mouth with kisses, and bury his manhood deep within her.

His reaction to her touch wounded Zerlina and she started to weep anew. Sigurd could not even bear her touch. Was she so ugly then, so repulsive to him?

"I wish I had died in his stead," she said bitterly.

Sigurd gripped her shoulders in anger. "Don't ever say such a thing, Zerlina."

"It's true. Wolfram had so much to live for. He loved and was loved in return. What mockery of the gods took him from this earth and left me here in my loneliness and misery?" she sobbed.

"The gods have willed that you live, Zerlina. Speak no more about it." His voice was harsh, yet her words had touched his soul, remembering what Deidre had told him. Was Zerlina really so very lonely?

She started back toward the hall, her eyes cast downward. She wished that she had the goddess Freyja's magic cloak so that she could fly like a bird through the air and be gone from Sigurd's sight.

"Zerlina!" Sigurd caught up with her in two powerful strides. "Don't go!"

She turned her red-rimmed eyes upon him and was surprised to see the softness in the depths of his. He was gazing at her as if he found her beautiful. Would he mock her now in her grief?

"I am lonely too, Zerlina," he said.

"You? A bold handsome Viking who could have any woman he seeks?" she asked in amazement.

"Any woman but the one I want. The one I love," he answered.

So Sigurd desired someone above all others then. Zerlina fought against her jealousy. Who was it?

"Is it Erika?" She had to know.

Sigurd threw back his head and laughed. "Erika? Surely you credit me with better taste than that, Zerlina."

His laughter shamed her. She had spoken foolishly. Who

Sigurd loved was no concern of hers. She turned her back upon him again and started to walk away, but Sigurd caught her from behind. "It is you I love, Zerlina," he said.

"Do not mock me, Sigurd," she gasped, pushing at his chest with her hands. "How could you love me?" Her voice was soft and filled with sadness.

"Because you are beautiful and good and kind. Oh, Zerlina." His resolve broke like a tidal wave and he covered her mouth again with his own, only this time the kiss was not gentle but instead filled with all his passion.

Zerlina stood unmoving in his arms. Never before had she felt the taste of a man's desire and it was for her that Sigurd was aroused. Her heart beat like the flutter of a bird's wing in her breast. Reaching up toward him, she wound her arms around his neck and sought to return those fiery kisses.

Sigurd lifted his lips from hers and stared down into her tear-stained face. "I love you, Zerlina. May the gods help me I do." His beard scratched her face as he bent his head to kiss the softness of her throat. His hand slid down to caress her hips and she could feel the hardness of his maleness pressing against her.

Zerlina moaned in Sigurd's arms as the blood pulsed through her veins. Awareness of her own woman's body was sweet yet left her aching with a need for something she was not yet certain of.

"I love you too, Sigurd," she whispered. "I always have, but I thought your kindness toward me was only pity."

Sigurd bent down then and lifting the hem of her gown took her foot in his large hands. Kneeling before her he kissed her ankle and gently caressed that part of her which Zerlina had always felt self-conscious about.

"You are beautiful in every way, Zerlina."

"No!" Zerlina tried to pull her foot away, but it was held fast in Sigurd's hands.

"Please don't pull away from me. Do you think that I could love you and not desire to touch every part of you?" He brought her down beside him on the ground and Zerlina felt his mouth moving hungrily against hers. She felt beautiful and warm in his arms. Never had she been so happy.

"Love me, Sigurd," she breathed.

Sigurd felt a surge of excitement at her soft cry for his love.

He held her closer against him, his hands caressing the curve of her waist, the thrust of her breasts. Her scent clung to him, of the spices and flowers her father had brought with him from the East.

Sigurd fumbled at the drawstring of his braccae, longing to do as she bid and make her his own, but a voice from beyond the shadows called to Zerlina.

"Zerlina!" It was Olaf's voice.

Sigurd broke away from Zerlina then and cursed himself for the fool that he was. Running a hand through his mane of silver-blond hair he looked at her with haunted eyes.

"I am worse than a Dane to treat you thus. Tumbling you like a common thrall. Your father would be right in demanding my life for this."

"I love you. It is not wrong, Sigurd. You have given me joy this night, made me feel desire like a woman." Her eyes were shining bright with her love.

"You deserve better than this. Oh, that I could claim you for my wife, but your father would never approve a marriage to one with my status, and I will not shame you by taking you like this." He stood up and straightened his garments, fighting still the desire he felt for her.

She looked at him from her place upon the ground. "What is it, Sigurd?" For a moment her old fears assailed her.

Sigurd's eyes looked down upon her and the tenderness written there could leave her no doubt of his love. Despite his protestations, her heart sang with joy. Taking his hand she tugged at him.

"Love me, Sigurd. I care not about shame, only about my love for you. How can it shame me to be so loved?"

He fought against his own desires. "I have killed many men upon the seas, Zerlina. I have raped many women and stolen many a man's treasure. I am not fit to kiss the hem of your gown, much less join with you. I am a bondi, you the daughter of a jarl. We are from two different worlds. There can be naught between us. I am worse than a snake for taking advantage of you with Wolfram's death still upon us."

He walked away from her before his heart could win the battle against his mind, but he called back to her. "I love you. Know that I will love you always."

Sigurd hastened to the hall and there made preparations to

leave the household of Olaf the Red, but a large hand upon his shoulder stopped him. It was Olaf who came up behind him as he was packing. "There you are, Sigurd."

"I must leave, Olaf. I cannot stay any longer."

"Leave? No. I ask you in the name of my son, Wolfram, to stay, Sigurd."

"Olaf, I cannot." Sigurd's eyes avoided looking at the other man. Too fresh upon his mind was the soft touch of the man's daughter.

"My daughter-in-law looks upon you as her friend. Perhaps you can help her through her time of sorrow. She called for you just now, and Zerlina too is fond of you. I ask you as your Jarl to stay, at least until after the baby is born."

He could not disobey. "All right, I will stay," Sigurd sighed. What was he to do when his Jarl asked him to remain in his hall? He would take Wolfram's place and look after Deidre and Zerlina and fight against his love and fondest desire.

33

The frost giants painted their pictures with snow and ice. The ground was blanketed in a white shroud and ice hung from the roof like large needles. Winter had come upon the Northland. Never had Deidre felt such cold. No matter how many fires stirred in the household, the chill was still about—the chill and the darkness.

Just as in summer the days had been an endless light, now in the winter they seemed an endless darkness. One could easily sleep their life away. And in truth, there were days when the pain of Wolfram's death made Deidre wish for such a sleep.

One winter storm was so severe that it froze the water in the soapstone bowls within the hall. Deidre thought it appropriate that the Vikings conceived of the realm of the dead as cold, rather than the flaming hell of the Christians. Putting all of her cloaks around her swollen body, she joined the others at night, sleeping around the fire in the kitchen area.

"Are you well, Deidre?" Olaf asked her from his place across the fire. "I would not want you to catch a chill. The baby will soon be coming."

Olaf had been so concerned with her welfare the past few weeks. Not just for the sake of the child, she knew. This big, flaming haired, gentle giant of a man really loved her. She was touched by that love.

"I am fine, Olaf," she answered, trying to control her chattering teeth. She did not want him to worry about something he had no power over.

"And how is my grandson?" He winked at her, for they each had foretold a different sex for the child, Deidre insisting that the baby would be a girl.

"He is fine," she answered, giving in to his playful mood. If

239

Olaf insisted the child would be a boy, what harm was there in that? There was always a chance that he was right. They would know soon enough.

Her bulging stomach made her feel unattractive and clumsy despite Zerlina's protestations to the contrary.

Feeling someone's eyes burning into her, Deidre looked beyond the fire to where Warrick stood. He was always watching her lately and this made Deidre strangely nervous. What was it about Warrick that bothered her lately? Although he had sought her out and tried to comfort her, the old bond between them seemed to be gone no matter how she tried to feel friendship for him.

"It it not good for a child to grow up without a father," he had said, and Deidre felt in her heart that come spring, he would ask her to wed him.

"That I cannot do," she thought with a sigh. Wolfram was her only love, dead or alive she would wish no other.

Deidre watched as Warrick went about instructing the thralls to keep the fire well supplied with wood and to go out of doors to the wells to fetch water. There was danger this time of year in being outside for more than a few moments and more than one thrall had been found frozen to death. With the harshness of winter, the female thralls spent the nights inside the hall, huddled near the outskirts of the big fire, while the male thralls spent the nights in the barns around the small fires that were kindled to keep the animals from freezing to death.

Feeling a hand touch her shoulder, she gave a start of alarm at the contact. She had not heard Sigurd come up behind her. He had been by her side constantly since the day she had learned of Wolfram's death at the hands of the Danes. He would not let her lift anything at all and always seemed anxious to be of help to her.

As usual Sigurd's eyes sought out Zerlina, and Deidre wondered how much longer it would be before his love won out over his misplaced honor.

"I've brought you another cloak, Deidre," Sigurd said, putting the garment around her shoulders. He sat down beside her and began to tell her favorite story about Day and Night. To the Viking mind, Day followed Night, not Night the Day. Night, Sigurd related, was a beautiful dark-haired young woman of strong character. Though beautiful, she wished to be even more attractive by wearing bright stars in her long hair. Mother of a son called Space, a daughter called Earth by her previous two husbands, Night was also the mother of Day, a blond son whose fondest desire was to drive about the sky in his chariot, casting a glow from his long golden hair.

"The gods decided that the hours should be divided into light and dark and decreed that Night should drive around the earth first, and Day the rest of the time," Sigurd said, looking over at Deidre. The Irish woman looked to his eyes as he imagined the beautiful Night would appear.

Deidre's eyes grew heavy with sleep as she listened to Sigurd's story. In the haze of her dreams it was she herself she saw driving the dark chariot and Wolfram who guided the golden horses of the dawn, his blond hair shining in the sun.

"Wolfram," she whispered, and reached out to him. Closing her eyes she fell asleep amid her many cloaks and blankets, with Sigurd's watchful eyes upon her.

Deidre slept peacefully until the early hours of the morning, but was awakened from her slumber by a sharp pain. She ran her hand over her swollen belly. She had been dreaming of Wolfram, but the pain she felt in her belly was no dream, it was real! She opened her eyes wide.

"The babe!" she exclaimed. She tried to get up but the pains tore at her. Biting her lip, she fought to keep from crying out and waking the others. Instead she said a prayer to the Holy Mother Mary.

Her eyes sought out Sigurd and she found him as usual positioned halfway between Zerlina and herself as if in his way to guard them both, the woman he loved and the woman who had loved his friend.

Deidre called out to Sigurd, but he was snoring loudly. Crawling on her hands and knees, she sought out Zerlina. "Zerlina!" she cried softly.

Zerlina opened her eyes and looked at Deidre crouching on hands and knees beside her. She had no need to ask what was happening; she read in Deidre's eyes the pain and fright of the coming birth of a first child.

"Frigg, Earth Mother, Wife of Odin, be with Deidre," she intoned to the goddess invoked by women in labor. Rising, she nudged the plump figure of her mother. She needed Adora's knowledge of birthing to help Deidre now. "The baby! Deidre's baby is coming!" she cried out. "Her pains have already begun."

Hearing Zerlina's words, the other women were up immediately, hustling about in an effort to be of some help. Deidre, meanwhile, sought a corner of the hall near another of the fires, a smaller one, where she could have some privacy to have her child. It took all her courage to move about while the knives of labor cut through her. The thought of dying entered her head, for it was not at all unusual for a woman to die in childbirth.

Surely unless I am dying, she thought, *I would not be in such great pain.* What she felt now was sheer torment.

"Boil the water!" she heard Gerda say.

Looking across the room she could see Erika watching her, but this time there was no jealousy written on her face. Erika did not envy her the pain.

Taking Erika's arm, Gerda herself led the blonde woman to where the cauldrons lay in wait. "Come, Erika, there is much to be done."

The entire household was awake and watching now. Deidre felt embarrassment at having the others witness her pain. As if sensing her feelings, her need to be away from prying eyes, Olaf set about to construct a makeshift tent in the corner of the large hall, using a large linen blanket draped over several poles set in the floor. In the corner Zerlina lit an oil lamp then came to Deidre's side to reach out her hand.

"Squeeze my hand when the pain becomes unbearable," she instructed Deidre.

Adora placed a cup of herb tea in Deidre's hands and bid her to drink of the liquid to soothe the pain. "It is a secret Olaf brought back from the East," she confided.

The hours dragged on as Deidre lay upon the cloak-strewn floor. Her labor was long, her pain severe. Adora and Gerda had kept her upon her feet, walking as long as it was possible, telling her that it would make the birthing easier, but now Deidre could stand no more.

"How is she?" Olaf asked, sticking his head inside the tent. "How is my Raven?"

"Still in labor!" Deidre heard Adora answer. "It is taking such a long time."

Again the agony came and Deidre wondered if she could

survive the searing torture. As the pressure increased, demanding all her strength, she pushed with all her might.

"That's right, bear down," Zerlina said. Deidre writhed in her agony and bore down in an effort to push the child out of her womb.

"The head is about to come. That's it, push down. Scream if you want to, it may help," Adora instructed.

"No. No. I will not cry out. I am a Viking now," Deidre breathed, clinging to Zerlina's hand to give her comfort. She felt the baby's head slide from her body and whispered her thanks to her God. One life had been taken from her, but tonight another had been given.

34

Olaf looked down at the raven-haired Irish woman. Her gown was soaked with sweat, her hair was matted around her pale face. She had been to Hel this night and yet had not uttered one scream. Truly she was a brave Viking. He watched as Adora wiped the child with a linen cloth then held the infant high in the air. "It is a male child, a son."

Looking upon the infant, at the proof of maleness, Olaf's eyes flashing with pride, he cried aloud, "I have a grandson."

Adora handed him the tiny bundle wrapped in swaddling cloth. "He is healthy and strong."

Olaf bent down and looked upon the face of his son's widow. "You have made me proud, Raven," he whispered.

Deidre lifted her chin proudly. "He pleases you. I am glad. I love you, Olaf. You have been a father to me truly." Olaf thrust the child into its mother's arms and Deidre looked upon the baby with eyes filled with love.

"He is much like you, the same dark hair," Zerlina said softly.

"He looks like Wolfram, the same strong chin and well-formed nose," Deidre answered. She sighed. "I'm so tired."

"You have been through a great deal tonight," Zerlina whispered, wiping the sweat from Deidre's brow. She marveled at the tiny toes and fingers of the babe. So perfect yet so small. The head of Wolfram's son was covered with thick, black hair that curled around his small face. Looking in Sigurd's direction she wished that someday she would have a child of her own.

Taking the baby from his mother's arms, placing it at the patriarch's feet for the ceremonial act of acceptance, Gerda asked, "Do you accept this child?" There was silence in the room. Deidre felt her heart nearly stop as she remembered

Erika's words. Her child was healthy and strong. Olaf would accept him. But what if the child had been otherwise? Could she have allowed this precious bundle to be taken from her? To be left alone out in the wilderness? She held her breath as Olaf took the child from Gerda's arms and watched in amazement as he poured water over the baby.

"It is to show that he has been admitted into the family," Zerlina whispered.

"He is baptizing my son," Deidre exclaimed, yet she knew that the Vikings did not worship her Lord. She had to admit that the ceremony, though pagan, was beautiful. Never again would she allow anyone to call these people heathen. They had shown her much kindness during her stay with them. No Christians could have shown her more.

"He shall be called Fenrir, after the son of Loki, who is bound by the gods until Ragnarok, the end of the world. Fenrir the Wolf, the son of Wolfram. Wolfsson. Fenrir Wolfsson."

Deidre did not speak, she merely looked at the child in his grandfather's arms. "Wolfsson," she repeated.

Erika looked upon the babe. What was all the fuss about? The infant reminded her of a dried apple. "Shall we send for a wet nurse?" she asked snidely.

Deidre's eyes met the hostile eyes of the blonde-haired woman. "I will nurse my own child." Looking at Olaf she bid him to give her her son. She held the baby tightly to her breast, feeling a special bond between them, a bond that could never be broken. He was her child, her son.

The baby sucked greedily upon Deidre's breast, his eyes closed to shut out the light of the oil lamp.

"I love you, my little one," she whispered. Remembering how Wolfram had called her his little one, Deidre felt tears sting her eyes. "How I wish your father could see you," she cried, holding the baby close as the infant pushed at her breasts with his tiny fists.

"Perhaps the child will ease the pain of Deidre's loneliness," Zerlina said softly to her father. "Wolfram's death has been a death blow to her."

They looked at the mother and son and remembered the face of Wolfram, so loved by them all. Would they see him again in the afterlife? Would Deidre find him in the heaven she always talked about? They could only hope that it would be so.

35

Wolfram sat on a rock looking out to sea. Beyond the waters his heart lay with a midnight-haired Irish woman who had given him her love.

"Deidre, what has become of you?" he whispered to the wind. "Have you given birth to our child yet? Does your heart remember me? Are you safe?"

The fear gnawed at him that perhaps Warrick might harm his wife or child. There was no end to the wickedness of his brother. A man who would sell his own blood into slavery and would seek to kill, would be capable of anything.

"And yet he often looked upon Deidre with eyes that were gentle," he said to himself. It was small comfort. But what about his child? Wolfram prayed to his gods and the God of Deidre's people that the infant would be safe.

He closed his eyes remembering so vividly that day when he had heard the death cries of his men after falling overboard his ship. If not for the bearded hermit he knew as Paul, he would now be dead. Paul had nursed him back to health, fed him and given him shelter. He owed his life to the man and much, much more. Paul had given him friendship.

Seeing the familiar form of the hermit coming his way, Wolfram got to his feet. He had tried to learn the story of Paul's journey to the island, but the bearded man had refused to talk about himself, preferring instead to ask Wolfram questions. Yet once, while looking for something to eat, Wolfram had come across the strange crossed poles that Deidre thought of as so sacred. She had called it her Lord's cross. Was this man named Paul then also a Christian?

"Plenty of fish. I have gotten us plenty of fish this day," Paul said with a smile, coming up to Wolfram. "It will be good after dried meat and grain.''

Wolfram tugged at his bearskin cloak wrapped securely around him to keep out the freezing cold. At times his hands nearly froze out in this cold, away from the fire. Never had he experienced temperature such as this, not even in the North-land.

"I'll gather some more firewood," he said, anxious to taste the fish. It was difficult to pick anything up with his hands bound in those rags that kept his fingers from freezing, but he somehow managed. Together he and the hermit sat before the fire in the small earthen hut and watched as the fish cooked on the stones of the fire.

"I must go home. My wife is with child. I have to be with her," Wolfram said. He was trapped here on this island with-out a boat or ship, or even a log to carry him back to his home.

"There is no way. You must wait until the spring comes, my son," the hermit answered. His deep-set eyes were filled with compassion and understanding.

"I can't wait!"

"You must. To venture out now would mean your death. When the thaw comes I will help you build a boat. It was not too long ago that I fashioned a craft for sailing." His eyes looked faraway for just a moment as if remembering. "I too had a woman that I loved."

Wolfram clenched his fists in frustration. What Paul said was true, it would mean his death to be out and about in this ice and snow. He could only hope that his father would watch over his wife and child until he could return to them.

So many things have happened, he thought. It seemed that every time happiness was to be his some obstacle appeared in its path. First his injury and loss of consciousness after his fall from the cliff, and now his separation from Deidre. And it was all due to Warrick's treachery.

"Something is troubling you, my son. Tell me about it," Paul's voice was soothing.

Wolfram told him the story, then of his love for Deidre, of their journey together from Ireland, and of his brother's hatred and evil. Paul listened with his head bent down to the floor, his eyes sparkling with light each time Wolfram men-tioned the emerald island known as Ireland to Wolfram's people.

"I must be with her. What if Warrick seeks to harm her?"

"Like Cain and Abel," the hermit muttered, moving away from the fire toward the door of the small hut. Looking out he said, "I know where there is an old ship. Perhaps with my help you can make it seaworthy again."

"A ship?"

"But you must wait for mild weather in which to sail."

"Agreed. I do not wish a speedy death. I want to see my wife and child and to avenge myself upon my brother who sought to take all from me." Rising to his feet, Wolfram joined the bearded man at the doorway.

"I think that the fittings and the keel can be salvaged. Perhaps the timbers too. I have a few tools with me here," Paul said.

Wolfram pounded the hermit on the back in a gesture of friendship. "I will make a Viking of you, my friend. And then who knows? Perhaps you will sail with me to my home. I owe you a great debt of gratitude."

Paul shook his head sadly. "No. My place is here, in solitude. It is a vow I took long ago. Never again will I walk among men." He turned and made his way to the fire, picking the cooked fish out of the embers with his calloused hands and putting them upon wooden plates fashioned by his own hands. Holding out a plate to Wolfram, they ate in silence.

"A ship," Wolfram mumbled. "I will have a ship. And then Deidre, my love, I will come home to you."

36

The winter days passed with happiness for Deidre. Fenrir, the child of her heart, took up her hours during the day and brought her much joy. Only when she thought of Wolfram, of how he would never see his son, did the child bring her pain.

"You will look like him, my son," she would say. Except for the dark thatch of hair, Fenrir did indeed look like his sire. Wolfram would have been so proud to have such a son as this one.

The weeks had been almost mild in the month following the baby's birth and Deidre had gotten back her strength. It was a good thing, for now there was even more work to be done. There was Fenrir's linen to be changed, his swaddling to be kept clean, household chores to be done, as well as Fenrir's feedings which often woke Deidre at night. With the coming of spring fresh rushes would need to be strewn upon the floor and the old rushes swept out and gathered for the fires of the Spring Equinox, or as Deidre knew them, the Beltaine fires. Although the thralls did much around the house, there was still much to be done. No hands could remain idle for long. The women went about the duties of the household while the men spent their hours working with wood and leather. Harnesses needed to be mended, shields fashioned, boats built as well as weapons and tools repaired and sharpened.

Every Northman was a craftsman and Deidre marveled at the workmanship the men of Olaf's hall wrought. An air of harmony surrounded the people as they waited for spring. There were, of course, scuffles and minor fights from time to time, being cooped up in such close proximity for so long, but basically there was more brotherhood among these Vikings than Deidre had seen among her own people. Everyone seemed to accept Olaf's leadership and none thought to un-surp his power as was often the case among her father's countrymen.

Olaf too was happy and content. His world centered now around his grandson. Deidre would often find him bouncing the baby upon his knee, holding the precious bundle in his large hands.

"He has the strong chin of a jarl," he would say to all those around him. "And see how he clings to my finger. He will have a mighty sword arm, this grandson of mine. Fenrir the Strong Arm, that's what he shall be called."

It seemed that everyone in the household loved the child, everyone except Erika. The baby reminded her of her own failing, her barrenness. Warrick, too, was often cold toward the child. Deidre supposed it was that memory of the baby's father brought sadness to Warrick.

Olaf showered gifts upon Deidre and she soon came to feel safe and content in the hall, an honored member of the family as the mother of the Jarl's grandson. But no amount of riches could take the place of the man she loved so dearly and had lost to the hated Danes.

Sigurd too seemed to adore the child, and Deidre wondered what she would do without this trusted friend when spring came and he left the hall. Zerlina also, she knew, would be upset to see Sigurd go. Some sort of bond had formed between Zerlina and Sigurd now as if each was certain of the other's love. Yet they never touched, never spoke, only looked at each other from afar. Deidre felt sorry for them but knew that only they, themselves, could break down the wall between them.

"Would your father ever let you marry Sigurd?" Deidre asked Zerlina one day.

"I have asked him and he has answered no. My father is overprotective of me, Deidre. He fears that I would in some way come to harm. I do not believe, as Sigurd does, however, that the reason is because Sigurd is bondi. No, my father will never give me over to any man. I have always been his fragile Zerlina."

"And yet in ways you are the strongest of us all, Zerlina," Deidre said as the two changed the baby. Zerlina picked up the small Fenrir in her arms and helf him closely, and Deidre could see in her eyes the desire to have a child of her own.

"My father, Olaf believes—" Zerlina began, but stopped

talking as she saw her father come up behind them. It was as if she had conjured him up with her thoughts. Olaf had his finger dipped in honey and he watched with a smile as the baby licked at the sweet confection.

"He is my greatest treasure," Olaf said with eyes filled with pride. "I would give my very life to make certain that he is safe and happy. He is the hope of the family. A new generation of Vikings."

"I fear lest you spoil him," Deidre chided. She did not know if honey was good for the babe. Her mother had never allowed sweets to be given her children.

"Bah! It is right for the grandson of a jarl to be at least a little coddled." He bid Deidre and Zerlina to fetch their cloaks and warmest woolens and come with him. "Adora can watch little Fenrir," he said.

The two young women did as he bid, then followed him outside to where a sledge stood harnessed to one black horse. The sledge was carved and had two runners instead of wheels.

Deidre raised her eyebrows in bewilderment. What was this contraption for? How would it move upon the ground without wheels? At her puzzlement Olaf threw back his head and laughed merrily.

"Ah, Raven, I see that you do not have this in your land, uh? It skims the top of the snow as the ship skims the waters. Come. I will show you what fun it is to ride in my sledge." He helped her into the sledge and then reached down a hand to aid Zerlina. "My daughter has often ridden in this."

"It is fun, Deidre," Zerlina agreed. Olaf took the reins while Deidre and Zerlina buried themselves in the furs.

Olaf pulled at the reins and the sledge took off with a jerk. The runners skimmed over the snow like magic and Deidre thrilled at the sights around her. She could see that the ponds and lakes were frozen over, looking like the glass Olaf had brought back from his travels. It was a fantasy kingdom of ice and snow.

"Look there!" Deidre gasped, seeing several people gliding about upon the frozen waters.

"They are skating," Zerlina said. "They have runners attached to their feet much the same as we have runners attached to this sledge. I have learned that it is much fun, although I have never tried it myself."

"Will they not fall through?" Deidre asked.

"If the ice is thin there is a chance for such a thing to happen. But usually one is careful," Olaf answered, amused at his daughter-in-law's enthusiasm. "Someday you will have to try."

Deidre felt so good to be out of the hall, in the outdoors. The air was fresh but cold, and her cheeks were chilled, yet she was enjoying herself. All too soon the adventure came to an end, and they found themselves back in front of the large building which housed the family.

Helping the two women he loved down off the wooden seats, he watched with laughing eyes as they walked back together toward the hall. Deidre was good for Zerlina; she brought happiness to his daughter as she had to his son. The Irish woman had brought joy. *And my grandson*, he thought with a smile.

Leading the horse back to the barn to give it over to his thralls, Olaf saw Warrick and another. He was about to greet his son when he heard him shout, "You fool! Coming here right under the very nose of my father. Go back to your ship where you belong!" The other man wore the garments of a Dane and he too waved his hands around in anger. Curious as to what was happening, Olaf ducked back into the shadow.

"You promised us silver. I am here to collect what you owe us."

"I promised you silver if you got rid of my brother for me. As it was I that killed him, I will not pay you for that which was not done." Warrick turned his back upon the Dane and started to walk away.

"I will tell all I know about what you have done. I am no fool. There is great shame and punishment for he who kills his own blood." The words were an angry threat and Warrick turned and fought with the man. They rolled over and over on the floor as Olaf watched.

"Warrick has killed my son, his own sibling," Olaf said beneath his breath, barely able to control his rage. "He has brought great shame upon me and my household and must be punished. I will not shield him, son or no son." Now all of the pieces of a puzzle suddenly fell into place as Olaf remembered all that had occurred during the last months. Warrick's charge that Everard had tried to kill Wolfram, the obvious attempts upon Wolfram's life, even the threat to Everard and Olaf coming home from the trial by ordeal.

Warrick reached for the Dane's sword and struck him down before Olaf's eyes, laughing malevolently as he finished the act. "You will say nothing now, Dane." He wiped off the sword, intending to slip back into the hall, but his father stepped out of the shadows to block his way.

"May Odin strike you down for what you have done," Olaf exploded as he confronted Warrick. "You who have committed the gravest of crimes are no son of mine."

Warrick drew back in alarm as years of awe of his father were remembered. Always he had seen Olaf as a powerful and mighty man. He thought quickly. "I have done no wrong, Father. I have merely killed a Dane. He sprang upon me from the darkness, no doubt there are many of his kind nearby. It was for Wolfram that I killed him."

"Lies! You are a liar," Olaf shouted bearing down upon his son. "I heard your words and now I know them to be true. It was one of Wolfram's brothers who so foully sought to kill him, only that brother was you and not Everard. You are a viper, a worm. You have brought shame upon my seed and upon my blood."

"You are wrong, Father. I don't know what you think you heard, but—" Olaf grabbed his arm so hard that Warrick stopped his babbling. "We will go back to the hall and there I will decide what to do with you." For just a moment Olaf turned his back, just one fleeting moment, as years of habit and of trust of his sons overshadowed his caution. It was just long enough for Warrick to strike, mingling the blood of his father with that of the Dane.

Like a giant tree, Olaf fell to the ground, his eyes wide with horror. "Odin!" he cried, knowing that he had been struck a mortal wound.

37

Deidre and Zerlina giggled like two children before the great fire as they warmed their hands and feet. Deidre's face glowed with excitement over their excursion. She had never realized that winter could bring so much fun.

"I want to go out in the sledge again," she confided to Zerlina. "I like to feel the wind in my face and see the world beyond these walls."

She looked toward the door to watch for Olaf's return, wanting to thank him again for the ride, but instead saw Warrick walk into the hall, his face set in a scowl.

How can anyone be angry on a day like today when the frost giants have painted such a glorious mural outside these doors? she thought, but she would not let Warrick bother her this day.

Feeling her breasts throb with milk, Deidre returned to her sleeping chambers to nurse Fenrir. The baby sucked contentedly upon her breasts, kneeding the soft mounds with his tiny fists.

"I hope that the world is kind to you, my son," she said softly. "You will always be loved and protected." She felt the sting of tears. It seemed that she would never get over the pain of losing Wolfram. As long as she lived she would mourn for him. Deidre could still see his face before her eyes, his face filled with love for her. Closing her eyes she sought the memories which were her only legacy from the man she had so loved.

Deidre heard an anguished cry and the sound of feet tramping past her door. Putting her baby down in his small wooden cradle, she opened the door a crack, peering out. She saw Adora, her face a mask of grief; Gerda, her eyes red with weeping, and Zerlina, brushing away her tears.

"What is it? What has happened?" Deidre cried out. A sense of foreboding gnawed at her heart.

"It's Olaf."

"Olaf?"

"One of the thralls found him out in the barn. He's been stabbed." Adora broke down with weeping.

Deidre knew the answer before she asked the question, but she asked it anyway, hoping against hope that her fears would not materialize. "Is he alive?"

"He is dead!" Gerda too began sobbing.

Deidre ran to Zerlina. "Say it isn't so. It can't be. We just left him. Who would do such a deed? Who?"

Zerlina was too choked with sobs to speak. Her father had been the person she loved the most, next to Sigurd.

"It was a Dane. The body of that foul murderer was found next to my lord's. They must have killed each other," a thrall said.

"A Dane! What would a Dane be doing here?" Anger flooded over Deidre. The Danes had killed Wolfram and now they had also murdered his father. "May Odin strike the guilty murderers down in his wrath!" She put a hand to her mouth, surprised at her words. Was she becoming a pagan here in the Northland, mimicking their talk?

Zerlina was weeping and Deidre put her arms around her and held the red-haired girl's trembling body close. "I'm so sorry this happened. Your father was such a good, kind man. I loved him too," Deidre whispered. Tears rolled down her cheeks for the man who had called her Raven. He had loved her and she him and now he too was gone from her.

Olaf was laid upon his large bed in all his finery as the members of the household, including the thralls, filed past to give their last respects to this great Jarl who had now gone to his glory in the realm of Valhalla.

As in life, also in death, Olaf was given the greatest respect. Deidre learned that Olaf would always be with the family and for that reason it would be the obligation of Olaf's loved ones to maintain his grave or burial mound so that he would never feel forsaken or obliged to become a vengeful ghost.

"A walker after death is dangerous and terrible," one of the thralls whispered to her. His eyes grew large in his head as he

talked, and Deidre imagined that many a tall tale had been
told round the fire of such a thing happening.

"Olaf loved us all," she said. "He would not seek to come
back to haunt us. We Irish have a saying that after death the
soul escapes from the body in the form of a white butterfly."
She hoped that this was true for Olaf and that even now he
was winging his way toward the heavens.

Zerlina, Adora, Gerda and Deidre had bathed Olaf's body
and clothed him in all his bracelets and Viking garments. Seeing Olaf lying there, so peaceful in his eternal sleep, was nearly
more than Deidre could take. She wanted to hear him laugh,
see him smile, watch him bounce little Fenrir upon his knee.
How she wished to hear him call her Raven again and gather
her into those large protective arms of his to still her sobs as he
had often done the many nights after Wolfram's death.

When the others had left the room and only the wives of
Olaf and Zerlina stood by her side, Deidre crouched down
near the red-haired Viking man and wailed her keening cries as
she had done for her dead in Ireland. Zerlina joined her as did
Adora and Gerda for it was a Viking custom as well. Through
her tear-blurred eyes Deidre looked upon the others realizing
that people all over the world were not all that different from
each other in many ways. All felt love for their families,
hatred for their enemies, rejoiced at the births of their children
and mourned their dead.

All through the night the women kept watch over Olaf as
did Everard and Warrick. Deidre tried several times to talk
with Warrick, to tell him how sorry she was at his father's
death, but much to her surprise he avoided her. Perhaps his
grief was just too much for him to bear, she thought.

Deidre left the room for just a moment and brought her
sleeping babe into the room to lay beside his grandfather for a
short while. It was her tribute to the man who had been so
kind to her.

"Your grandson, too, bids you good-bye, Olaf," she
sobbed, and wondered what the days would be like without
this strong loving man to guide the household.

38

For miles around the mourners flocked to the burial of Olaf the Red. For the Vikings, death after a lifetime of combat was thought to be the beginning of a glorious hereafter of feasting and fighting in Valhalla. Olaf's body was to be placed in a longship, the same ship he had commanded during the days of his youth, which would carry his soul to Valhalla.

Deidre watched in silence as Olaf's possessions were put aboard the ship. Everything that he would need in the next world was taken on board; a wagon, chest, buckets, a sledge, even food for his long journey. Olaf's treasures were also piled upon his ship, including his favorite swords and battle axe. Even a horse was killed and placed on board so that Olaf would have the animal in the next life. With a shudder Deidre noticed that it was the same horse that had drawn the sledge the day Olaf had taken them outdoors.

Deidre was dressed in her finest garments, her silk gown and her jewelry, including the bracelets Olaf had given her and the brooch that symbolized her love for Wolfram. All the others at the funeral were also wearing their finest clothing, Everard, Warrick and the other men decked out like warriors but wearing the many silver and gold bracelets.

After bidding her last good bye to her husband's father, Deidre watched as friends and warriors of the dead Jarl carried aboard the ship the rest of his personal belongings. Somehow today she felt like an outsider as she watched the traditions so foreign from her own Christian teachings. Father Finian had told her that a man had to leave behind his worldly possessions to enter the kingdom of God. Was he right? Deidre had begun to doubt for the first time in her life. Who

257

really knew what happened when death gave its kiss of eternal sleep?

Olaf's ship had been placed in a huge trench sixty yards long and fifty wide and on that ship the body of Olaf was placed upon a bed, his arms folded across his chest. The roughly hewn burial chamber would be completely buried to keep Olaf comfortable during the long voyage which loomed ahead.

"The prow of the vessel points in the direction of the sea," Zerlina whispered in Deidre's ear. "An anchor lies on the ship ready to be dropped when Father reaches his destination."

"May he have a smooth voyage," Deidre said softly, making the sign of the cross. Be it Valhalla or Heaven, she knew that being a just man, Olaf would find his reward.

Seeing one of the elder chieftains walking slowly around the ship, repeating a chant, followed by four men of the household, Deidre tugged at Zerlina's gown and looked upon her with questioning eyes.

"He is preparing to make animal sacrifice to please the gods," Zerlina answered, nodding in the direction of the older man. "And the four following him bring statues of my father's favorite gods, including Odin with his spear and Thor with his hammer. He will need their help in guiding him on his journey."

Deidre nodded her understanding. No doubt Father Finian would have been shocked that she had taken part in a pagan ceremony, but the kind father was far away and Ireland another realm, a part of the past she had forsaken to be at Wolfram's side. She would stay and give Olaf the respect that was his due.

After the sacrifices were completed, the workers began to bury the funeral ship, shoveling a layer of sand and blue clay around it. The mast had been chopped off so that it would not rise above the burial mound.

"Once the ship is covered with the sand and clay, layers of moss and twigs will follow, and then a top layer of peat sods will make the mound airtight. All of us will carry one of the many carved memorial posts to set up as boundaries of the grave site," Zerlina told Deidre. Her eyes were dry now and her chin was held high with pride for her father. Deidre had seen such a burial mound once with stones outlining a ship upon the hillside. Now she knew what that outline of stones had meant, no doubt another Viking hero on his way to Valhalla.

At the end of the ceremony, the women of the household returned to the hall to set out food and drink for the many guests. The men would stay behind to oversee the mounding of the grave which Deidre assumed would be accomplished by the thralls. In so many ways these slaves were important to the well-being of their Viking masters.

Much as the Irish did in their land so far away, the Vikings too stayed up long hours feasting and toasting the dead Viking Jarl.

Seeking the solitude of her own chambers, Deidre nursed her baby, needing the comfort of his little outstretched arms.

"What will happen to you now, little one, without your grandfather here to look after you?" she whispered, holding him close. The child had no father and no grandfather. Like her he was alone, with only Sigurd and Zerlina to love and cherish him. Everard would now be the Jarl and Erika, the Jarl's first wife. Deidre had no doubt that the woman would seek to taunt her.

Reaching out his tiny hands, Fenrir touched his mother's brooch, tugging at it with fascination. Flooding Deidre's mind came visions of Wolfram's face, his smile and the sea blue of his eyes. With a sudden flash, she felt Wolfram's voice calling to her, but she shook her head. It was impossible; Wolfram was dead.

"No, I feel it again as I did the night Warrick brought me the news of the raid of the Danes. Wolfram is not dead." She prayed to her God to let it be so, to let Wolfram be among the living. Putting Fenrir back in his crib, she closed her eyes and slept peacefully for the first time in a long while.

39

Wolfram Olafsson gazed with pride at the magic he and the hermit Paul had wrought upon the old wrecked ship that Paul had taken him to. It would only be a matter of weeks now before spring would shine down upon them, and when that time came Wolfram would be ready to set sail for his home.

"I will never be able to repay you for all that you have done for me," he said to the bearded man at his side who chopped with his axe at one of the trees. The hermit had been by his side in the cold helping Wolfram to repair the ship.

"I was glad to help you, my son," Paul replied with his usual grin. It seemed that he had smiled more since the Viking had come than before. It was good to have someone to talk to. He would miss the companionship when the Viking sailed away.

Wolfram pulled at the old nails in the ship, trying to straighten them out. They could be hammered in again and used to hold the new wood. This ship would not be as handsome as the *Sea Wolf,* but it would get him where he wanted to go.

"Just think, Paul, my child has already been born. I wonder if I have a son. I hope that Deidre is well." He smiled at the man next to him. Now he knew that Paul had once been a priest of the god Deidre worshiped. Paul had read to him in the evenings from the Holy Book Deidre had told Wolfram about. The story of the man named Noah had impressed him the most. In Viking legend too there had been a great flood. This Noah had been wise to build his great ship, although Wolfram grimaced to think of the mess all the animals would have caused aboard such a vessel. No doubt Noah took many thralls with him to care for the animals.

"We have prayed for her, my son. She will be well," Paul answered, pausing to wipe the sweat on his brow from his exertions. When one worked hard the body continued to dew the skin with its moisture.

"Ah, how I long to see her. I love her, Paul. She is everything a man could want in a woman. Wise like your Ruth, loyal like your Esther and beautiful like Sarah." Thinking about Deidre, Wolfram's eyes closed as he imagined her face before him. So intent was he upon his thoughts that he injured his thumb with the tongs he held in his hand and issued a curse.

"Careful, my son," Paul said with concern. He stopped his chopping to look again at the handiwork of the ship. With a new sail, and a bit more work it would be ready. "We will have to gather some pitchy logs to tighten the seams. The tar will work wonders and make the ship airtight."

"I'm surprised that you know so much about ships, Paul," Wolfram said. "One would almost think that you had been a Viking and not a priest."

Paul's eyes clouded and the smile faded from his face. He seemed again in his own private world and Wolfram wondered what thoughts tortured this kind man.

After a time Paul looked at Wolfram. The young man reminded him of himself many years ago. He had been so filled with excitement and with his passion for adventure. Now the bond of their love of the sea drew him to Wolfram. He was glad that the skills he had learned in his youth could help the Viking return to his homeland. Picking up a chisel he began to work at the spintered oar holes. No doubt this vessel had been a Viking's pleasure ship for it held few oar holes and was a small craft. Just the perfect size for a man alone.

"I wish you would come with me, Paul," Wolfram said after awhile. He hated to leave this man alone in this wilderness. A man could die out here of so many causes. Animals or the freezing cold could quickly claim a life.

"No. It is here that I must stay. I promised my Lord that I would do so in penance for my great sins." Again the hermit had that faraway look in his eyes.

Hearing the cry of a wolf, Wolfram looked in the direction of the sound. He could see many eyes upon them, watching

them build their craft. It reminded him that at all times they
had to be close to their weapons in case one of the animals attacked. Food was scarce in the winter and any starving animal
would prey upon humans for food, although Wolfram had
heard that the meat of humans was not a favorite with the
creatures. "It is said to be too stringy," he joked with Paul as
they saw the creatures from afar.

Thinking of food made the two men hungry and putting
down their tools for the day they set out for the hermit's small
hut. A warm fired awaited them and Wolfram drew from the
snow outside the door two large fish that he had caught the
night before along with some roots that Paul had gathered.
The two had a feast then read again from the Holy Book. This
time Paul read to Wolfram about Judas and his betrayal of the
gentle Christ.

Wolfram's eyes blazed with anger. "This Judas. He was
just like my brother. All the time smiling while he planned to
betray your Jesus. How could Jesus ever forgive such
treachery?" It was more than he could fathom.

"Because he loved us. Love is a very powerful thing, Wolfram, as is faith. Faith can move mountains they say." He
closed the book. "It is love and faith that kept you alive in the
waters out there, not your hatred. All these weeks it has not
been your vengeance toward this Warrick that has motivated
you, but your love for your wife, your child, your sister and
your father.

Wolfram thought a moment. "Yes, that is true. Are you
then asking me to forgive my brother as Jesus forgave this
Judas?"

"Yes. If we live by the sword, we die by the sword, my son.
Believe me I know this to be true. Think upon my words this
night, that is all that I ask you."

Wolfram pulled the warm furs over his body and closed his
eyes. "Forgive Warrick? So strange these Christians and their
ways and yet he admired this Jesus that the Holy Book talked
about. Truly the man had been given much courage. He would
think about what Paul had said but he would not make any
promises. When he told his father, he would see what Olaf
would say to this matter of forgiveness."

The next day bright and early, Paul and Wolfram were up
and out of doors to work on the ship. Slowly the skeleton of

timbers was taking on the shape of a sailing vessel held together with iron nails and pine tar. The sail was fashioned from an old woolen blanket of Paul's and if it was a crude craft it would serve Wolfram's purposes well.

Every night Paul read to Wolfram from the Holy Book and Wolfram would carefully notch a stick to keep track of the time until he could return to his wife and his homeland.

40

The old Jarl was dead and a new Jarl had taken his place. Everard Olafsson now wore the circlet and carried the sword of his father. Among much pomp and ceremony and feasting he had been proclaimed the leader of his people. Everard's first deed as Jarl was to search for the murderer of his father, scouring both land and sea for any sight of the hated Danes. He had found no sign of them and so it was supposed that the Dane found beside his father had been the one to do the dastardly deed. Still the hall clucked with gossip. What had brought a Dane upon their shore? Only Olaf the Red knew and he was dead.

Deidre did not hold much love for Olaf's son, but Everard seemed to ignore her most of the time, more interested in the men of the hall than the women. Once or twice, however, Deidre did see him looking in her direction with a lustful gleam in his eyes and feared lest he decide to make a claim upon her. Much to her relief he did not.

Now that the baby was born and Deidre's body had returned to its former slimness, Warrick hovered constantly at her side. At first, she had been flattered and had endured his stories and attentions. It had been like the days when she had first arrived here. She saw in him a great resemblance to Wolfram and felt somehow comforted to have the brother of the man she loved nearby. But it soon became clear to her that Warrick was becoming far too possessive. It was as if he had an obsession where she was concerned, as if he assumed that she would soon become his wife. Indeed he acted now as if he were her husband, taking his place beside her in the hall and even calling her "wife" upon occasion, though she sought to discourage him. Deidre determined that she must make Warrick understand that her denial of marriage to him was a firm one. They were friends, nothing more.

Now as she entered her room to feed Fenrir after the evening meal she saw him deep in the shadows, standing over her baby. The sight angered her. Never before had he entered her sleeping rooms, except once when Wolfram was injured.

"Hello, Deidre," he said cheerfully, extending his hand to her. She brushed his hand away.

"What are you doing here, Warrick?" she asked, her voice sharp with annoyance.

"I came to see my son."

"Your son?" Deidre cast him a wary glance. What game was this that he was playing? Did he mean that he would adopt Fenrir as his own if she married him? "What do you mean, Warrick. Fenrir is not—"

"You are beautiful, Deidre. Like a goddess. I've always thought so. My eyes can never get enough of your beauty. It makes me proud to have you by my side. Your hair is like the velvet black of the night." He took a step toward her but Deidre backed away. She heard the faint whimper of Fenrir and hoped that his uncle would not frighten him with his presence.

"Warrick, please. I must nurse my child. Leave me be." Her voice was trembling with a mixture of anger and fear. Something in his behavior troubled her, though his words were pleasant enough.

His smile faded. "No. I will not leave. I want you to marry me. Tomorrow. I have waited long enough."

Deidre sighed. They had been over this before. "I love your brother, and want no other as my husband. Wolfram still lives, I feel it in my heart. Surely you can find another more anxious to be given the honor of your wedding rings." She started toward the door with the intention of calling Zerlina, but Warrick reacted quickly and moved to block her way. He put both hands on her arms.

"You don't understand, do you. You belong to me. You have always belonged to me. No other man is good enough for you. Wolfram was not."

She tried to pull away but he held her with a strength born of madness. "Warrick, you are hurting me. Let me go!"

"No. Not until you call me husband!"

Deidre closed her eyes in pain as he held her wrists in a

bruising grasp, but suddenly she felt his hold on her loosen
and opening her eyes saw Sigurd holding Warrick by the hair,
pulling his head backward. He had heard her voice and had
come to her rescue.

"What are you doing here?" he growled, pushing Warrick
down.

"I came to see Deidre, bondi. She belongs to me." Slowly
Warrick got to his feet, his eyes blazing hatred.

"She belongs to you, does she?" Sigurd shouted. "Is that
why she was cringing away from your grasp. You dog. You
are unfit to call yourself Olaf's son." Sigurd touched his
sword, a reminder to Warrick that he was prepared to fight.

"I am better than you are, bondi," Warrick responded. He
took a step forward but at the look in Sigurd's eyes backed
away. "I am the son of a jarl and you are a peasant."

"I would rather be a peasant than one such as you. Sneak-
ing in here and frightening Deidre is cowardly. She does not
welcome your attentions."

Warrick laughed then, deep and dangerously. "And are you
her guard dog? You, a raper of women, raider of villages. You
call me coward and I call you one as well. It is much like the
pot calling the cauldron black."

Sigurd's eyes flashed, his teeth clenched, but he did not
respond. How could he? What Warrick said was true. In
his youth he had done many things for which he was now
ashamed. Loving Zerlina had changed him. Now he regretted
the things he had done.

Warrick brushed at his clothes. "You dared to push me
down. Know well that I will take my revenge for this insult,
bondi. Do not think that I have not seen the way you look
upon my sister. She is too good for the likes of you, crippled
or not. If you ever touch her I will kill you!" With that he
turned and left.

The sound of his voice had frightened Fenrir and now he
cried his protestations at the intrusion. Deidre picked him up,
cradling him in her arms as she turned her eyes upon Sigurd.

"I am sorry to have involved you in this, Sigurd. I do not
think that he would have harmed me."

"One never knows what can happen," Sigurd answered
shaking his head.

"I hope that Warrick does not retaliate for your actions.
There is something about him that worries me. I thought

I knew him well, but lately he is like a different man." She rocked Fenrir in an effort to soothe his wailing.

"I do not fear him. He is as I have always said, a pup though he has been acting strangely of late. How Zerlina could have come from the same womb as he, I do not know. She is so good and fine and he, I fear, is touched with evil." He put a gentle hand upon Deidre's shoulder. "I will stay outside your door this night, Deidre. He will not come back. In the morning I will speak with our new Jarl about Warrick. If you do not want his attentions, then Warrick should leave you alone."

"No. Do not speak with Everard," Deidre said with a toss of her raven hair. "I do not want to cause trouble between the brothers. I will just remember to barricade my door at night. And really, I do not think Warrick would ever harm me. There are times when he can be so gentle."

Sigurd was not convinced. "I think Everard should know. He is not a bad sort, Deidre. He is not as wise and gentle as Olaf was, but he is strong and just in his own way."

Deidre remained firm. "No. I would not have more bad blood between the Jarl and his brother. It is for me to take care of this and for you to give me your friendship."

"It will always be yours. Rest now and feed your strong son. But please remember not to stray from my sight, for only if you are near me can I protect you."

Deidre smiled. "I will do as you say, Sigurd. Again, thank you." She watched him go, then bared her breast to her son. "I will just have to wait until you grow up, Fenrir," she said softly to the child. "I know that then I will be protected. Isn't that so, little one?" As if understanding her words, Fenrir looked upon his mother with his blue eyes, eyes like the sea. He cooed to her and waved his small arms in the air and in spite of what happened, Deidre smiled.

41

Warrick troubled Deidre no more, but from time to time as she looked across the table in the big hall, his eyes were upon her. His look held anger and a veiled threat and even though she was surrounded by the family, Deidre felt apprehension not only for herself, but for Sigurd as well. She had made an enemy of Warrick and there was no Olaf the Red to keep her from harm. Now she had two enemies, for Deidre well knew that Erika bore her no love either.

Since Everard had been proclaimed Jarl, Erika acted more like a queen than the first wife of the head of the household. Neither Adora nor Gerda put on such airs. Erika strutted around the hall in all her finery, refusing to allow her hands to be dirtied by household chores.

"She imagines herself to be the goddess Frigg, Odin's wife," Zerlina said one day in annoyance as Erika went about ordering the thralls to do her bidding.

"She has always wanted to be wife to the Jarl. Now she has her wish," Deidre said wearily. With spring fast approaching there was so much to do in the great house. But Erika kept the thrall women so busy with her own personal needs and desires that much of the work once done by them was now given to the women of the hall to do.

"Perhaps now that Erika has what she has always longed for, it will turn to dust in her hands," Zerlina said with a sigh.

With her father dead, Zerlina had no reason to stay in the hall except for her friendship with Deidre and her mother. She had meant to ask Everard to allow her to wed Sigurd, for she well knew that Everard considered her more of a burden than anything else—an unmarried lame sister. She had made up her mind that if by some chance Everard refused she would travel

the world over with Sigurd at her side. Life was too short not
to reach out for happiness. She had thought about going with
Sigurd to the settlement of Dubh-Linn in Ireland to there
share his bed and his life, but he had been acting so strange of
late. Always before he had looked at her with love in his eyes,
and she had felt secure just knowing that he cared about her.
But now his eyes avoided hers.

Deidre saw Zerlina's eyes as they sought out Sigurd, saw the
look of pain cross her face and knew that she had to confide to
her friend what had happened with her brother several days
ago. It was not right for Zerlina to think that he had stopped
caring for her.

"Sigurd is being overly cautious right now," she whispered,
then told her about the heated words between Sigurd and Warrick in her chamber.

Zerlina's eyes were wide with surprise. "I had no idea that
my brother could be like that," she said. "He has always been
the quiet one of the family. Could it be that he has put on a
mask before us to hide the seething inside him?" She thought
long and hard, "Now that I think about it, he has always
coveted all that belonged to Wolfram."

"He insisted I marry him and if not for Sigurd, he might
have hurt me," Deidre answered.

"Then I am glad for you that Sigurd came. No woman
should be forced to do that which she does not want. He
would do well to remember that you are my friend and the
mother of our brother's child," Zerlina said, scrubbing at one
of the black cooking pots to get it clean, her frustrations being
absorbed by the object in her hands.

"But now Sigurd cannot even look upon you without risking Warrick's wrath. I know it is not his fear of your brother
which keeps him from seeking you out, but his honor. Men are
so foolish at times. He should carry you away with him, Zerlina, and end this barrier between you."

Deidre wondered at the smile which curved Zerlina's
mouth. She raised her eyebrows and was about to ask Zerlina
what so amused her when Erika came strutting up to the two
of them.

"You prattle on and on like two old women," Erika
taunted. "I want Deidre to go to the barn and fetch some
rushes for the floor in my bedchamber. The rushes there are
old and dusty and offend my nose."

Zerlina stood up with her hands upon her hips. "Let one of the thralls go about your errands, it is not for Deidre to wait upon you. Besides, you should wait for spring to gather up the old rushes for the bonfire."

Erika smiled. "I want them now. My thralls are busy elsewhere." She stood towering over Zerlina, her hands set upon her ample hips.

"I will go," Deidre said with a shrug of her shoulders, anxious to avoid more trouble between the two women. It was not right for Zerlina to fight her battles, and she did not mind the walk to the barn. It would be good to get out in the fresh air.

Deidre did not see the eyes watching her, nor did she see the smile curve Warrick's lips. He had waited for just such a chance to find Deidre alone. He remembered her telling him about the husband she had left in Ireland. Now he would get his revenge upon her for shunning him, as well as gold to fill his chests. Her return would herald a great ransom from her husband, no doubt.

Warrick laughed at his cunning. He had been wise to keep the Danes about for just such a chance. Their ship was hidden in a cove of the fjord. He had only to run and fetch them to see all his plans fulfilled. They trusted him, the foolish bastards, and would do anything he asked in their greed.

As she walked along, Deidre looked at the green of the new blades of grass peeking out from under the thin layer of snow, which was nearly all melted now by the warmth of the coming spring. Overhead she could hear the chirp of the birds and welcomed their return. There was even more reason to be happy this day. Soon the world would be reborn again, and when spring arrived there would be no reason why Sigurd and Wolfram's men could not go out in search of him. She would see Wolfram again, of this she was sure.

Entering the barn, Deidre bent over to gather the rushes stored there, but a sudden sound made her turn around quickly. A man stood behind her wrapped in furs and wearing a double-edged sword at his waist.

"Hello," she said in greeting, lifting her hands in the gesture of friendship. He did not return the greeting but merely took a step closer to her. Deidre did not know this man, he was not of the hall. His garments were unfamiliar to her and as she gazed at him a feeling of apprehension came over her. "Who are you?" she asked.

The man babbled at her in a tongue which was similar to the language Wolfram and Hildegard had taught her, yet with just enough difference to make it difficult for her to understand. Another man stepped out of the shadows, then another and another.

"Danes!" she shrieked as the truth came to her mind. The first man grabbed her from behind and stopped her cries with his hand over her mouth. Deidre could hear the words "ship" and "seas" but the rest escaped her ears.

Remembering the scissors and small knife that always hung by a golden chain from her gown, Deidre reached her hand up to grab one of the tiny weapons, but before she could do so, the man had yanked the chain from her garments. The scissors and knife clanked as they hit the ground. A wave of terror washed over her.

"Are you going to kill me?" The face of Fenrir flashed before her eyes and she began pleading for her life. "My child. He needs me!" She gestured with her hands to try and make the man understand.

A grunt escaped the lips of one of them. "Silver," he said. "Irish husband."

Deidre fought them even harder now. They were not going to kill her; they were going to sell her for silver, separate her from her baby, take her from Fenrir.

The Danes tied her wrists and ankles together with ropes, then pushed her toward the door.

"No! My son, my son. I cannot leave my son!" she screamed. A cloth was stuffed in her mouth, she was hoisted over one of the Dane's shoulders, jostled and manhandled as they fled the barn. They climbed down a steep cliff to a ship awaiting them in the waters of the fjord. Deidre was thrown to the deck and watched helplessly as the ship moved slowly away from the landing. Panic overwhelmed her. These men were taking her away from her son. She couldn't leave him—he was her heart, her soul.

A moaning, a keening sound came from Deidre's throat, tears filled her eyes, and her body shook with her sobbing. She was leaving this land on this ship perhaps never more to lay eyes upon her baby.

The water of the fjord was rough, the current swift as it carried the ship far away from the shore. Deidre fought against her fate with every ounce of strength she had, but it was useless. She was caught like a fish in a net, helpless against these men who had taken her.

"How I once longed to see Ireland again," she thought, as tears coursed down her cheeks. "But not like this. Not like this." Once again she was to travel across the wide ocean, but this time she would not have Wolfram's love to shield her.

42

Zerlina paced the hall. Deidre had been gone overlong just to gather some rushes. Remembering the recent assault on Deidre she scolded herself for letting her go out alone, even to the barn. What if Warrick had forced himself upon her again? She went in search of Deidre and saw her brother sharpening his sword by the front door of the hall. It had not been Warrick then who had detained her. She sighed in relief.

Zerlina made her way toward the barn. All was quiet. She poked her head inside the door. "Deidre? Deidre are you in there?" There was no answer. Stepping inside the door Zerlina's eyes beheld the sparkle of something on the ground. Bending she reached her hand out for the shiny objects and gave a sharp intake of breath as she saw Deidre's scissors, knife and a Danish coin. She could see rushes strewn about the floor and the signs of a scuffle.

"Something is amiss here!" Zerlina exclaimed, rising again to her feet. "Deidre! Deidre, answer me."

Zerlina left the barn, searching in desperation for her friend. She had not returned to the hall, no one had seen her for at least an hour. Zerlina sounded the alarm and told everyone that Deidre was missing. They searched for hours, then Zerlina made her way toward the woods. Perhaps Deidre had strayed in that direction, or if someone had taken her, they might have headed toward the forest.

Deeper and deeper into the woodland Zerlina pressed, heedless of her own safety, only concerned with finding Deidre.

"Deidre!" she yelled over and over again.

The howl of a wolf stopped Zerlina in her tracks. She had traveled too far. She could see a shadowy form in the distance and realized too late her plight. It was a wolf. What had Wol-

273

fram told her to do if ever confronted by these animals? A tree, yes. He had told her to climb a tree.

Zerlina turned around in her path and began to run as fast as she could with her lame leg. Suddenly her foot caught in the roots of a tree and she fell to the ground. She could hear the bushes behind her rustling and could feel a pair of eyes at her back. Turning she saw the wolf, its fangs glistening like snow. With a snarl it edged closer to her.

"Help me!" she sobbed. "Someone help me." She was too paralyzed with fear to move.

The beast sprang but at that instant Sigurd appeared and grappling with the ferocious wolf, he raised a knife and plunged it into the beast's throat.

"Sigurd!" she cried. The next thing she knew she was held against a strong firm chest, a hand was smoothing the hair from her brow.

"Are you all right, my love?" he asked.

"Yes, yes!" she sobbed, clinging to him. It felt so good to be in his arms. "Have they found Deidre?" Even in her fear, she remembered the fate of her friend.

"No. They have searched everywhere! I fear that the Danes have taken her. It's the only explanation. Their ship was spotted not far from our shores."

"The Danes! Oh no. When will this all end?" Zerlina began weeping then as her fears and sadness tugged at her heart. Sigurd hushed her, raining kisses upon her face and running his hands over her body. He had almost lost her. How could he have lived if she were gone from the earth? Even just seeing her from a distance had been a balm to his soul.

"Oh Zerlina, I love you so," he crooned, rocking back and forth as he held her.

"Take me away with you, Sigurd," she pleaded. "Take me to Dubh-Linn. I don't want to be without your love any longer." Her arms clung to his neck and their mouths came together in a fiery kiss which left them both breathless.

"Dubh-Linn," he said finally when their lips had parted. "You would be happy there in that foreign land?"

"I would be happy anywhere with you," she breathed and he knew her words were true. They had been separated too long. It was only right that they be together. "And will you be my wife?"

"Yes, Sigurd. Yes, yes, yes." She held him to her once

again, their bodies touching, their hearts beating as one.

"Then we will set out right away, but first I must find Deidre." They walked along the pathway to the great hall hand in hand.

"I'll go with you, Sigurd. We will sail around the world if we have to in order to find Deidre and return with her. We have much reason to follow these Danes. They have taken Wolfram, my father and now Deidre I fear."

They walked along making their plans. Zerlina would pack all her belongings and be ready to sail with Sigurd aboard the *Dragon's Head* on the morrow.

"Should we take Fenrir with us?" Zerlina asked.

"No. He is next in line after Warrick as Jarl. He belongs to our people here. Adora will care for him as if he were her own. She loves the babe."

"And perhaps Diedre will return," Zerlina whispered, hope reflected in her voice.

They opened the door to the great hall but were met by Warrick who stood with crossed arms in front of the door. "I told you to stay away from my sister, bondi. Are you deaf?" He motioned to several armed men, his warriors, who wrestled with Sigurd and bore him to the ground.

"No, Warrick. No. I love him. I want to be with him. You can't do this," Zerlina begged on her knees.

"Lock him up. I will decide his fate." Warrick pushed the sobbing form of his sister out of his way and left the hall. It would take some convincing to get Everard to agree to kill Sigurd, but somehow he would manage it. His elder brother was all brawn and little brain. Perhaps, after he had disposed of this Sigurd—the only one who opposed him, he could turn his attention to Everard—the only one who now stood in his way to being the Jarl.

With a deep laugh Warrick thought of all the future held in store for him. First he would rule as Jarl. He could imagine what it would be like to wield so much power. Of course it would have meant much more to him if Deidre were at his side. She was meant to be the wife of a jarl. Erika was awkward and ugly in comparison to her. Deidre was so lovely.

"But she scorned me," he whispered. "She had to be punished. She was so foolish to anger me, to turn her back on her destiny. Now she is with the Danes." He felt a sudden regret for what he had done when he thought about Deidre being returned to her husband. He hated to have another man touch her. "She could have been *my* wife."

Perhaps he would one day have himself crowned king. It was rumored that Halfdan the Black had such ideas. Well, Warrick would beat him to it and become Norway's first king. Maybe then he would sail to Ireland and bring Deidre back. "A Viking Queen." His laughter sounded through the night as he made his plans.

43

The weather turned from its sharp blast of cold air to the warmth of spring and the wind whispered to Wolfram that now was the time to depart.

"It is time for me to seek my wife," Wolfram said to Paul. In some ways he would be sorry to leave, for a great friendship had sprung up between the Viking and the hermit priest. If only he could take the man with him, but Paul would have none of that.

"I will tell you my story, my son," he had said the day before as Wolfram had stubbornly refused to leave him behind. "I was a priest once long ago, young and foolish in my pride and my ambition. I felt the world was mine, with little thought to the God I was supposed to serve. I thought that I could live two lives, one for myself and one for my God. To make the story short I fell in love with a married woman."

"There is no sin in that, Paul. I did the same," Wolfram said softly.

"Aye, but this man was wont to beat my lovely Maria just for the fun it gave to him. One night he nearly killed her with his brutality and I stilled his life with my bare hands." Paul's eyes closed as he recalled that day so long ago. "I fled from the country in fear for my life, thinking only of myself and my reputation. A year later I learned that my lovely Maria had been convicted of the crime and put to death. No one believed her words that she had not killed her husband. My cowardice and selfishness had caused the death of the one person in this world I had loved. It was then I stripped myself of my priestly trappings and retired to this island in an effort to punish myself. For it is glad that I would be for death and that is why

I must live my life here alone to atone for the great wrong that I once did."

Wolfram could not understand the hermit's reasoning. All that had happened so long ago. Did Paul not deserve a second chance to serve the God he had betrayed? He had taught him so much about the Holy Book and made him understand so many things. He owed him his very life. Paul had taken a life but he had also saved a life in return.

"Perhaps some day I will leave this island, but not now, my son," Paul whispered. The two clasped each other in the warmth of their friendship as Paul bid Wolfram "good-bye." "Take care my son."

Wolfram huddled in the stern of the small boat as it rocked to-and-fro upon the waves. He felt like a leaf in the wind as the boat plunged through the seas. More than once Wolfram feared that the ship would capsize, but his fears were never put to the test.

When at last after three days Wolfram saw the shores of his homeland before him he wanted to leap for joy, but instead jumped into the icy waters of the fjord and swam toward the rocks. He went under instantly but fought his way to the surface, stepping at last upon the bank. He ran up the path leading to the cliff and knew that he would have indeed crawled had it been necessary.

"Paul is right. It was love for Deidre and not the thought of vengeance which saved my life," he whispered, yet he would seek punishment for what Warrick had done. But first he wanted to hold Deidre in his arms.

Laughing and crying, Wolfram stumbled toward the familiar shape of the great hall. How surprised his father would be to see him and Deidre too. He would pick Deidre up in his arms and carry her to their bed and never let her go again. Soon, soon they would have another baby and this time he would be at her side as she pushed the head from her womb.

"Deidre!" His cry rocked the hall as all eyes turned his way. He could see the fear in the eyes of the thralls who thought him to be a ghost. "Fools, come and touch me. I am flesh and blood, no being from the grave."

Erika was the first of the family to see him, and in her shock fainted dead away upon the floor of the hall. Wolfram chuckled at the impression he was making. It was rather fun to be brought back from the dead. He roamed the hall in search of Deidre, laughing as thrall and bondi alike ran in terror from the sight of him. When at last he came to the room where he had shared his love with Deidre, he looked down upon the baby sleeping there and was filled with awe.

"My child!" he exclaimed, picking the baby up in his arms. So tiny was this child of his loins. He looked at the face of the baby with the dark thatch of hair and was surprised to see his own face mirrored there. Anxious to know the sex of the child, he gently parted the swaddling and gazed at the tiny male organ. "A son!"

Wolfram's ministrations woke the child who set up a lusty wail. He rocked the child, feeling clumsy and foolish to be so inept at quieting his own baby.

"What are you doing in here? Leave the child alone!" It was Zerlina's angry voice he heard.

Turning, Wolfram gave his sister a boyish grin. "I wanted to see my son. He is a strong tyke, is he not?"

Zerlina felt the ground whirl beneath her as she gazed into her brother's face. "Wolfram! We thought you dead! The Danes. Warrick told us that they had killed you!"

"I live. I was thrown into the sea but a kindly old Christian priest saved my life and sheltered me these long winter months. It is a long story and one that must be told." His eyes looked behind her as if expecting Deidre to come in the room at any moment. "Where is Deidre? Where is my wife?"

Zerlina turned her back upon him so that he would not see the tears in her eyes. She started for the door, but Wolfram called her back.

"Where is Deidre, Zerlina? Answer me." All sorts of thoughts ran through his mind. Deidre had died in childbirth, or of childbed fever. All these months he had thought of nothing but her, her lips, her body, her gentle loving, he could not bear it if she were dead.

"The Danes took her, Wolfram. She disappeared about a week ago. I found her scissors and knife in the barn. We have heard no word of her since, though Odin knows that Everard has sent men to search for her."

"Does father know about this? Has he sent out his own men to find her?" Somehow Wolfram trusted his father more than his brother because of his wisdom.

"Father is dead, Wolfram." Her voice was soft as if in a wish to spare him pain.

"Dead?" His face turned pale. "No. Not Father! He was so strong." For a long moment he mourned him silently, barely controlling his sorrow. "How?"

"A sword wound in the back. He was a victim of the Danes as were you. He has long ago been buried. Everard is now the Jarl." Zerlina took the baby from his arms and quieted the child's whimperings, calling for a wet nurse who put the child to her breast.

"The Danes? It was not the Danes who sought my life," Wolfram said bitterly. Somehow he knew in his heart that Warrick was responsible for all that had occurred. Had their father found out about his treachery? Had Warrick sought to silence him? And what of Deidre? Had she too gotten in Warrick's way?

Wolfram took hold of his sister's shoulders. It would be painful for her to hear his words but she must. "It was our brother Warrick who killed my men and tried to kill me too. It was Warrick who sold me as a slave and who no doubt slew our father."

"No!" Zerlina exclaimed, wanting to believe the words to be untrue. But she knew by the look upon Wolfram's face that he spoke the truth. Hadn't Warrick acted with treachery these last few days in keeping Sigurd locked up? And hadn't he threatened Deidre? He was not the same brother she had once loved so dearly.

"I heard it from his own lips. No doubt Everard too is in danger. He is the only one who stands in Warrick's way now."

"Everard!" Zerlina said breathlessly. "He and Warrick went hunting together just a little while ago."

"Hunting?" Wolfram's blood ran cold. What a perfect opportunity to murder a man. Without another thought Wolfram ran from the hall in search of his brothers before another tragedy ensued.

Heading toward the forest on horseback, Wolfram soon came upon Warrick. Jumping from the horse, he grabbed his brother by the throat. He squeezed at his neck much as he had done once before but this time Paul's words came to his mind. "Forgive. We must forgive." Twisting the spear from Warrick's grasp, Wolfram stood with flashing eyes before him.

"I would kill you right here and now but in truth your blood is not worth spilling."

"I thought you dead!" Warrick's eyes were wide with surprise. Was this some demon come to haunt him?

"No thanks to you I am still alive, though I have heard that our father is dead. Did you kill him? Was he on to your tricks and treachery? And what of Deidre? Is she too the victim of you madness as well?"

Warrick laughed then, certain that this was no demon. He was not afraid of Wolfram. "Deidre is far away by now. I sent her back to her husband in Ireland where she rightly belongs. You will never see her again, though my chests will be full of silver and gold for her return. It is all that I ever got from her, though I would have given her the world!"

"In Ireland. Then she is safe?" The words were like a balm to Wolfram's heart.

"Unless her husband sees fit to punish her for her unfaithful ways." Warrick's eyes squinted against the sun. He sought some way to take his brother unawares, then he could continue in his plans for Everard. He would use the very spear Wolfram now held to end both their lives, Wolfram's and Everard's.

"Did you kill Olaf? Did you end our father's life?" Wolfram pushed the tip of the spear close against Warrick's throat until a thin trickle of blood appeared. "Did you?"

"Yes, I killed the old fool. He was getting soft. No longer was he fit to be the Jarl. He thought to punish me for my hand in your death, but I could not let him do that."

"Murderous dog! I will see you pay for this, Warrick. With my every breath I do so swear."

"And who will believe you? I will deny everything you say. All of the people know that it is the Danes who are responsible for all that has happened."

"Not everyone," Everard said, stepping out of the shadows where he had been listening. "No doubt I was next on your list." Everard's eyes were filled with loathing.

"What will you do with him?" Wolfram asked.

His voice was cold. "The punishment is well known for patricide. Warrick will be hung by his heels next to a live wolf suspended in like manner. Let them claw each other to pieces. It is Odin's law."

"No!" Warrick groveled at his brothers' feet begging their forgiveness and mercy. Wolfram thought about all that Paul had taught him. He could forgive Warrick, but he could not forget what he had done.

"Do what you want to with him, Everard. I want no more to see his face before my eyes. He sickens me. I wash my hands of his fate." Tears for his father flooded his eyes but he wiped them away.

Wolfram strode off in the direction of the hall, calling back over his shoulder. "I go to seek Deidre, Everard. I would wish to take Sigurd with me. Is that to your liking?"

"Yea," Everard called out. "He has been punished unjustly."

Wolfram left the forest then, ignoring the piteous cries of his brother Warrick, who sought pity where he had given none. Looking out toward the sea Wolfram knew what he had to do. He would take the *Dragon's Head* to Ireland and there he would claim his wife. None would ever part them again be it brother, father or husband. Deidre was his and no ocean could keep them apart for long.

PART III

A Treasure of the Heart

IRELAND
SPRING, 846

"Where your treasure is there will your heart be also."

NEW TESTAMENT, Luke, XII, 34

1

The rain clouds hovered high above the emerald isle releasing the rain upon the wooded hils and granite mountains. The air smelled of life reborn and the growth of grasses, flowers and leaves. It boded of the promise of spring and the joy and happiness that the season would bring, but to the dark-haired woman who looked out the window of the stone abbey, it boded ill. Although she was back in her homeland, she mourned for her son.

"Ah, Bridget," Deidre said to the nun standing before her, the sister of her blood, "how can I cry any more tears? I have wept them all out with my sorrow and still I cannot forget my child. I will never cease grieving that I am parted from my son. I would as well cut off my right arm."

The holy woman put a gentle hand on her sister's arm. "You will see him again, Deidre. I will do everything I can to sway Phelan's steadfast mind."

Deidre shook her head. "Nay, it is to punish me that he refuses to send me back to where my baby is. Even now he has not come before me. I have been back now almost two weeks and yet he has not seen fit to tell me of my fate." Deidre closed her eyes and remembered all that had happened to her since she had last held her son. The ocean voyage had been a nightmare of torment for her. Being dragged away from her son had been a torture to her soul. She had spent the entire time aboard the ship in a limbo between sleep and wakefulness. No doubt the Danes had drugged her so that she would be an easier passenger aboard their craft. Very little food had touched her lips. She was ill, not from the pains of her body, but from those of her heart. Upon reaching land she had been transported by horseback to the abbey at Muskerry, a big round stone building overlooking the rolling hills of Eire. At the abbey, she had been met by her sister, Bridget, now a nun. Bridget had forfeited her long flaming hair for the veil of a holy sister.

It had been a bittersweet meeting, filled with memories, a meeting that would have made Deidre happy if not for her anguish at being parted from her son. She remembered all that Bridget had suffered and mingled her tears with those of her sister.

"But I am content now," Bridget whispered. "Ian is with God and I have found forgiveness in my heart for those who killed him."

"There is much we have to learn about the Vikings," Deidre said softly. "They are not the heathens they are said to be, despite what they have done to us. You would have liked Zerlina and Olaf." She lowered her eyes. "And Wolfram." She told her sister all about the Viking customs and laws and about her love for Wolfram and knew that she understood.

Deidre was pleased with the look of peace she saw upon her sister's face. Bridget had not changed much, although her eyes seemed larger and more blue, her face a little paler. Her nose still had the sprinkling of freckles that Deidre had teased her about when they were younger. The smile upon Bridget's full lips told Deidre that here in the abbey her sister had found the calm and tranquility to help her forget the terrible nightmare of all that had happened that fateful day when Ian had been killed.

"We too have changed, haven't we?" Deidre asked softly. "You have found your Lord and I have found my heart. Only to lose it."

"That which was lost will be found again," Bridget answered, walking over to the window. She gazed out at the ground below. "When Ian died I wanted to die too. I shut my mind to the truth of my loss, yet God opened up my heart and with it my eyes. I know now that we must trust in the Lord in all things."

Sudden irrational anger took hold of Deidre. "Trust in the Lord. Words, only words. I have had everything taken from me. The man I loved more than life itself and the child of my womb. I find myself thrust into the hands of a man who once spoke vows before God claiming me to wife but now scorns and seeks to punish me, though he has no courage to face me.

Surely the Lord too has turned his face from me."

Bridget took her sister's hands in hers. "I too have suffered, Deidre. But my faith made me strong. It is not for us to question the wisdom of God. We can only fill our hearts with love and do as he bids us. We must forgive our enemies."

"Forgive our enemies," Deidre repeated. It was much easier said than done.

Bridget straightened her wimple with her small freckled hand, looking all the while deep into her sister's eyes. "Forgive and trust."

"Trust," Deidre repeated. She thought of Warrick. She had trusted him. Surely it was his treachery which had brought her such pain.

"And look forward to tomorrow with hope. Only God knows what tomorrow will bring. I will pray for you, Deidre, that you too may find peace and contentment as I have."

The bell sounded for Matins and Deidre silenced her words as she walked behind her sister toward the small chapel. It was cold and damp as she knelt before the altar, listening to the chanting voices of the service. Deidre's mind was in turmoil. How much longer would she be confined behind these walls? It was peaceful with the nuns, but it was not where she belonged. She wondered if her mother knew of her whereabouts. How she longed to see her again. Bridget had told Deidre that after she had disappeared the family had mourned her as one dead, certain that the Vikings had either murdered her or sold her into slavery. Only Tara had refused to believe that her daughter was gone from the world of the living. It was just how Deidre had thought about Wolfram. An inner voice still whispered he was alive.

Deidre tried to concentrate upon the service, but it was nearly impossible. What if she were to live out her days here, much as Queen Guinevere had in the days of King Arthur? What if she were never more to look upon Fenrir's tiny face, to see his sweet smile? Even his crying was dear to her. And what of Wolfram? What if he came back when she was away. Would she know where to search for her?

"What am I to do?" she cried out softly. An older nun nudged Deidre, bidding her to silence.

When Deidre thought that her knees could stand no more of the cold, damp floor, another bell rang out heralding breakfast. It would no doubt be the usual porridge and herb tea, but somehow Deidre found herself walking faster than usual, anxious to eat and be on about her day. She planned to send another message to Phelan and a letter to her mother.

The refectory-kitchen buzzed with the voices of the sisters who welcomed this time to break their silence and talk with each other.

Picking up her bowl and standing in line, Deidre searched for Bridget. Where had her sister gone? Was she in her cell-like room upon her knees in private prayer?

"Deidre," called the voice of one of the novices, a round-faced young girl who was constantly chastised for her giggles. She motioned to Deidre to come with her.

Putting down the bowl and casting a wistful eye upon the porridge, Deidre followed the young girl. Many thoughts flooded her mind as she hurried to keep up with the novice. "Am I to be scolded for whispering in the chapel?" she wondered. What could they possibly want with her?

Quickening her pace even more, she finally caught up with the young woman. Putting a hand upon the novice's arm she asked, "What do you want with me?"

"There is someone here to see you. He waits below with your sister." The novice nodded in the direction of the stairs then turned her back and left.

"Someone to see me?" Apprehension took hold of Deidre. Who was it below? Was it Phelan? Her father? Father Finian? Who?

Descending the steep, winding stairs, tripping upon her long gown, Deidre nearly fell in her haste. Dare she hope that it could be Wolfram waiting for her below? Her heart hammered in her breast at the thought.

Stepping through the courtyard archway, Deidre saw the black and white of her sister's form and behind her the short stocky physique and red hair of the man who had once claimed her hand. Disappointment coursed through her as she tried to smile.

"Phelan!" She thought of all that she could say to her visitor, all the ways she could plead to make him understand her love for her son.

He smiled at her, the smile too broad, however, to be sincere. His brown eyes squinted in the early morning sun, making his nose appear even flatter than it really was. He held out his hand to her as if nothing amiss had ever passed between them, as if nearly two years had not gone by since they stood before Father Finian and said the marriage vows.

Although the air was fragrant with the smell of wildflowers and herbs, Deidre did not notice. Her voice was barely a whisper. She stood frozen, pondering what words she could say to this man to let her go. Finally she asked, "Why have you come?"

Phelan crossed to her, his eyes riveted to her face. "Why? Why indeed. You are my wife, Deidre, no matter what sin you have committed. Your place is by my side."

"I have committed no sin," she answered stubbornly. Truly her love for Wolfram had been something pure and right.

"You have born a bastard, I hear, a child by a heathen." His eyes flashed and his lip curled.

"My child is no bastard! I love him. He was grandson to a noble Jarl, son of a brave and gentle man, a child of love. Do not slander him before me, for I will not allow it." She stood with her chin held high and her shoulders thrust back.

Phelan gestured for Bridget to leave. "There are some things that must be spoken only between husband and wife," he said. Bridget looked at Deidre, hesitating before she made ready to go. Deidre nodded. She was not afraid of Phelan. When Bridget had climbed the stairs, Deidre turned her attention to Phelan.

"I want to go back, to be with my son."

"I will not argue with you, Deidre. I came here to mend the hostile feelings between us. You have been through a trying time. I will try to understand and be patient with you."

"If you want harmony between us, send me back to the Northland. I want to be with my son." Her voice was firm, her eyes unwavering.

"The only place you will go is to the hall with me to live there as my wife," Phelan answered. By the tone of his voice it was apparent that his patience was wearing thin.

"I cannot go with you, Phelan. I'm sorry. But fate has intervened in our lives and in my heart you are no longer my husband."

He folded his arms across his chest. "You are talking nonsense, Deidre. We spoke the vows. You are my wife. Now you can either come peacefully or I will drag you back to the hall. It is your choice, Deidre. You are my wife and the laws of God and man are on *my* side. You belong to me as the land in the meadow belongs to me, as the sheep which graze upon that land belong to me and there is nothing you can do to change that fact.''

He moved toward her, pushing her in the direction of his waiting horses. Deidre realized that he would not listen to anything she might say. His mind was made up. There was nothing she could do but go with him and bide her time until she could think of a way to escape.

2

The thunder of hooves against the hard ground echoed through the quiet of the abbey courtyard as Deidre rode behind Phelan's black stallion on a red-gold mare. Her horse was tied bridle to bridle to her husband's horse to insure that she would not ride away.

"I am the prisoner of a man who is supposed to be my husband," she reflected bitterly, seeing the irony and resenting Phelan's treatment of her. The uncertainty of her fate was like a sore, festering as she rode along.

Phelan looked straight ahead as they rode in silence. The landscape looked familiar to Deidre and with surprise she noted that it was toward her father's hall that they traveled. Her heart leapt with joy at the thought of going home. Would her mother be sitting at the hearth at her spinning? Had her father recovered from his wounds? Was he out riding the lands he so loved? Colin and Brian, where were they? Did she dare hope that Phelan had changed his mind and decided to take her to her home?

"Phelan," she said aloud, trying to capture his attention. "Are you taking me to the hall of my father?"

"No. We are merely passing through his land on our way to my lands to the North," he answered curtly.

You mean my lands, Deidre thought in anger. Since their marriage had not been consummated, they still belonged to her. Was it any wonder Phelan was anxious for her to assume her duties as his wife. No wonder he had ransomed her. His treatment of her today proved beyond a doubt that it was not for any affection toward her that he had paid the Danes their silver.

Looking up at the sky she could see the sun directly overhead. They had been riding a long while already. Deidre's backside attested to the many miles they had traveled.

Deidre looked behind her at the seven men riding at her horse's flank. All were armed as if she were a dangerous enemy. Would they slay her if she tried to get away. No. At least not until Phelan could attest that their marriage was finally consummated. No doubt he wanted to make certain that she could not petition the church for an end to her marriage vows. Were she to do such a thing the lands they now rode through would be Deidre's according to the law.

Deidre thought about the laws. If a woman could show just cause for legal separation, a wife could take all her marriage portion, her marriage gifts and also receive a certain amount of damage money. No wonder Phelan felt the need to keep her tied to him!

That's it. That is what I must do. I must somehow reach the safety of my father's hall and beg him to give me shelter until the matter of my marriage to Phelan is settled. Surely Father Finian will help me when he understands my feelings, she thought.

Deidre looked behind her at Phelan's men. She had no doubt but that she could outdistance them on the long-legged mare. She was much lighter of build than they and had often ridden horseback. The problem would be with Phelan. How could she loosen the ropes which bound them together. Never had she longed for her knife and scissors as much as at this moment.

"Phelan," she called in a voice meant to sound weak with fatigue. "Can we rest? I am hungry and thirsty and swear that I can go no further." Putting a hand to her head, she made as if to swoon.

Phelan signaled for his men to halt. Dismounting from his horse, he yanked Deidre down from her mare none too gently. "We have to eat and quench our thirst as quickly as possible. There are many miles yet to travel." His eyes seemed to search the road behind them. Of what or whom was he afraid? Did he fear encountering her father or brothers? The Vikings? That she might escape?

Taking advantage of Phelan's lack of attention to her, Deidre slipped away from his watchful eyes. Slipping through the underbrush she came to a place where the woodland met the river. How many times as a child had she sat on this very bank and watched Colin and Brian frolic in the rough waters? She knew every rock and blade of grass near the river.

I'll soon be home again, she thought with a smile. Hoisting up her gown and chemise and tying them round her waist, Deidre made ready to flee.

"Deidre! She's gone!" Phelan thundered. Deidre could see him waving his arms frantically about as he gestured to his men to look for her.

Deidre looked wildly about her for a means of escape before she was once again in the clutches of Phelan's men. The only escape was by plunging into the roaring waters of the river. Hesitating only a moment, Deidre found her courage too late, a hand reached out to claim her. Turning around she found herself face to face with Phelan.

"Running away, Wife?" he asked with a growl.

Forcing a smile, Deidre looked upon him with eyes wide with innocence. "Why . . . no . . . I . . . was just . . . bathing. I could not abide the filth from the road one moment longer. Surely you cannot begrudge me a dip in the waters?"

Phelan searched her face for the truth of her words and found no guile there. With a shove he pushed her up the hill. "We have no time for your vanity, Wife," he said.

Deidre swore beneath her breath. Next time he would not catch her unawares.

Phelan thrust a piece of undercooked rabbit into Deidre's hands. She ate slowly, hoping that perhaps he would leave her again, but he stayed right by her side.

"What I can't understand," he grumbled, "is why those Vikings carried you off." It was obvious that it angered him beyond reason, as if in some way he had been betrayed.

Deidre shrugged her shoulders, thinking his pique was for the inconvenience her absence had caused in not being able to claim her lands. Would he have been less annoyed if they had killed her? She remembered that none of Phelan's men had been around at the time of the Viking raid to aid her father. Nor had Phelan thrown himself into the battle, coward that he was.

"They did not carry me off," she answered, fighting her anger.

"They did not? Did you go willingly with them?" The look of shock upon his face was nearly comical and if not for the danger she might have laughed.

"We were betrayed. I heard the Vikings talking. I wanted to find out who the traitor was. I hid in a barrel and by mistake ended up on board the Viking ship." Her eyes swept over him. "I would give everything I own to find out who that traitor was."

He grunted in answer, taking her by the arm. "Hurry. We can tarry no longer here," he ordered. If she had expected him to swear vengeance upon the one who had betrayed them, she was disappointed. Surely then he *was* a coward.

They took to the road again, riding just as swiftly as before. Deidre gazed about her at the greens and browns of the hillside as they passed by. The gently rolling hills were covered in lush green grass and dotted with gnarled trees, the branches reaching up toward the sky as if seeking to touch the bright orb of the sun. Soon, all too soon, they would leave this land behind them and then Deidre's chance at freedom would be gone.

Deidre cursed the rope which bound her to Phelan like a child to its mother. She had nothing with which to cut it. Somehow she had to find a way to rid herself of its bonds.

"Phelan," she said after a time, "I fear my horse has gone lame. May I ride with you?"

Issuing a curse Phelan climbed down from his horse. "Women! God curse them all. They are a bother and a nuisance." Untying the rope which joined her horse to his, he reached for his sword to put the animal out of its misery.

"Get down!" he exclaimed, this time doing nothing to aid her dismount.

Deidre took a deep breath. It was now or never. Digging her heels into the horse's flanks, she guided the animal away from the raised sword of the man who would claim her. Heart beating wildly, she crested the top of a hill. There was nothing but grass and hills before her.

"Damn you, woman, come back!" she heard Phelan shout. She turned around only long enough to see him jump upon the back of his stallion. He rode over the rough ground yelling in anger at the top of his lungs.

Trying to confuse her pursuers, Deidre wheeled her horse around. The dense thicket of forest behind her offered a hiding place and she plunged deep into the shadows of the foliage there. The sound of horses' hooves echoed in her ears, coming closer and closer. Just as she judged that her followers were deep within the shadowy woods, Deidre again changed direction, this time heading for the green hills. She plunged down the hillside, the thought of freedom a balm to her soul. No one could catch her now.

The wind tore at Deidre's face as she rode onward, but she did not notice. All that mattered was that she was free of this man who sought to entrap her. She had won this time. Now, all she needed was to seek the safety of her father's hall, the love of her mother's arms and the wisdom of Father Finian.

3

Deidre tethered her horse and ran toward the door of the hall of Llewellyn. Never had she been so out of breath as she was now. Phelan and his men had pursued her the entire way, nearly catching her twice. Even now she could hear the thunder of hooves as Phelan and his men approached.

Tara was the first person Deidre laid eyes upon as she ran through the door. Her mother was noticeably thinner but still maintained her regal bearing. She looked up from her loom, her eyes wide with amazement as she saw who stood before her.

"Deidre! The Lord has answered my prayers. He has sent you safely back to us." Rising from her weaving she stretched out her arms and gathered her daughter safe within the warmth of her embrace. "How? When? Are you all right?" she cried aloud.

Laughing and crying at the same time, Deidre explained all to her mother, her words moving so quickly that she was soon out of breath again. She told her mother of the traitor, the man called the "Irishman" by the Vikings; how she had sought his identity and been transported aboard the *Sea Wolf;* about her love for Wolfram whom she had first met when he was a slave on their shores; and lastly about her child.

"A child?" The shocked look upon her mother's face was more than Deidre could bear. Surely she too would not think ill of her.

"His name is Fenrir. He is all that I could wish for in a babe, more dear to me than my very life." She broke away from her mother's embrace to stand and look into her eyes.

"A son. But child to a heathen? Deidre, daughter, what are we to do?" Tara hugged her arms around her body, not knowing quite what else to say.

"Wolfram, the Viking leader, was my husband, Mother. We were joined by Viking law." Tara began to speak but Deidre silenced her. "You cannot say one word to me that I have not already said to myself over and over. Wolfram took me in love. Never did he force himself upon me. I foolishly thought myself tied to Phelan by my vows, but there is a deeper commitment than the words spoken to bind two people. That is the love one feels for another in the heart. We have a son who is the fruit of that love and the treasure of my heart."

"And so he shall be the treasure of my heart also," Tara said, gathering her daughter in her arms once again. "Ah, Daughter, it is so good to have you back again. Where is my grandson?"

Deidre started weeping then. "They took me from his side! The Danes fell upon me while I was gathering rushes and brought me back to Phelan's side. They sold me for gold and silver. I must go back to my child! I must!"

"They forced you to come back? It was not by your own free will?"

"Nay. I have been back two weeks now. Phelan seeks to punish me. It is only to keep hold of his lands that he wants me. I am not so naive or foolish as not to know why he bought me back. There is no love between us. In truth there never was. Please, I beg of you to shelter me from his wrath, by the love you bear me." Taking her mother's hand and kneeling before her, Deidre pleaded with the woman who had borne her.

Tara gently lifted her daughter up. She would not have her humble herself so before her. "By the love I bear you it shall be so. No one shall take you from this house unless it is by your desire."

No sooner had the words been spoken than the two women saw through the tiny window slits in the walls that Phelan and his men were approaching the great wooden door.

"Bar the door!" Tara ordered to one of the servants, who lowered the large log into place. "Deidre, stand behind me. Phelan may be your husband but I am lady of this hall and as such will have a say who goes here." Head erect, Tara stood before the door.

Deidre could hear the sound of pounding as Phelan tried to break down the door, furious that it should be locked to his entrance. When at last he realized the door was a strong one he beseeched those inside to let him in. "I have a right to entry," he called loudly.

"Why do you come armed to my husband's hall?" Tara asked defiantly. Her instincts now told her that this man, husband or no, did not bode well for her daughter.

"I come for my wife. It is my right as her husband," Phelan shouted back. Deidre could hear the sound of swords hacking at the wood and clutched at her mother's hand in fear. She knew that she would rather die than suffer Phelan's touch.

"Put down your swords at once," Tara demanded loudly, incensed that they should seek forceable entry. Turning to the few guards and servants who stood nearby, she bid them take up arms.

"Let me in and I will do as you ask." Phelan was stubborn in his pride.

"You will not enter here, husband or no husband. My daughter seeks safety under my roof and she shall have it," Tara called through the door. The hacking sound ceased.

"Woman, you interfere where you have no business! This is between husband and wife. It is no concern of yours. I have every right to take my wife back with me. She has led me a merry chase and has angered me greatly, yet I will be merciful in my punishment of her."

"My daughter will not be punished by your hand or any other. She has suffered greatly these past few weeks. I will grant her peace now and the safety she so deserves." Tara looked upon Deidre and smiled. There had always been a bond between them but never was it stronger than at this moment.

"By the laws of God I demand you turn her over to me. I am bountiful in not casting her from me in disgrace. She has committed adultery and spawned an evil seed. I agree to forgive her and take her back within the bosom of my heart. God commands it and it must be so." Phelan's voice had softened now.

"God commands that we love one another and show mercy. No, Phelan, I will not let you in. Go now before there is bloodshed. Deidre will stay here as is her wish."

There was silence outside the door and for a moment Deidre and her mother thought that Phelan had left, but once again he spoke. This time with renewed fury.

"I will seek Llewellyn. He will see to it that my demands are satisfied. I will not leave this land until I go with my wife back to my hall. Deidre is mine."

This time Phelan ordered his men away from the door. It would be only a matter of time until Deidre was in his clutches again. He had no doubt that her father would give in to his demands. Llewellyn had always been afraid of him and this fact made him smile.

After he had gone, Deidre sat down upon one of the wooden benches. It had been a trying day and she was exhausted. "Will Father do as Phelan says, Mother? Will he make me go with a man I do not love? Am I then just chattel?"

Tara gently stroked her daughter's hair. "I care not what your father says. As long as you want to stay here you shall do so. It is as I told Phelan."

"And my child?"

"We will seek to find him, but first there is the matter of your marriage vows."

"I must sever the tie which binds me to Phelan. I will never love another man but Wolfram. He is the father of my son and the love of my life. Somehow I know within my heart that he is not dead. He will find me, of this I feel sure, and when he does only then will I truly be alive again."

"Then Godspeed him," Tara whispered.

4

It was a starless night, the sky black and mysterious as it waited for midnight to descend upon the earth. Only the full moon gave light to the world below as it struggled to escape from the veil of clouds which covered it like a cloak. Making their way through the blackness, Wolfram, Sigurd and Rorik made use of the darkness as they headed up the Irish coastline on foot.

Wolfram tried to calm his impatience, but that was no easy feat. His arms longed to hold Deidre again and his eyes to look upon the glory of her beauty. It had been a long journey across the sea, but now he was but a mile from the hall of Deidre's father. He could only hope that she was there; he could not know for certain.

Was it nearly two years ago that Wolfram had set upon these shores in quest of the riches the Irishman had promised would be easy prey? He thought about the Irishman with disgust. How could a man deceive and betray his own people? The man, Phelan, had been a greedy one all right. Wolfram had remembered the name because it meant "wolf" or "brave" in the Gaelic tongue, although he supposed the man should have been better named Guthrie, "war serpent."

"And to think that Deidre was bound by Christian vows to such a one as he," he thought. So many times he had been tempted to tell her the truth about the man she had once called "husband," but each time he had feared that he would in some way hurt her. He had wanted to win her heart not by accusations but with love. So he had kept silent and in the end had triumphed and won her love. Had this Phelan come forward to claim his husbandly rights now that Deidre had returned to her own land? Wolfram wondered. The thought made him seethe with rage. She was *his* wife now.

"Odin's teeth!" Wolfram heard Sigurd swear as the two collided in the darkness. Wolfram was nearly toppled to the ground by the impact of the other man hitting him from behind. They both heard Rorik's laughter and felt his hand help them to their feet.

"Enough of this stumbling around in the dark. Come, let's rest a bit and light a fire. We have come a long way," Rorik said.

Sigurd fumbled for the flint he always carried upon a ring at his belt and struck it to cause a spark to ignite the twigs and branches that Rorik had gathered. Wolfram felt ill at ease about starting a fire for fear the Irish might see them from afar, but Rorik set aside his fears with soothing words.

"The Irish never have lookouts near the water. Remember how easy it was the last time we came upon them?" he said.

"Aye, I am tired of crawling around like some creature from the night, Wolfram," Sigurd agreed.

Wolfram paced the ground nervously. The fire boded ill. It was not wise to let down one's guard in enemy land. They could not afford to be overconfident or foolish. When they came before the lord of the hall, Deidre's father, and made their peace with him, then they could walk openly upon the land without fear, but now was too soon.

"I think we should put out the fire and go about our journey," Wolfram said aloud.

"You are our leader," Rorik consented with disappointment, kicking dirt upon the glowing embers. The fire had been a welcome boon on such a dreary night.

"We will soon be before a larger fire than this," Wolfram said as they walked along. He could only hope that Deidre's family would not be hostile toward him. The touch of his sword at his side gave him confidence, but he knew that unless his life were threatened he could not strike out with it. There had been enough killing once before. He only wanted to fetch Deidre and no more.

"I for one will be glad when we can return to Dubh-Linn with Deidre. I am lonely for Zerlina already," Sigurd whispered. Zerlina had come with them on the journey, bringing with her Deidre's and Wolfram's child, Fenrir, but the ship had stopped at the Viking settlement at Dubh-Linn, where Zerlina and the baby had stayed for safety's sake. It was to that settlement that the *Dragon's Head* would shortly return.

"And I for Helga," Rorik added.

The screech of an owl sounded through the night and Sigurd stopped in his steps to touch his sword, but he soon laughed at his folly. "The night bird."

Brushing aside the heavy foliage of the bushes, Wolfram thought he heard more than just a crackling in the underbrush, more than just the wind sweeping through them. The very leaves seemed to be trying to tell him of some secret. But he had no time to stop and listen.

Rorik seemed not to hear. "Would that we had Thor's goat-driven chariot with us this night to fly above this rocky ground to this hall of Deidre's father."

It was then that the rocks lunged at them from the shadows. The rocks turned into the dark shapes of men alerted to the Viking presence by the small fire.

"Wolfram, watch out!" Sigurd shouted as he watched two of the shadow figures fall upon his friend. He himself narrowly escaped a knife in the back.

Wolfram felt a pain in the back of his head as someone hit him from behind. Then he felt his arms pinioned from behind as he was pushed down into the dirt.

"It's the Vikings!" shouted a voice. "I told you if we watched upon the hillside long enough we would find our quarry. These bastards always return in the spring."

Wolfram saw Sigurd spring at the two, pummeling with his fists. But he too was laid low. They were outnumbered.

"Rorik run! Alert the ship," Wolfram yelled out.

"No. I will not leave you," Rorik screamed back.

He started forward but Wolfram cried out again, "Do as I bid you. I will not have us all captured. Run!"

Rorik did as he was bid, dashing in and out among the trees like a wounded deer, to be followed by one of the Irishmen who guarded the hillside.

"Don't let him warn the others, Brian," shouted a voice. Wolfram and Sigurd watched as Rorik easily outdistanced the young Irishman, then breathed a sigh of relief. At least Rorik had gotten away.

Wolfram cringed as a torch was lit and thrust into his face.

"Let's see these two, Colin," said a deep booming voice.

Wolfram gazed into a pair of burning eyes, eyes mocking

and angry. "It's him! That Viking who led the raid in spring two years ago. The one who no doubt took our Deidre from us!" said a voice.

"The Viking dog!" shouted another.

"Let's hang them right now," said still another.

"No!" The voice was that of a red-haired youth. "We must keep them alive until we find out what has happened to my sister."

Wolfram tried to speak but was given an elbow in the stomach for his trouble. He looked again at the red-haired youth. So this was Deidre's brother. He felt a liking for the young man despite the situation. Truly he could not blame him.

"Let's take him to our father! He will know what to do with him," said the man who looked upon Wolfram's face.

Wolfram thus found himself being shoved and pushed along behind Sigurd. He would come not as a friend to the hall of Deidre's father, but as a prisoner.

5

Wolfram and Sigurd could see the hearth fires of Llewellyn's hall shining through the small window slits in the walls. The hall looked like a small box in the distance. They were coming closer and closer to the dwelling of wood and stone, and Wolfram wondered if this night would bring him great joy in seeing Deidre or the ending of his life.

All around the two Vikings, the men of Llewellyn's clan brandished their swords and called out to the two men from across the seas with taunts and threats, as they walked along.

"Feed them to the wolves. I hear that's what they do in their country," said one large man.

"Hang them from the trees and let the birds feed upon their carcasses," said another. "Chopping off their heads would be far too merciful. Let them suffer for what they did to us two years ago."

"Ha! Child's play. I tell you we should give them the blood eagle. That is how my father died by Viking hands, his entrails cut and spread out before him as he lay helpless," taunted still another. The heavyset man pushed Wolfram violently to the ground. He spoke and laughed as Wolfram tried to get up only to find that same man's foot in his back.

From his place upon the ground Wolfram looked up and was met by a pair of eyes so familiar to him. Yet they were not Deidre's eyes, but those of another. He read compassion in those eyes and kindness.

"Leave him alone, Cedric. We do not have to act like brutes in this matter," the young man said, giving Wolfram his hand.

"Who are you?" Wolfram asked, knowing the words as he spoke them. The man had to be kin of Deidre's to have such eyes.

"Brian. It was my sister you so ruthlessly vanquished and disgraced then carried off with you. May God forgive you for what you did that day, for I cannot."

"Brian," Wolfram repeated. He had often heard Deidre speak of this brother. They were close, he knew that. This one was the gentle sibling; Colin the fiery one. The red hair suited Colin.

The dark-haired brother with the unusual shade of blue eyes started to stride away, but Wolfram raised a hand to stay him. "Please. We must talk. You must help me," Wolfram exclaimed.

"Help you? Why should I help one such as you?"

"Because your God, your Christ wanted you to forgive your enemies and because I love your sister and therefore her kin," Wolfram answered.

"My sister? You have defiled her and taken her from her husband. For this and many other things you must be punished. I want to hear no more of your words." Brian stood with his arms folded across his chest but his eyes belied his feelings. He was torn between listening to this Viking and joining the others who called for the man's blood.

"Is she here in your father's hall?" Wolfram breathed. "Please, I have to know. I must speak with her."

"Quiet, Viking. The young lord told you he didn't want to hear any more of your words." He lashed out at Wolfram as Sigurd fought the men who surrounded him to come to his friend's aid. Sigurd too was dealt a brutal blow.

Brian looked confused. "My sister is not here in Ireland. Why do you ask me such a thing?" He motioned to the man who held Wolfram to let him speak.

"Your sister and I were married under Viking law and lived as man and wife in the Northland. We sired a son together of our love and were happy until we were separated. When I returned I found her gone, taken from my shores by the Danes. I hoped that they brought her here to ransom her and that is why I dared to come back. It was because of my love for your sister that I risked my life. Can't you see that?"

"The Danes? Here?" Brian looked upon this Viking with different eyes. Was it possible that perhaps he had spoken the truth? Could Deidre, if alive, be in some sort of danger?"

"Shut your lying mouth, you heathen dog!" The man named Cedric shouted pushing Wolfram once more to the ground. "You no doubt killed the woman and now expect us to believe your stories."

Wolfram once again struggled to his feet, his eyes riveted upon the dark-haired brother of Deidre's, his only hope now. Brian was deep in thought.

"Don't believe him, brother." The speaker was Colin who had shown all too well his hatred of the Northmen. He had been occupied with Sigurd, but now he stepped forward to take command. "Throw them into the pit like the dogs that they are!"

Wolfram and Sigurd were taken a few feet away and there given a shove which sent them falling into a deep dark pit. They struck the bottom with a jolt which sent their teeth rattling in their heads.

"A fine cauldron of herring we have gotten ourselves into!" Sigurd said beneath his breath, brushing himself off as he stood upon legs covered with bruises. "We will be lucky if we escape this place in one piece."

Wolfram examined his arms and legs to make certain that he had no broken bones. He could not help but remember the time he had fallen down the cliff when he had gone in search of his father. Finding himself sore but not severely injured, he set about trying to escape. The dirt was too soft to allow them to climb upward, and overhead there were logs placed like bars upon a cell. Above them they could hear the voices of their captors celebrating the victory of their "hunt."

"We are caught like bears in their pit!" Wolfram swore, hitting his hand against the moist earthen wall of his prison.

"There will be no escape for us," Sigurd sighed.

Wolfram thought about Deidre's brother. He could only pray to the Christian God that the one named Brian would in some way aid them—or it was possible he would never lay eyes on his beloved Deidre again.

6

A honking of geese and the whining of the wolfhounds in the yard announced Llewellyn's return home from his yearly tribal clan meeting. Deidre could hear his booming voice as he chastised the dogs.

"Chasing the geese again, eh, Fomor? And you too, Finn?" He strode into the hall with the dogs close behind him. He did not see Deidre sitting in the corner of the room, his eyes were only for his wife as he strode across the floor and embraced her in his arms.

"Glad I am to lay eyes upon you. I am overly tired from my journey." He broke away from her embrace and looked at the two dogs. They hung their heads and headed for the out of doors. "Blasted dogs. Always chasing the geese! How many times do I need to scold them?"

"They are only animals, Llewellyn, not people," Tara said, shaking her head in amusement.

"They are as naughty children," Llewellyn answered. Looking out the doorway, he saw the geese waddling about as the dogs flung themselves once again into the flock, barking and snapping at the feathery host. "Fomor! Finn!" Llewellyn waved his arms around and turned crimson in the face as he always did when annoyed. From her seat in the shadows, Deidre was shocked at her father's appearance. No more was his hair reddish brown, but now almost completely gray. His usually clean-shaven face showed the shadow of a beard. Her heart went out to him as she thought, *"He is getting old before his time."*

"Llewellyn," Tara began, glancing behind her at Deidre.

"Those dogs! No discipline. Just like the younger generation I tell you." Still blustering, he walked toward his favorite

chair. Seeing Deidre for the first time he opened his mouth
wide in shock. "Deidre? Deidre? Is it really you?" His steps
faltered as he gazed upon his daughter's face. He looked as
white as a ghost.

"I tried to tell you. A miracle has occurred. Deidre is alive. I
knew in my heart that the Lord had spared her, though I fear
her return to us is not altogether a happy occasion for her. She
was kidnapped yet again—" Tara exclaimed.

"Deidre," he interrupted.

Deidre smiled. "It's I, Father. I have come home." She ran
to his outstretched arms and clung to him.

"Ah, Deidre, my lovely daughter. God has truly wrought a
miracle and sent you home to us." Stepping back from her
after a time, Llewellyn took her arm and led her toward the
tables. "Have you eaten, child? Have you rested?" She
nodded. "Then tell me all. I want to know how you escaped
from those heathen Vikings." He remembered how she had
fought so bravely in the hall that day and his head was filled
with wild imaginings.

"I did not escape father. It was the Danes who brought me
here, not the same seamen who attacked our hall."

"The Danes. I do not understand. I thought it was the Vikings from the land of Norway who had taken you from us."

"I was not abducted, Father. It was by accident that I found
myself aboard the *Sea Wolf*." She told him the same story she
had related to her mother of that fateful day two years ago,
and of the traitorous Irishman. "I will find out some day who
this traitor was. He brought death and destruction upon all of
us."

"Bah! It was the Vikings who were to blame. None of our
own would sink to such treachery. But no more talk about
this. What has happened to you all of this time?"

Deidre hesitated a moment. It was one thing to tell her
mother all about her love of Wolfram, another to tell her
father who was so very strict and unyielding in his thinking. "I
lived among the Vikings," she began.

"Ah, I knew it. They took you as a slave. My poor Deidre."
He reached for her hands, holding them palm up as if to see
for himself the blisters and welts the heathens must have in-
flicted upon her. Seeing no traces of hard work or calluses
there, he touched the golden rings upon her fingers and looked
up at her in surprise.

"I was not a slave, Father, but an honored member of the household," Deidre whispered.

Llewellyn raised his eyebrows. "And . . . and did these Vikings force you to their bed?"

"No!"

Llewellyn sighed in relief. "Good. Our blessed Lord shielded you after all." He looked about him. "Where is Phelan? Surely your husband must be rejoicing in your return."

"It is about Phelan that we must talk with you, husband," Tara began.

"He has cast her aside? Tell me he has not." Llewellyn sat down upon his chair as if he could no longer stand.

"No, he has not cast her aside. He wants her to go to his hall and there consummate their marriage vows. It is Deidre who has turned from him," Tara said softly. She walked toward her husband, wishing to calm the outburst she knew was coming.

"Turned from him!" His brows furled in a scowl as he looked at Tara. "What foolishness is this? Deidre cannot turn from him. They are married. Stop this silly prattle and let me talk with my son-in-law." He pushed his wife's arms away from him in irritation.

"I do not love Phelan, Father," Deidre exclaimed, coming forward to stand before him.

"Love? Bah. What has love to do with it? I promised you to Phelan long ago. You know that. So speak no more to me of love." He started to turn his back upon her, shaking his head in bewilderment at her words. Never before had this daughter given him cause for anger.

"I love another. I was married to him by Viking law."

He whirled around, his face drained of all color. "Viking law? They have no laws. They are heathen. They worship false gods. How dare you speak to me of their laws!"

"Their laws are just. You do not understand them as I do. I lived among them. I bore the son of my Viking husband. A son. Your grandson."

"A child? God help us. If you bore a child from such a union I will call it bastard! It be no grandchild of mine!" He grabbed at his chest, his face writhed in pain. For a long moment he was silent and Deidre feared that her words had killed him.

"Father! Please! I want no bitterness between us," Deidre cried.

"Calm yourself, Llewellyn," Tara scolded. "It is your heart again. You cannot work yourself into these rages." Quickly Tara ran to get her herb pouch, brought forth the dead nettle, called by some angelica, and pressed it to her husband's lips. When at last Llewellyn had recovered, the pain gone, he turned again toward his daughter.

"Whore!" he spat at her. "Viking's harlot!"

"Llewellyn!" Tara gasped. "Hold your tongue."

"You should have killed yourself rather than submit to such degradation. Better for me and for you that you had died rather than bring this shame upon the family," he said to Deidre, ignoring his wife's interruption.

Deidre looked upon her father with stunned disbelief. She had known that he would be angry, but she had never realized that he could despise her so. Could he not understand that she had been in another land, governed by laws different from their own?

"Father. Don't say such things to me. Try to understand."

"Understand?"

"Let me explain," she sobbed. "I never loved Phelan, you know that. Nor has he ever loved me. We said vows before Father Finian, that is true, but we never slept together as man and wife. The Viking showed me kindness. I fell in love with him. Yet even then I kept from his bed, remembering the words I had spoken before God. But my heart was joined to his heart and became as one, and my soul merged with his soul. Our love was strong and our bodies too were finally joined together. We had a child from that love, a son. There is no shame in such a child, nor in such a love as we shared."

He refused to listen. "You belong to Phelan," he said between clenched teeth, "by my word!"

"No. Not to Phelan. Never to him. I will not go back with him. Let him do what he wants, I will never go back to him. He does not love me any more than I love him. His only concern is the lands my dowry will bring, and the silver and gold he was forced to pay as my ransom." Deidre's hands trembled as she stood before her father, fearing his anger. She remembered all the days of childhood when she had sat upon his knee, listening to his every word. She respected his wisdom, but in this she would remain steadfast.

"You will go back!"

"No!" Deidre whispered.

Tara walked toward her daughter and put her arm around her waist and held her tightly. "I have given Deidre my word that we will give her shelter here."

"Here?"

"I will not allow Phelan to take her. I have made a vow. A vow is a vow."

"Yes, a vow is a vow! What about the vows your daughter spoke before Father Finian?" Llewellyn stubbornly refused to yield.

"Those vows have been canceled by what has befallen. I will seek Father Finian out and tell him to petition the Holy Father in Rome for an annulment to the union between Phelan and Deidre. It was never meant to be. You and I both know that your only reason for wanting the marriage was to merge the adjoining lands and clans. But Deidre is no parcel of land. She has a heart and a mind and a right to happiness."

"Foolish women and their talk of happiness. You will cause trouble for us all. Phelan will strike out at us in an effort to regain his honor," Llewellyn snorted.

"And so it is fear and pride that turn your heart so cold," Tara said scornfully. "Well, I am not afraid of Phelan. If need be I will fight him myself to save my daughter."

Llewellyn's eyes were cold as he looked upon the mother and daughter standing there in defiance. "Then your daughter she will be. From this moment on I have only one daughter, Bridget. Deidre is as dead to me. Though my eyes look upon her I will not see her."

"No!" Deidre fought against the tides of sorrow in her heart.

"Llewellyn, you know not what you are doing," Tara choked. "Deidre has been through so much. How can you turn your back upon her? How?" Tears rolled down Tara's face, not for herself but for her daughter.

"Close your mouth, woman. I will hear no more. It is enough that I will not turn the harlot out of doors where she belongs. She may stay here but I refuse to have anything to do with her. You may pray that her coming here will not bring hardship to us all. That Phelan will not seek retaliation for your stubbornness." With that Llewellyn left the sobbing women in the hall.

7

In her bed, Deidre tossed and turned, weaving in and out of her dreams. She was upon a ship floating along the coastline, stretching out her hands toward another ship with the figure of a man standing at the prow. She cried out for him, murmuring in her sleep, "Wolfram." Ever closer they came to each other as the waves whipped and thrashed about them. Deidre was tied securely to the mast, she struggled with her bed linen imagining them to be the ropes which bound her.

"No! Let me go to him," she mumbled.

Deidre could see Wolfram's face swimming before her eyes. She knew that he had not died. As the ships passed she could see that he held her son in his arms. Closing her eyes in this land of her dreams she felt a hand grasp hers, felt arms enfold her, lips touch hers. As if by magic the ropes around her were tossed aside.

"Wolfram!" she called again, but instead of the sea-blue eyes of her beloved Viking, she saw the small, cold eyes of her Irish lord, Phelan. Holding her child in his arms he threw the baby into the sea, laughter issuing from his throat.

"My God!" Deidre cried out, sitting up in her bed. She buried her face in her hands still trembling from the pictures in her dream. "It was only a dream. A dream."

It was too soon for her to rise and be about the day, yet she could not stay in bed after her nightmare. Fumbling around in the dark, she lit a candle and was comforted by its warm glow. Like one of the little folk, the fairy people, she went about from room to room. Hearing the snores of her father coming from his chambers, she felt an ache in her heart as she remembered his words to her. If not for the love of her mother

312

she would surely have wanted to die.

Dressed in her white sleeping gown, her arms bare, Deidre shivered despite the warmth of the season. In Ireland the air was moist and the nights often chilly. Instead of going back to her room to cover her shoulders, Deidre plunged onward. She could see her mother's form in one of the guest rooms and felt sadness that her coming back had caused anger between her parents. Tara had abandoned Llewellyn's bed and had vowed to sleep apart until he reneged upon his stubborn vow to consider his daughter as one dead. Was it her imagination or could she hear the soft sound of her mother's weeping? She started to go to her but a loud crash in the hall caused her to go in that direction.

"So we have caught two in our trap," she heard a voice say and knew it to be Colin's. She hurried toward him but a sudden thought caused her to stop in her tracks. Would Colin shun her too?

"It doesn't matter," she said to herself. "All that matters is my love for Wolfram and my son." Again she started toward the hall holding the candle before her.

Colin was holding high his drinking cup as if in toast to Brian as Deidre came into the room. Seeing the vision dressed in white, a vision that looked like his lost sister, Colin dropped the cup to the floor.

"Go away!" he said, as if to a ghost. Deidre could see that he was quite drunk.

Deidre took another step forward as Colin shrank from her. "Colin!"

"Away I say. For the love of God leave me be and return to your—" Colin began only to be interrupted by a smiling Brian.

"This is no ghost, it is our Deidre. She is here." Brian wound his arms around his sister, kissing her on both cheeks. Stepping away he looked at her curiously. "You have blossomed, sister. You were always a beauty, but now there is none that can rival you." Brian remembered the blond Viking's words to him, that he had risked his life to come after Deidre. He had asked if she were in her father's hall. Had the Viking then spoken truly in all things? "Deidre, we caught two—"

"We caught two wolves in our trap," Colin said quickly,

regaining his senses and seeing that truly this was his sister and
no apparition. He gave Brian a look which warned him to hold
his tongue.

"Wolves?"

"They have been attacking our sheep, but will do so no
more." He cast a meaningful look at Brian, then took hold of
Deidre's hands. "But enough about such matters. How is it
that you come to be here in the hall? We all feared you dead at
Viking hands."

One more time Deidre related all that had happened to her
that fateful night. How many times must she tell this tale? She
was weary and sad and longed to see her son again and tell no
more of the traitorous Irishman and his evil.

"And you lived among those heathens?" Colin asked in
shock. Unsteady on his feet, he took a seat by the roaring fire.

"As wife to the man I loved, yes," Deidre responded,
watching his face to see if he too would turn his back upon
her. "I bore him a child. My baby is in the Northland. The
Danes abducted me and brought me here for ransom. Somehow I must get back."

"Colin!" Brian exclaimed. "He told me true. He said
that—"

"Shut up, Brian, and listen to our sister," Colin scolded.
He again gave his brother the sign to keep silent. He wanted
no hysterical woman demanding freedom for a man she
thought to love. His sister had no doubt been through such a
trying time that she had lost her wits. After a time she would
forget all about this Viking and the child she had borne in the
Northland. There was no more need to keep those two
heathens alive. Deidre was here. When he thought about the
wound he had received at the hands of those marauding
Northmen, the rape of his sister and the death of his brother-
in-law Ian and others, Colin seethed with rage.

Heedless of her brother's cunning and of the danger which
hovered over Wolfram, Deidre chatted on. It was good to talk
to her brothers again. She told them about Zerlina and Sigurd,
about Olaf and Erika and tried to make them see that in reality
the Vikings were truly no different from the people of Eire.
Colin in turn told his sister of his wedding plans.

"I have finally decided to wed the golden-haired Alana. It is
time that I brought forth sons to this land."

Deidre smiled her approval. "Alana will make a good wife

for you, Colin," she said. "Her weaving is known all around
the countryside for its beauty and her cooking is rumored to
be fine as well."

They talked for a long while, Brian holding his tongue
about the captives. It bothered him that they were keeping
such an important secret from his beloved sister. Surely she
had a right to know that her lover was being held by them as a
prisoner. His eyes sought out Colin's from time to time, but
always he read caution in them. Years of idolizing his brother
caused Brian to hold his tongue, yet all the while his conscience
was at war with the loyalty he held for his sibling.

At last Colin rose from his chair by the hearth. "Ah, it is
good to have you home again, Deidre." He grinned. "Now I
will have someone to tease again."

Deidre smiled, but her thoughts soon sobered. "Father has
turned his back upon me. He thinks of me as one dead because
of my love for the Viking and my refusal to go back to Phelan.
Will you still claim me as sister knowing of his anger?"

Colin stiffened a bit but shook his head. "Yea, I will always
claim you as sister. You were not to blame for what those
murderous Northmen did. You are but a woman, weak and
fragile. It is time that you need right now. Time and our compassion."

"I need my son in my arms," Deidre whispered, remembering the feel of tiny hands at her breasts.

Seeing the look of grief in her eyes Brian once again opened
his mouth to speak. "We must tell her, Colin," he began.

"Tell me what, Colin?" Deidre questioned.

Colin pushed at his brother, maneuvering him out the door.
"That if after a time it is still your wish to recover your child,
that we will do all we can to help you," he said. "As for now
there is a small matter we must attend to. We need to see about
those wolves." Thus said he and Brian were gone, leaving
Deidre alone once again in the hall she had known since
childhood but that now seemed foreign and cold to her.

"God willing I will enlist your aid, my brothers, and once
again see my son." Lighting her candle from the glowing
embers of the hearth fire, Deidre walked to her sleeping
chamber.

8

The light from the moon shone through the cracks in the logs high above Wolfram and Sigurd as they lay on the cold ground of their prison. Both Vikings had tried to sleep but in this foul pit with the shadow of death hovering over them, it was impossible.

"Shall we try again?" Sigurd asked, rising to his feet. Bending down on hands and knees he waited patiently while Wolfram stood upon his shoulders. Only then did Sigurd rise to his feet with Wolfram balancing upon him. He thanked the training they had received in the Northland. Both had learned to swim, hunt, wrestle, fight with bow and arrow, sword, spear, and balance upon even the thinnest of beams and jump sometimes fully armored above their own height.

Wolfram reached as far as he could, trying to grab a firm hold on one of the logs in the hope of pulling himself out of this Helhole and then helping Sigurd, but it was useless. They had tried it with Sigurd standing upon Wolfram's shoulders, but that too had come to no good.

"Only about the length of a man's hand. That is all we lack and we could be free of this place!" Wolfram swore, jumping down from the other Viking's shoulders.

"It might as well be the depth of the ocean for as much good that it does us, my friend," Sigurd answered. "We must face the truth. We are at the mercy of the Irish unless Rorik comes to our aid, and I doubt that he would be able to find us down here. We are doomed."

"No. I will never give up. I remember a story the hermit Paul told me about a man named Joseph, the son of a man with twelve sons. Out of jealousy his own brothers stripped him of a bright coat his father had given him and flung him into a pit. He did not give up, not even when he was sold into slavery by these very same brothers. In the end he triumphed over them and was even made ruler of that land called Egypt."

"Was it Odin then who gave him this power?" Sigurd asked. He had never heard this story before.

"No, it was the God the Christians worship," Wolfram answered. "I learned much about this God of theirs and about his son."

"The Christian God is weak, not powerful like Odin," Sigurd retorted.

"No, he is strong. I used to think as you do but Paul taught me that brute strength is not always a show of power. Sometimes wisdom is more important. And Sigurd, my friend, we must truly use wisdom at this moment."

A grinding noise sounded above them as one of the logs was rolled away. High above them they could see the grinning face of Colin.

"Hey Viking dogs!" he shouted. "I just came to let you know of your fate. My sister has come back to us, she is in the hall so we do not need to keep you alive any longer. What do you say to that?"

"Deidre? Deidre is safe?" Wolfram exclaimed.

"She waits in my father's hall for the return of her husband, Viking. She is lost to you forever and you will be in the fiery pits of hell where you and your kind belong!"

"Please, give her a message for me," Wolfram said loudly. "Tell her that our son is safe in the settlement of Dubh-Linn and tell her . . . tell her that I love her."

There was no reply from above but Wolfram could hear the sound of arguing and thought he could hear Brian's voice. At last he heard the sound of another log being rolled away. Was there a chance that his words had softened the fiery one's heart?

From above came a shower of vegetables and fruit. Wolfram and Sigurd ducked out of the way of the barrage.

"Your food, you stinking dogs." It was the voice they recognized as Cedric's. As always he was filled with hatred for them and they wondered if it was because of the raid upon these shores or because of some deeper, darker reason.

Again the face of Colin came before them. "I have no liking for you, Viking," he said, "but likewise I have no disliking for your son. He is my blood and so I shall do all within my power to bring him back to my sister. I do not want her to mourn his loss any longer. But as for you, in two risings of the sun you will be taken out to the rocks of the cliff, both you and your friend, and there tied securely. As you wait for the tide to come in you will know that the same waters you have sailed over in your terrible ships will be the very waters which will bring your death."

"You will drown us, without a chance to fight?" Sigurd was indignant. With a growl like that of a wolf he jumped as high in the air as he could. "Oh that I could lay my hands upon you."

"Easy, Sigurd," Wolfram counseled. "We must save our strength." He wondered if he were to pray to this Christian God if that God would help him.

"Two days, Vikings. Two days. Think about it and remember the Irish lives you took that day." Colin withdrew his head and motioned for his brother to come with him back to the hall.

"No, I want to stay here for just a moment," Brian answered. He peered down into the dark depths of the pit. Seeing his face gave Wolfram hope.

"You," Wolfram said. "I know you are more compassionate than the other brother of Deidre's. Please, take her a message for me. Don't let me die without first seeing her, touching her. I love your sister and she loves me."

"She is another man's wife," Brian said curtly, all the while tormented by what he had heard Deidre tell him about this man they held prisoner. She loved him, and they were going to take his life.

"Would you have her married to a traitor?" Wolfram asked. He could not bear to think of Deidre in the arms of one who had betrayed his own kind. Who was to say what a man whose only love was money would do to the woman he loved and to their child.

Confusion came into Brian's eyes. "A traitor? What do you mean?"

"How do you think we knew that your coast would be unguarded and all your warriors at their drink? Did you think it was by accident that we stumbled into your hall. No. It was one of your own kind who led us there and told us of the wedding feast. He told us that we would take you unawares and for his help he was given much silver and gold."

"You lie!" Brian exclaimed.

"I have no reason to do such a thing. You will kill me anyway. All I ask is that you keep the truth from Deidre, I would not want to hurt her and let her know that the traitor whose identity she sought the night she came aboard my ship was that of her very own husband. Just keep her from his clutches if you love her as I do."

"Phelan would not do such a thing. I don't care what you say!" Brian exclaimed. "I will not stay here and listen to any more of your slander. My brother is right. You both deserve to die." He stormed away into the night leaving Wolfram and Sigurd once again at the mercy of the man named Cedric. They had two days, two risings of the sun, to live and hope that help would come.

9

The still of the early morning hours was broken by the excited cries of one of Llewellyn's servants running through the hall, waking the household from their slumber.

"There is an armed band approaching. To arms! To arms!" he shouted, waving his arms wildly. Running into the bedchamber of his lord Llewellyn, he shook him until he was awake.

Llewellyn shook his head and ran his fingers through his thick mat of hair. "What the devil are you yelling so about?"

"A band of riders on horseback approach us from the north. There are many of them my lord," the servant babbled, his eyes wide with fear.

Rising from his bed, hastily donning his garments and grabbing for his sword, Llewellyn prepared himself for battle. "Be they Irish or Viking?" he asked.

"I could not tell, they were too far away. I only know that there were about thirty of them riding toward the hall."

From the doorway Deidre heard the servant's words. It was Phelan. It must be. No doubt he had ridden to his lands for added manpower and would now use force to take her back with him.

Seeing the look upon her face her father said, "This is your doing. If they be Viking, they be your lover's men come to fetch you, and if they be Irish, they be your husband come to claim his wife."

"Father, I meant no harm in coming here," she whispered in an agony of grief.

"The blood that is spilled this day will be upon your head," he replied angrily, brushing past her. Deidre followed him through the hall and out the large door.

Llewellyn shaded his eyes against the early morning sun. "If they be Viking, where in hell could they have gotten so many horses?" he wondered aloud.

"No doubt they are stolen. Those devils take anything they want as they march inland," answered one of Llewellyn's men at arms.

Llewellyn looked again toward the hills. He could perceive the forms of the riders coming at a furious pace toward them and realized at that instant that these were in truth no Vikings, but Phelan's men. He was sorely tempted to fetch his daughter and thrust her out the doorway and have done with it, but the knowledge that his wife would never forgive him ate at his heart.

Phelan held his hand up in a gesture of peace as he rode forward. "Llewellyn, father of my wife, I bid audience with you," he shouted.

Feeling a sense of apprehension in his gut, Llewellyn nodded for the man to come forward. He had always feared Phelan. He cursed his daughter beneath his br   ...
    ...nging this upon him.

    ...helan rode forward at a slow pace as if he wer...
    ...d inspecting his lands. He smiled to think tha...
what happened this day he would be the victor. When they reached the walls of the hall he dismounted and strode forward to meet Llewellyn.

"I come to claim my wife and take her back with me. Your wife has denied me this right and thus I seek you out, since you are lord here and not she." He smiled at Llewellyn, sure of himself and the imposing figure he must make in all his finery.

Llewellyn clenched his hands as he spoke. "I cannot let you take Deidre from these walls. I am sorry, my son."

The smile faded from Phelan's face. He had been so certain that this show of force would cause Llewellyn to give in.

"You spineless old man!" he shouted. "You let a woman dictate to you. Your wife then is the lord here." His eyes sought out the familiar form of Deidre. "Bring my wife before me. I would speak with her."

Llewellyn started to refuse, but before he could get the words out, Deidre was by his side.

"I am here, Phelan," she answered. "Speak your mind." She stood with her head held high. She would not let this one cower her.

"You know what I seek," he answered. "Will you come with me and avoid this bloodshed?"

"There need be no bloodshed if you but let me have my freedom. I beg you for mercy. It is not these people," she swept her hand before her, "that you have cause to be angered with, but me. Let us come to terms, Phelan. It is not your wife that you seek to claim, but the lands that were my dowry. Keep those lands. I have no need of them. They are yours if you will only leave me be."

Phelan laughed sourly. "And what about my pride?"

"You do not fool me, Phelan. It is not your pride that has been wounded but your purse. You bemoan the gold and silver you were forced to pay for my return. Would that I had the equal in coins, I would gladly give you recompense." She eyed him coldly, her eyes mirroring her dislike for him.

Phelan looked upon Llewellyn, playing with him like a cat with a mouse. "And what say you, Llewellyn? Will you turn over the lands of her dowry to me legally? Will you pay me in gold and silver for your daughter's freedom?"

Llewellyn's face turned pale, knowing well that he could not. "You may keep the lands, but I have no gold and silver give to you. We are a pastoral people, not traders as the Vikings are. I am rich in land and livestock. I can pay you in sheep and goats." He looked so old at that moment that Deidre pitied him.

Phelan threw back his head and laughed. "You lie, old man. There are treasures in this very hall that the Vikings did not take with them. Holy relics in your chapel, tapestries that were untouched by those raiding heathens, flagons and swords of metal. I have no use for sheep and goats, I have enough of my own."

Llewellyn stood tall before Phelan, all fear gone now as he strove to protect his hall. "Those are not for your touch. They are mine and my family's, passed down from generation to generation."

"Then give me your daughter."

"I cannot," Llewellyn answered. He had seen a side to Phelan this day that he had never witnessed before. He knew now that Phelan would never be gentle with Deidre. It was as she had said. Greed was a demon in Phelan. By his words he had given himself away. His eyes looked toward Deidre and they were filled with pride. No matter what she might have done or the shame she might have brought in coupling with a heathen, she still had strength and courage. He would not give her to this man's care so that she could be mistreated as he knew she would be. "My answer is no."

"Then prepare to fight, old man." Phelan strode toward his horse. He would win this day and have it all; Deidre, the lands and this very hall. Even the church would not censor him in this. To the victor now belonged the spoils. Mounting his horse, Phelan rode up the hill toward his men.

"Where are Colin and Brian? We need them here among us?" Llewellyn asked as he called his own men together, preparing to fight. He could see his sons nowhere. He was unprepared for this.

"They left early this morning," one of the servants explained, "though I know not what has captured their fascination of late."

"Perhaps it is well," Llewellyn sighed beneath his breath. "At least there will be sons to carry on my name after this day." He had no doubt as to the outcome of this fighting. All of his men were old and sickly. The younger men were all away, no doubt with his sons. He laughed at the irony of the fact what while these young men watched the shoreline for signs of the Vikings, their families were to be engaged in fighting other men of Eire.

Deidre watched as the two small bands of armed men assembled to fight. Could she allow this to continue? Was her own happiness worth the price? How could she watch men die for her? If the sacrifice of her own contentment would stop this carnage, then she had to offer herself after all.

"Father!" she yelled, running after him as fast as her legs could carry her. "Wait. I cannot allow this. I never knew it would come to this. I will go back with Phelan. I will be his wife."

Llewellyn shrugged her clinging hands from his arms. "No, daughter. It is I who was wrong, I can see that now. You are not something to be bartered, but someone to be cherished. You are my flesh and blood, Deidre, not the silver and gold that this man covets. How I could have ever given you to him is beyond me. Know that if I live through this I will stand behind you in your efforts to be well rid of him." He mounted his horse and lifted his sword to prepare for the fight.

As the two bands of armed men came face to face upon the

hillside, hacking and thrusting at each other, the clang of sword against sword echoed down the hill. Deidre and her mother stood holding each other's hands praying to their God to be merciful.

Phelan ordered the torching of several of the outlying houses, which flamed and smoked as they burned to the ground.

"Even the Vikings did not set fires," Tara said in anger. She was thankful that she had stood steadfast in not giving her daughter to a man such as this. How could Phelan have fooled them all these years?

"I fear all is lost!" Deidre sobbed as she watched one man after the other fall to the ground. She covered her face in her hands and wept.

"Look! Toward the west," an old woman shouted.

Deidre lifted her head and glanced in that direction, amazed at what she saw. It was a band of Vikings and if her eyes did not deceive her, they were Wolfram's men.

"Vikings!" came the shout as all the people gathered together, running in terror toward the safety of the hall.

Deidre watched in wonder as the Viking band took to the hillside, their swords raised not against her father and his men but in defense of them.

"The Vikings!" came the shout again as the frightened crowd peered from behind the doors of the hall. A cheer arose as they saw that those they called heathens had this day come to their aid.

From his point at the hillside Phelan shouted aloud in anger. "You fools! It is I who am your friend. Have you forgotten so soon who has been your friend these past months."

"You are no friend of mine," shouted Rorik. "It is for the woman Deidre that I have loyalty. Her son will one day be Jarl! It is for her family that I fight this day, not for a traitor to his own." He pushed toward Phelan with upraised sword.

Phelan fought wildly, knowing that the tide of this battle had turned. "I will pay you. Silver and gold to turn against this old man and fight beside me. I can help you in your raids as I did before!"

Rorik laughed in his face. "Our loyalty cannot be bought." Pressing forward he struck out at Phelan, wounding him in the shoulder. Despite the fact that Phelan and his men were on horseback and Rorik and the Vikings fighting on foot, Phelan was wise enough to know that they were the losers in this battle.

"Retreat!" he commanded.

From her place at the doorway of her father's hall, Deidre watched as Phelan and his men galloped their horses back in the direction from which they had come. Her heart was thumping wildly in her breast. They were saved. All was well, all was well.

10

There was much celebration in the hall during the day, long into the night as Viking sat beside Irishman in the bond of newfound friendship.

"I never thought to be happy to seé the Norsemen!" Llewellyn said with a laugh. "But surely you have saved our hides this day." He turned to Deidre. "Can you speak their language?" he asked.

"Yes, Father."

"Then tell them of my gratitude. As far as I am concerned there is now friendship between us. I will forget all about the raid two springs ago. Tell them that."

Deidre spoke to Rorik of her father's message and he smiled. "Tell him that we welcome his friendship. Tell him that he has a brave, beautiful daughter and that it was for her that we came this day."

Deidre translated Rorik's message with a blush and watched as her father and the young man grabbed left hands in a gesture of friendship. Llewellyn went about the hall then, raising his glass to the others of Rorik's band. At last Deidre was left alone with Rorik to ask the questions she so needed to ask.

"How did you know that I would be here?"

"We didn't. Wolfram only supposed that it would be here that the Danes would bring you."

"Wolfram!" Deidre's eyes were filled with joy. "He is alive? I knew it. In my heart I knew it. Where is he? I must see him." Supposing him to be aboard the ship which had brought the Vikings to the shores of Eire, she ran out the doorway and headed for the path which would take her to the seashore.

Rorik caught hold of her. "Wolfram is not aboard the ship,

Deidre. He was captured by Irishmen on our way to your father's hall. I had thought them to be your father's men but if you have no knowledge of the deed, then I was wrong."

"Captured! By Irishmen! No!" Deidre felt the world spin about her.

Rorik did not have the heart to tell her that he feared his two friends were dead. Instead he said, "I got away to warn the others. Sigurd and Wolfram were set upon as the three of us came in peace up the coastline."

"We must find him! We must move heaven and earth to find him!" Deidre was nearly hysterical now in her grief. So much had happened this day and now to find that Wolfram had come after her only to be taken prisoner was too much to bear.

"Deidre, you must be prepared in case the worst has happened." Rorik's eyes were deep with compassion for her misery and Deidre remembered that first time she had seen him in this very hall. He had showed h̶̶̶̶̶̶̶ even then and Bridget as well.

"No. He is alive. I will not even thin̶̶̶̶̶ ̶ere is any ̶ssibility that he is not. Round up some o̶̶ ̶̶ Vikings, we ̶o out now to search. I will not rest until we f̶ ̶im."

Deidre, Rorik and six others took to th̶ ̶ horses and searched far and wide for Wolfram. Riding to neighboring halls and huts alike they asked about the two Vikings, but none had seen them. It was as if Wolfram had vanished in the very mists of the lands of Eire. In disappointment Deidre headed for home.

"We will rest this night but with the first crow of the rooster we will start out again. I will search forever if need be for Wolfram. As God is my witness let it be so."

11

Wolfram and Sigurd watched from their cold, damp prison as the sun rose over the horizon bringing with it their death. From above them they could hear the jeers of the Irish guards as they returned en masse to witness the spectacle. A rope was tossed down and they were bid to climb up to meet their fate.

Hand over hand Wolfram climbed, reaching the top only to be set upon by three Irishmen and bound amid much laughter and taunting. Sigurd was also bound with his hands behind his back, uttering a curse at his fate.

Seeing the familiar form the Deidre's dark-haired brother standing on the edge of the group of men, his eyes showing his discomfort at witnessing such a scene, Wolfram fought to gain his attention, struggling further with the men who held him.

Brian's eyes met Wolfram and for a moment he was tormented by guilt. "Colin, I have no stomach for this," he said sternly. "How can we take the life of this man and not tell Deidre? He is the father of our nephew. Can we look the child in the eye some day and calmly tell him that we killed his father? Viking or not they deserve better than this."

"These men led the raid which killed Ian, do you deny that? What of our sister Bridget? We owe her our loyalty as well as Deidre. It is for Bridget then that we do this thing." His voice was bold, but Colin too had begun to doubt this action.

"Bridget would not want this," Brian answered, his eyes blazing with sudden conviction. Gone now was his fear of Colin's anger. "What you do is wrong! I will have no part in it." He turned to leave but was stopped by another of his brother's followers.

"The Vikings attacked your father's hall just yesterday. I watched from the tree over there and saw from a distance as

328

the huts were burned to the ground around your home. Do you still beg clemency for these Northmen?"

"My father's hall. And we were not there to fight beside him?" To think that such carnage had occurred only a mile away. Brian took to his heels.

Wolfram watched Brian leave and with him the last shred of hope that his life would be spared. "Brian! For the love of your God help us!" he cried. But it was too late.

"Come, Viking!" Wolfram heard a voice say as he was pushed forward. He remembered one of the hermit Paul's stories from the Holy Book. He had told him that the son of God had climbed a hill to his death; now he too was facing execution. His hour had come.

"I will face it with as much courage as did Deidre's Christ," he vowed, wondering why in this time of despair he should be moved toward the Christian God in his thoughts.

Across the meadow, down the long pathway to ⸺ they walked as the sun beat down upon their head ⸺ pom wished for the cool mists of Ireland to come ⸺ gem bringing the rain. All about him was silence as the ⸺ alked ⸺ ng.

Wolfram gloried in the rustling and twittering ⸺ the birds as they flew about. To hear their chirping remo ⸺ some of the burden from his heart. It was strange how ⸺ he took so many things for granted in life. How he wou'd miss those things now, but most of all he would miss Deidre and her love.

"Deidre," he whispered, and her name was like a prayer.

As they walked along, Wolfram looked down at the foot of the rocks as the sea foamed and thrashed. He thought about how easy it would be to end it all now by leaping to those rocks below, but his pride would not let him do such a thing.

At the foot of the cliff the sea pounded, slowly receding bit by bit, but it would return, bringing death with it. Seeing two large rocks, slim and smooth, he knew that this was to be his final resting place.

"You will be tied to those rocks to think about the evil you have done and to ask your many gods to help you," the man named Cedric said with a snarl. "Your kind sold my daugher into slavery and she killed herself rather than bear such a burden. Think about her as you wait."

"Yes, call upon your gods. We want to hear you," shouted a voice.

The feel of ropes sliced into Wolfram's arms and legs as they bound him to the rock. He looked out at the ocean imagining how it would be as the tide crept ever closer, choking him. First it would come to his knees, then to his chest, finally to his nose and mouth.

Without really knowing why, Wolfram began to say a prayer the hermit Paul had taught him. It was a Christian prayer, yet it soothed his soul and made him feel at peace. "Our Father, who art in heaven . . ." he began.

"What is he saying? Listen, it is one of our prayers that he spouts. What kind of mockery is this?" Colin shouted. "If he is a Christian we cannot kill him." He stepped forward with the intention of setting Wolfram free, but was stopped by another of the men.

"It is a trick. I will not stop until they are both punished," Cedric raved. He pushed Colin so hard that the young man fell to the ground. "I will be in command here now if you are too squeamish," he said.

Sigurd now was bound beside Wolfram, looking out upon the ocean he had often sailed upon. His thoughts were of Zerlina. How sad that he would never more feel her arms about him, never claim her as his own.

The waters sloshed and whistled at Wolfram's feet, rising ever higher as he closed his eyes in silent farewell to the woman he loved more than life itself. The very wind seemed to whisper the name, Deidre.

12

Deidre was weary as she rode back toward her father's hall beside Rorik. They had ridden deep into the woods this day in search of any sign of Sigurd or Wolfram but had found none. She had almost begun to give up hope of finding them.

"What are we going to do, Rorik?" she asked. "What are we going to do?"

"There is nothing we can do, Deidre," he answered. He did not want to tell her that he feared Wolfram already dead, a victim of her own people.

All sorts of thoughts were tumbling through Deidre's brain as she dismounted from her horse. There had to be some way to find out Wolfram's whereabouts. She swung open the heavy wooden door and peered within. The Vikings had left the hall now and gone to their camp nearby. It was silence that Deidre expected to find but instead she could hear the sound of voices raised in argument. She recognized one of the voices as that of her brother Brian.

"It cannot be. You must be wrong," Brian shouted. "Why would Vikings come to our aid, they are no friends of ours."

"For love of your sister. It was Deidre they wished to guard. She is considered to be one among them," Llewellyn answered. "I too thought them evil and barbaric, but I have learned much these last few days. Perhaps it is true that we are, every one of us, after all brothers."

"And Phelan, what of him?" again Brian's voice.

"He would have destroyed me in his anger. He is greedy that one. I would not put anything past him. I wonder how long he has had his eyes upon my holy relics and treasures? Your mother has gone to the monastery to fetch Father Finian. As soon as it can be arranged the marriage vows will be

331

dissolved between your sister and her husband.''

Deidre walked into the room as her father was speaking. Brian's eyes were upon her as he rose from his seat by the fire. Running to her, he knelt at her feet.

"Forgive me, Deidre. I did not mean to hurt you. I hated the Northmen for what they did during the raid. We should not have done what we did, Colin and I and the others, but we sought recompense for Ian's death.''

Deidre took hold of her brother's shoulders, confused at what he was talking about. He was babbling and talking so rapidly that she could hardly understand him.

"What are you talking about, Brian?" she asked.

"The Viking. The one who sired your son. We killed him. This morning.'' He stood upon his feet, his head hung in remorse. "I could not stay and watch him die. If not for the coward in me I would have tried to save him.''

"No! No!'' Deidre was screaming now, losing all control of herself. "In trying to avenge Bridget's husband you have killed mine!'' She was too late. Wolfram was dead. Her eyes were the eyes of a wounded animal. "The wolves!'' she sa? remembering the night Colin and Brian had talked to about catching two in their trap.

"Yes. It wasn't wolves but Vikings that we captured.''

"How did he die? How did the father of my son, the love of my heart leave this earth?'' She closed her eyes, knowing that she would feel his pain as if it had been her own.

"We secured them to the large cliff stones, there to await the incoming tide. Colin thought it only fitting that they should die by drowning since it is the sea which brought them here.'' Again Brian hung his head. It was so obvious how much his sister loved the Viking. Why hadn't he done something to save the man's life?

"The tide!'' Sudden hope came to Deidre. "Come with me, Brian. It can't be too late. Oh, God, please let it not be too late!''

Without another thought about her own well-being, driven only by the necessity of saving Wolfram from the ocean, Deidre mounted her horse and rode at breakneck speed, outdistancing her brother as he rode swiftly in an effort to catch up. To Deidre it seemed to take forever to reach the cliffs, but at last she could smell the sea. Cresting a hill, she jumped from her horse running down the path to the sharp rocks below.

The sight which met her eyes made her cry out. Wolfram was still alive, though she could see the water was now up to his chin. He was coughing and sputtering as the waves assaulted him. Sigurd, being the taller of the two, was not in as deadly a peril, though his life too hung in the balance.

There were no Irishmen around now, the rocks were deserted except for the gulls circling overhead and the crabs clinging to the banks as the tide pressed inward.

"Wolfram!" Deidre shouted, running toward him. Ripping off her shoes in order to have better footing on the slippery rocks, she frantically struggled to reach the man she loved.

Wolfram heard his name being called and thought that his mind was playing tricks on him. He had longed to hear Deidre's voice call to him. Or was it that he had already died and was listening to the voices of the angels Paul had told him about, calling to him? He choked as the water got into his mouth and knew that he was still alive.

"Wolfram!" Again the voice called to him. He fought to turn his head but the chill of the water had numbed and weakened him.

Deidre was but a short distance from Wolfram. She was in time, if she acted quickly he would be saved. The quickest way to rescue him was to swim toward him. Heedless of her own danger, Deidre eased herself out into the water. She would save Wolfram's life or die trying.

Deidre felt the cold of the sea engulf her as she fought against the waves. Every nerve in her body was on alert. She was aware of danger, sensed that someone was watching her. Whirling around to face the intruder she felt as if a knife had been thrust into her breast.

"Phelan!"

He had the look of evil personified, grinning at her like a satanic pagan god from the shore. Her eyes locked with his as he too plunged into the icy depths.

"Please, Phelan," she cried. She could hear his laughter as he reached out for her. She screamed, kicking out at him all the while to keep him away from her but he caught her tightly within his grasp. She felt herself being drawn toward the shore. "No!"

She struck at her captor, hitting him over and over again with her fists. All the while one thought kept reeling through her brain. Wolfram would die. Wolfram would die, if she did

not free herself. She fought like a wildcat, but Phelan was a
man of great strength and easily imprisoned her in his embrace.

"Please, let me go to him, Phelan," she begged. Time was
running out quickly.

"Go to him. I think not, dear wife. I prefer that we wait
here and watch the sea take him. Cursed Viking that he be."

At that moment Deidre hated Phelan as she had never hated
another human being before. To stand by and watch another
man die was heartless beyond belief.

"I'll give you anything, Phelan. Anything."

He laughed and hit her viciously. "I've wanted to do that
since you came back."

Deidre's eyes flashed. "I thought that our beloved Saint
Patrick drove all the snakes out of Ireland, but I see that he
left one upon our shores. You are lower than a snake. May
God curse you," she shrieked.

"You bitch! You will join your lover this day." Grabbing
her neck, he dunked her head beneath the waters in an attempt
to drown her.

At last catching up with Deidre, Brian stood upon the
and watched as Phelan tried to kill his sister. Jumping into
waters he pulled Phelan's hands from his sister's neck, wre
tling with the man amid the thrashing waters.

Free of Phelan's arms, Deidre once again fought to come to
Wolfram's aid. She could hear him choking. The water was
past his mouth. She swam to his side, pulling at his bonds
frantically. It was no use. The ropes were engorged with the
water from the sea.

"Wolfram, help me," she cried. "If you can hear me, hold
your hands closer together so that I may get you loose."

Wolfram heard her pleas as if through a tunnel. Only by
holding his breath was he still among the living. His chest
burned with the pain yet with all the strength left to him, he
pushed his wrists together.

"If only I had something sharp. Something with which to
sever these ropes," Deidre sobbed. She had no knife, no dagger. "My brooch," she cried out. With trembling fingers she
removed it from her wet gown, bobbing up and down in the
water as she fought the waves. Working with the sharp metal
against the ropes she struggled to free Wolfram, pausing from

time to time to gently lift his head so that he could catch a breath of air through his nose.

At last she had him free. Wolfram breathed a sweet elixir of air into his lungs. "Sigurd," he choked. Deidre freed Sigurd from his bonds as Wolfram struggled to keep his head above the water. In her efforts, Deidre lost the brooch to the waters of the ocean. She stretched out her hand searching for it, but the brooch was gone forever.

Swimming toward the shore, they all watched in horror as Deidre's brother fought with Phelan. Brian was skilled but not as cunning as Phelan. As the two men fought, one tall and thin with the grace of a deer, the other short and stout with the strength of a wild boar, they moved onto the rocks of the cliff. As if moving in some pagan dance high above the sea, Brian and Phelan fought. Again and again they collided, Phelan reaching out to gouge the other man's eyes, kicking with his feet and lashing out at Brian.

Deidre watched in agony as Brian fell. She struggled against Wolfram's arms to come to her brother's aid, but Wolfram held her securely knowing well that there was nothing she could do.

Phelan moved in for the death blow, jumping at Brian with a loud shout of victory, but misjudging the distance he slipped upon the wet rocks, and fell to the jagged stones below. His screams rent the air as he was killed upon the very rocks which had held Wolfram and Sigurd captive.

Soaked to the skin, Deidre clung to the man she loved more than life itself.

"It's over now, Deidre. Oh, my love, it is over," he whispered. "We have found each other once again."

13

Soaking wet, but happy to be alive, Brian, Sigurd, Wolfram and Deidre returned to the hall. Stepping inside the doorway they headed for the roaring fire in the hearth, shivering as they sought to dry off.

Like sweet music Deidre heard over and over again the words, "We are alive. Wolfram is free. We are together." Wolfram swept her into his arms, heedless of all else but the rapture of her kisses, as his mouth claimed hers.

"What is this?" called a voice as Deidre broke away from Wolfram's embrace. Father Finian walked across the hall meet them. "Surely there are more important things a than a dip in the ocean." He eyed Sigurd and Wolfram, wo dering who they might be.

"Father Finian," Deidre began, "this is my husband, Wolfram, and this is his friend—"

"Phelan is your husband, Deidre, until the Holy Father says otherwise." He scowled, his bushy white eyebrows shaped in a "V."

"Phelan is dead. Killed by his own wickedness," Brian exclaimed. "He was the traitor who betrayed us all to the Vikings."

"I knew he was evil," Deidre said in shock. "But I never knew how evil. It is well he is dead."

Brian told the kindly priest all that had occurred that very morning. "I only regret the part I played in Wolfram's and Sigurd's harrowing experience. Phelan's death was of his own doing. He sought my sister's death and my own."

"May God forgive his soul," Father Finian whispered, hastily crossing himself. Taking hold of Deidre's small hands, he pulled her from before the fire to sit beside him on one of the long benches of the hall. "Your mother tells me that you love this man and that you have a son. What are we to do, Deidre? What are we to do?"

"I love him, Father. Surely if our kind, heavenly Lord did not approve of that love, he would not have saved Wolfram." Her eyes met Wolfram's in a caress. "And given us Fenrir. Our son is a fine boy. I look forward to your baptizing him, though he has already had the waters poured upon his head."

"I cannot do so, my child. The boy, no matter how you love him, is bastard born. Only if you were married by our Christian laws could I legitimize him and that would be impossible since this Viking does not know our ways." His eyes looked upon Wolfram, then returned to Deidre again.

Wolfram took a step forward. "But I do know. Not only has Deidre told me about her God, but Father Paul as well. We read the Holy Book, he and I."

Deidre looked at Wolfram with surprise. Not knowing where he had spent his time while others thought him dead, she had no idea that the man she loved was familiar with the scriptures. "Father Paul?" she asked.

Sitting down beside Deidre and the priest, Wolfram told them the tale of his rescue and of his friendship with the hermit who had saved his life. He recounted the stories he had heard, adding that the story of Jonah in the whale's belly had been his favorite tale. "I have seen many whales up near the Northland. They are bigger than this hall. Jonah was a brave man and lucky to have escaped. This God of yours is mighty indeed."

"This Father Paul, was he Irish?" Father Finian asked. A light had come into his eyes as if perhaps he thought he knew the man.

"No, he came from lands to the south, but he lived in a monastery not far from a province he called Ulster." Wolfram described his friend in detail and told the sad story of the priest who had become a hermit.

"I knew him. I thought him dead. He was one of the priests who helped me translate the Holy Scriptures and set them down upon the scroll which even now lies in the abbey chapel." Father Finian had a faraway look in his eyes as if remembering another place, another time. At last he rose to his feet. "Would you agree then to be married by Christian vows to Deidre?" he asked Wolfram.

Wolfram nodded. "I have much respect for your God and for his Son. I prayed to him and here I am alive. Not Odin but your Jesus saved me. Deidre and I are already married by my people's laws, but if it would make her happy, then I agree to your ceremony."

"Then let us begin," Father Finian said softly.

Deidre ran from the hall to seek her parents, laughing like a schoolgirl. It was as if her nightmares had suddenly turned to dreams. What more could she wish for? Wolfram was alive, he had brought her son to safety in Dubh-Linn and soon she would be wed to the man she loved by the Christian vows.

She found her parents outside. Llewellyn and Tara were shocked by Phelan's death, but filled with happiness to think that Deidre had found the man she loved in time to save his life.

"I must meet the man who stole my daughter's heart so completely," Llewellyn said with a laugh. "If he can tame you, daughter, he is a better man than I, for God knows I never could."

"If you are happy, then I will be happy," Tara whispered in her daughter's ear. "Llewellyn does not know it, but it will be you who will do the taming. Your father does not know the ways of women, nor shall I tell him." She winked at Deidre then enfolded her in her arms. "Now, let us prepare for this wedding."

14

Deidre soaked in the warm tub of water. She let her long black hair float about her, washing the sticky sea salt from its silky strands. A fire blazed nearby filling the room of the sleeping chambers with warmth. She was lost in her dreams. Soon she would again marry Wolfram only this time there would be no guilt of prior vows to spoil the moment for her. Wolfram was to be her husband before all the laws of her church and with the blessing of her family. Oh, Colin had been a little angered at first to find that the man he had tried to kill was shortly to be his brother-in-law, but he had soon been soothed by Deidre's happiness.

Tara poured a mixture of herbs and flowers in Deidre's bath water and stood back to look upon her daughter.

"You are positively glowing, my child," she said. "Your contentment radiates to all who are about you."

"Yes, I am happy, Mother. Wolfram and I have been separated for so long that it is almost as if I come to him a virgin bride." In truth she was a bit nervous. She could almost see Wolfram standing tall before her in all his splendid nakedness. She ached to be in his arms.

As if reading her thoughts Tara said, "It will not be much longer before you are with your Wolfram." Deidre blushed then, but her mother only smiled. "Even now I too am like a young bride after your father has been away for a time. I think perhaps all women in love are the same."

Tara helped her daughter out of the tub, drying her long thick dark hair with the soft woolen, then wrapped the wool around her daughter's body. She brushed Deidre's shining raven locks, braiding the hair down the back and fastening gold rings at the end.

At last Deidre dressed in her wedding gown, a pale-blue gown embroidered with flowers by Tara's own hand. It had been Bridget's wedding gown too, envied by all of the other women in the province for its beauty and fine stitchery. The draped sleeves hung to the floor exposing the under-tunic. Upon Deidre's head was placed a veil as thin as an angel's wing.

Walking solemnly through the hall, Deidre headed for the small chapel. Even her brothers who, as brothers often do, ignored their sister's beauty, looked at her in awe. Before the altar stood Father Finian, beckoning to her with a smile.

"You are beautiful," Wolfram whispered in her ear, giving her hand a squeeze. He was dressed in one of her father's best tunics and looked magnificent in white trimmed in scarlet.

Father Finian began the familiar Latin words in his rich voice. Wolfram looked bewildered, not being familiar with the Latin tongue, but he reached out and took Deidre's hand firmly in his own as she whispered the words. As the Mass progressed, Deidre felt peace and love in her heart.

Father Finian bid her sink to her knees to receive the wine from the brimming chalice while Wolfram stood behind her, he too receiving the communion. At last the priest motioned for Wolfram to take his place upon his knees at Deidre's side. The blessing came and they were wed.

Wolfram kissed her then, his lips caressing hers. "Come, my wife," he whispered. "It is time we tasted of each other again." As they ran from the chapel and through the hall, Brian, Colin and the others bid the couple a lusty wedding night.

Arriving in Deidre's bedchamber, Wolfram smiled. This time the candles and new linen sheets scented with sweet herbs were there for him. Closing the door behind them, he took Deidre in his arms.

"Deidre." He kissed her long and hard, savoring the soft sweetness of her mouth. Her hand lay flat against him, twining in the golden hair of his chest. Stepping away from him, Deidre stripped off her gown and tunic and stood naked before him. The breath caught in his throat as he beheld her beauty. He ran his hand over the softness of her shoulder, down to the peaks of her full breasts. A blazing fire consumed them both as their bodies touched and caressed.

"Come!" Deidre bid. Wolfram cast away his garments then

followed Deidre to the bed. With hands and lips and words they gave vent to their love, reaching a shattering ecstasy much like the crashing of the waves of the sea.

"I love you, Deidre. You are the treasure of my heart," Wolfram whispered.

"And I, you, my bold warrior, my flame from the sea. This night we have truly been blessed. If I have my way there will soon be another son of your seed."

"Or daughter," he laughed.

"And this time you will be with me to see the miracle of what our love has wrought." Deidre nestled within the warmth of Wolfram's arms. As long as they were together they could face whatever the future held in store for them.

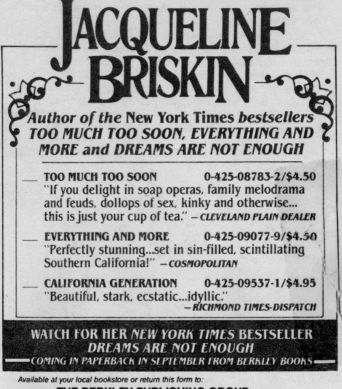